W8 - BUF - 573

D0013758

CLICK

BY KAYLA MILLER

HOUGHTON MIFFLIN HARCOURT
BOSTON   NEW YORK

FOR DAD, MOM, AND JEFFREY —KM

Additional color by Katherine Efird

Copyright © 2019 by Houghton Mifflin Harcourt

www.hmhco.com

The illustrations in this book were done using inks and digital color.
The text type was set in Kayla Miller's handwriting.
The display type was hand-lettered by Kayla Miller.

Design by Andrea Miller

ISBN 978-1-328-70735-2 hardcover
ISBN 978-1-328-91112-4 paperback

Manufactured in China
SCP 16 15 14 13 12 11 10
4500799929

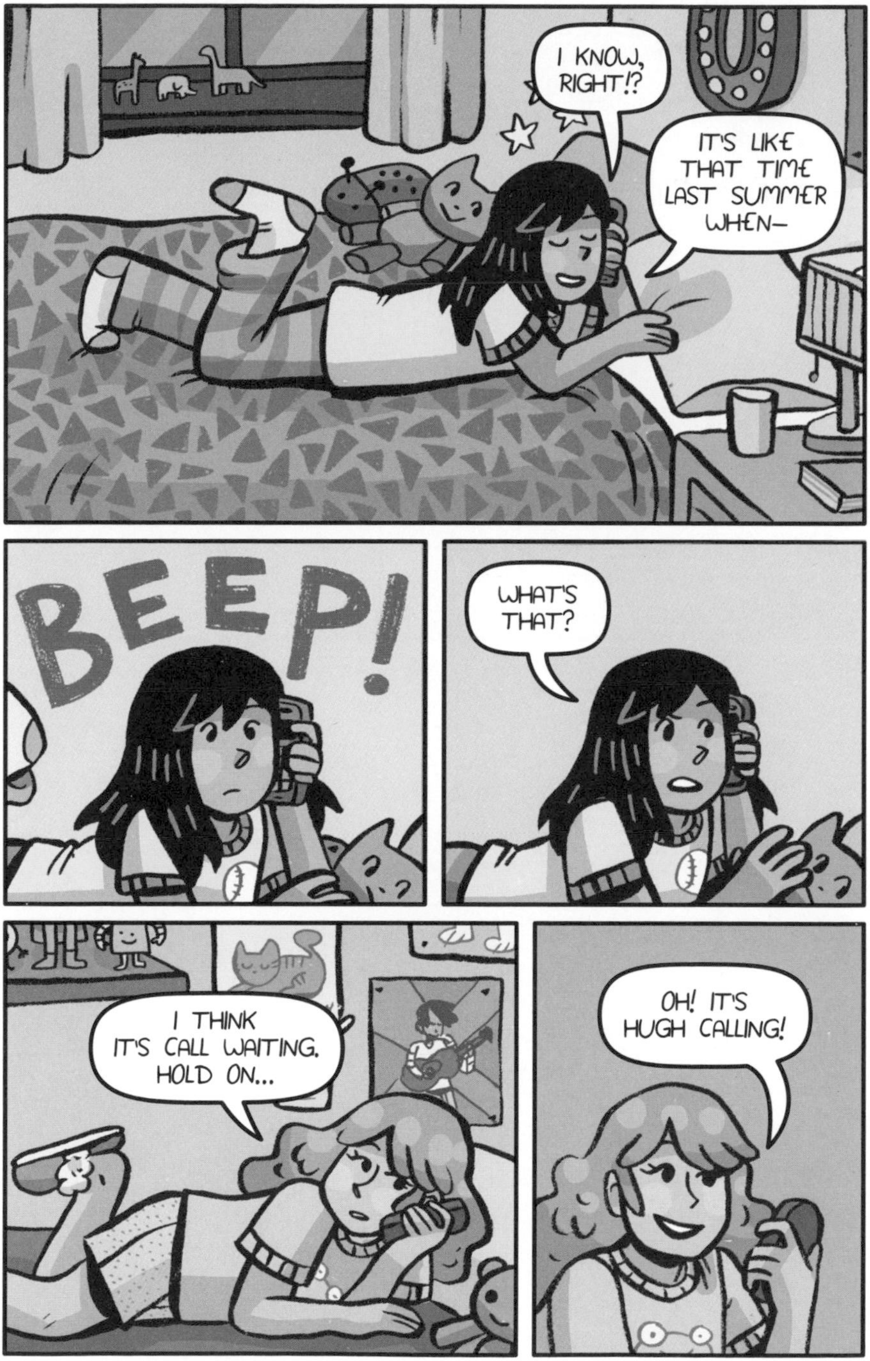
I KNOW, RIGHT!?
IT'S LIKE THAT TIME LAST SUMMER WHEN—
BEEP!
WHAT'S THAT?
I THINK IT'S CALL WAITING. HOLD ON...
OH! IT'S HUGH CALLING!

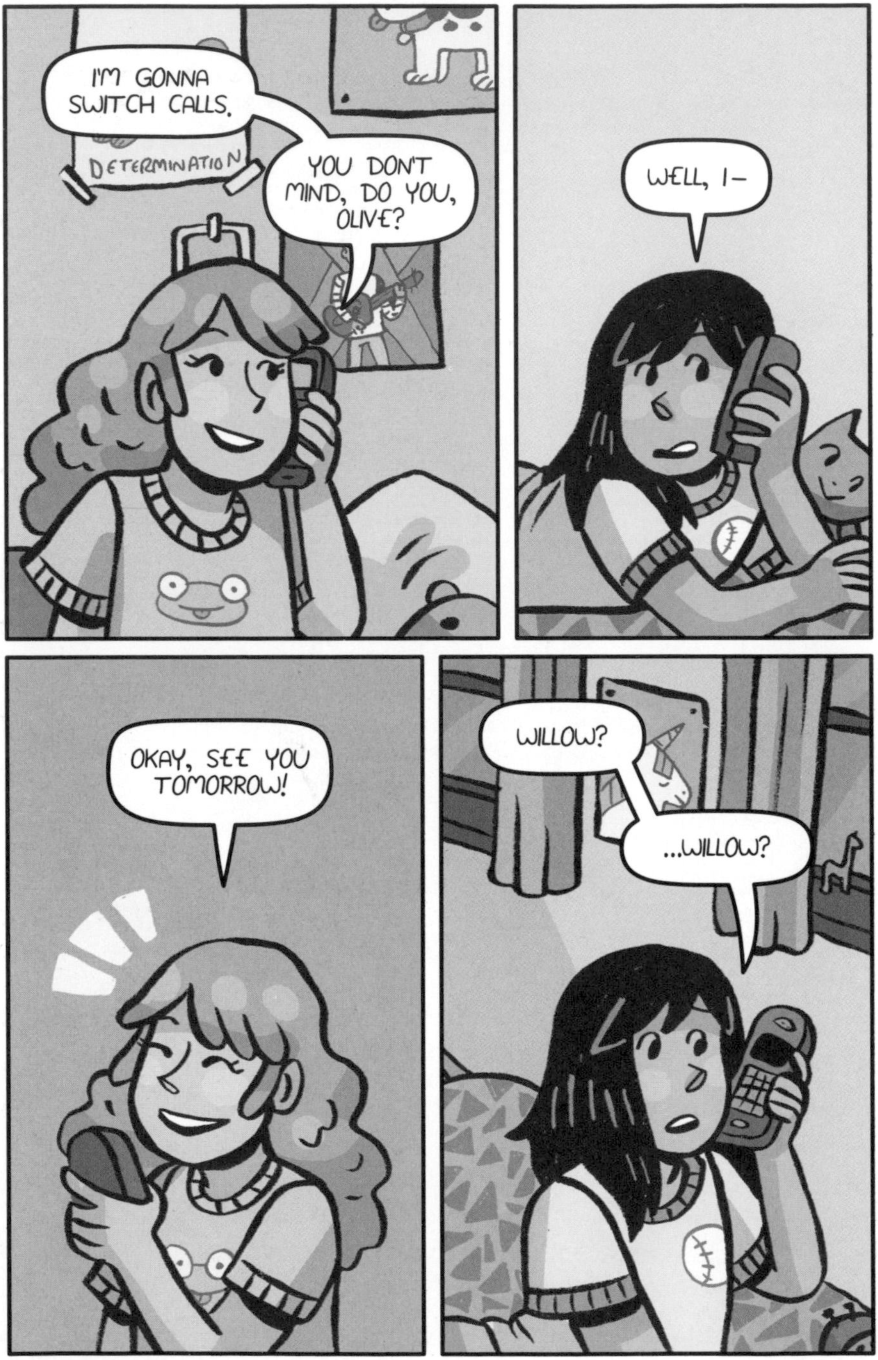
I'M GONNA SWITCH CALLS.
DETERMINATION
YOU DON'T MIND, DO YOU, OLIVE?
WELL, I—
OKAY, SEE YOU TOMORROW!
WILLOW?
...WILLOW?

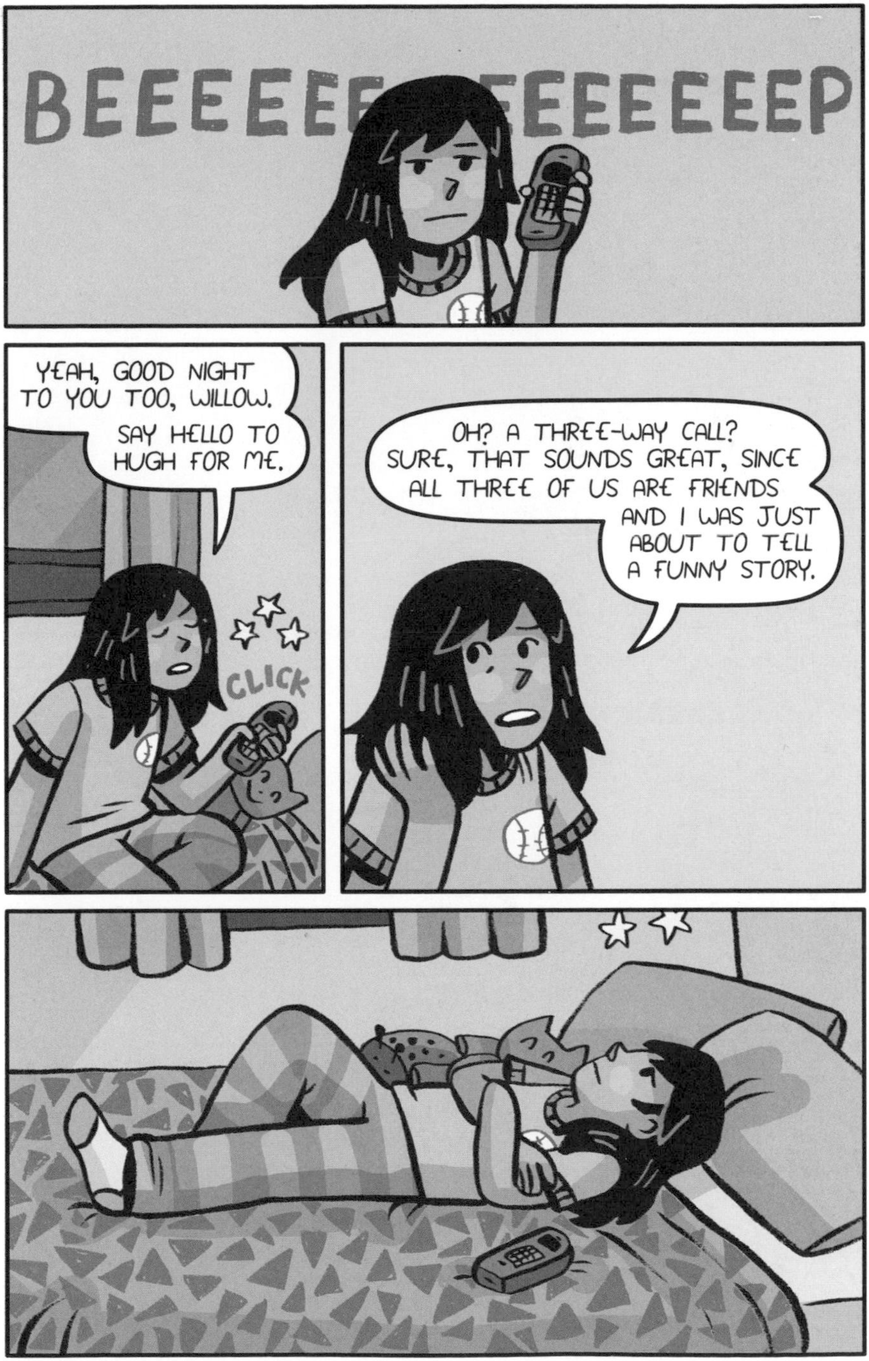
BEEEEEEEEEEEEEEEP
YEAH, GOOD NIGHT TO YOU TOO, WILLOW.
SAY HELLO TO HUGH FOR ME.
CLICK
OH? A THREE-WAY CALL? SURE, THAT SOUNDS GREAT, SINCE ALL THREE OF US ARE FRIENDS
AND I WAS JUST ABOUT TO TELL A FUNNY STORY.

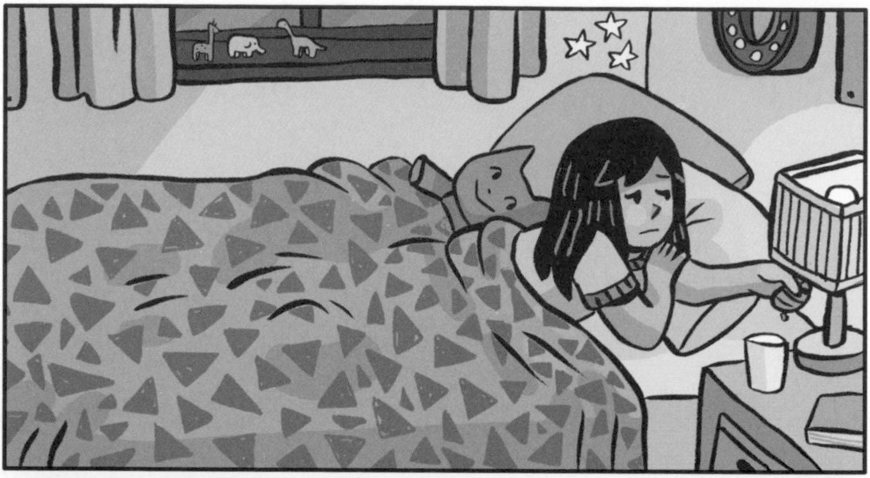

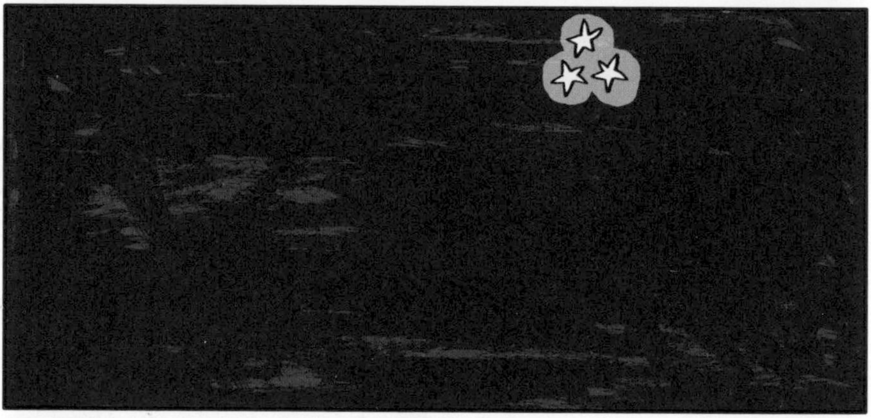

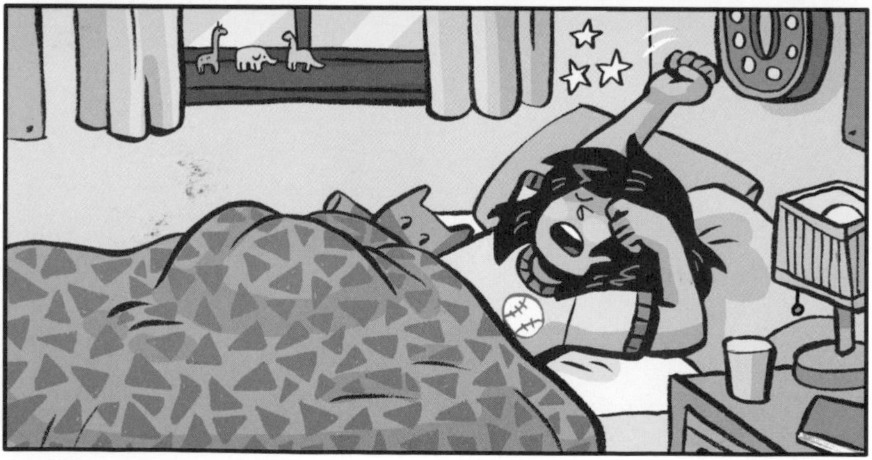

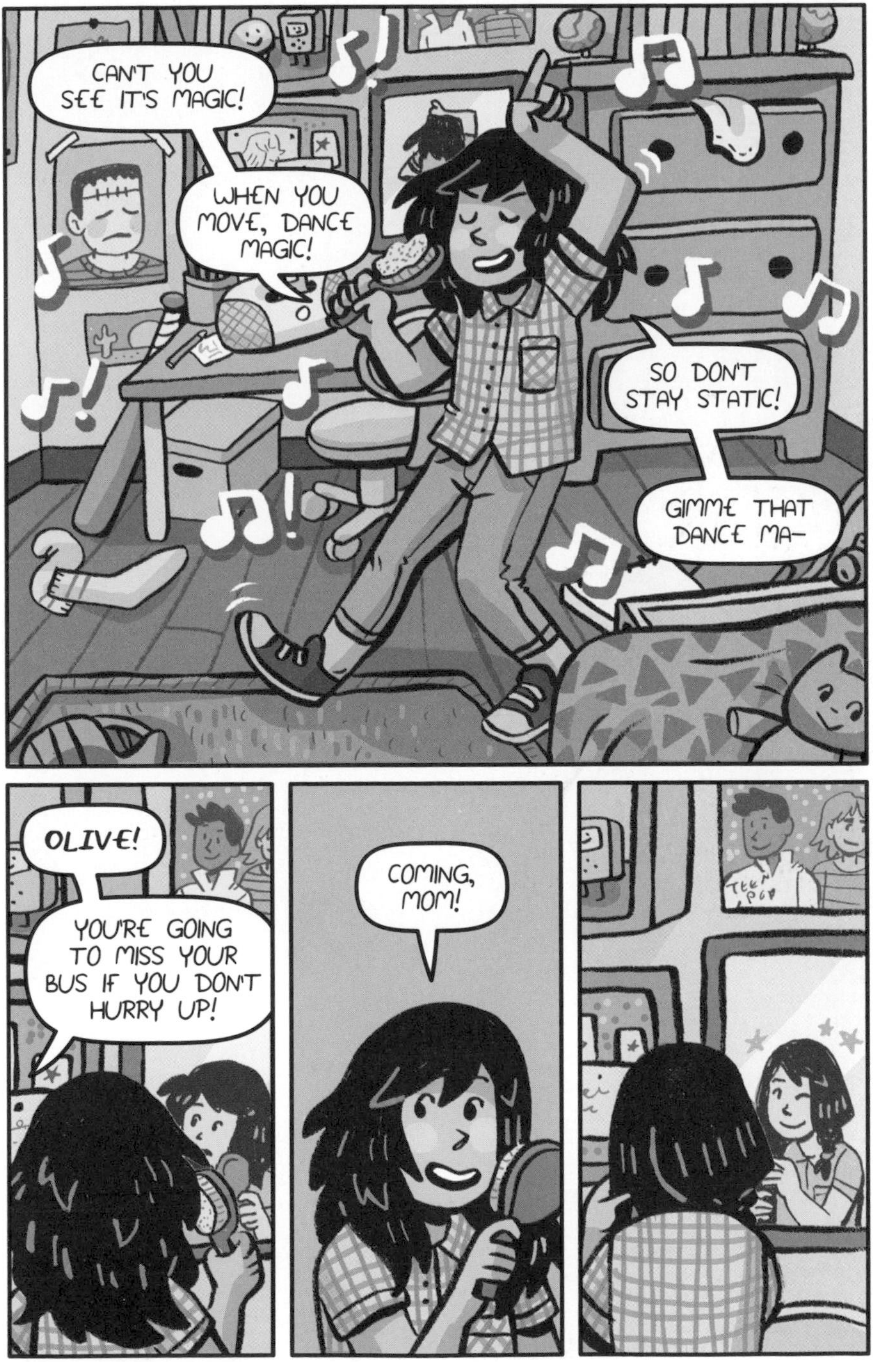
CAN'T YOU SEE IT'S MAGIC!
WHEN YOU MOVE, DANCE MAGIC!
SO DON'T STAY STATIC!
GIMME THAT DANCE MA—
OLIVE!
YOU'RE GOING TO MISS YOUR BUS IF YOU DON'T HURRY UP!
COMING, MOM!

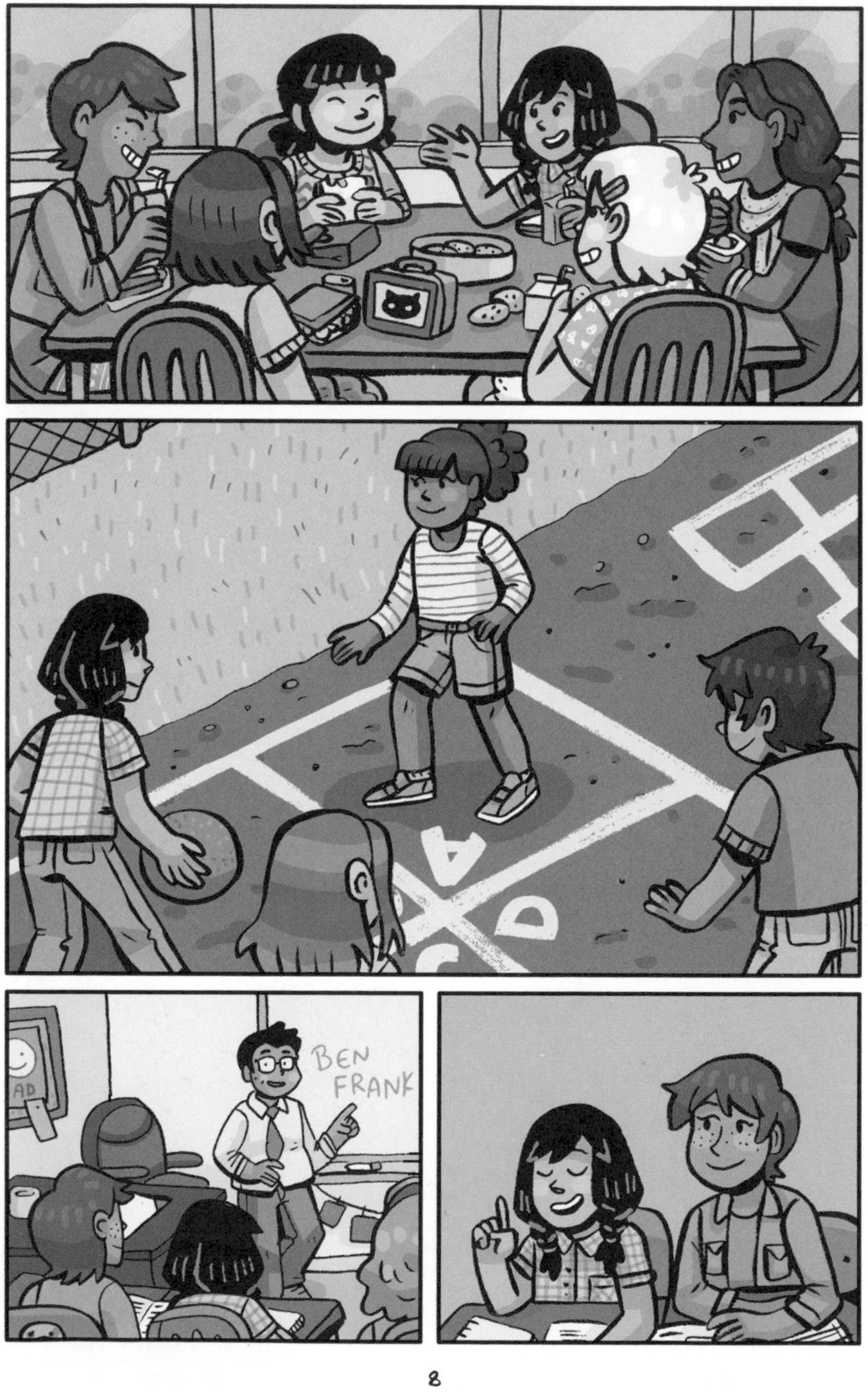
AD
BEN
FRANK

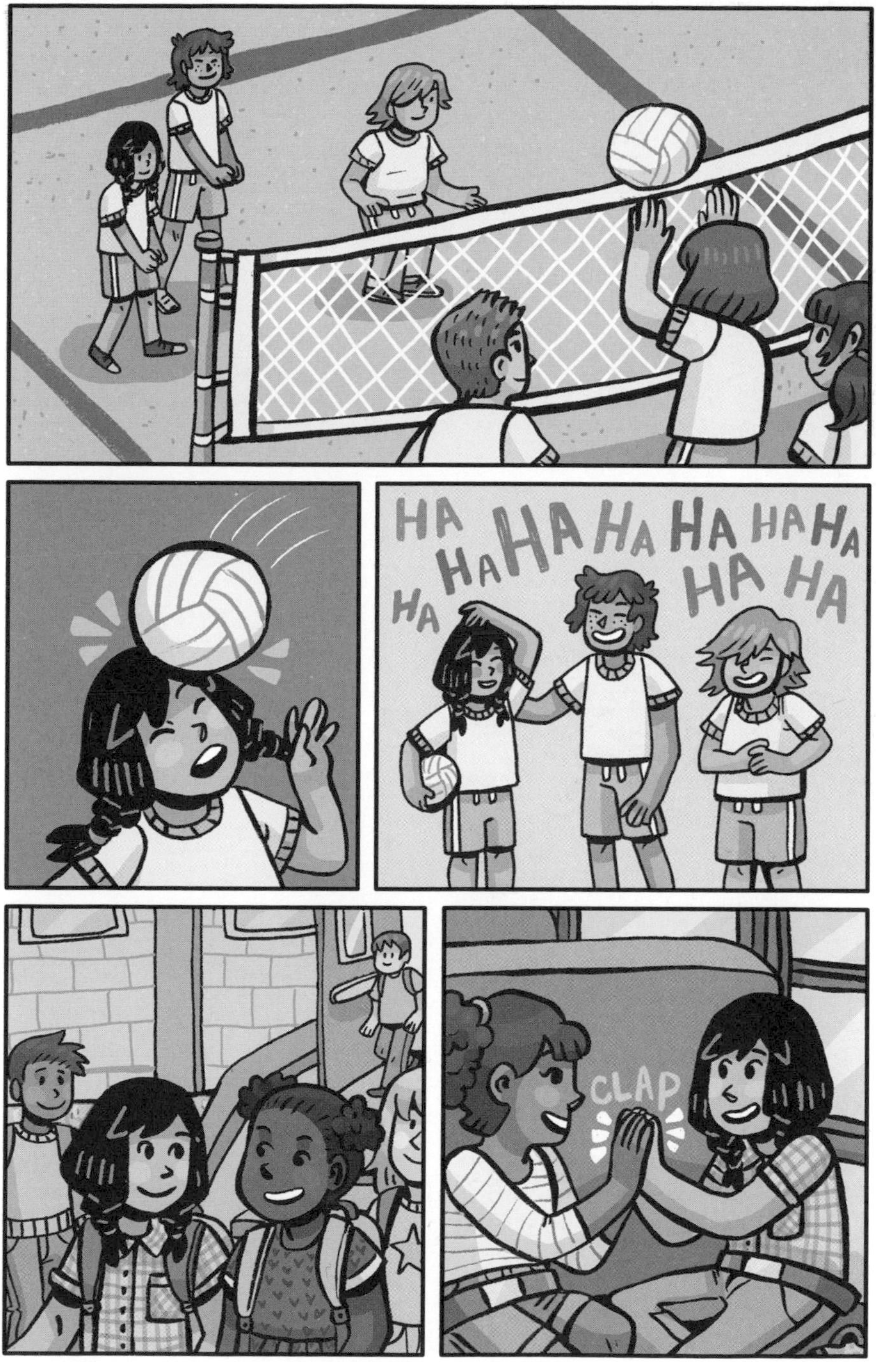
HA HAHA HA HA HAHA
HA HA HA HA HA
CLAP

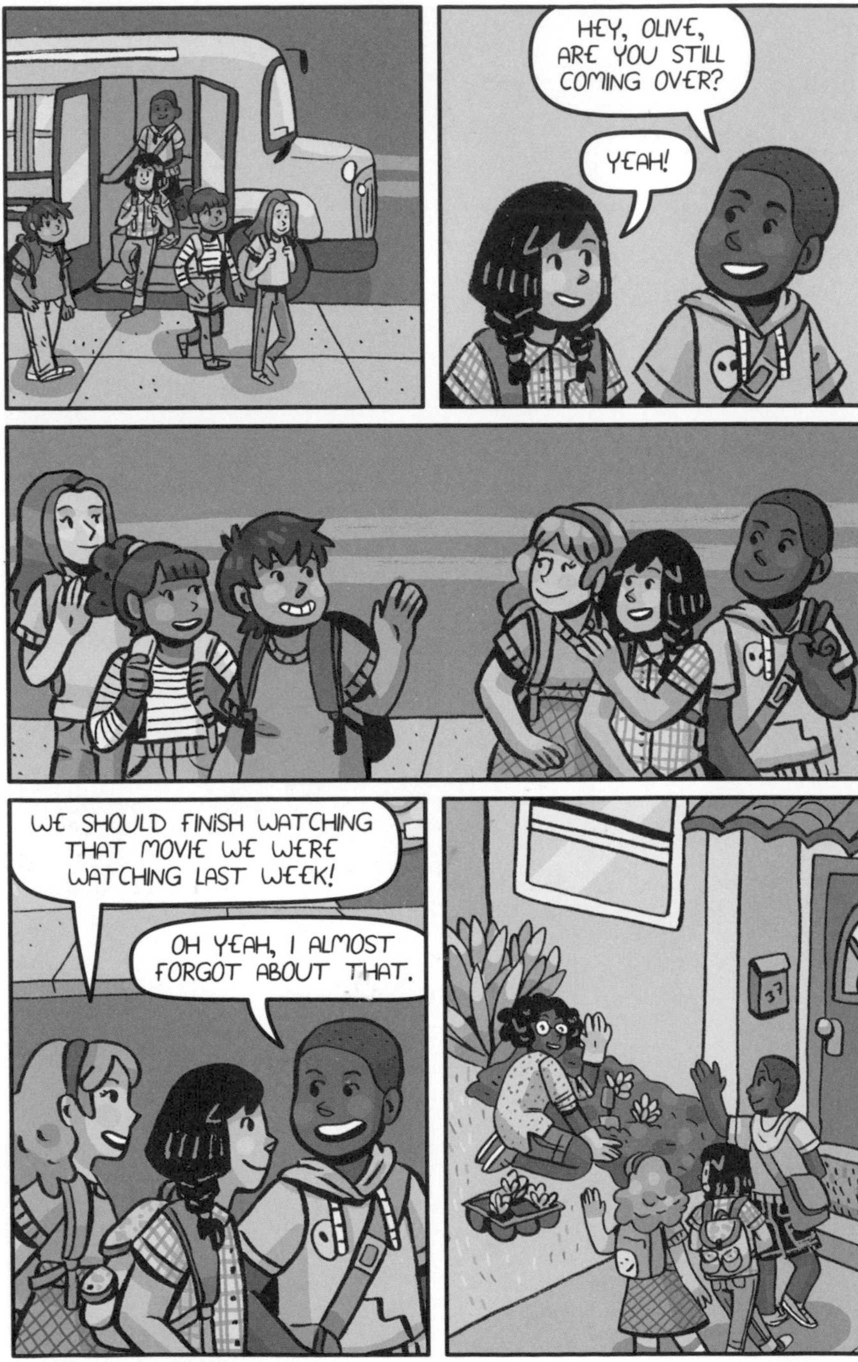
HEY, OLIVE, ARE YOU STILL COMING OVER?
YEAH!
WE SHOULD FINISH WATCHING THAT MOVIE WE WERE WATCHING LAST WEEK!
OH YEAH, I ALMOST FORGOT ABOUT THAT.

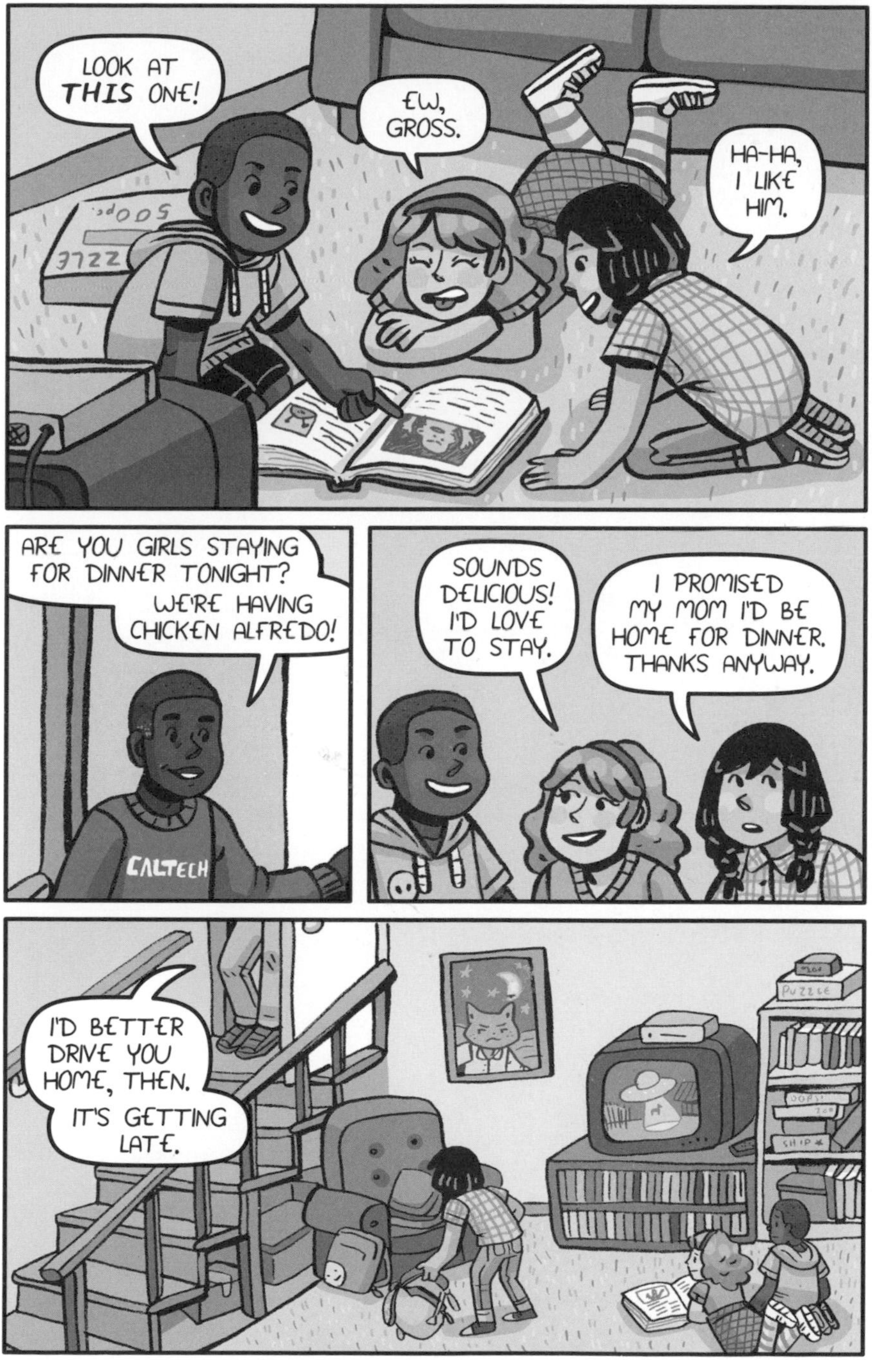

LOOK AT THIS ONE!
EW, GROSS.
HA-HA, I LIKE HIM.
ARE YOU GIRLS STAYING FOR DINNER TONIGHT?
WE'RE HAVING CHICKEN ALFREDO!
CALTECH
SOUNDS DELICIOUS! I'D LOVE TO STAY.
I PROMISED MY MOM I'D BE HOME FOR DINNER. THANKS ANYWAY.
I'D BETTER DRIVE YOU HOME, THEN.
IT'S GETTING LATE.
PUZZLE
SHIP

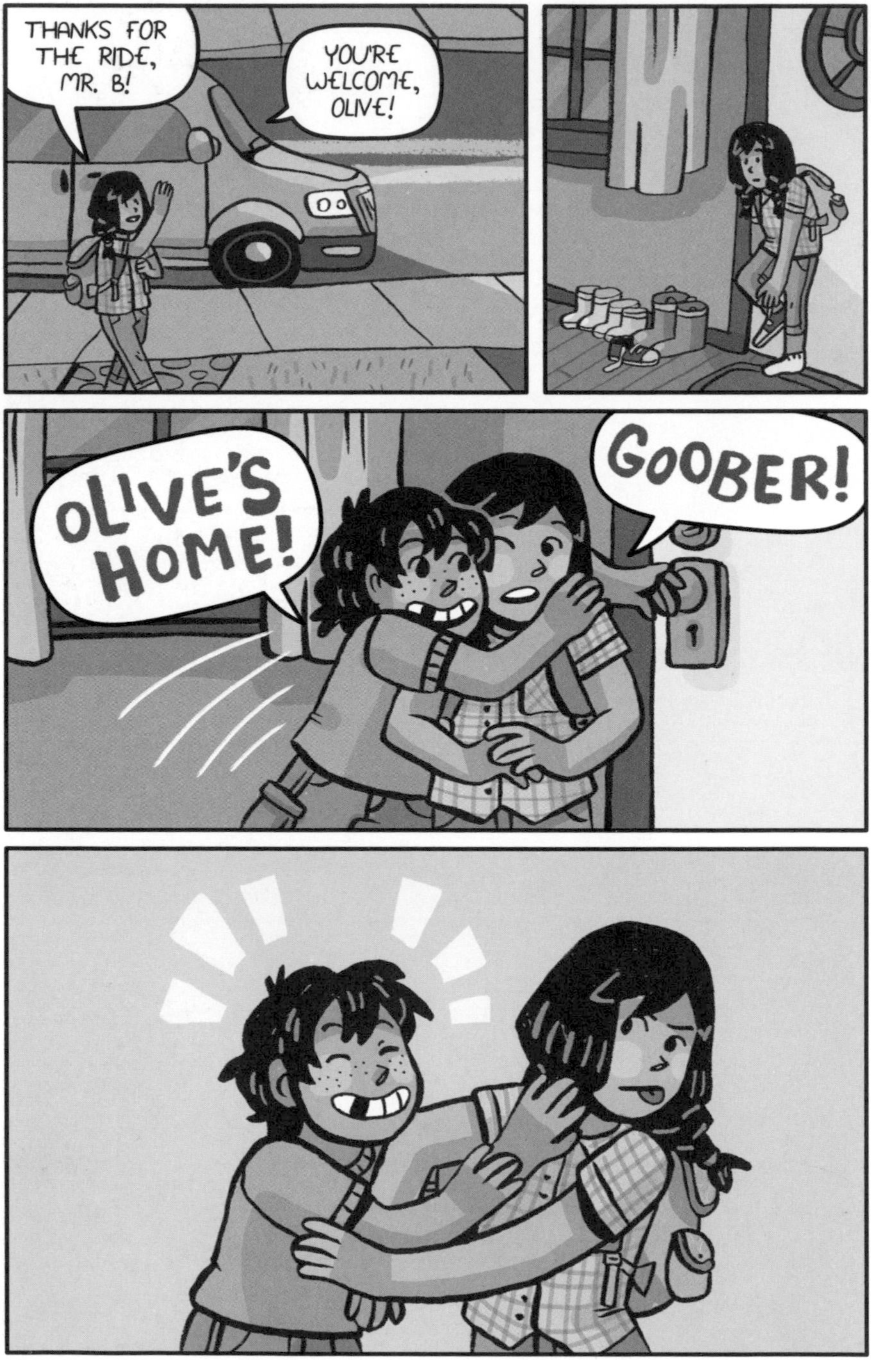
THANKS FOR THE RIDE, MR. B!
YOU'RE WELCOME, OLIVE!
OLIVE'S HOME!
GOOBER!

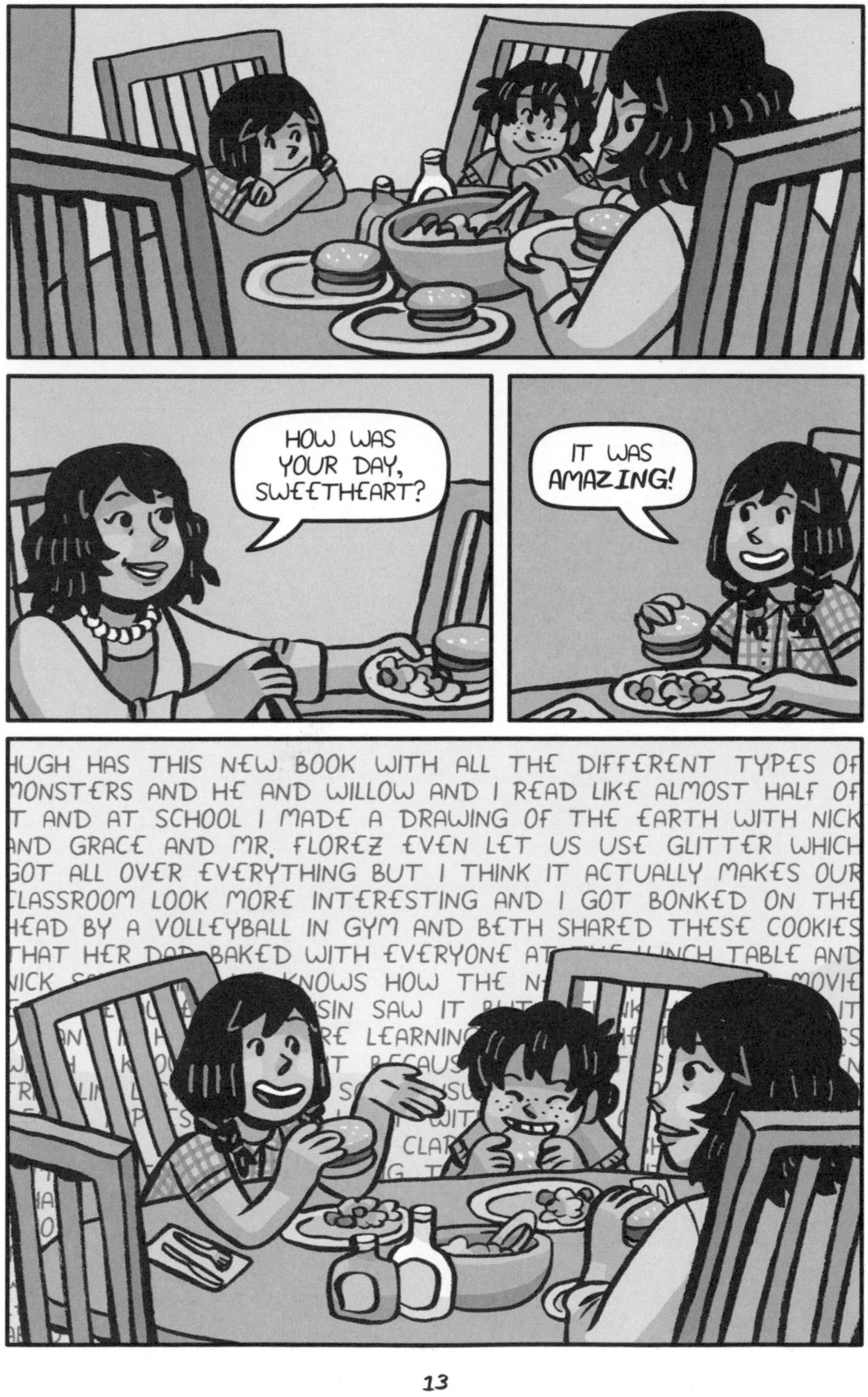
HOW WAS YOUR DAY, SWEETHEART?
IT WAS AMAZING!
HUGH HAS THIS NEW BOOK WITH ALL THE DIFFERENT TYPES OF MONSTERS AND HE AND WILLOW AND I READ LIKE ALMOST HALF OF IT AND AT SCHOOL I MADE A DRAWING OF THE EARTH WITH NICK AND GRACE AND MR. FLOREZ EVEN LET US USE GLITTER WHICH GOT ALL OVER EVERYTHING BUT I THINK IT ACTUALLY MAKES OUR CLASSROOM LOOK MORE INTERESTING AND I GOT BONKED ON THE HEAD BY A VOLLEYBALL IN GYM AND BETH SHARED THESE COOKIES THAT HER DAD BAKED WITH EVERYONE AT THE LUNCH TABLE AND

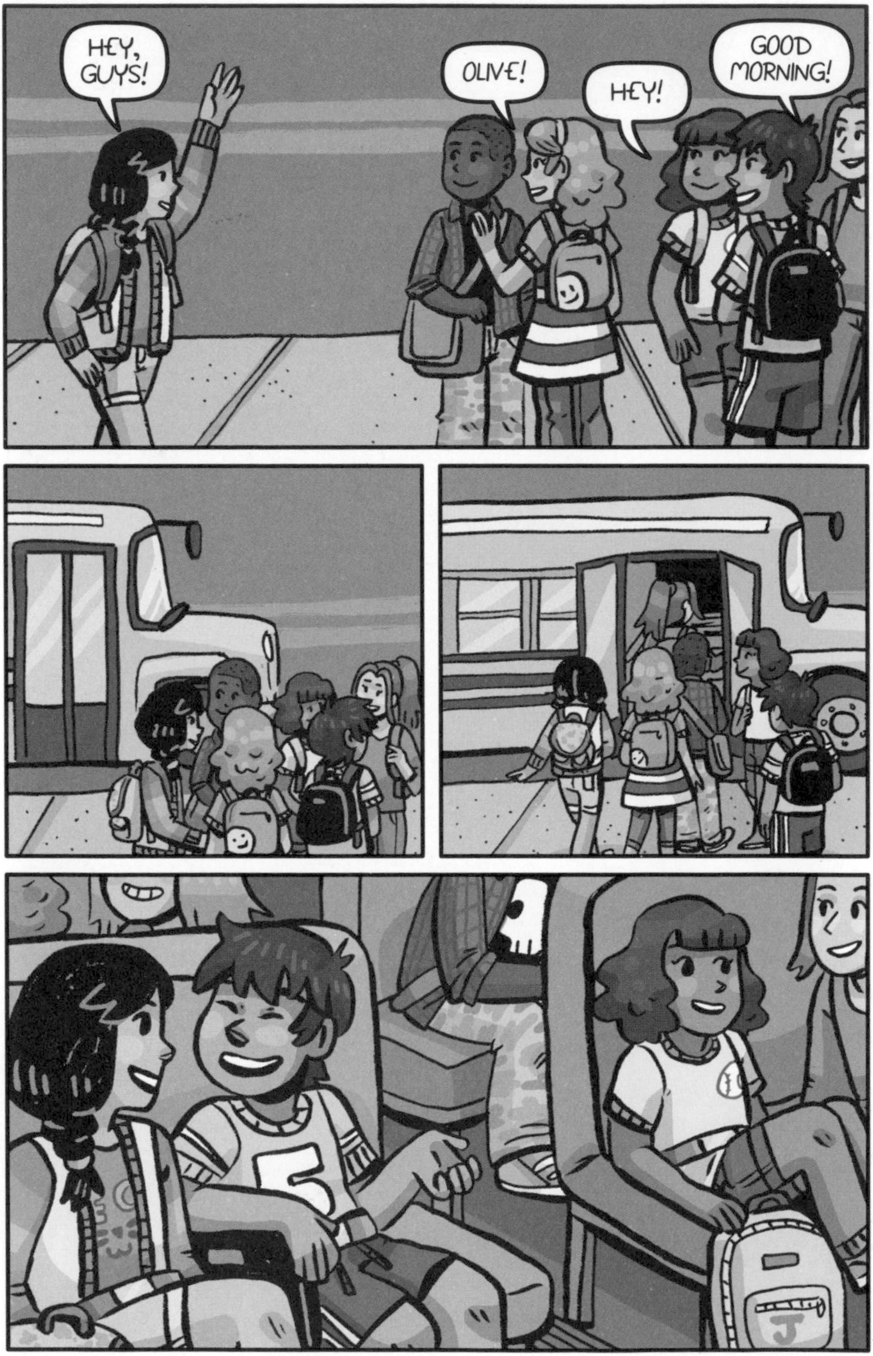
HEY, GUYS!
OLIVE!
HEY!
GOOD MORNING!

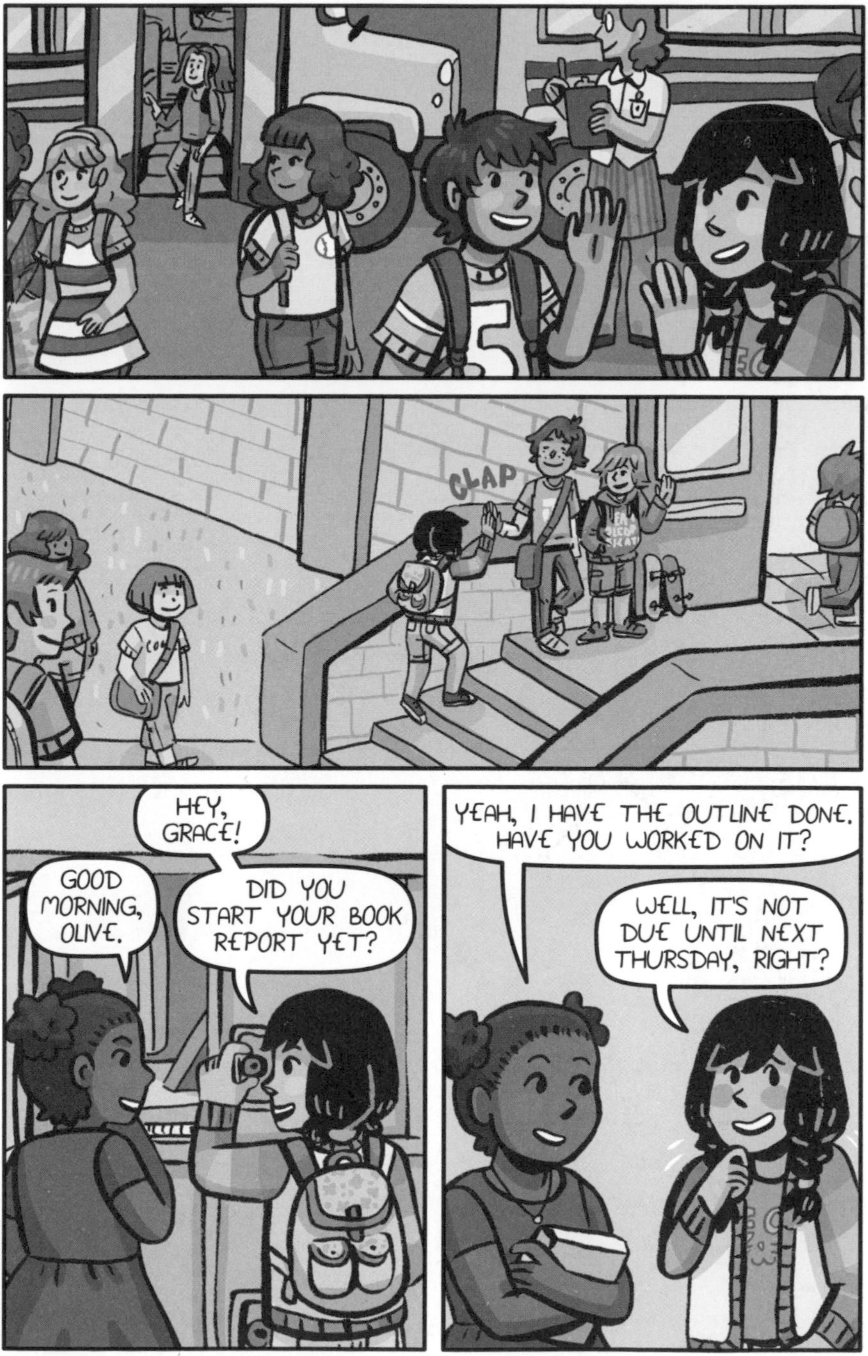
CLAP
HEY, GRACE!
GOOD MORNING, OLIVE.
DID YOU START YOUR BOOK REPORT YET?
YEAH, I HAVE THE OUTLINE DONE. HAVE YOU WORKED ON IT?
WELL, IT'S NOT DUE UNTIL NEXT THURSDAY, RIGHT?

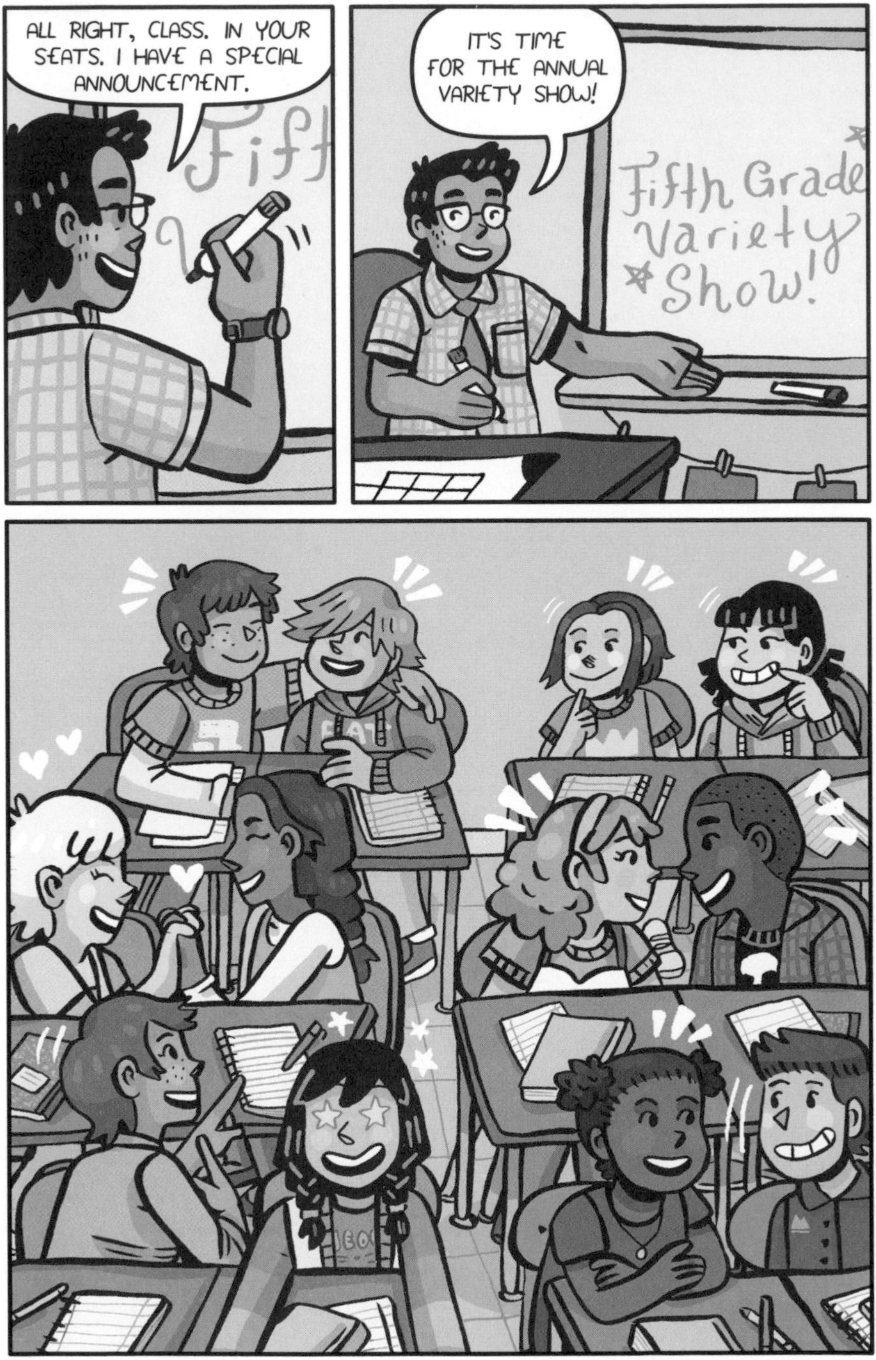
ALL RIGHT, CLASS. IN YOUR SEATS. I HAVE A SPECIAL ANNOUNCEMENT.
IT'S TIME FOR THE ANNUAL VARIETY SHOW!
Fifth Grade Variety Show!

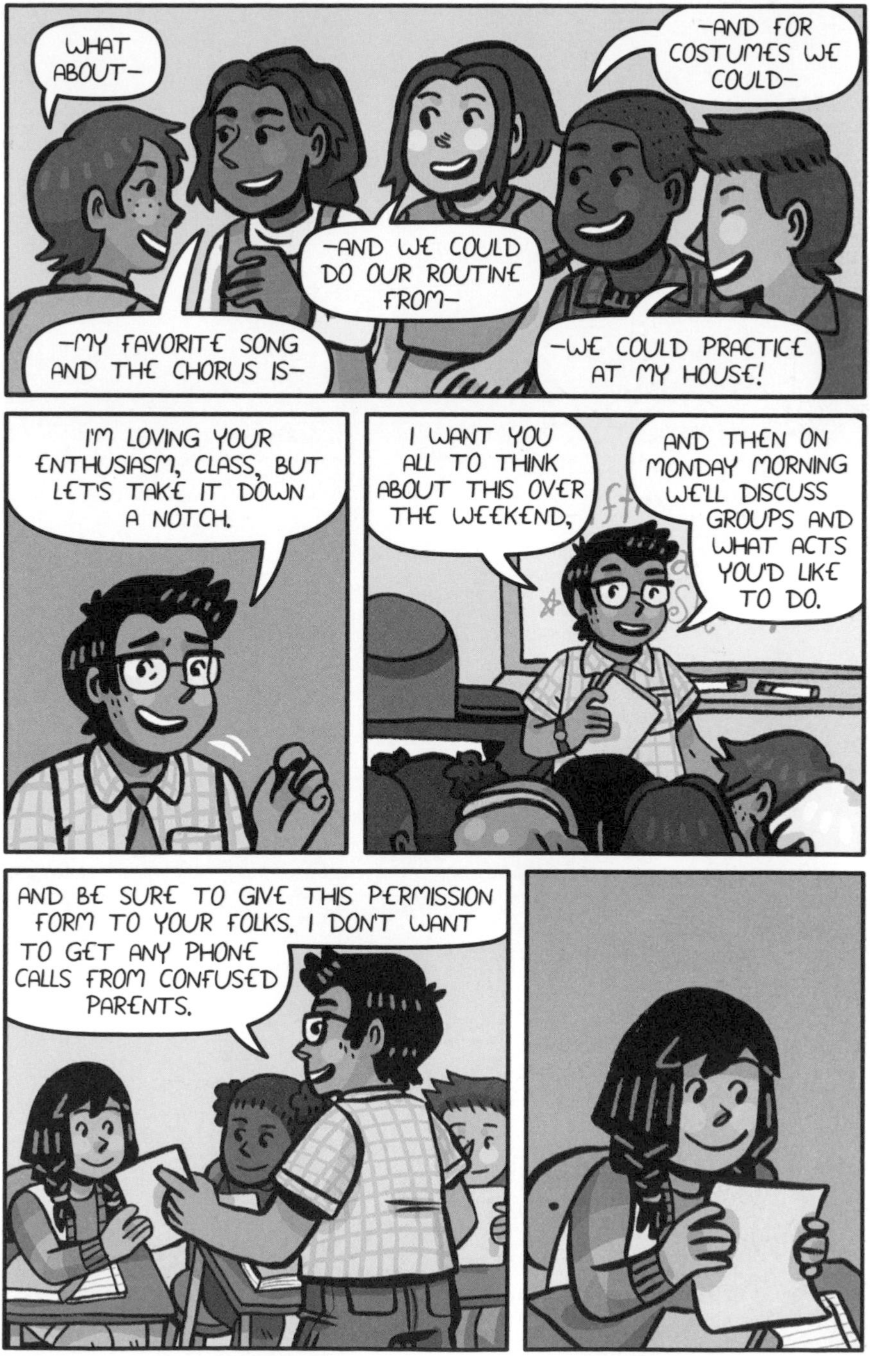
WHAT ABOUT–
–MY FAVORITE SONG AND THE CHORUS IS–
–AND WE COULD DO OUR ROUTINE FROM–
–AND FOR COSTUMES WE COULD–
–WE COULD PRACTICE AT MY HOUSE!
I'M LOVING YOUR ENTHUSIASM, CLASS, BUT LET'S TAKE IT DOWN A NOTCH.
I WANT YOU ALL TO THINK ABOUT THIS OVER THE WEEKEND,
AND THEN ON MONDAY MORNING WE'LL DISCUSS GROUPS AND WHAT ACTS YOU'D LIKE TO DO.
AND BE SURE TO GIVE THIS PERMISSION FORM TO YOUR FOLKS. I DON'T WANT TO GET ANY PHONE CALLS FROM CONFUSED PARENTS.

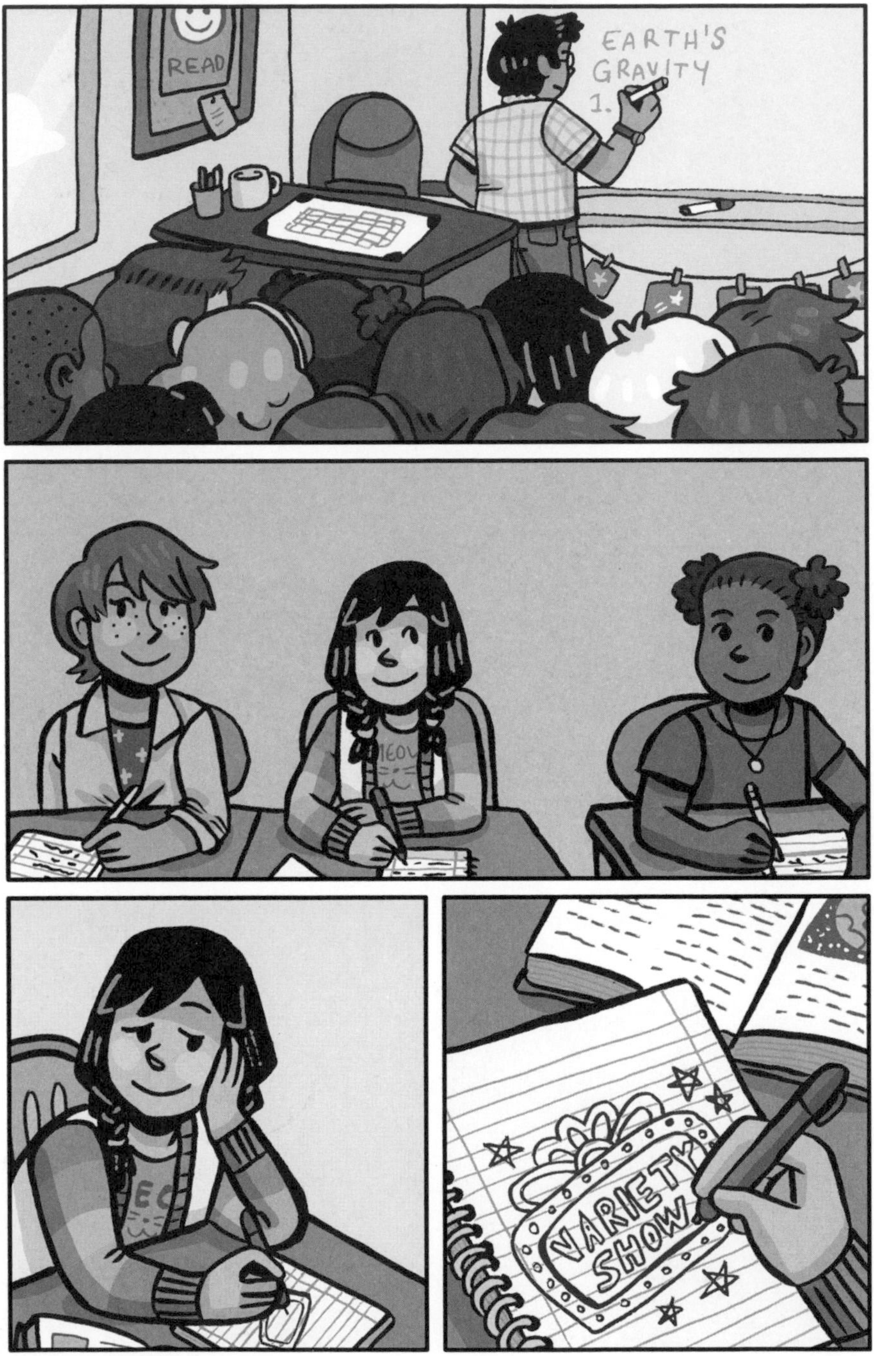
READ
EARTH'S
GRAVITY
1.
VARIETY
SHOW

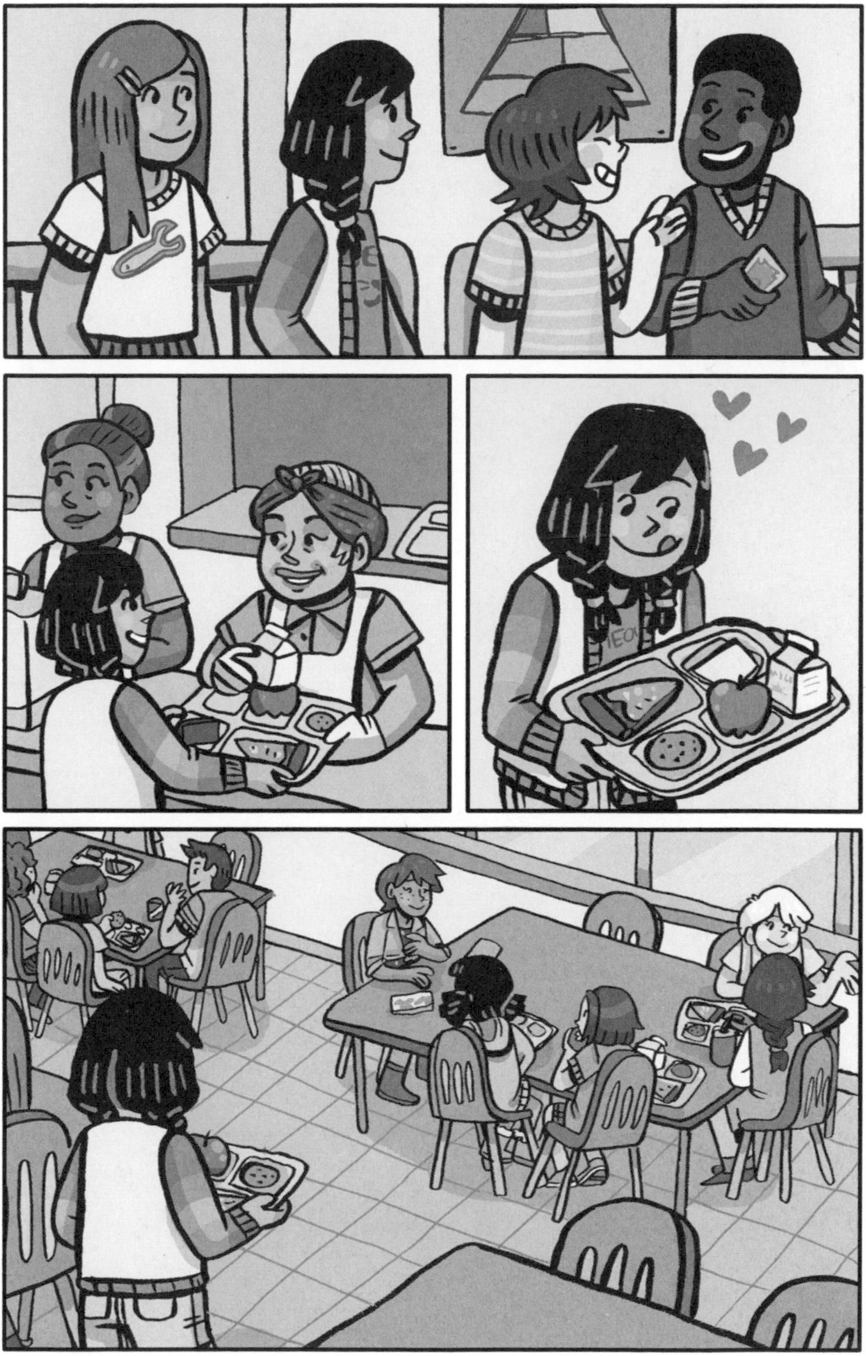

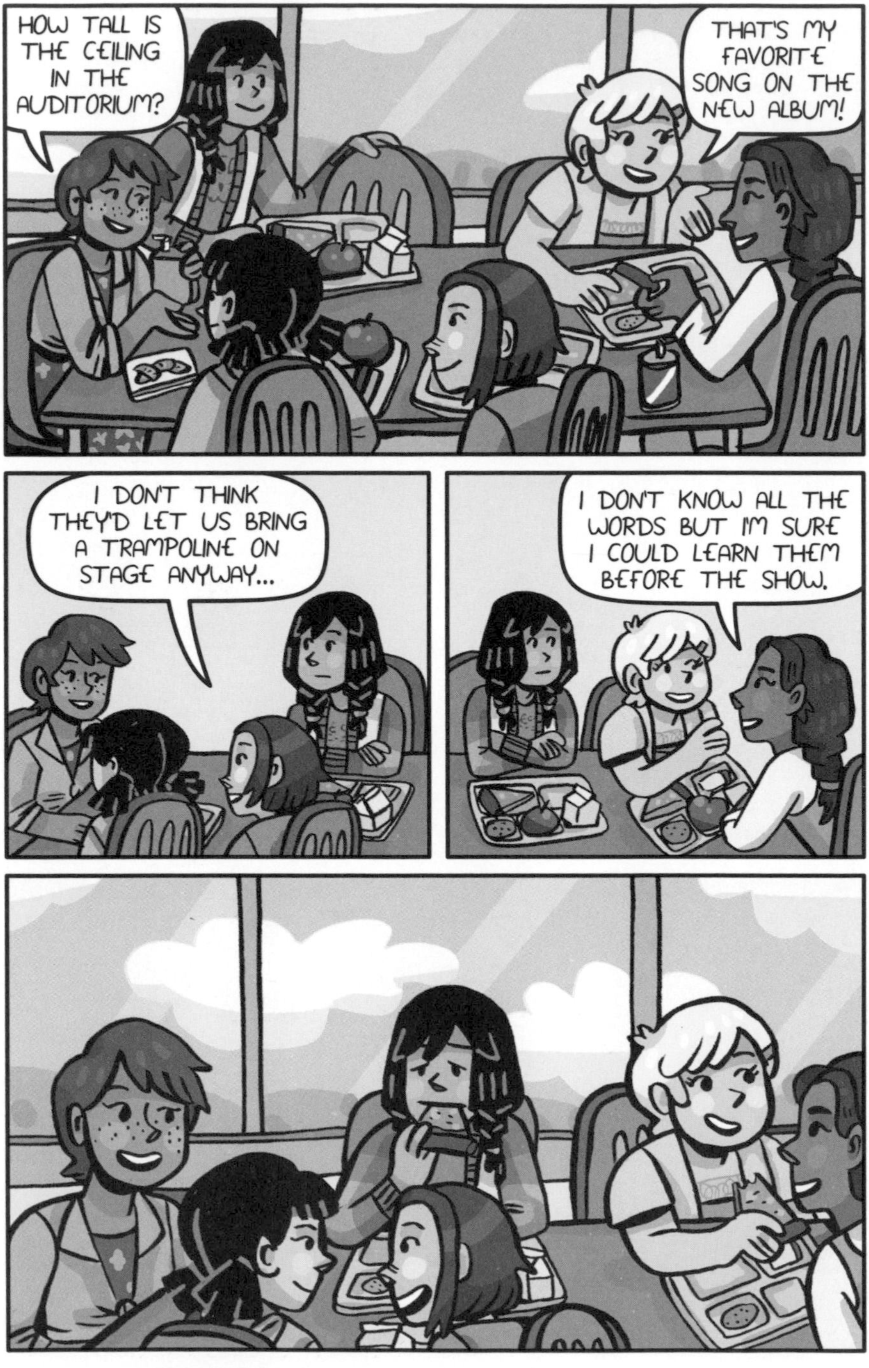
HOW TALL IS THE CEILING IN THE AUDITORIUM?
THAT'S MY FAVORITE SONG ON THE NEW ALBUM!
I DON'T THINK THEY'D LET US BRING A TRAMPOLINE ON STAGE ANYWAY...
I DON'T KNOW ALL THE WORDS BUT I'M SURE I COULD LEARN THEM BEFORE THE SHOW.

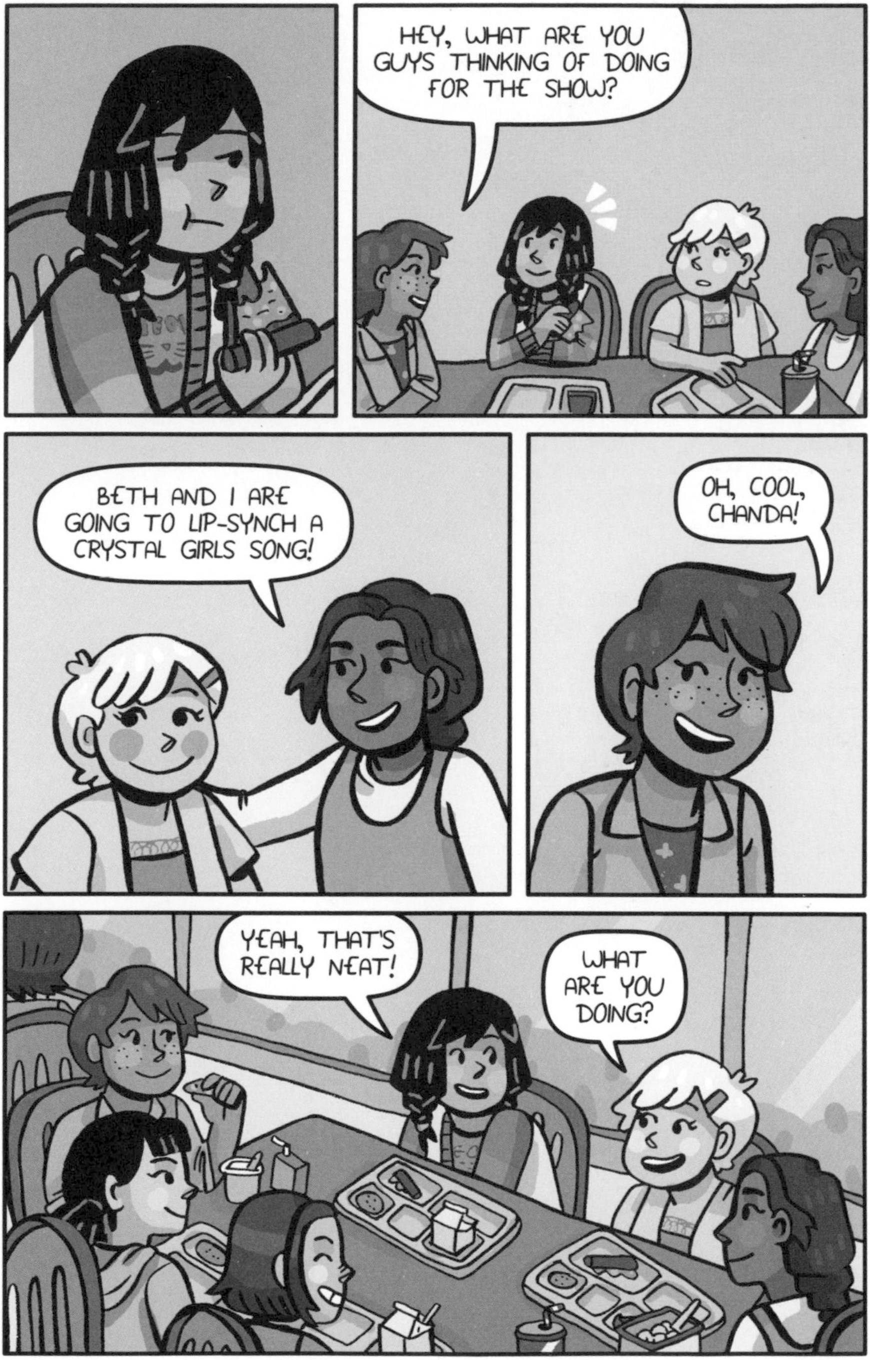
HEY, WHAT ARE YOU GUYS THINKING OF DOING FOR THE SHOW?
BETH AND I ARE GOING TO LIP-SYNCH A CRYSTAL GIRLS SONG!
OH, COOL, CHANDA!
YEAH, THAT'S REALLY NEAT!
WHAT ARE YOU DOING?

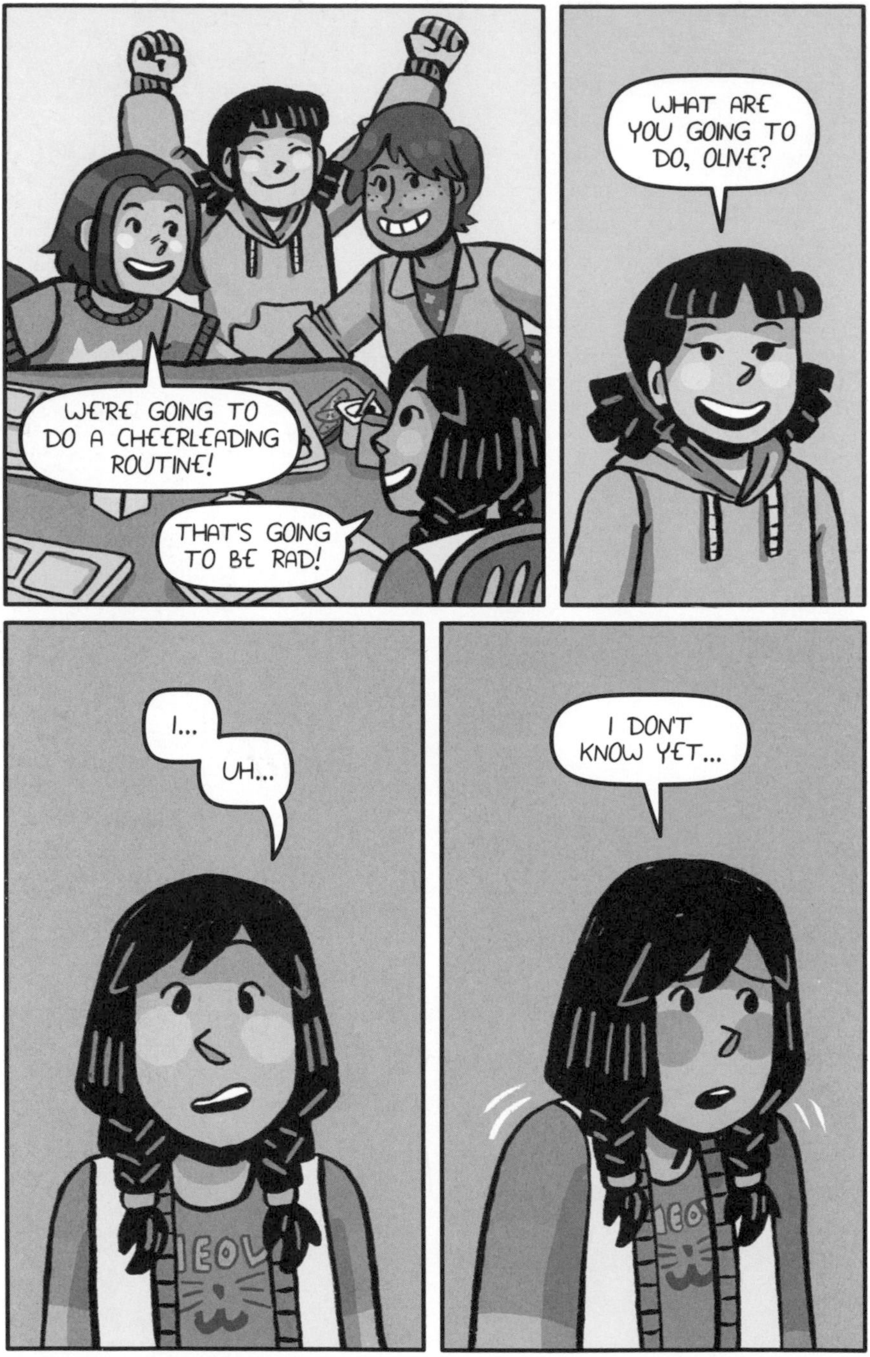
WE'RE GOING TO DO A CHEERLEADING ROUTINE!
THAT'S GOING TO BE RAD!
WHAT ARE YOU GOING TO DO, OLIVE?
I...
UH...
I DON'T KNOW YET...

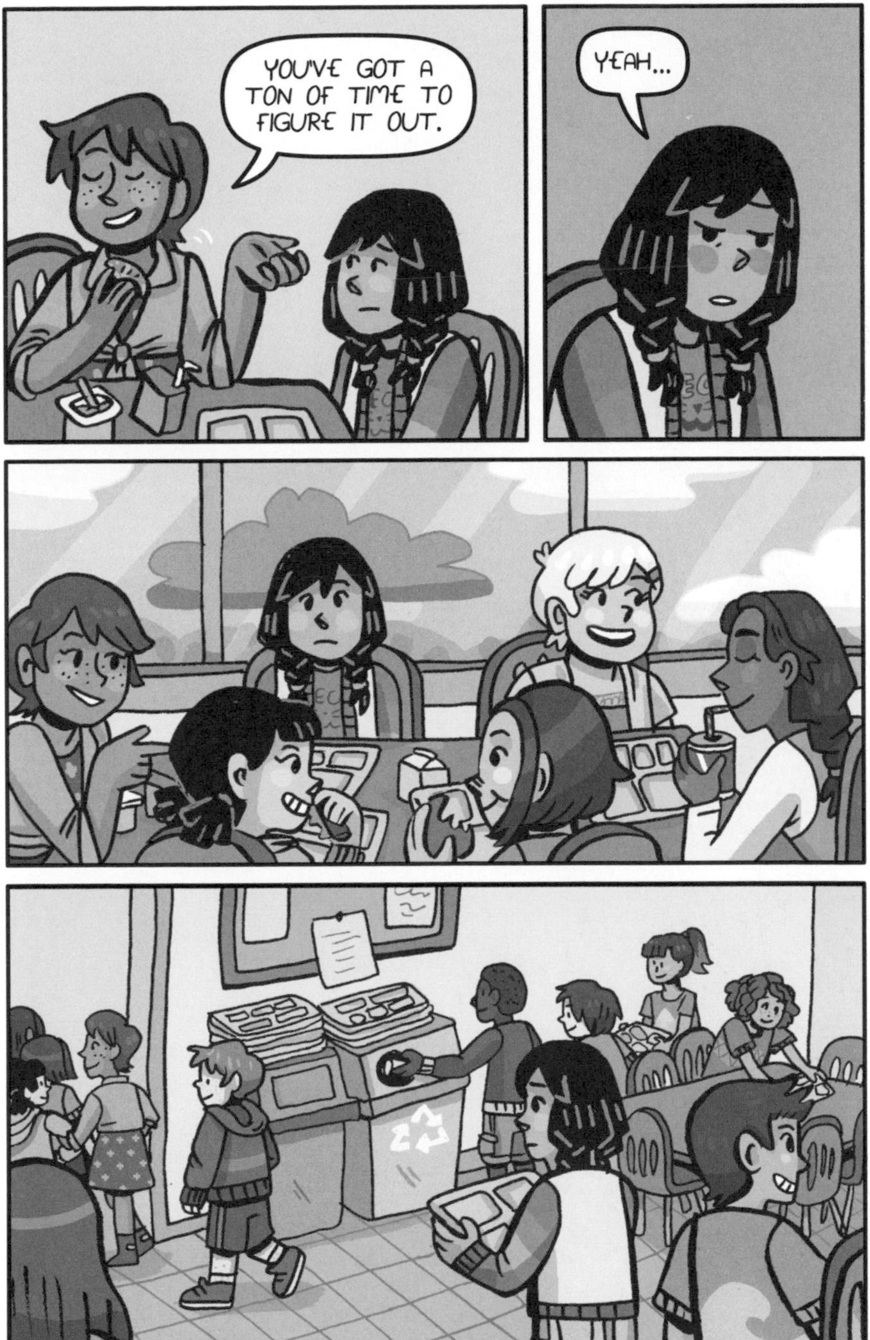
YOU'VE GOT A TON OF TIME TO FIGURE IT OUT.
YEAH...

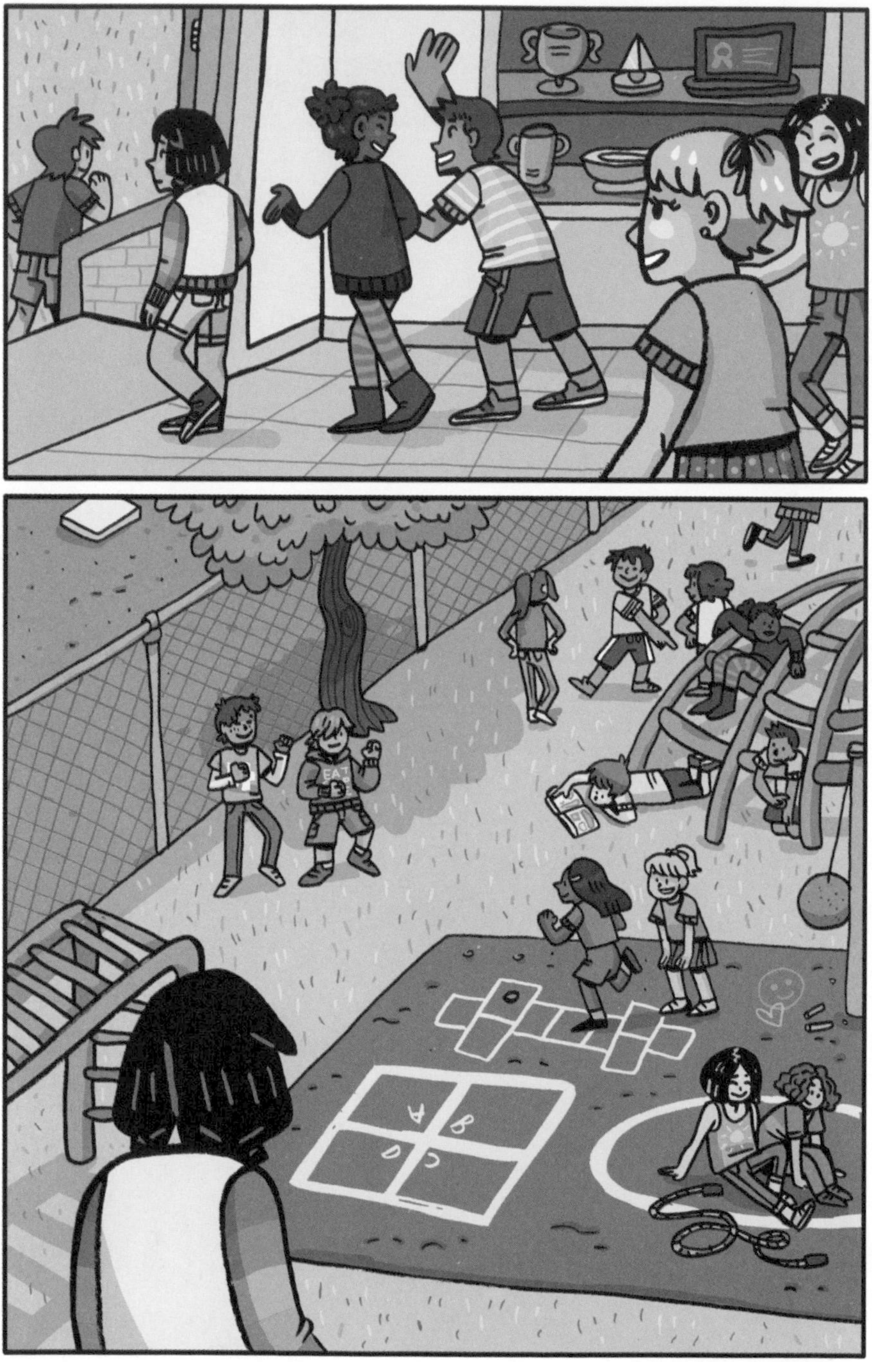

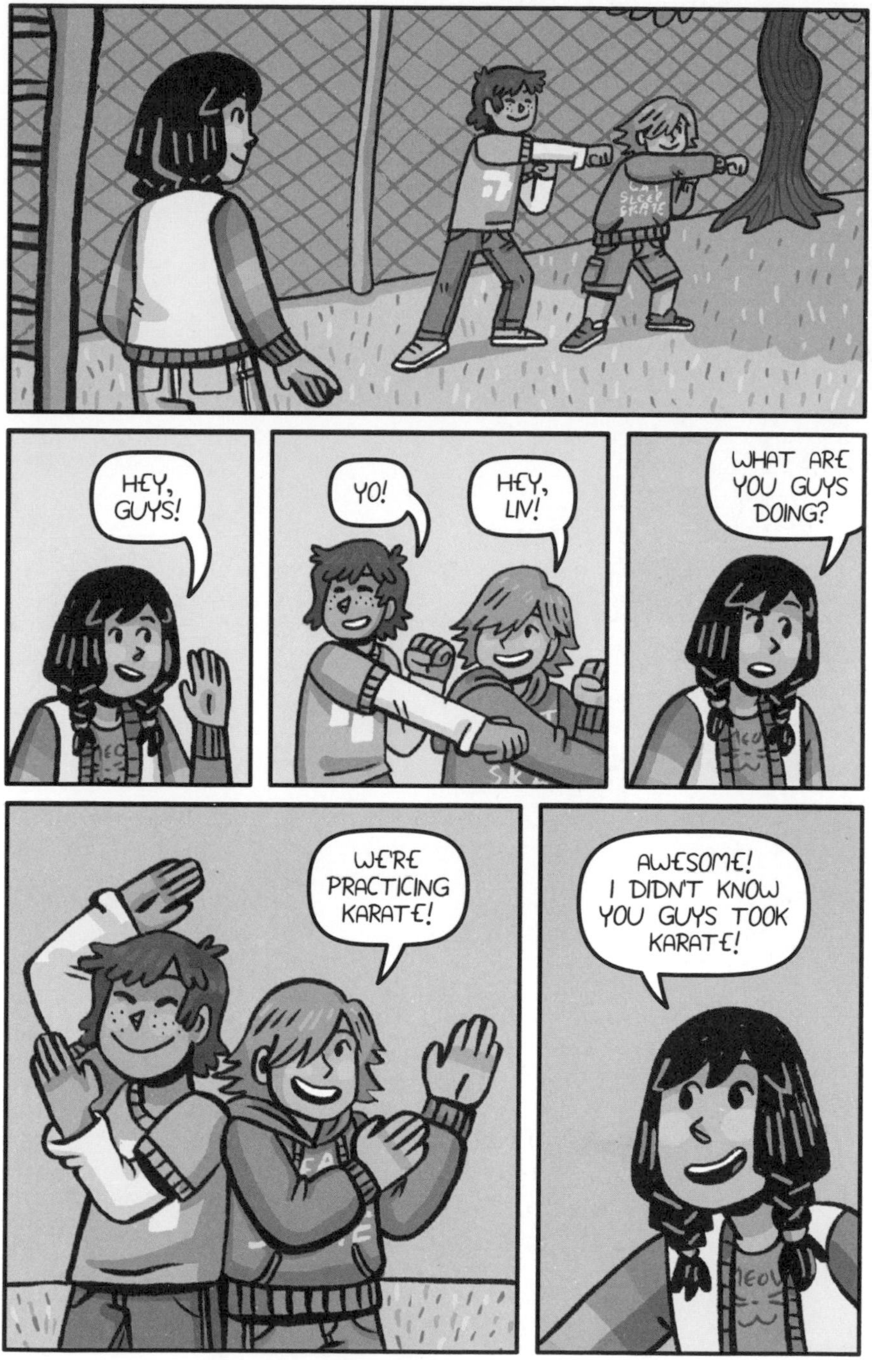
HEY, GUYS!
YO!
HEY, LIV!
WHAT ARE YOU GUYS DOING?
WE'RE PRACTICING KARATE!
AWESOME! I DIDN'T KNOW YOU GUYS TOOK KARATE!

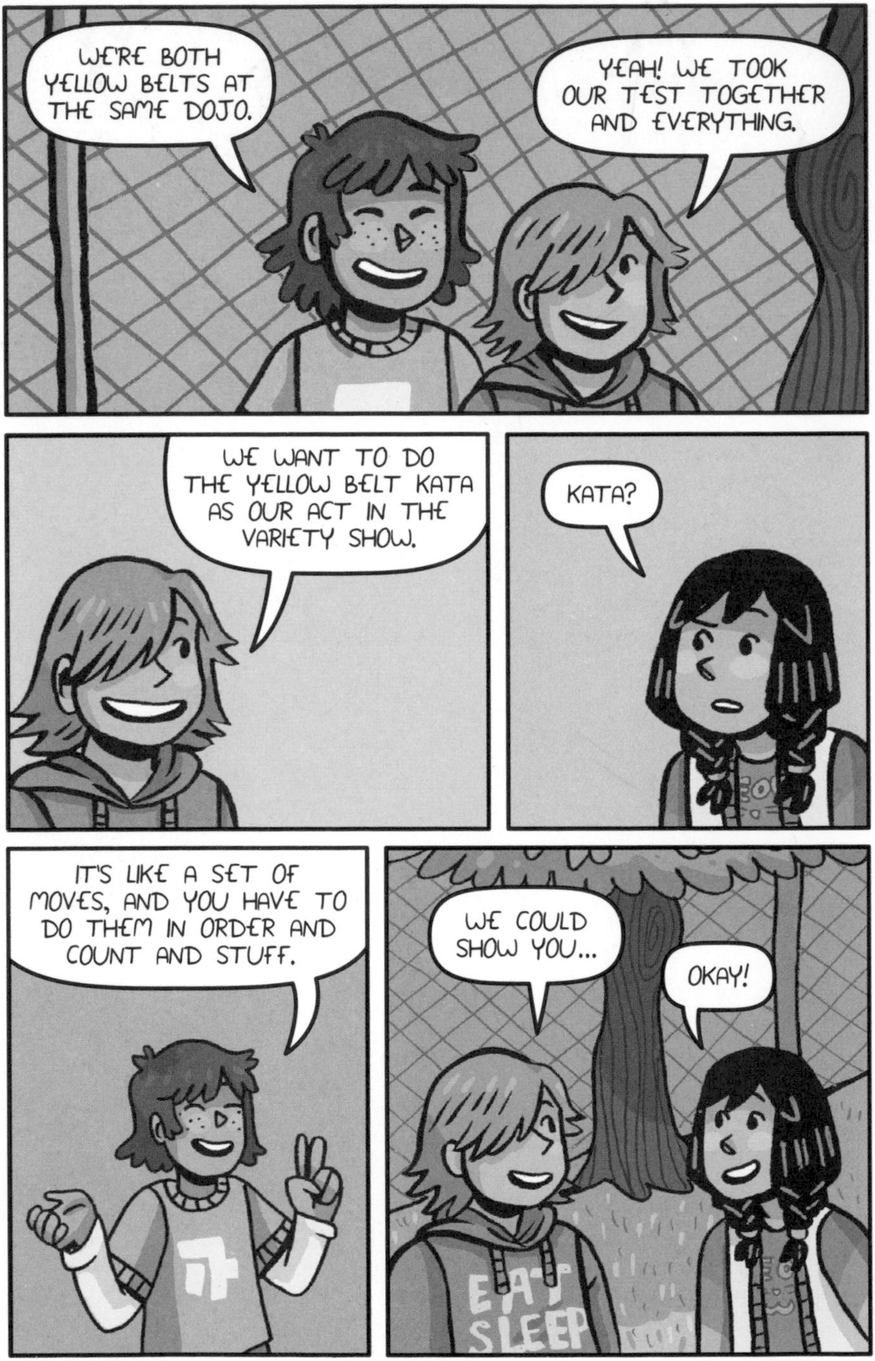
WE'RE BOTH YELLOW BELTS AT THE SAME DOJO.
YEAH! WE TOOK OUR TEST TOGETHER AND EVERYTHING.
WE WANT TO DO THE YELLOW BELT KATA AS OUR ACT IN THE VARIETY SHOW.
KATA?
IT'S LIKE A SET OF MOVES, AND YOU HAVE TO DO THEM IN ORDER AND COUNT AND STUFF.
WE COULD SHOW YOU...
OKAY!
EAT SLEEP

THAT WAS GREAT!

YOU CAN KEEP WATCHING US PRACTICE IF YOU WANT.

OH...

YOU'RE NOT DONE?

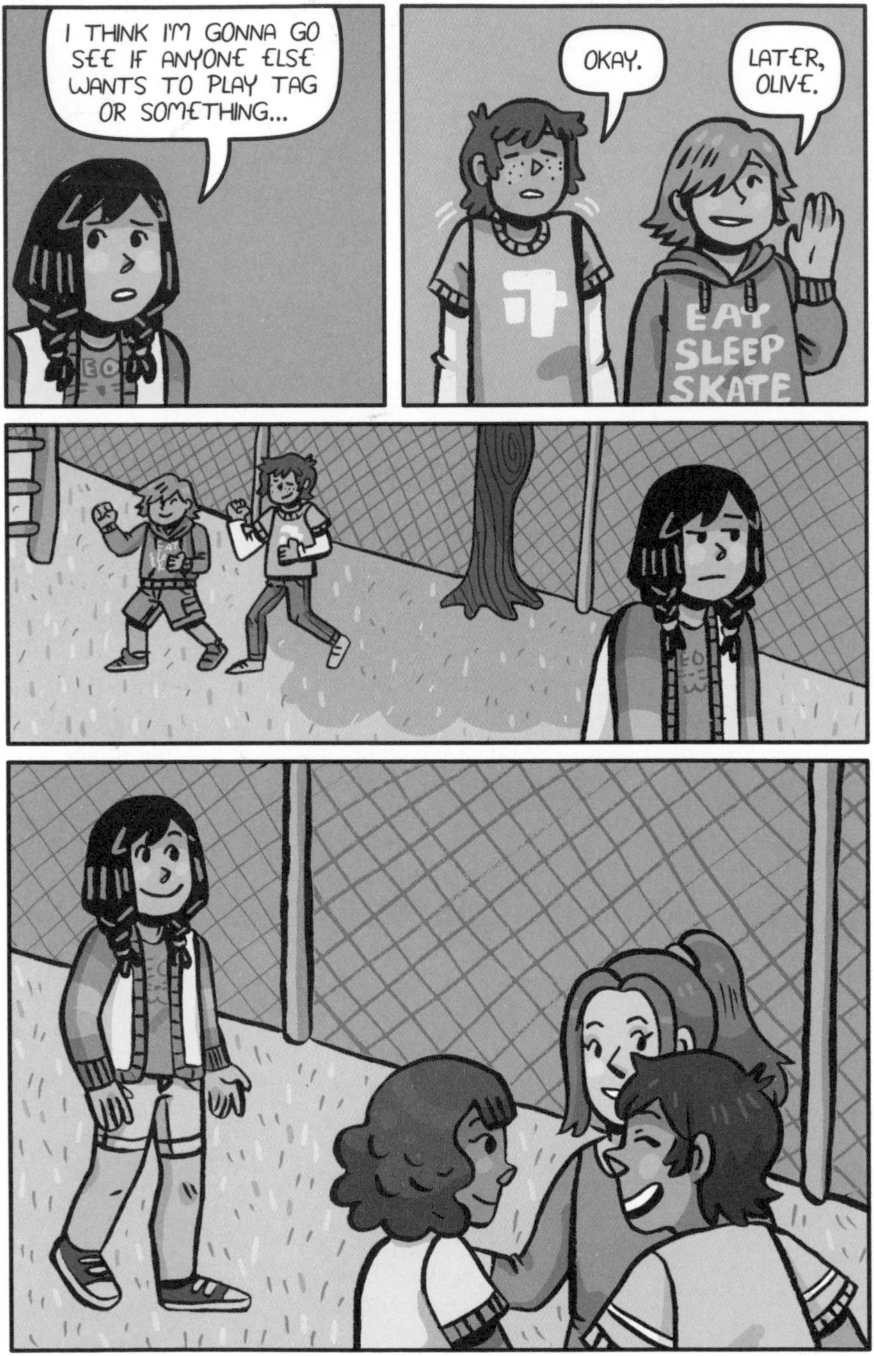
I THINK I'M GONNA GO SEE IF ANYONE ELSE WANTS TO PLAY TAG OR SOMETHING...
OKAY.
LATER, OLIVE.
EAT SLEEP SKATE

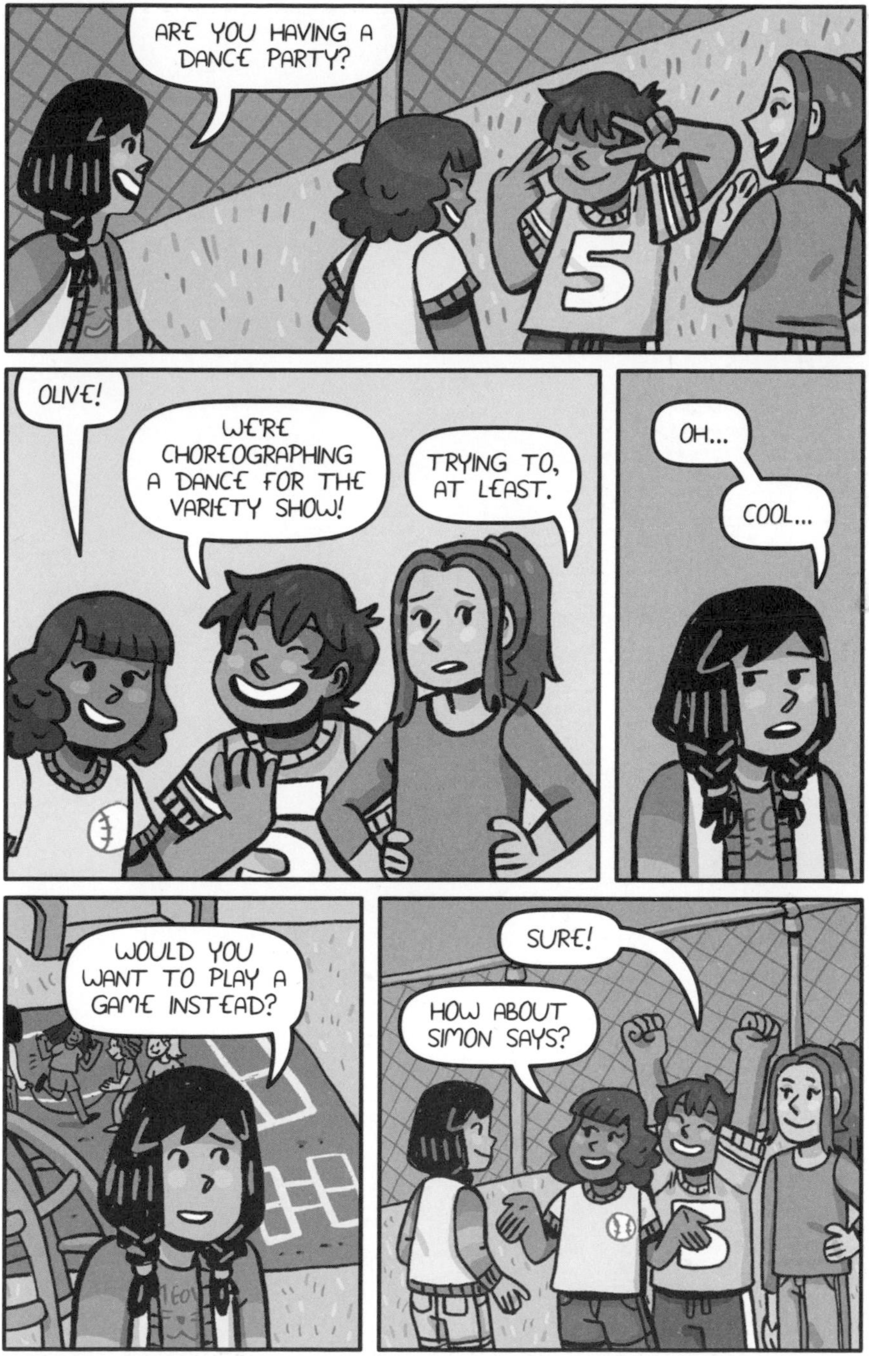
ARE YOU HAVING A DANCE PARTY?
OLIVE!
WE'RE CHOREOGRAPHING A DANCE FOR THE VARIETY SHOW!
TRYING TO, AT LEAST.
OH...
COOL...
WOULD YOU WANT TO PLAY A GAME INSTEAD?
SURE!
HOW ABOUT SIMON SAYS?

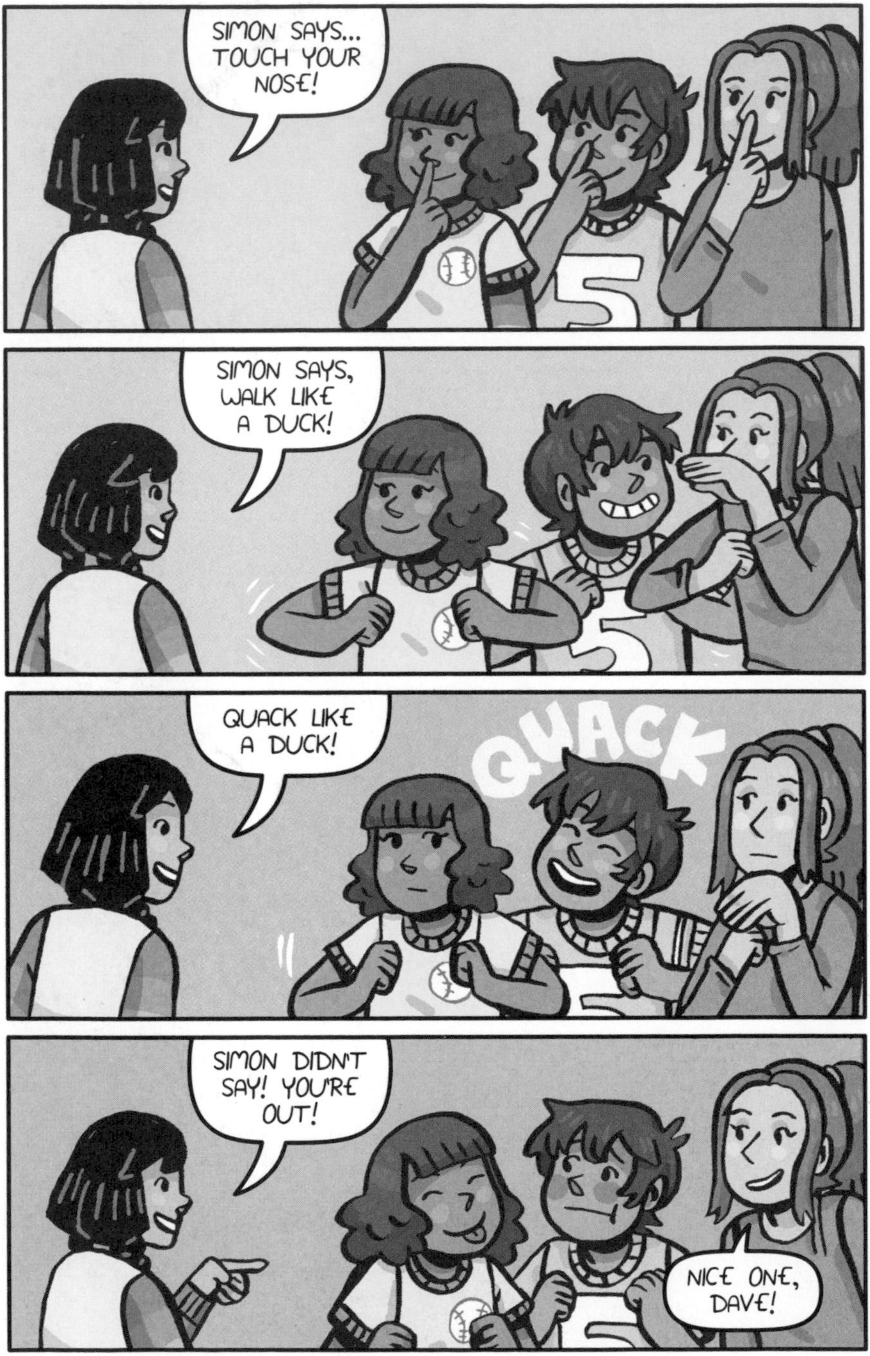
SIMON SAYS... TOUCH YOUR NOSE!
SIMON SAYS, WALK LIKE A DUCK!
QUACK LIKE A DUCK!
QUACK
SIMON DIDN'T SAY! YOU'RE OUT!
NICE ONE, DAVE!

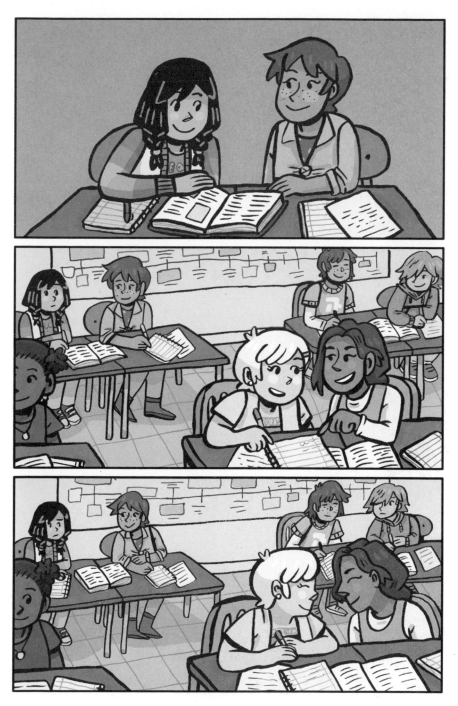

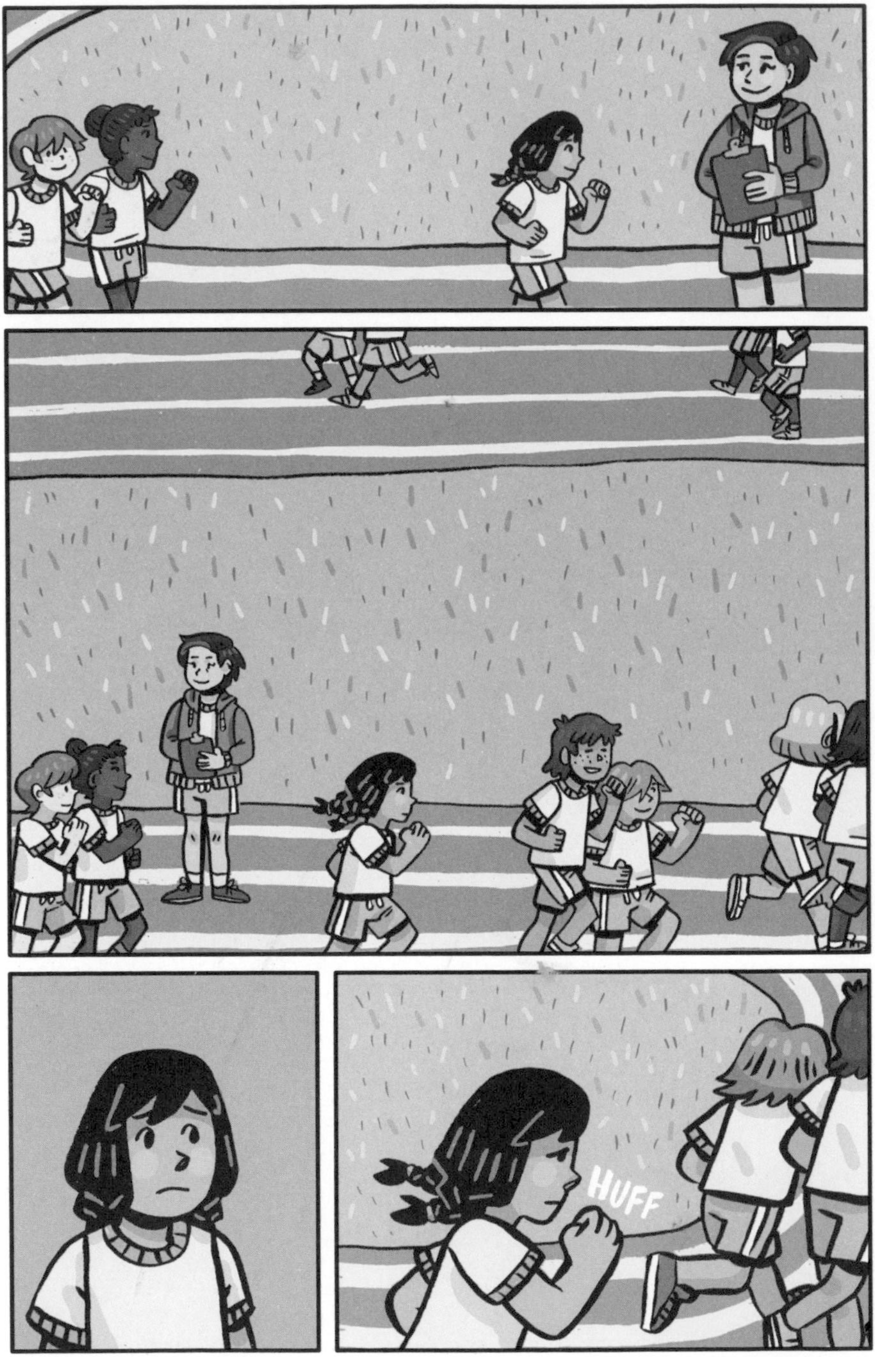
HUFF

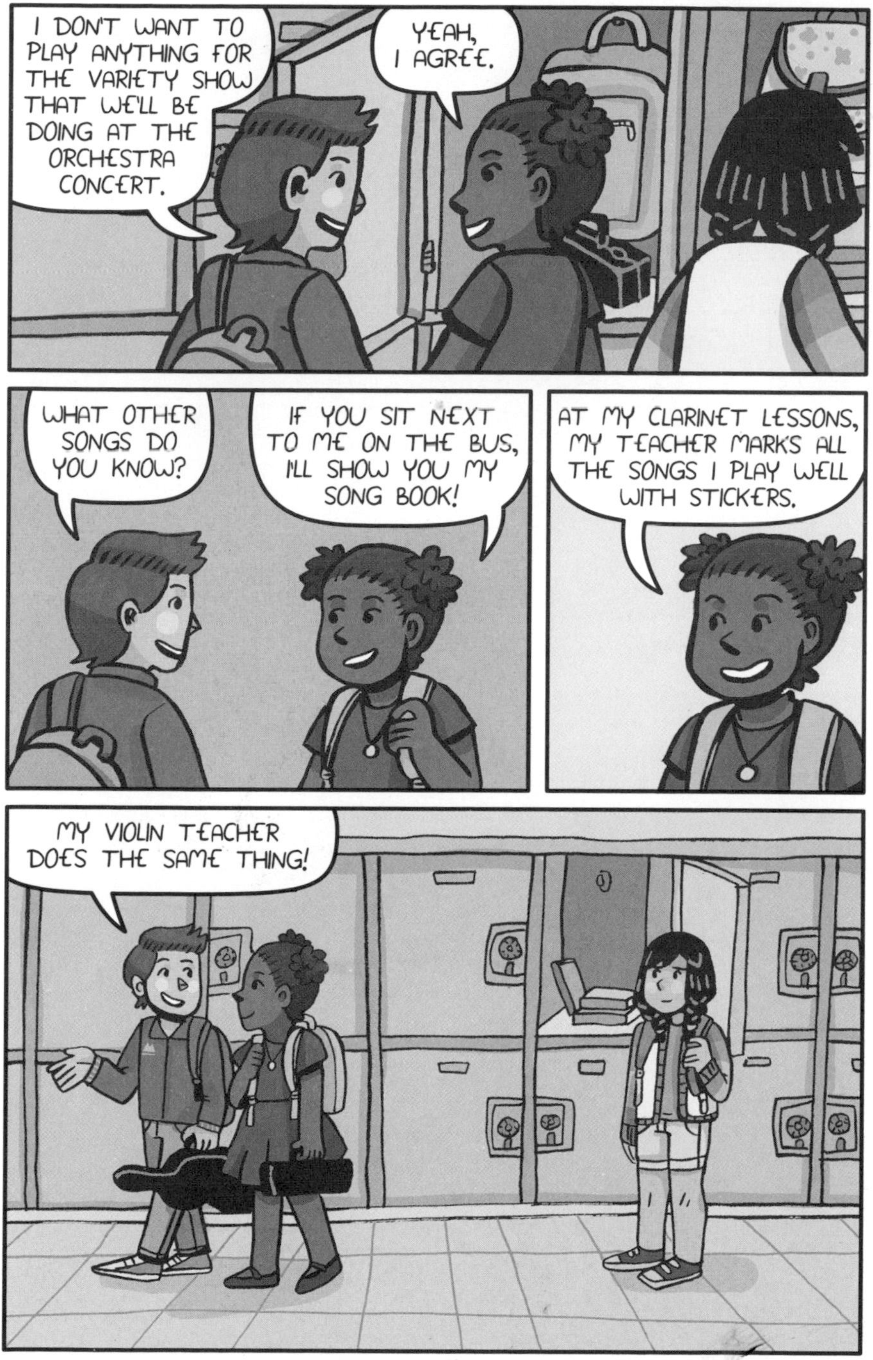
I DON'T WANT TO PLAY ANYTHING FOR THE VARIETY SHOW THAT WE'LL BE DOING AT THE ORCHESTRA CONCERT.
YEAH, I AGREE.
WHAT OTHER SONGS DO YOU KNOW?
IF YOU SIT NEXT TO ME ON THE BUS, I'LL SHOW YOU MY SONG BOOK!
AT MY CLARINET LESSONS, MY TEACHER MARKS ALL THE SONGS I PLAY WELL WITH STICKERS.
MY VIOLIN TEACHER DOES THE SAME THING!

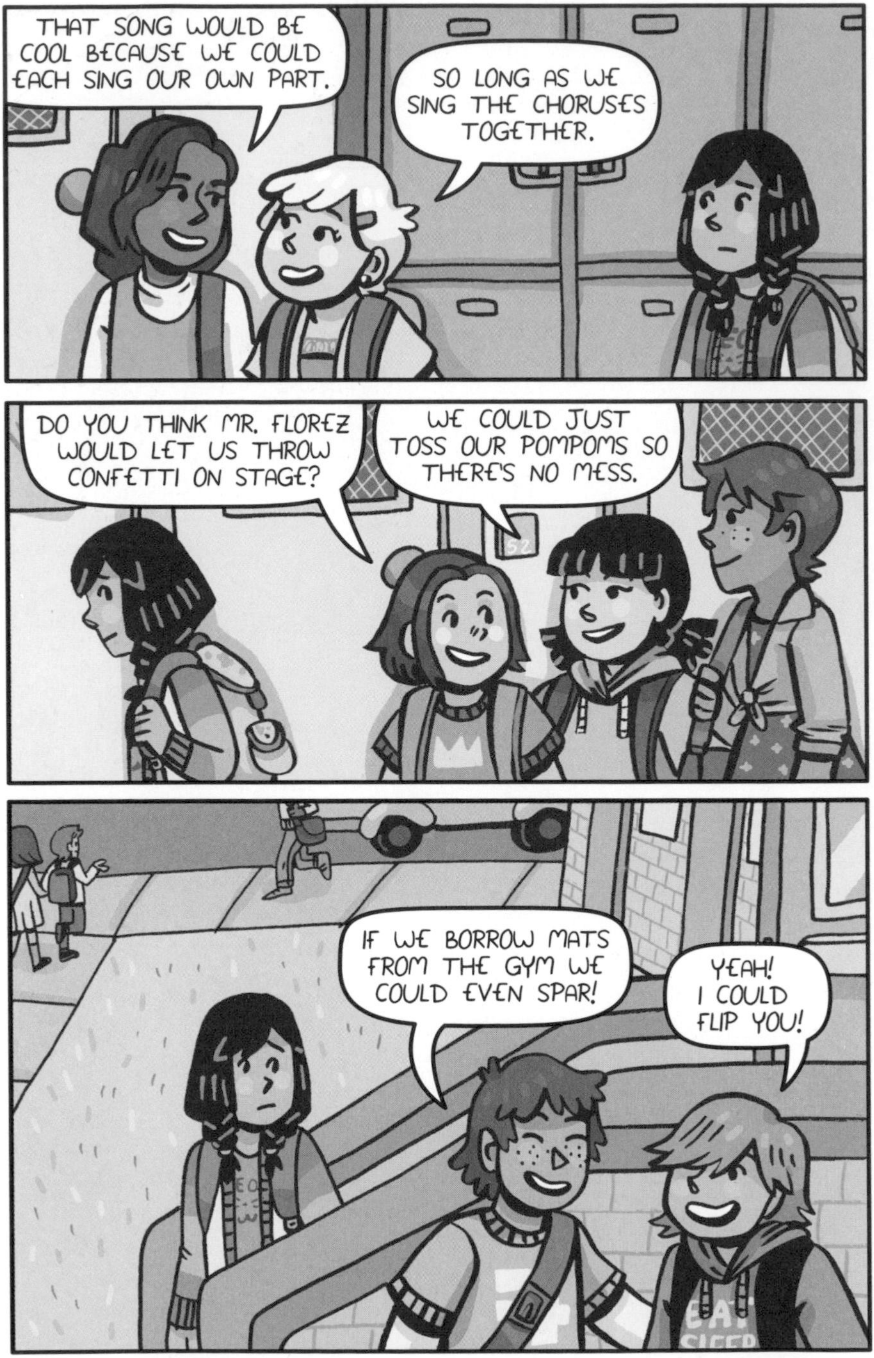
THAT SONG WOULD BE COOL BECAUSE WE COULD EACH SING OUR OWN PART.
SO LONG AS WE SING THE CHORUSES TOGETHER.
DO YOU THINK MR. FLOREZ WOULD LET US THROW CONFETTI ON STAGE?
WE COULD JUST TOSS OUR POMPOMS SO THERE'S NO MESS.
52
IF WE BORROW MATS FROM THE GYM WE COULD EVEN SPAR!
YEAH! I COULD FLIP YOU!

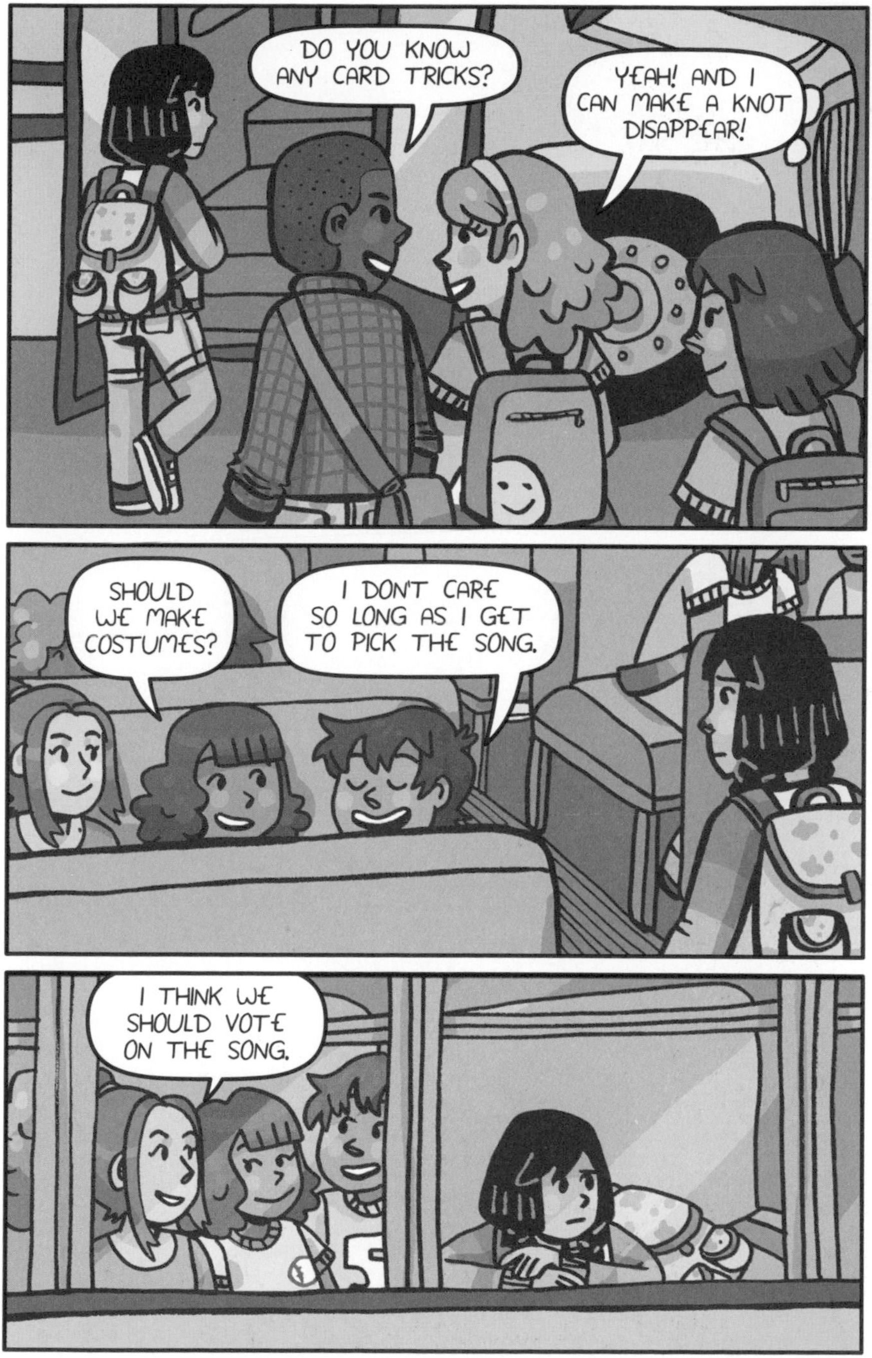
DO YOU KNOW ANY CARD TRICKS?
YEAH! AND I CAN MAKE A KNOT DISAPPEAR!
SHOULD WE MAKE COSTUMES?
I DON'T CARE SO LONG AS I GET TO PICK THE SONG.
I THINK WE SHOULD VOTE ON THE SONG.

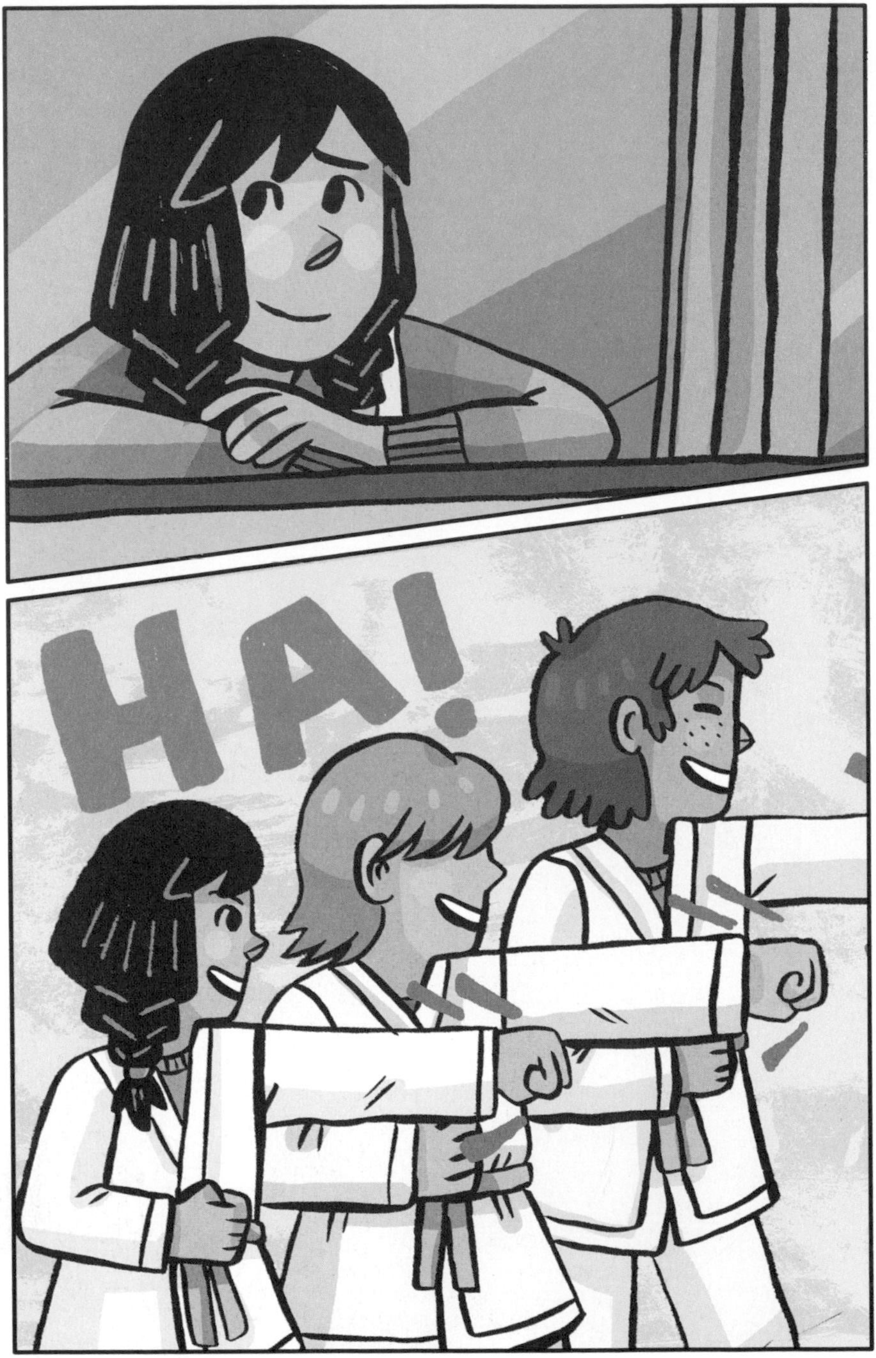
HA!

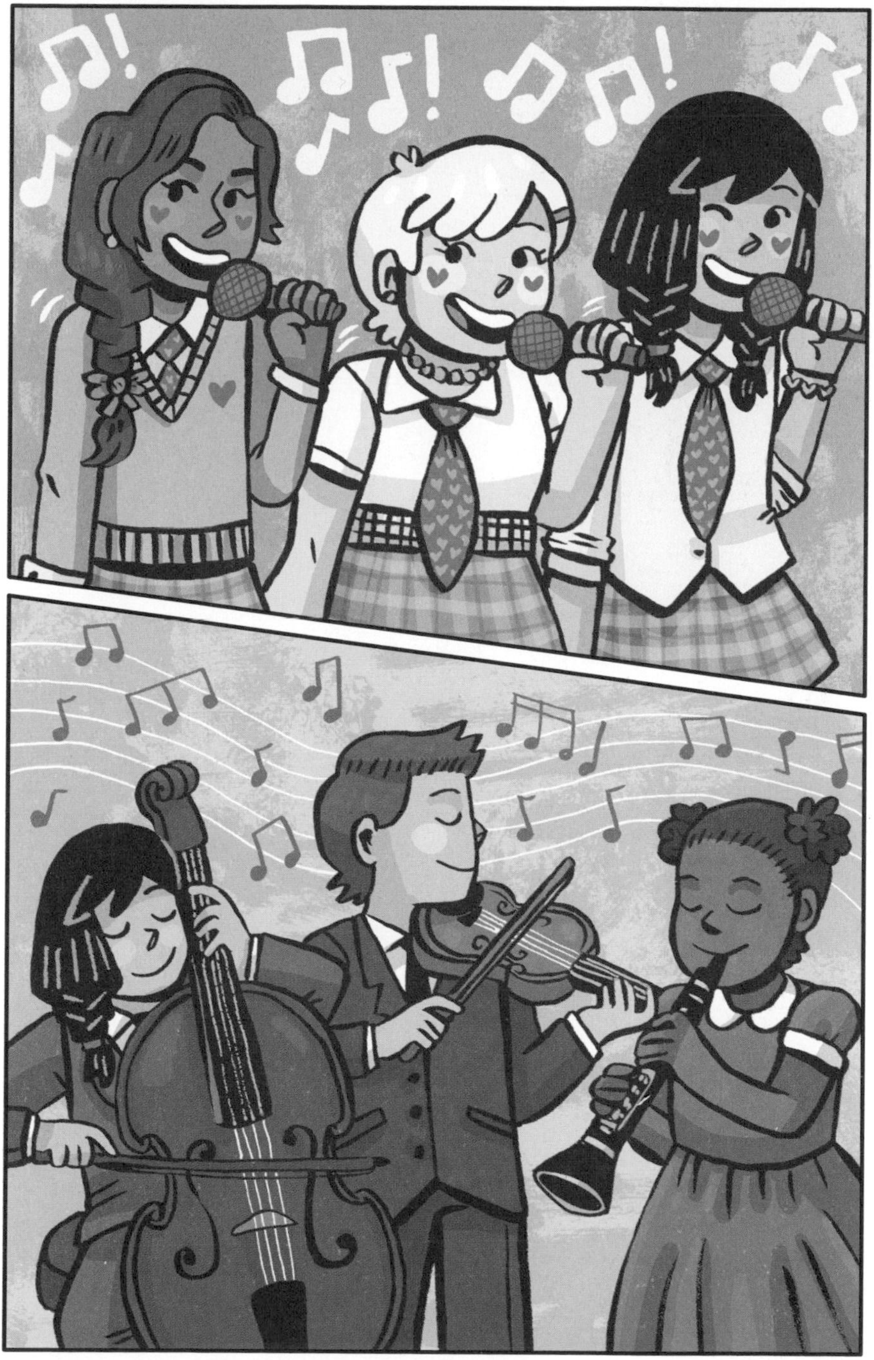

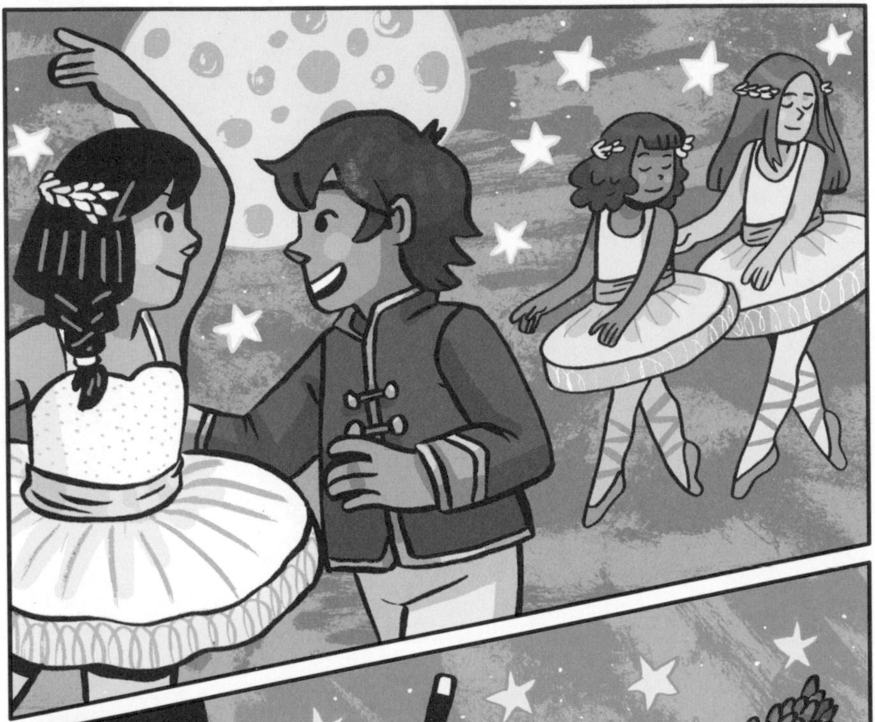

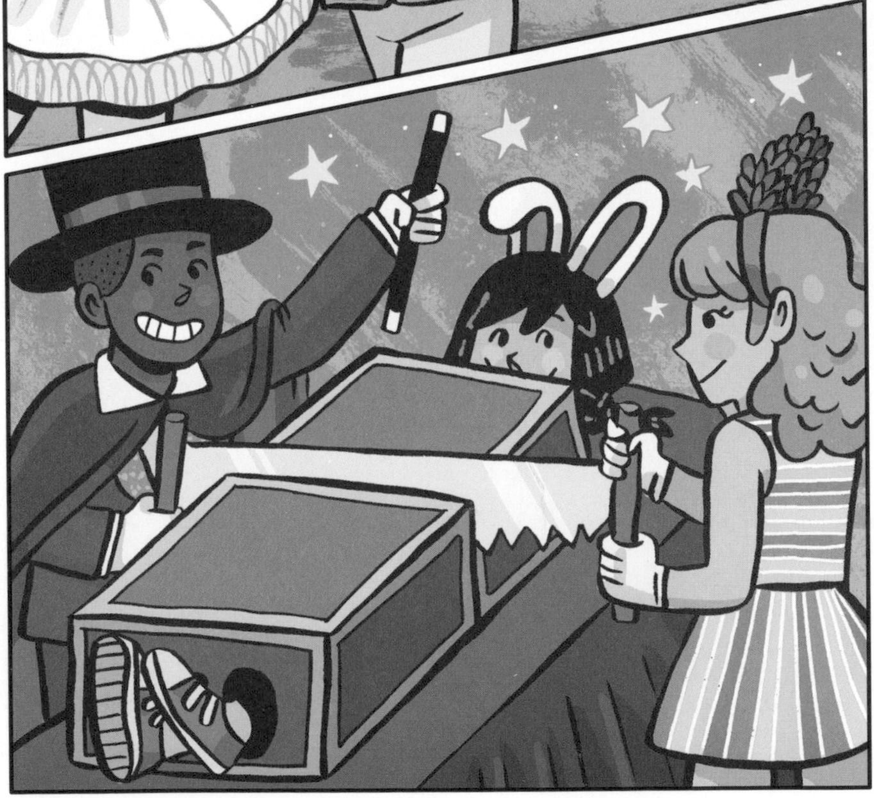

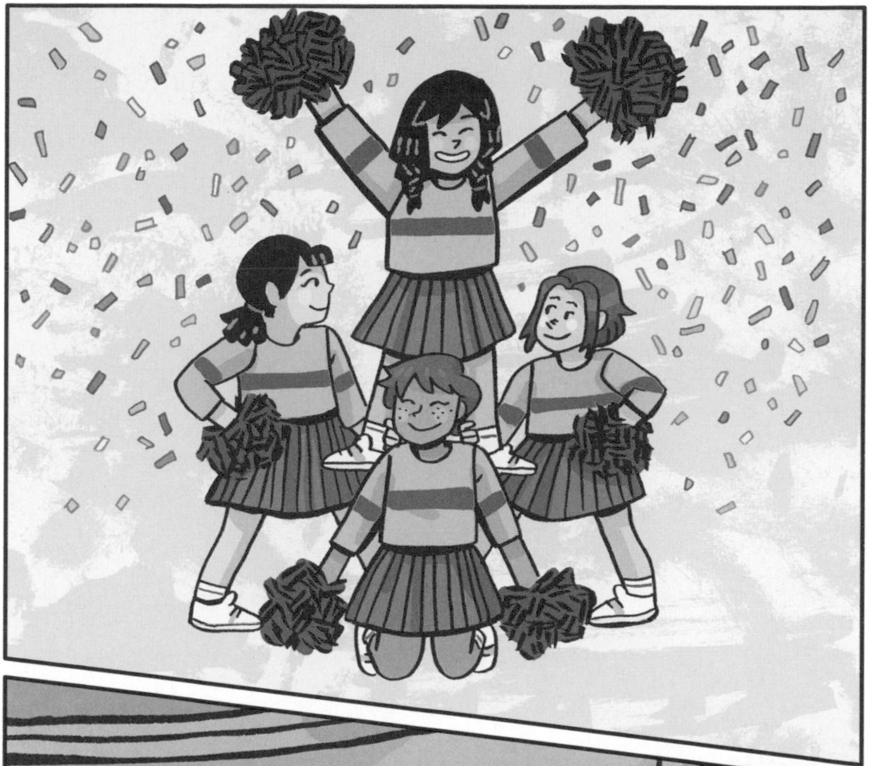

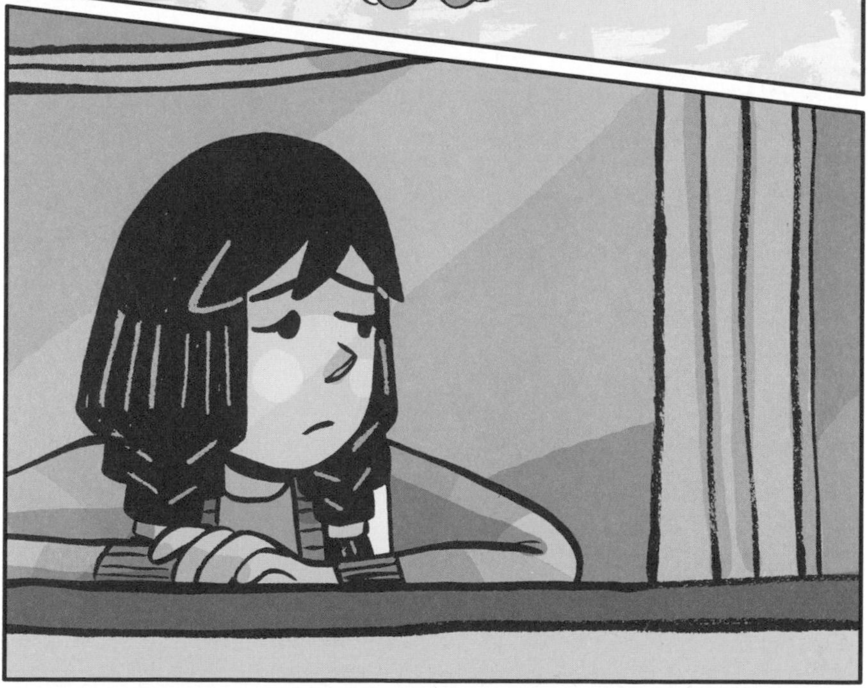

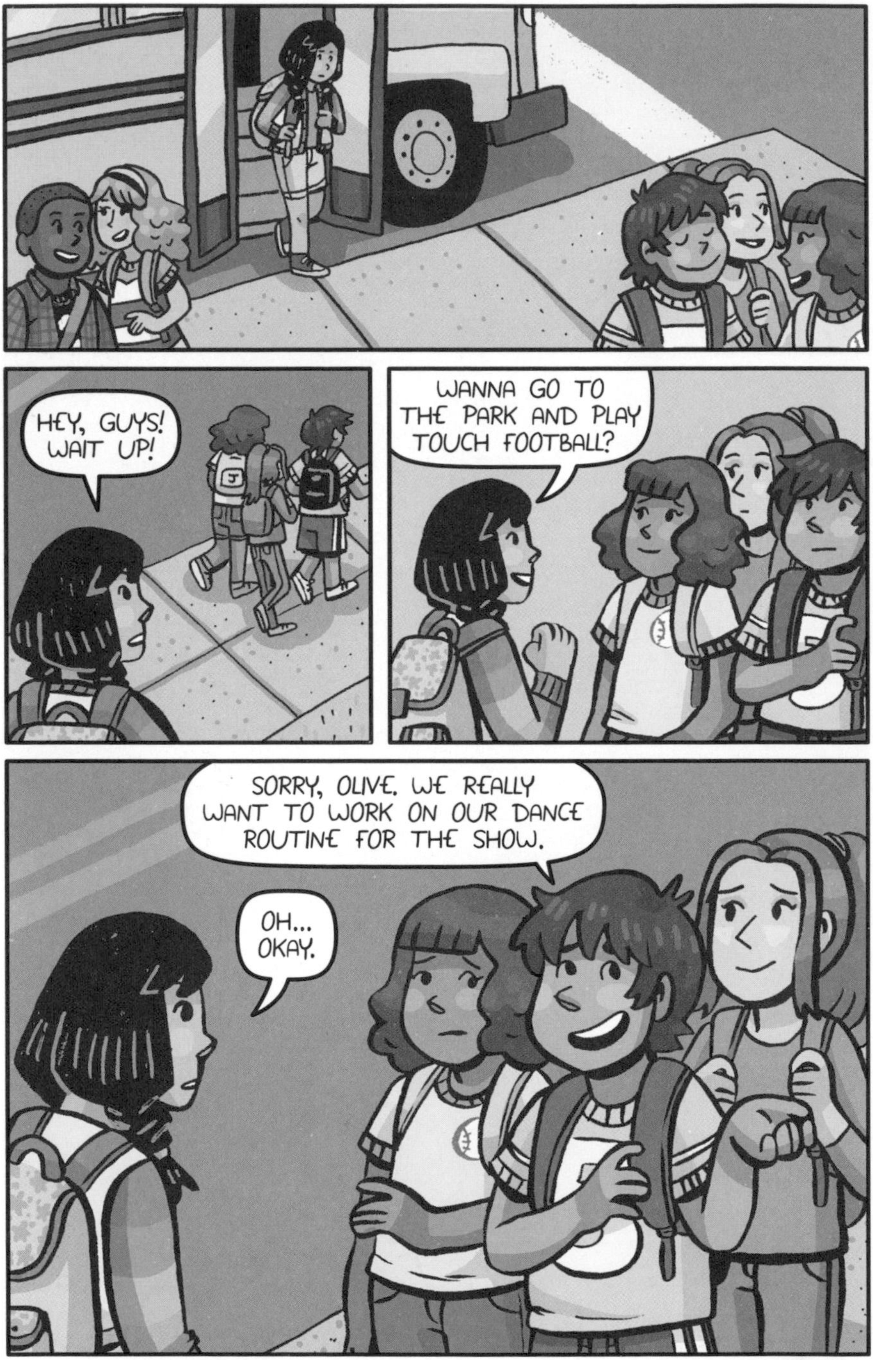
HEY, GUYS! WAIT UP!
WANNA GO TO THE PARK AND PLAY TOUCH FOOTBALL?
SORRY, OLIVE. WE REALLY WANT TO WORK ON OUR DANCE ROUTINE FOR THE SHOW.
OH... OKAY.

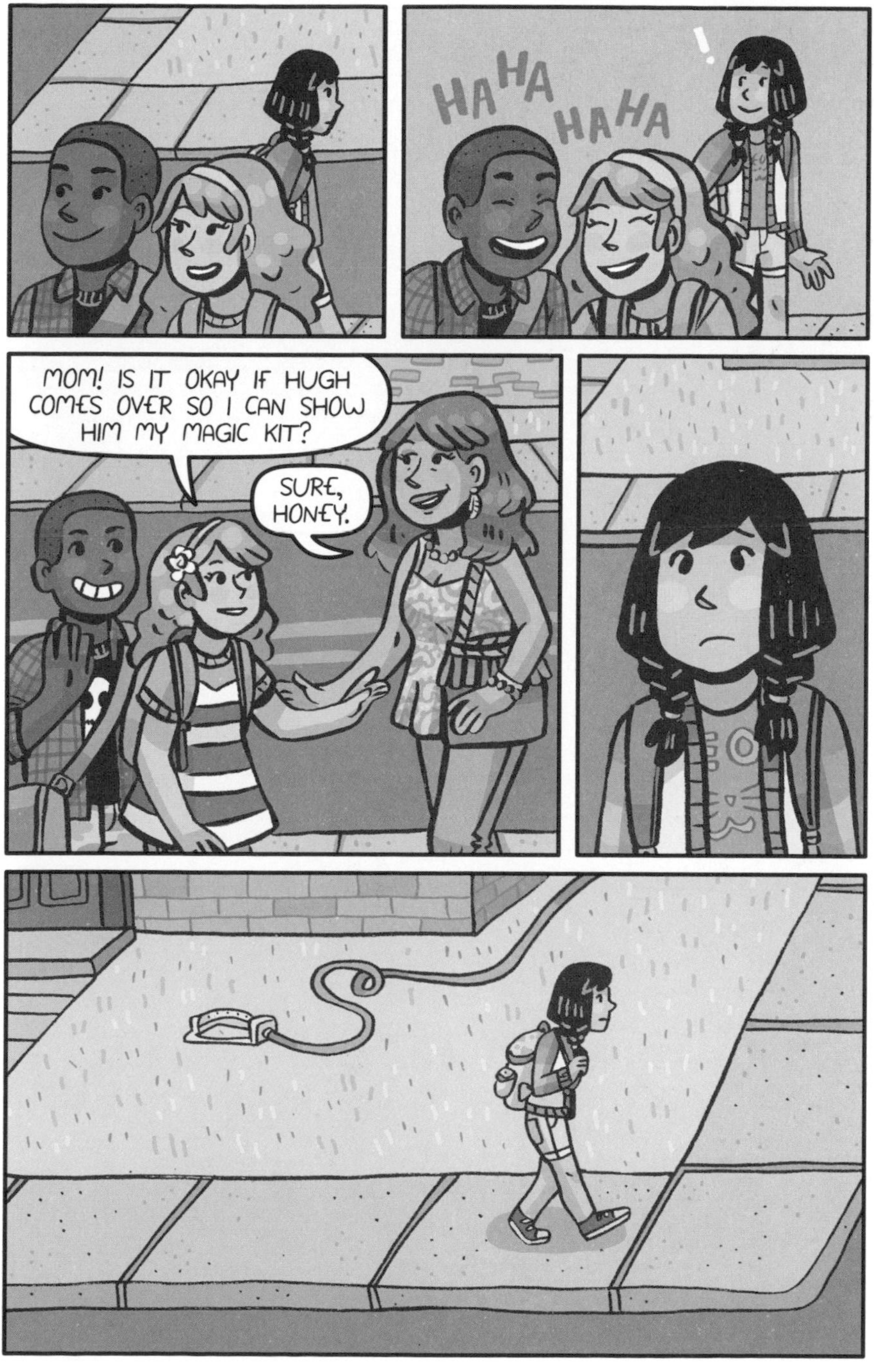
!
HAHA
HAHA
MOM! IS IT OKAY IF HUGH COMES OVER SO I CAN SHOW HIM MY MAGIC KIT?
SURE, HONEY.

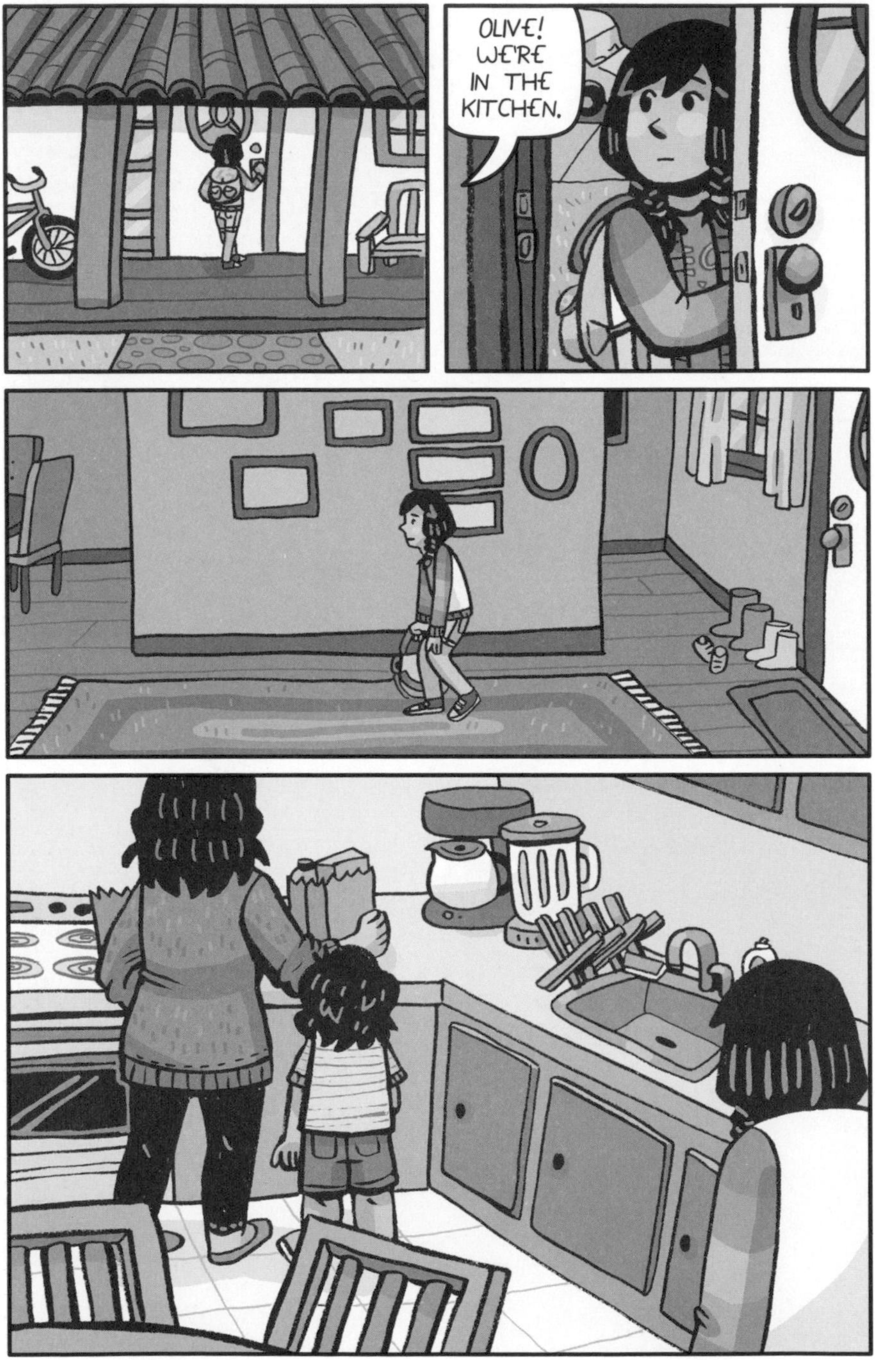
OLIVE! WE'RE IN THE KITCHEN.

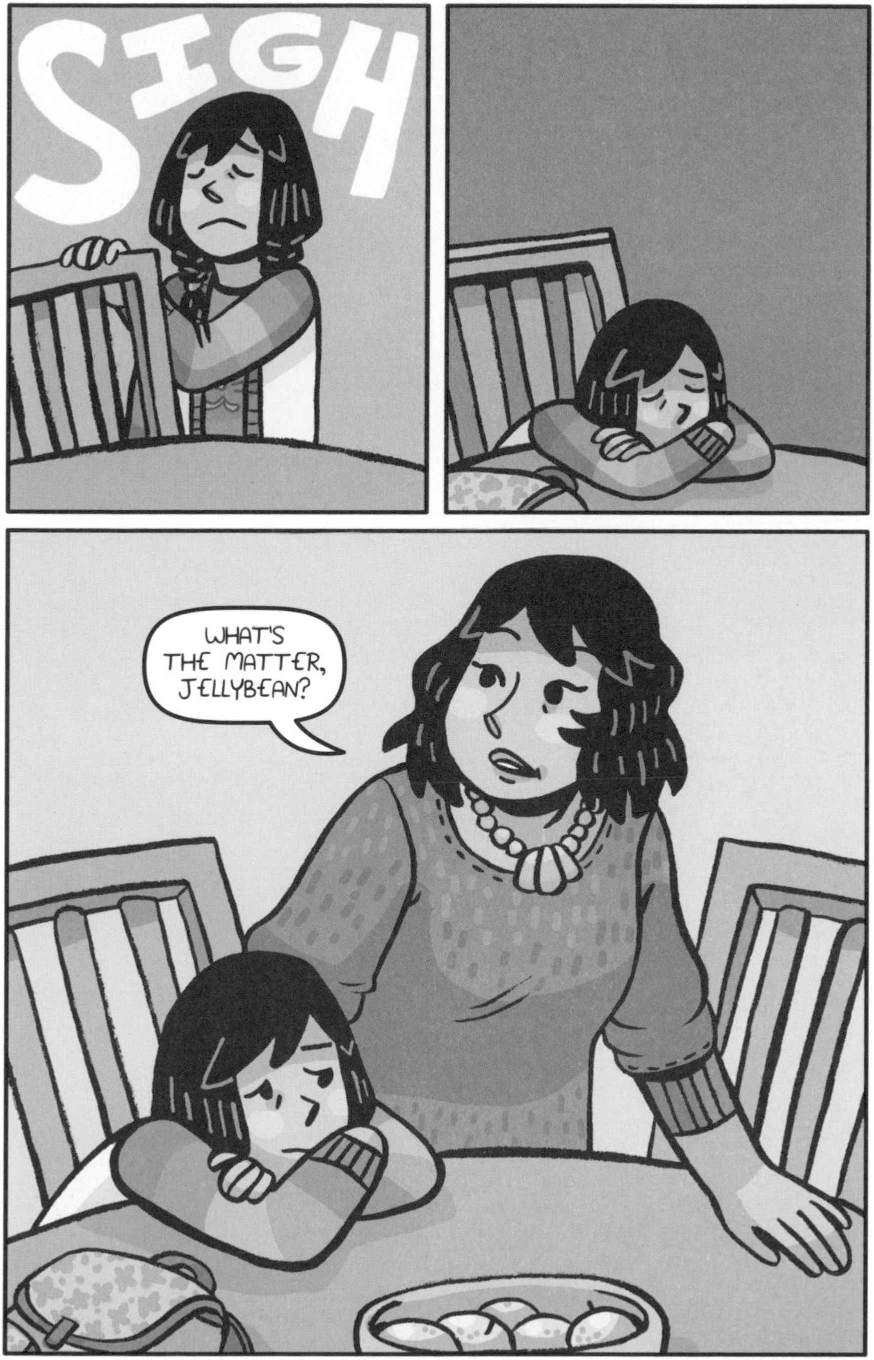
SIGH
WHAT'S THE MATTER, JELLYBEAN?

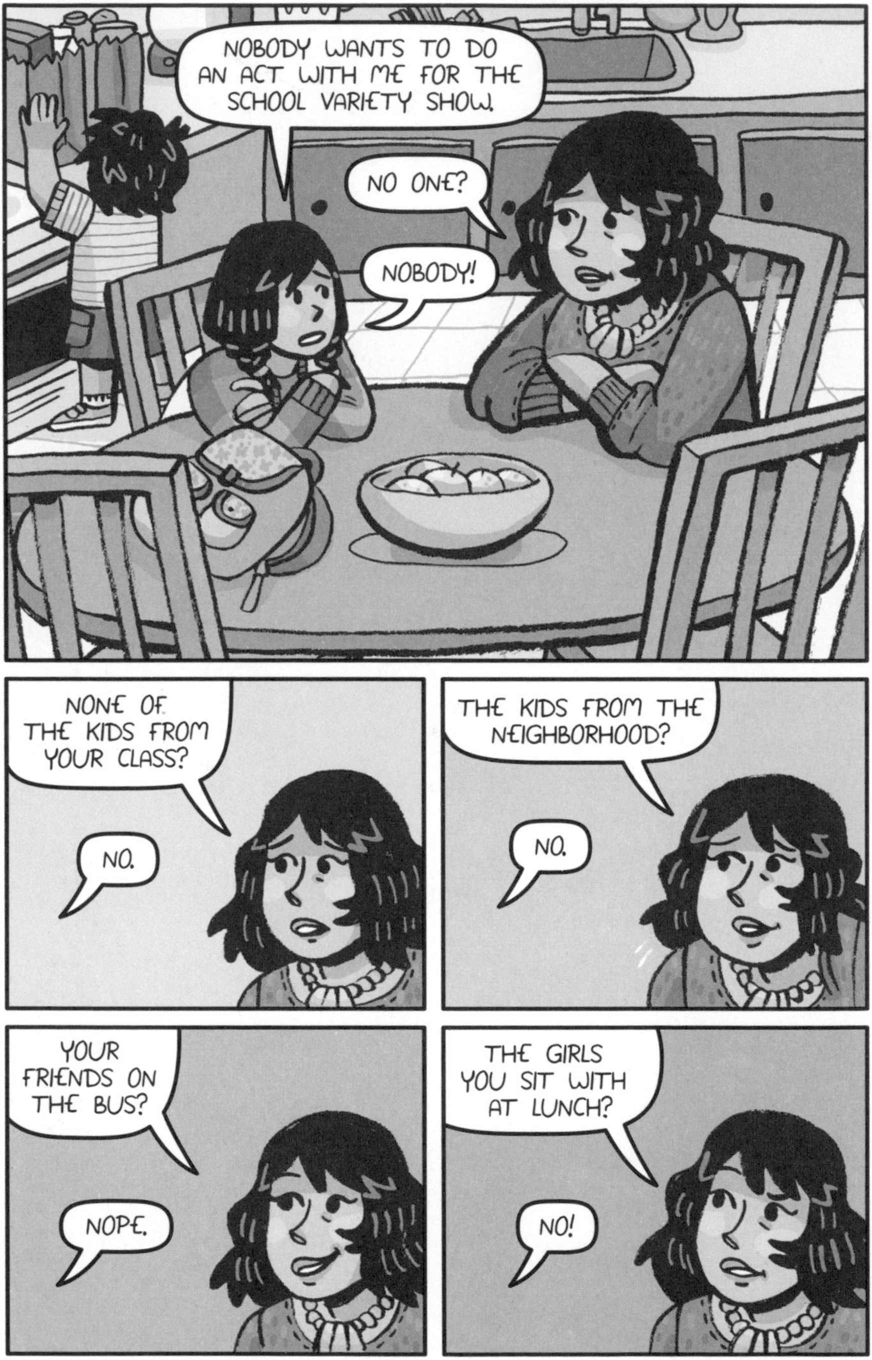
NOBODY WANTS TO DO AN ACT WITH ME FOR THE SCHOOL VARIETY SHOW.
NO ONE?
NOBODY!
NONE OF THE KIDS FROM YOUR CLASS?
NO.
THE KIDS FROM THE NEIGHBORHOOD?
NO.
YOUR FRIENDS ON THE BUS?
NOPE.
THE GIRLS YOU SIT WITH AT LUNCH?
NO!

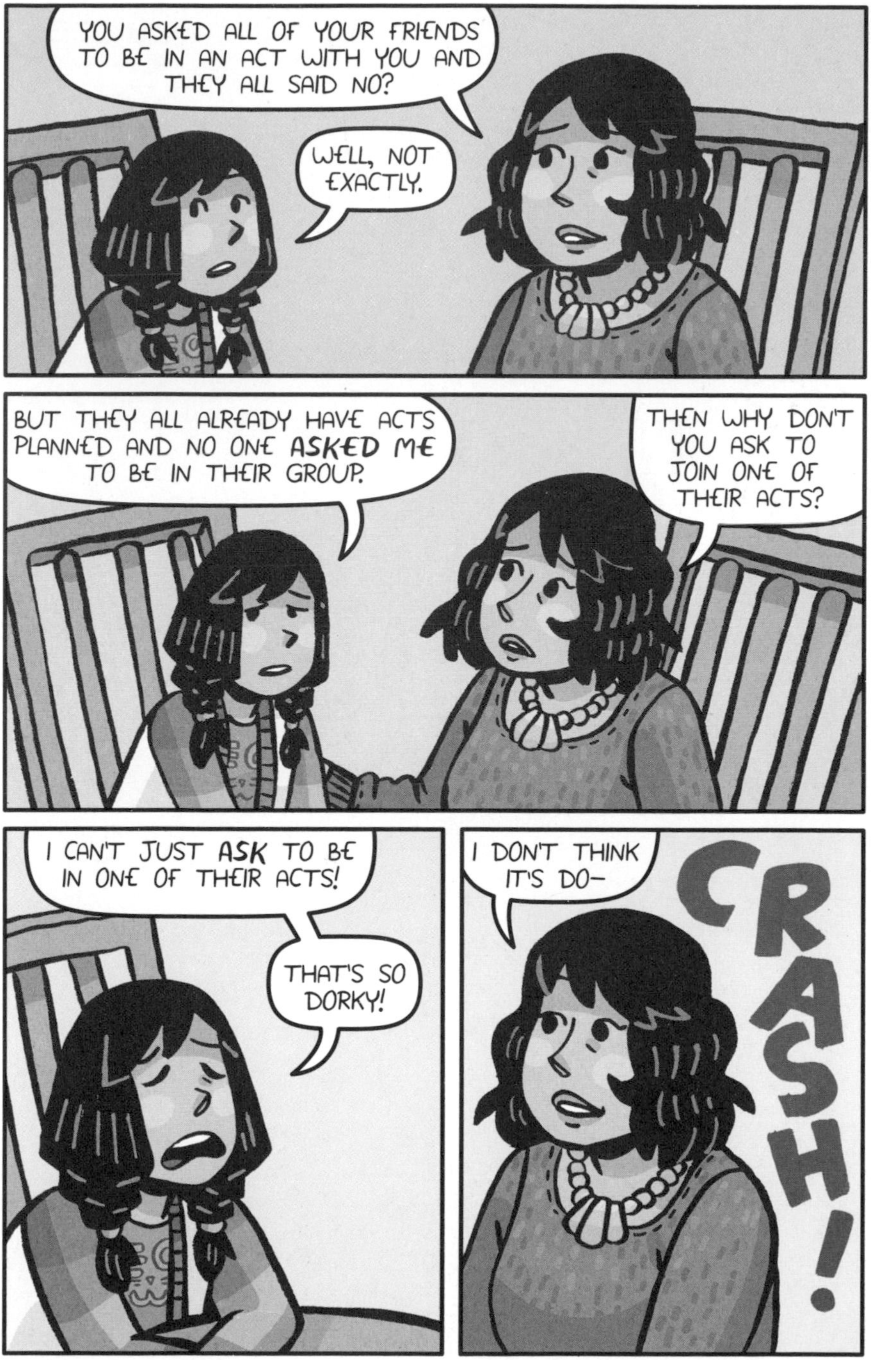
YOU ASKED ALL OF YOUR FRIENDS TO BE IN AN ACT WITH YOU AND THEY ALL SAID NO?
WELL, NOT EXACTLY.
BUT THEY ALL ALREADY HAVE ACTS PLANNED AND NO ONE **ASKED ME** TO BE IN THEIR GROUP.
THEN WHY DON'T YOU ASK TO JOIN ONE OF THEIR ACTS?
I CAN'T JUST **ASK** TO BE IN ONE OF THEIR ACTS!
THAT'S SO DORKY!
I DON'T THINK IT'S DO—
CRASH!

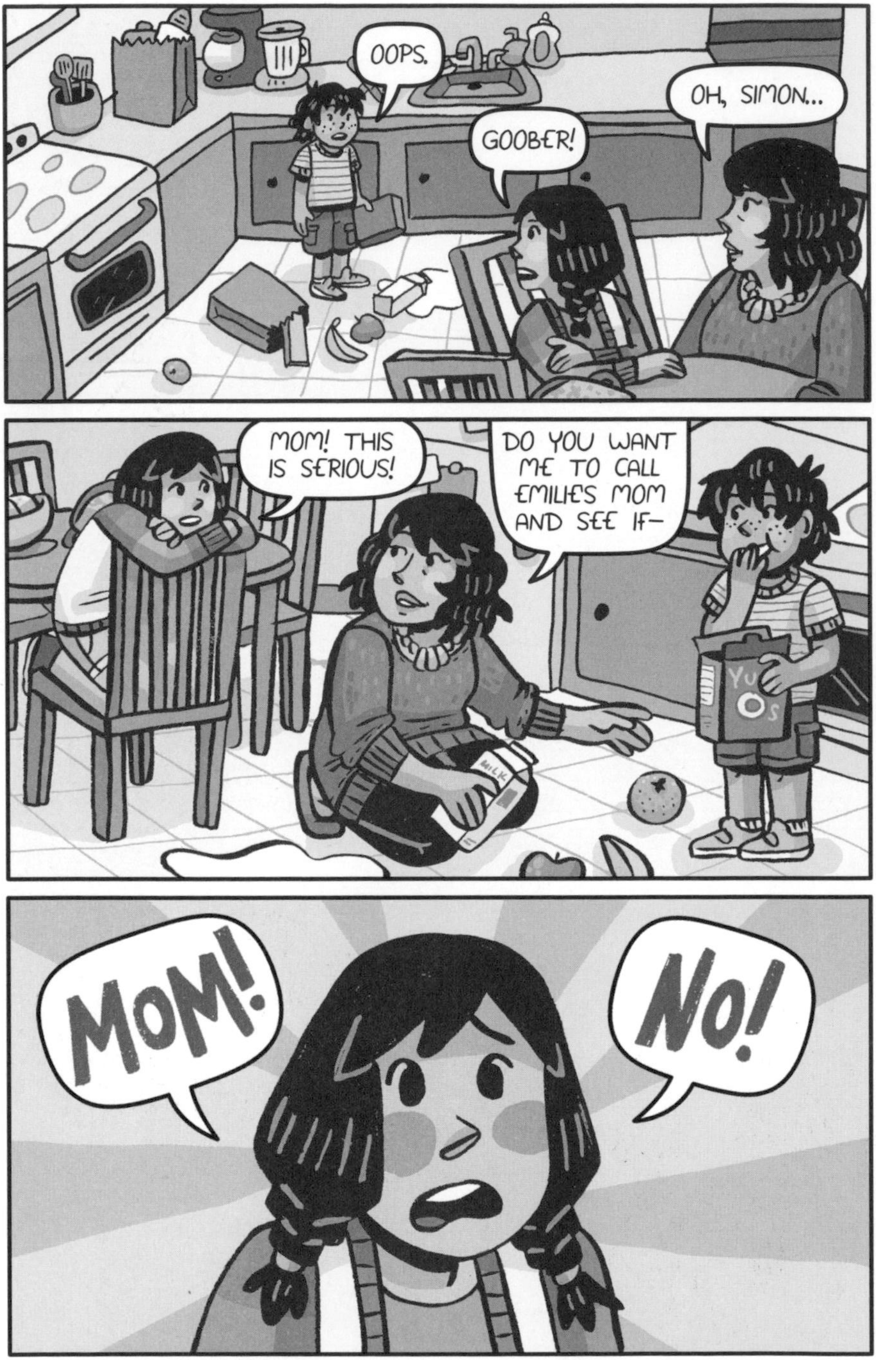
OOPS.
GOOBER!
OH, SIMON...
MOM! THIS IS SERIOUS!
DO YOU WANT ME TO CALL EMILIE'S MOM AND SEE IF—
MILK
YUM Os
MOM!
NO!

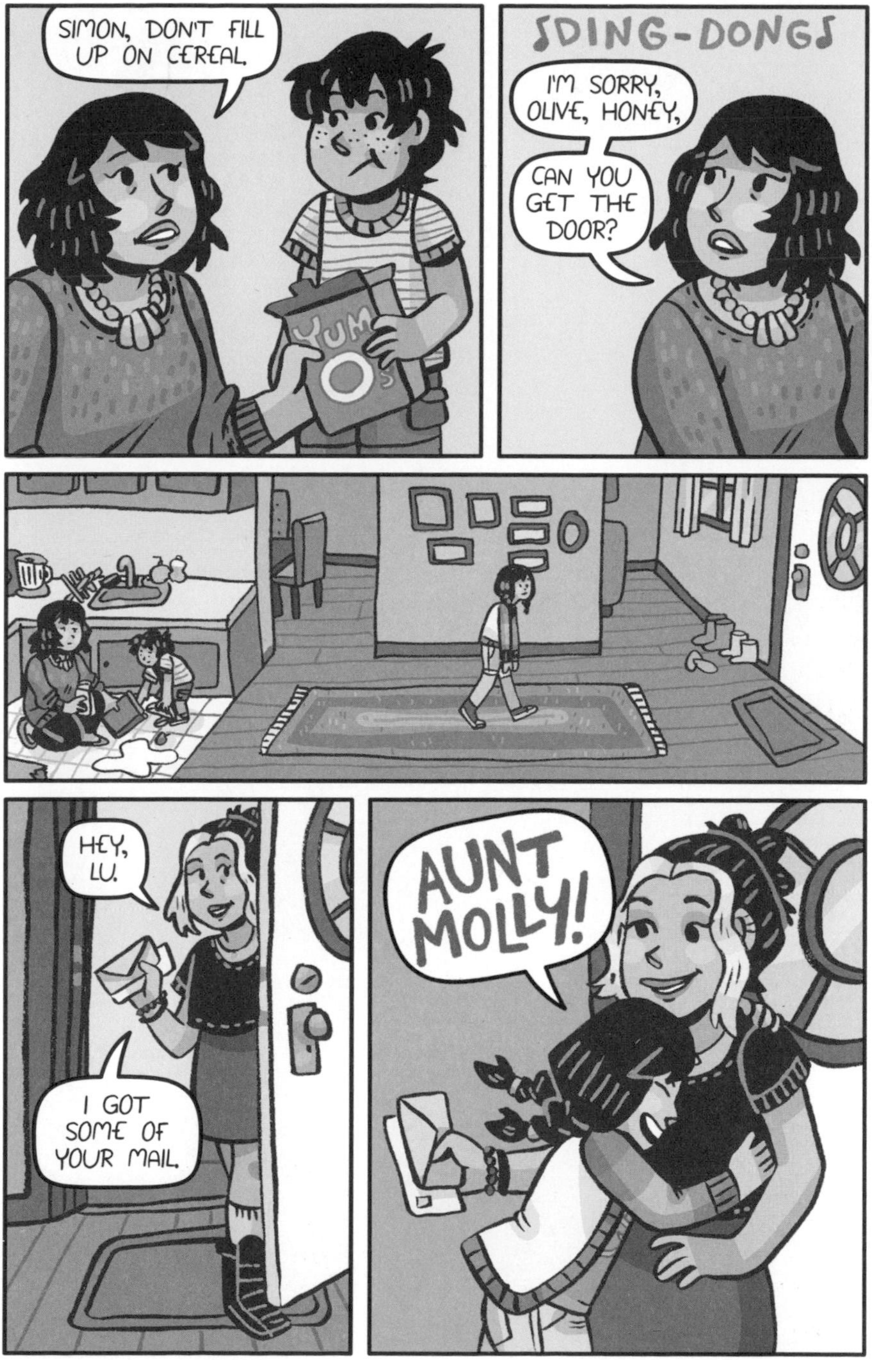
SIMON, DON'T FILL UP ON CEREAL.
YUM OS
DING-DONG
I'M SORRY, OLIVE, HONEY,
CAN YOU GET THE DOOR?
HEY, LU.
I GOT SOME OF YOUR MAIL.
AUNT MOLLY!

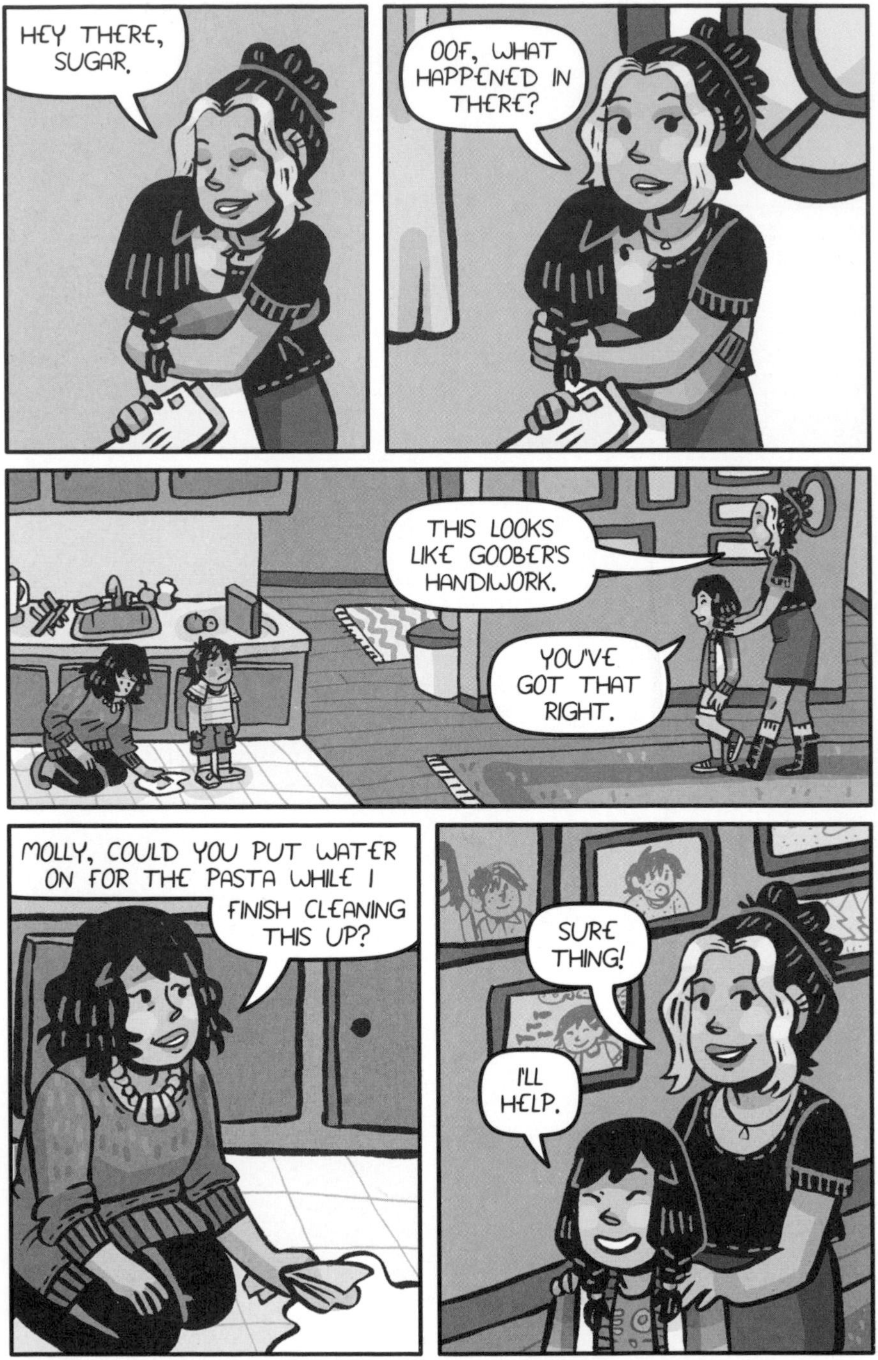
HEY THERE, SUGAR.
OOF, WHAT HAPPENED IN THERE?
THIS LOOKS LIKE GOOBER'S HANDIWORK.
YOU'VE GOT THAT RIGHT.
MOLLY, COULD YOU PUT WATER ON FOR THE PASTA WHILE I
FINISH CLEANING THIS UP?
SURE THING!
I'LL HELP.

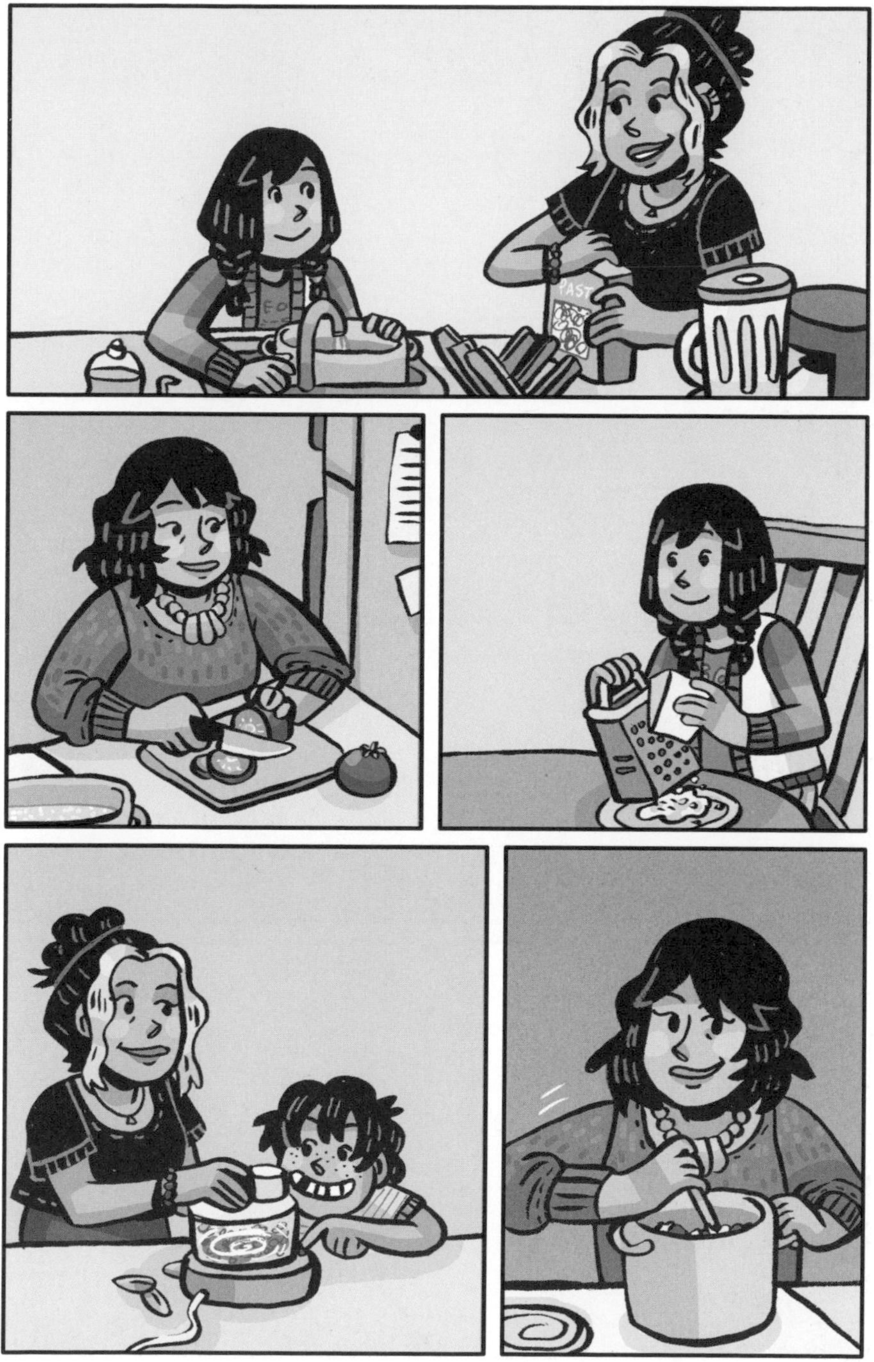
PAST

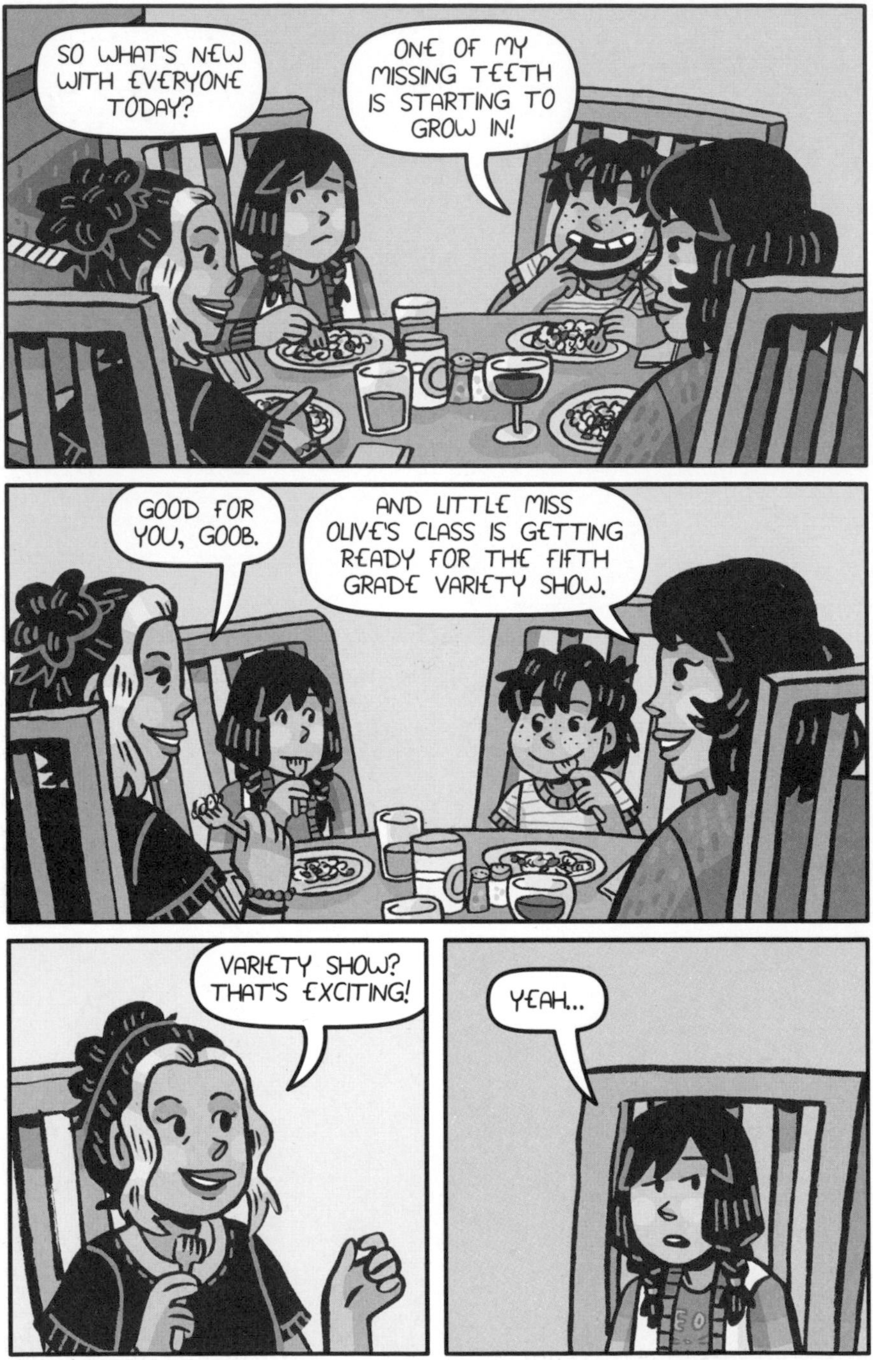
SO WHAT'S NEW WITH EVERYONE TODAY?
ONE OF MY MISSING TEETH IS STARTING TO GROW IN!
GOOD FOR YOU, GOOB.
AND LITTLE MISS OLIVE'S CLASS IS GETTING READY FOR THE FIFTH GRADE VARIETY SHOW.
VARIETY SHOW? THAT'S EXCITING!
YEAH...

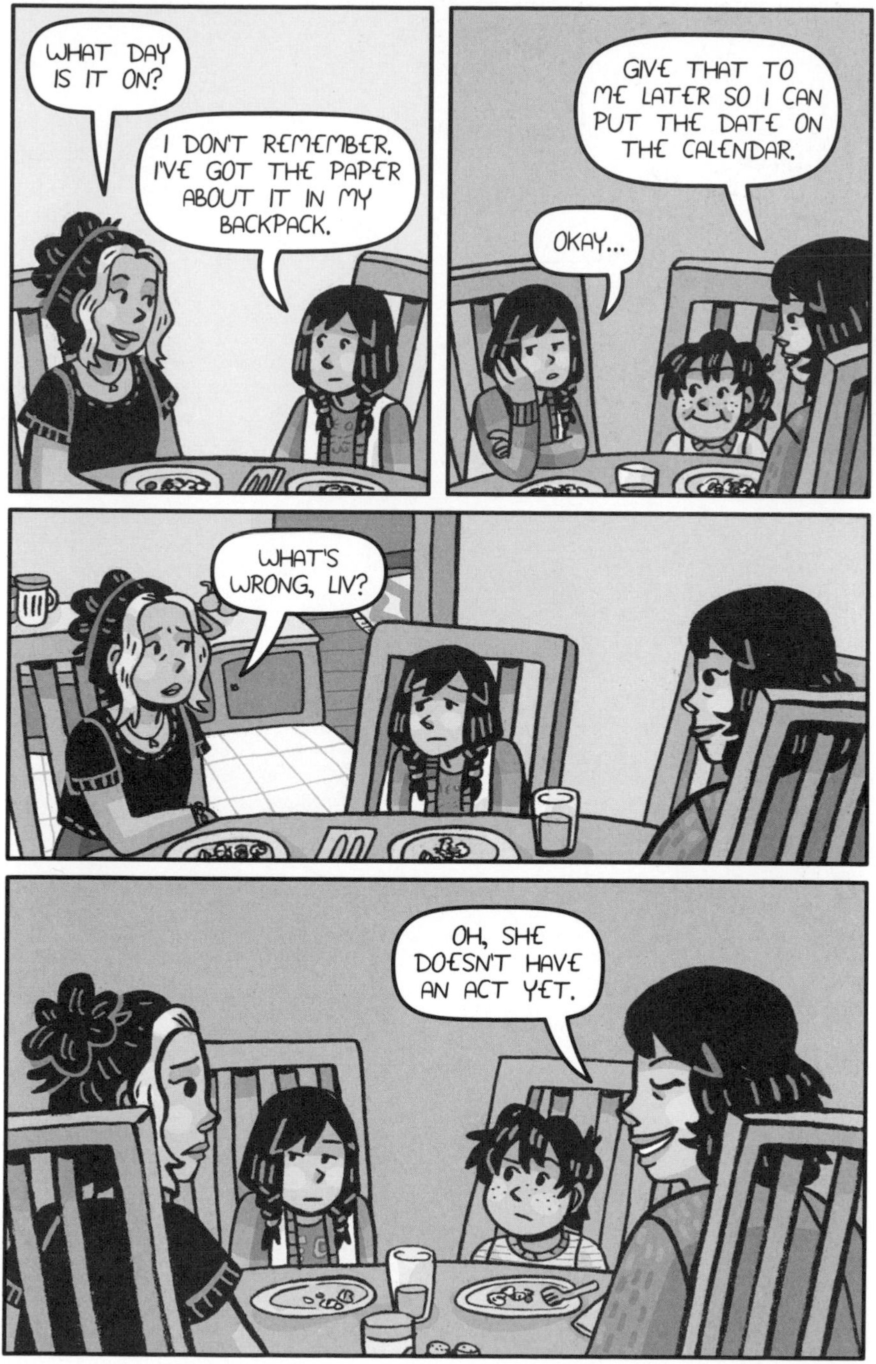
WHAT DAY IS IT ON?
I DON'T REMEMBER. I'VE GOT THE PAPER ABOUT IT IN MY BACKPACK.
GIVE THAT TO ME LATER SO I CAN PUT THE DATE ON THE CALENDAR.
OKAY...
WHAT'S WRONG, LIV?
OH, SHE DOESN'T HAVE AN ACT YET.

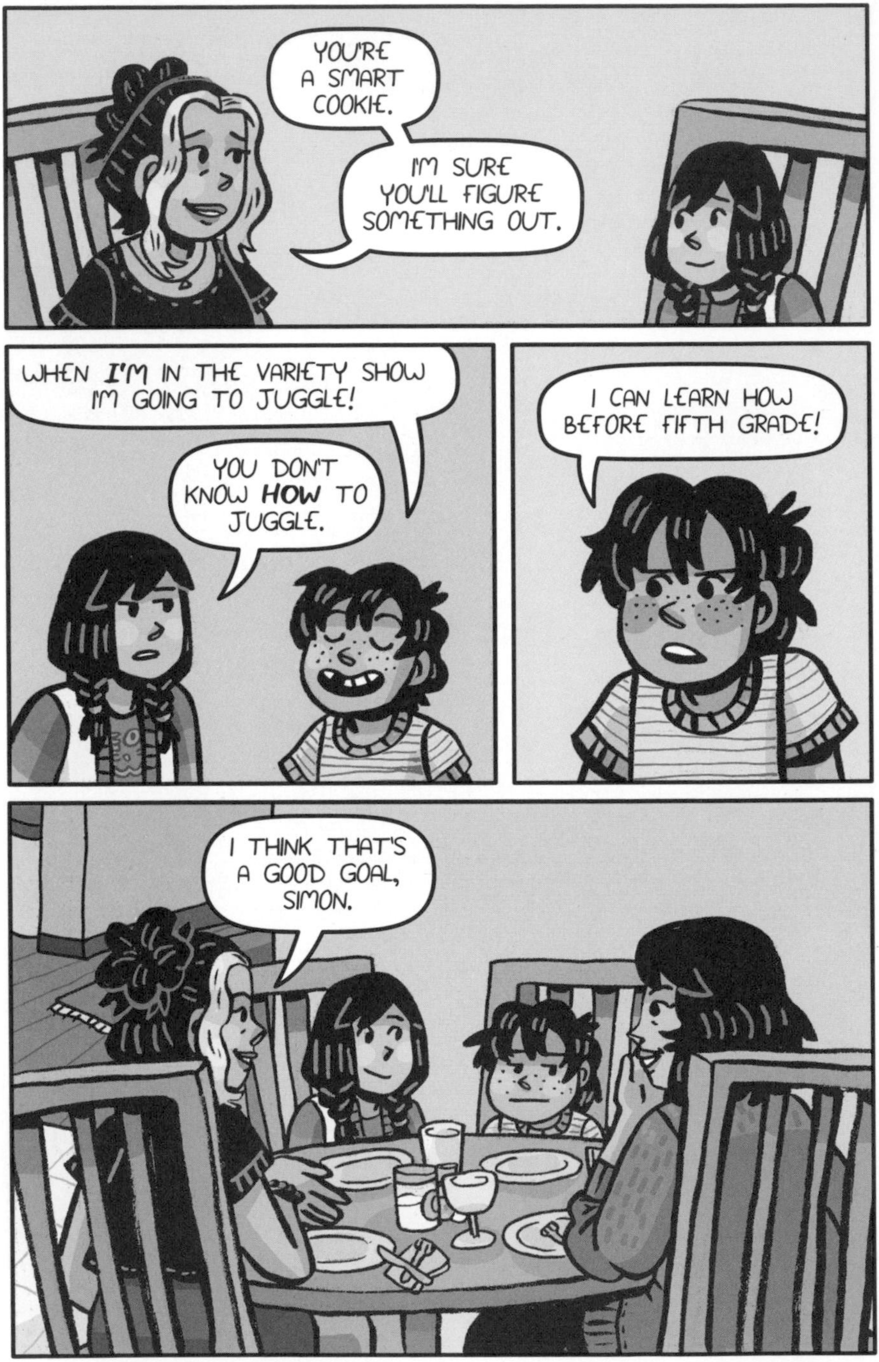
YOU'RE A SMART COOKIE.
I'M SURE YOU'LL FIGURE SOMETHING OUT.
WHEN I'M IN THE VARIETY SHOW I'M GOING TO JUGGLE!
YOU DON'T KNOW HOW TO JUGGLE.
I CAN LEARN HOW BEFORE FIFTH GRADE!
I THINK THAT'S A GOOD GOAL, SIMON.

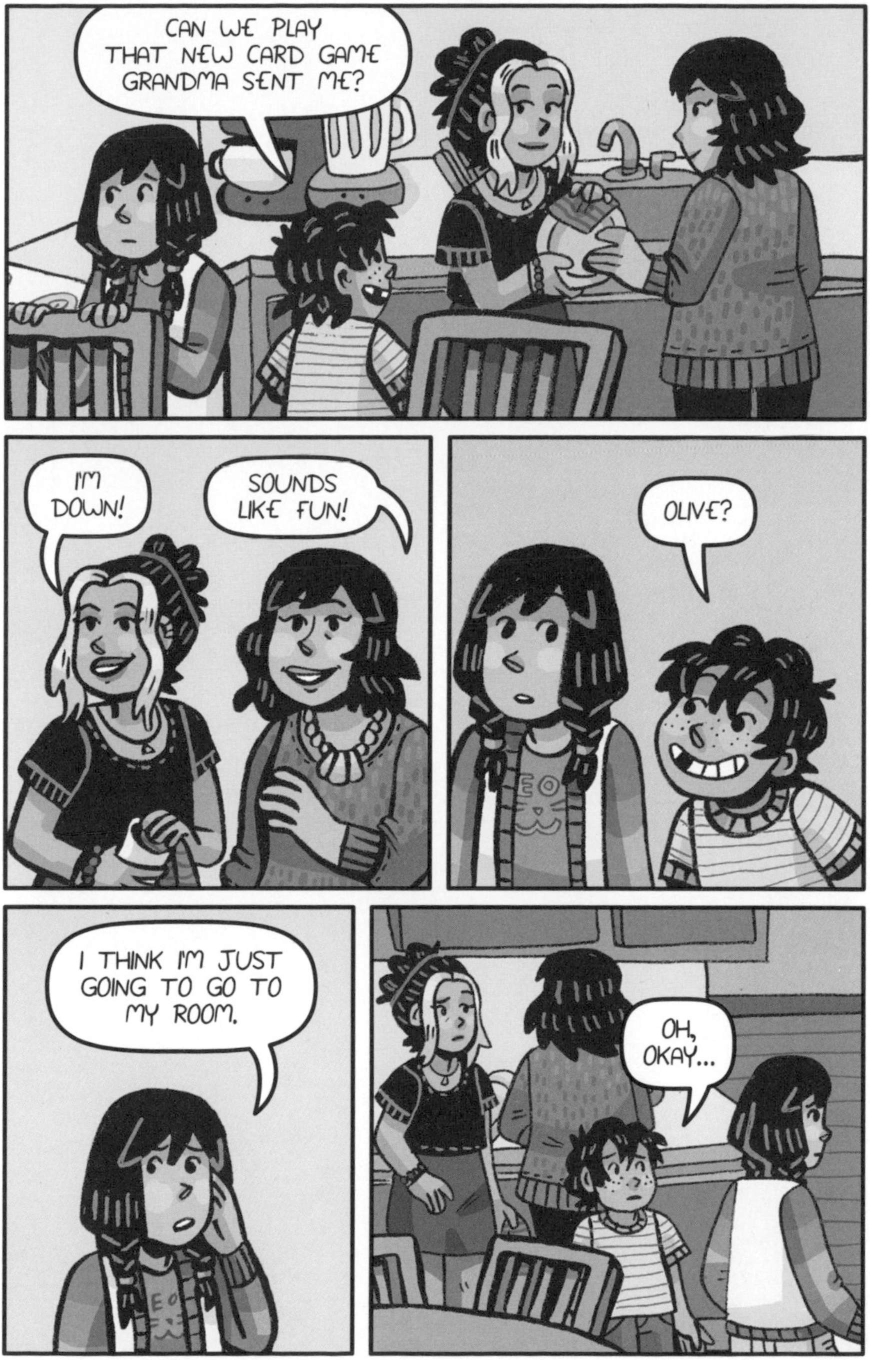
CAN WE PLAY THAT NEW CARD GAME GRANDMA SENT ME?
I'M DOWN!
SOUNDS LIKE FUN!
OLIVE?
I THINK I'M JUST GOING TO GO TO MY ROOM.
OH, OKAY...

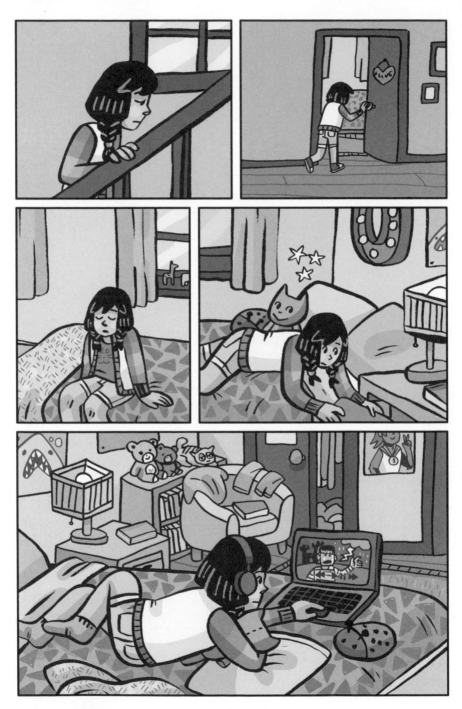

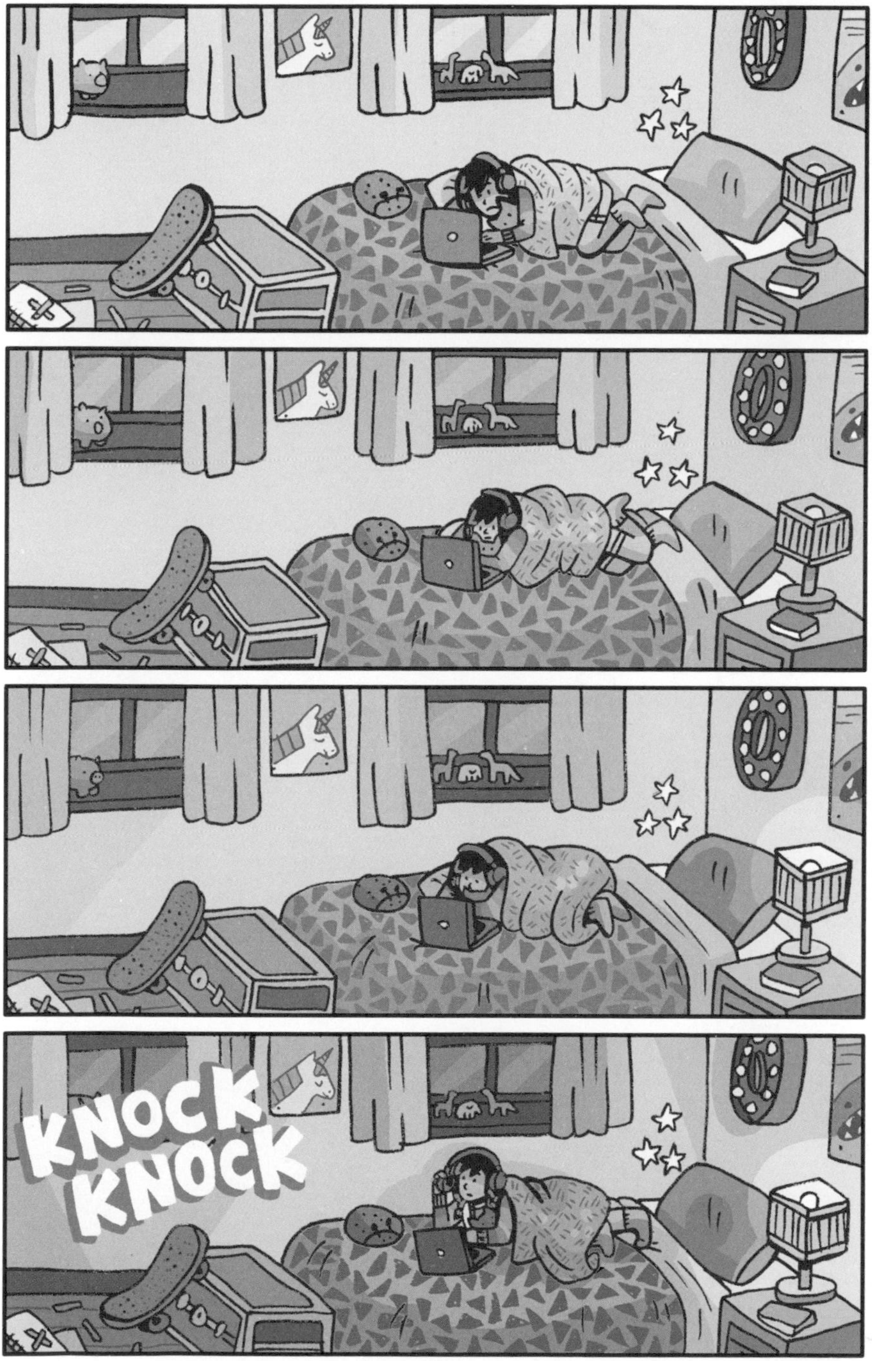
KNOCK
KNOCK

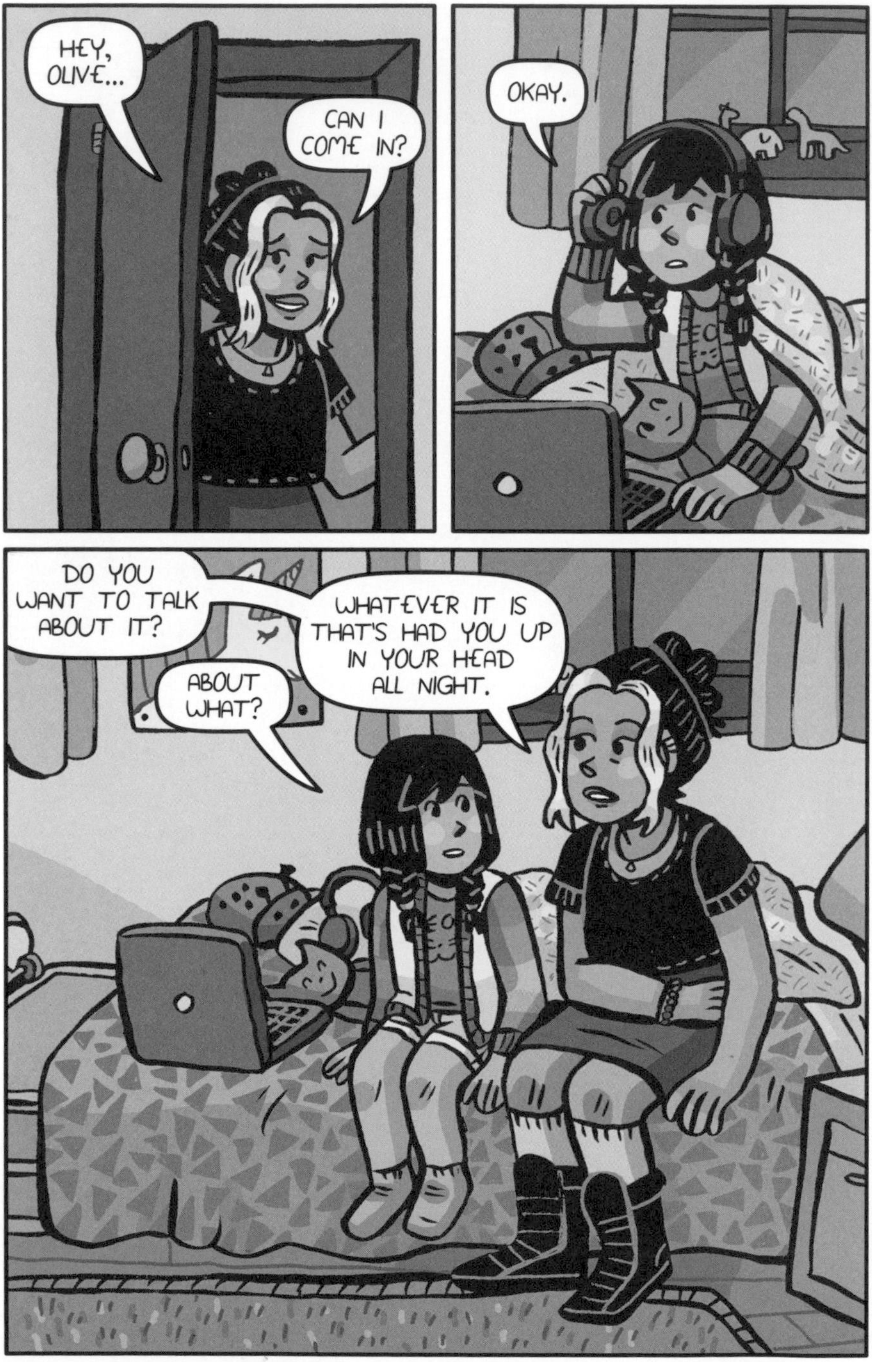
HEY, OLIVE...
CAN I COME IN?
OKAY.
DO YOU WANT TO TALK ABOUT IT?
ABOUT WHAT?
WHATEVER IT IS THAT'S HAD YOU UP IN YOUR HEAD ALL NIGHT.

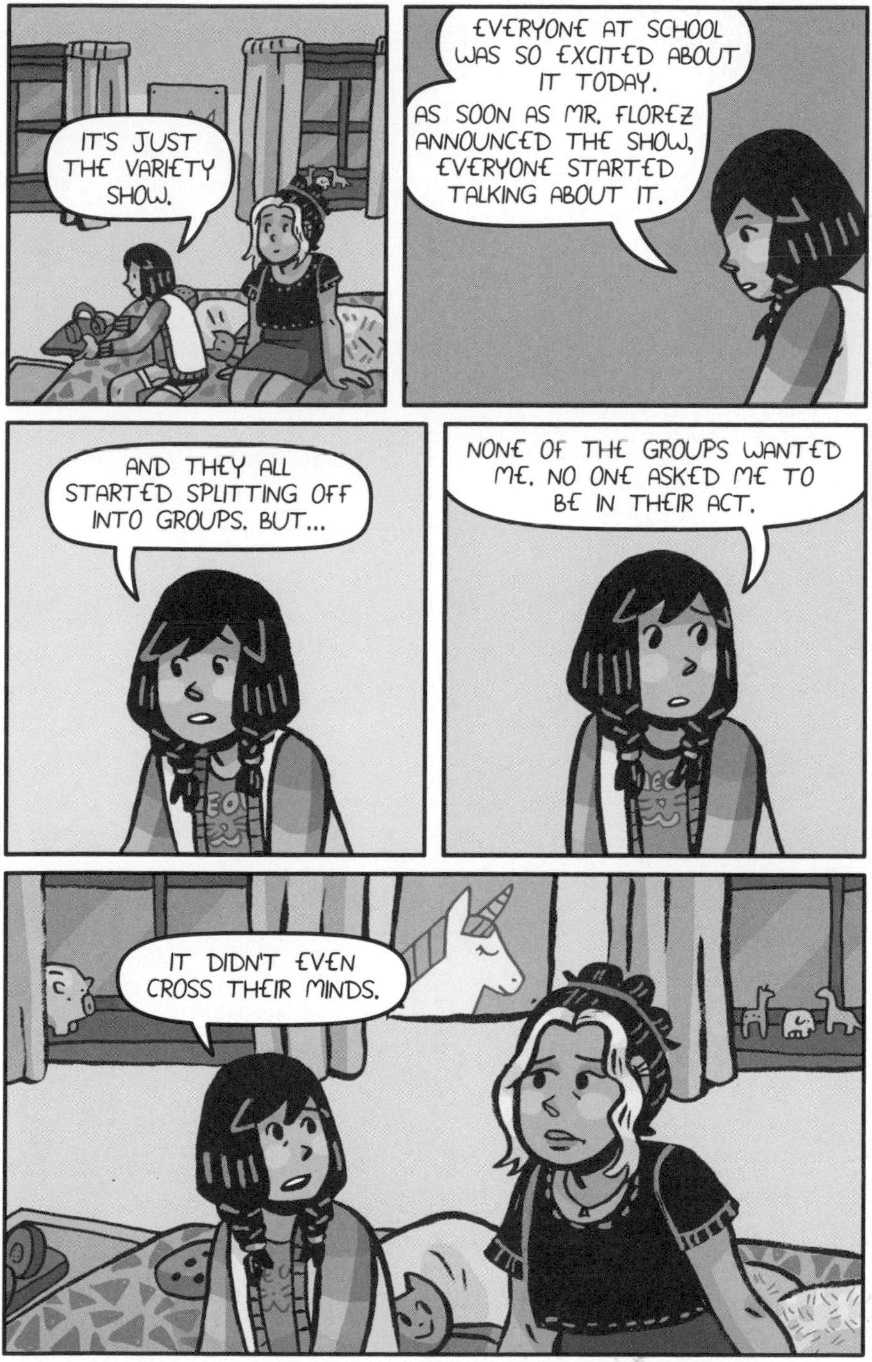
IT'S JUST THE VARIETY SHOW.
EVERYONE AT SCHOOL WAS SO EXCITED ABOUT IT TODAY.
AS SOON AS MR. FLOREZ ANNOUNCED THE SHOW, EVERYONE STARTED TALKING ABOUT IT.
AND THEY ALL STARTED SPLITTING OFF INTO GROUPS. BUT...
NONE OF THE GROUPS WANTED ME. NO ONE ASKED ME TO BE IN THEIR ACT.
IT DIDN'T EVEN CROSS THEIR MINDS.

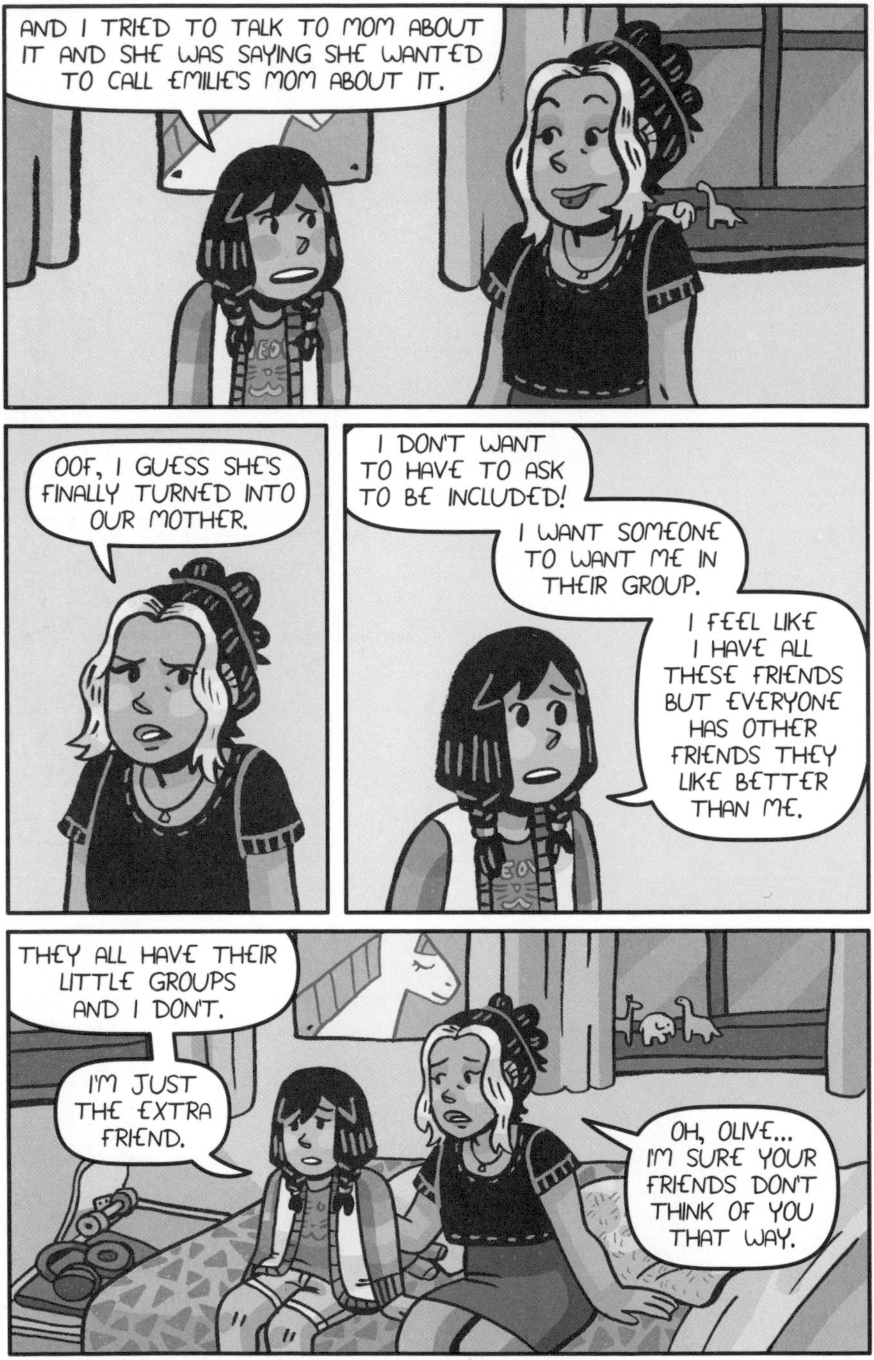
AND I TRIED TO TALK TO MOM ABOUT IT AND SHE WAS SAYING SHE WANTED TO CALL EMILIE'S MOM ABOUT IT.
OOF, I GUESS SHE'S FINALLY TURNED INTO OUR MOTHER.
I DON'T WANT TO HAVE TO ASK TO BE INCLUDED!
I WANT SOMEONE TO WANT ME IN THEIR GROUP.
I FEEL LIKE I HAVE ALL THESE FRIENDS BUT EVERYONE HAS OTHER FRIENDS THEY LIKE BETTER THAN ME.
THEY ALL HAVE THEIR LITTLE GROUPS AND I DON'T.
I'M JUST THE EXTRA FRIEND.
OH, OLIVE... I'M SURE YOUR FRIENDS DON'T THINK OF YOU THAT WAY.

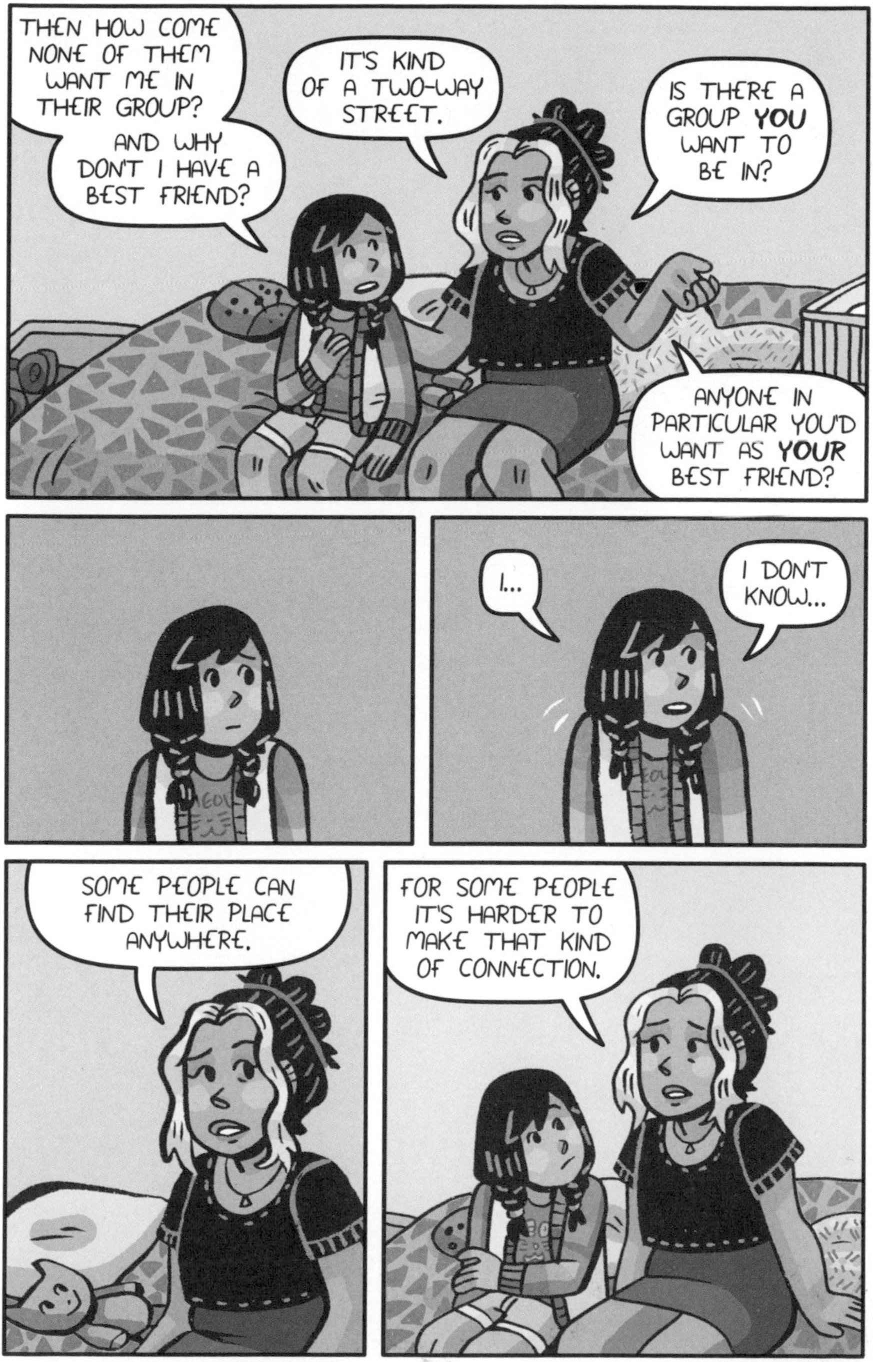
THEN HOW COME NONE OF THEM WANT ME IN THEIR GROUP?
AND WHY DON'T I HAVE A BEST FRIEND?
IT'S KIND OF A TWO-WAY STREET.
IS THERE A GROUP **YOU** WANT TO BE IN?
ANYONE IN PARTICULAR YOU'D WANT AS **YOUR** BEST FRIEND?
I...
I DON'T KNOW...
SOME PEOPLE CAN FIND THEIR PLACE ANYWHERE.
FOR SOME PEOPLE IT'S HARDER TO MAKE THAT KIND OF CONNECTION.

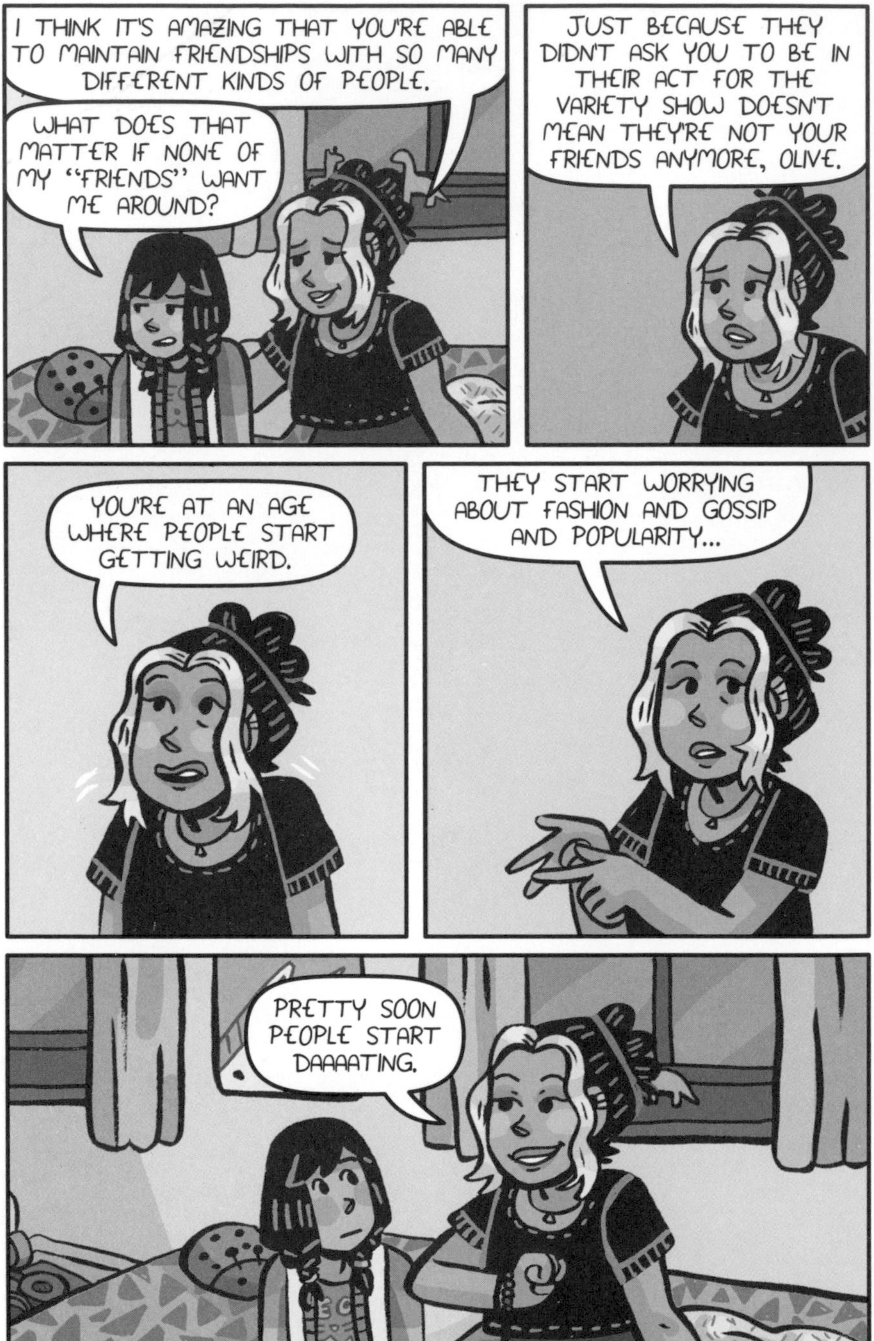
I THINK IT'S AMAZING THAT YOU'RE ABLE TO MAINTAIN FRIENDSHIPS WITH SO MANY DIFFERENT KINDS OF PEOPLE.
WHAT DOES THAT MATTER IF NONE OF MY "FRIENDS" WANT ME AROUND?
JUST BECAUSE THEY DIDN'T ASK YOU TO BE IN THEIR ACT FOR THE VARIETY SHOW DOESN'T MEAN THEY'RE NOT YOUR FRIENDS ANYMORE, OLIVE.
YOU'RE AT AN AGE WHERE PEOPLE START GETTING WEIRD.
THEY START WORRYING ABOUT FASHION AND GOSSIP AND POPULARITY...
PRETTY SOON PEOPLE START DAAAATING.

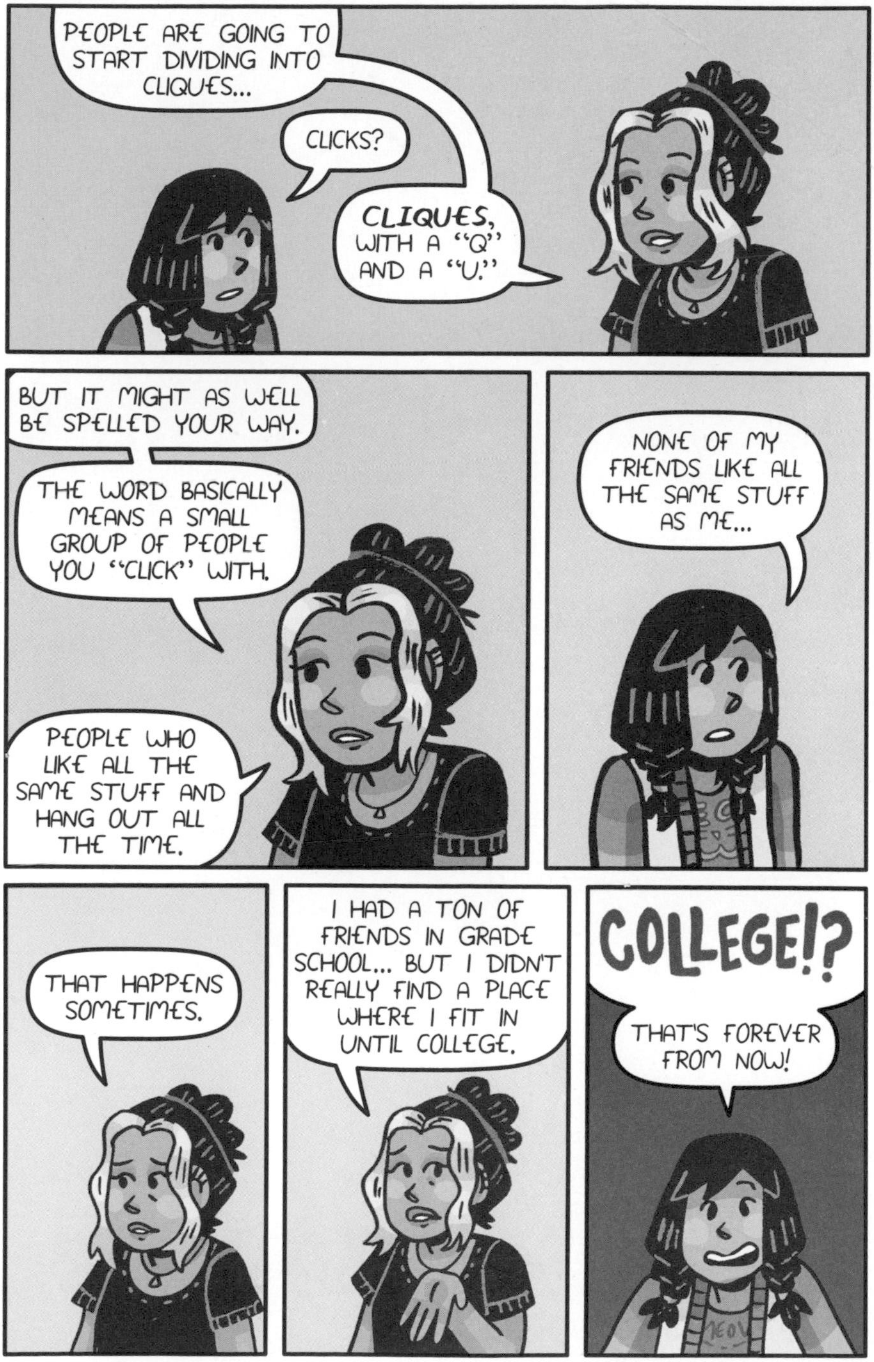
PEOPLE ARE GOING TO START DIVIDING INTO CLIQUES...
CLICKS?
CLIQUES, WITH A "Q" AND A "U."
BUT IT MIGHT AS WELL BE SPELLED YOUR WAY.
THE WORD BASICALLY MEANS A SMALL GROUP OF PEOPLE YOU "CLICK" WITH.
PEOPLE WHO LIKE ALL THE SAME STUFF AND HANG OUT ALL THE TIME.
NONE OF MY FRIENDS LIKE ALL THE SAME STUFF AS ME...
THAT HAPPENS SOMETIMES.
I HAD A TON OF FRIENDS IN GRADE SCHOOL... BUT I DIDN'T REALLY FIND A PLACE WHERE I FIT IN UNTIL COLLEGE.
COLLEGE!?
THAT'S FOREVER FROM NOW!
MEOW

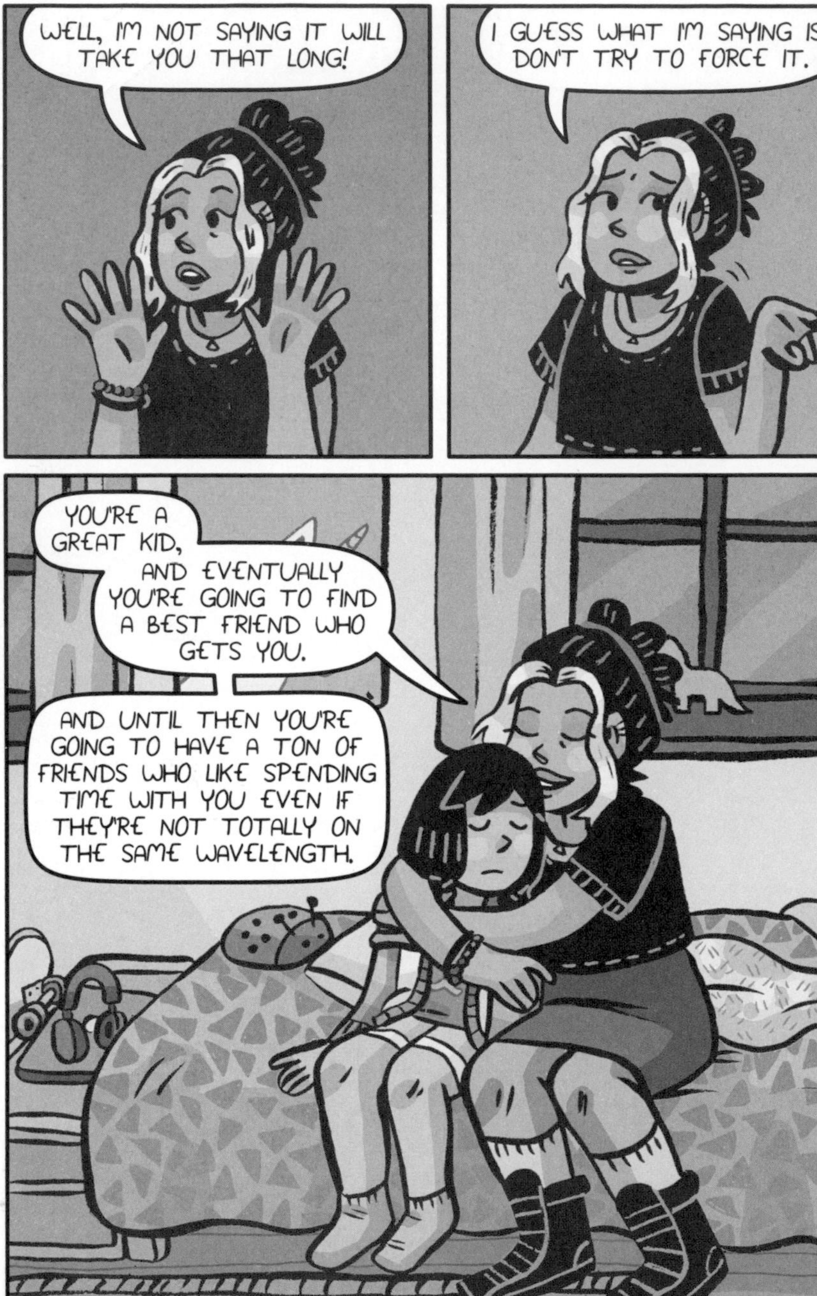
WELL, I'M NOT SAYING IT WILL TAKE YOU THAT LONG!
I GUESS WHAT I'M SAYING IS, DON'T TRY TO FORCE IT.
YOU'RE A GREAT KID,
AND EVENTUALLY YOU'RE GOING TO FIND A BEST FRIEND WHO GETS YOU.
AND UNTIL THEN YOU'RE GOING TO HAVE A TON OF FRIENDS WHO LIKE SPENDING TIME WITH YOU EVEN IF THEY'RE NOT TOTALLY ON THE SAME WAVELENGTH.

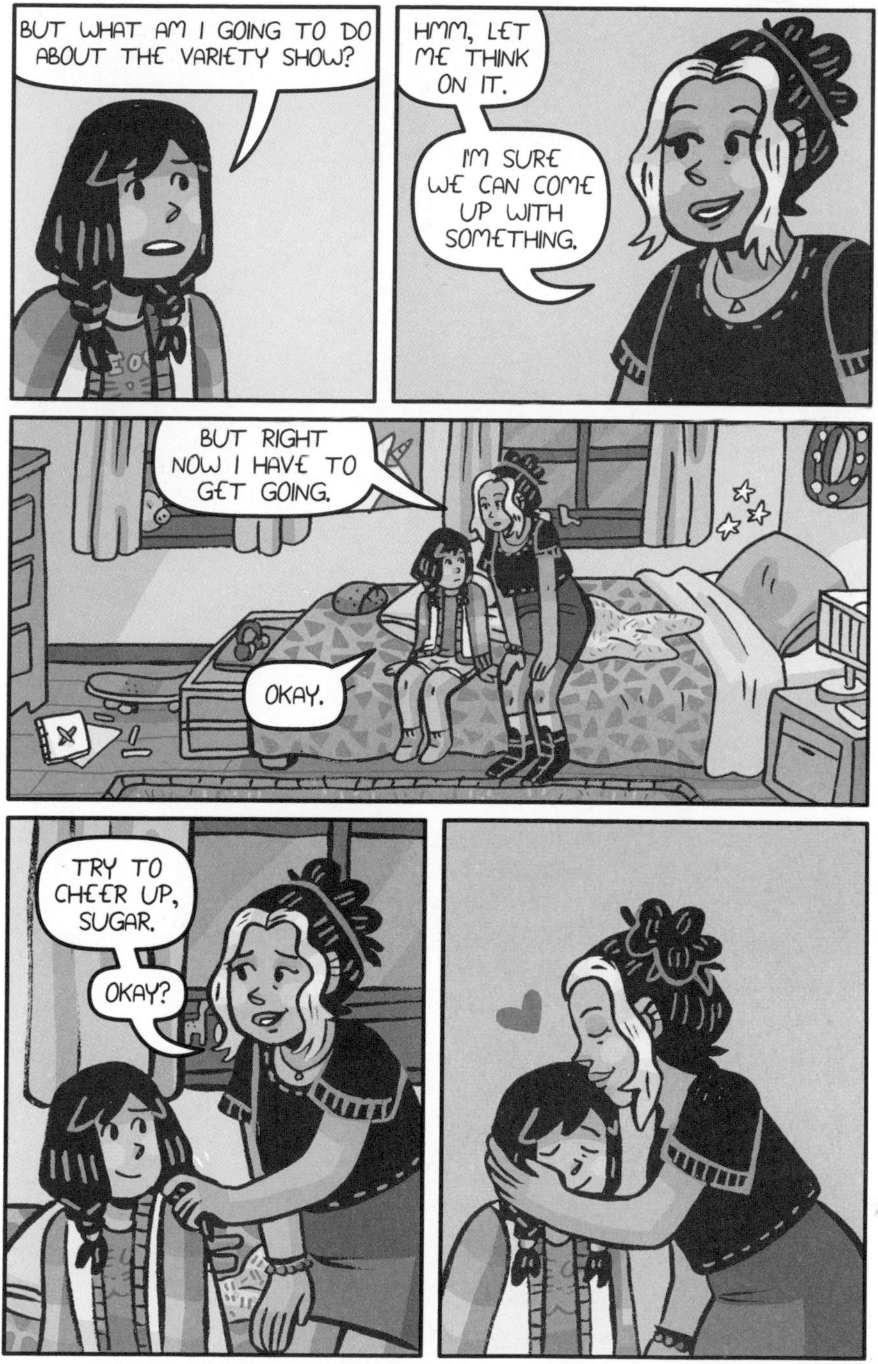
BUT WHAT AM I GOING TO DO ABOUT THE VARIETY SHOW?
HMM, LET ME THINK ON IT.
I'M SURE WE CAN COME UP WITH SOMETHING.
BUT RIGHT NOW I HAVE TO GET GOING.
OKAY.
TRY TO CHEER UP, SUGAR.
OKAY?

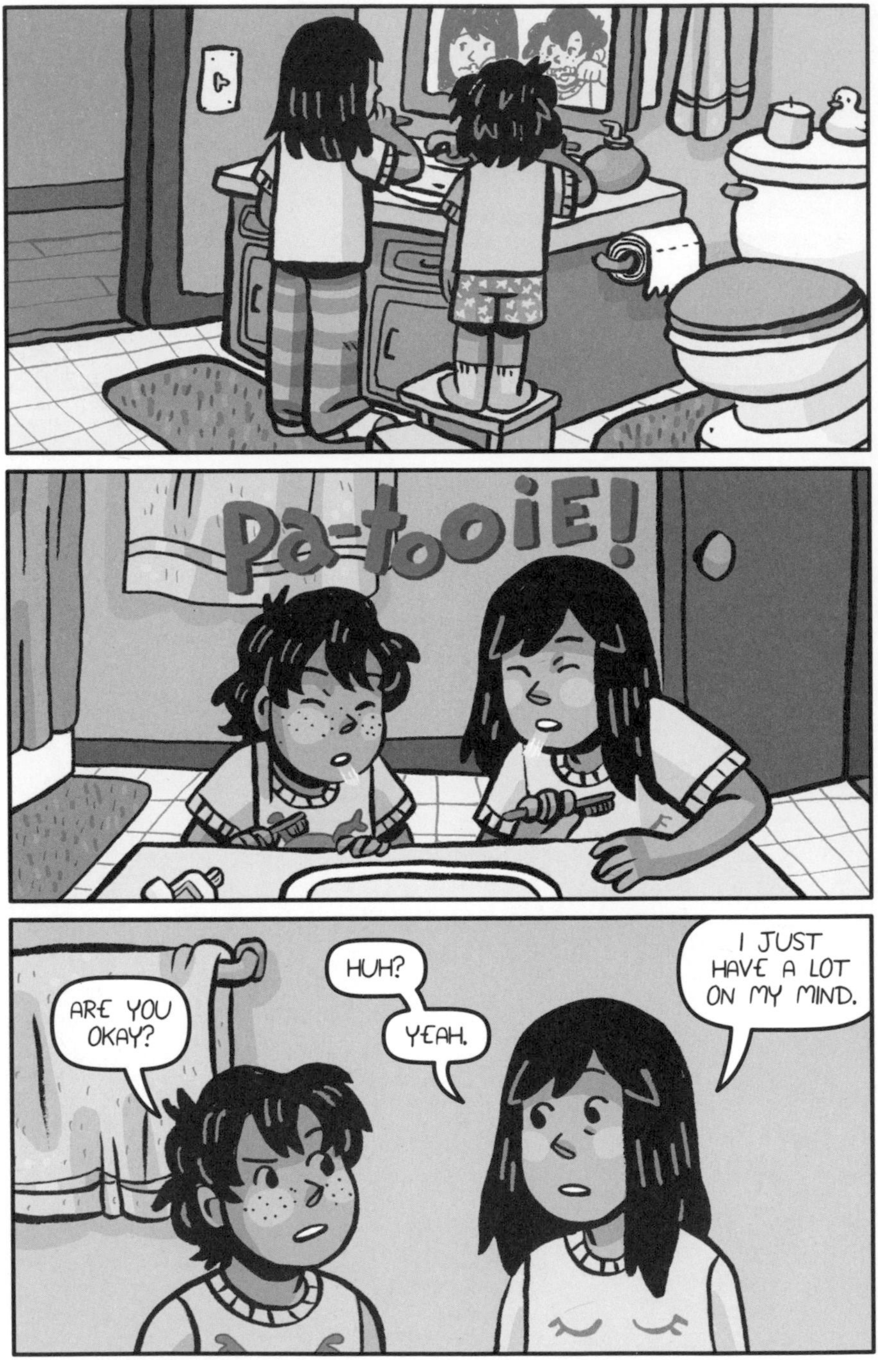
PA-TOOIE!
ARE YOU OKAY?
HUH?
YEAH.
I JUST HAVE A LOT ON MY MIND.

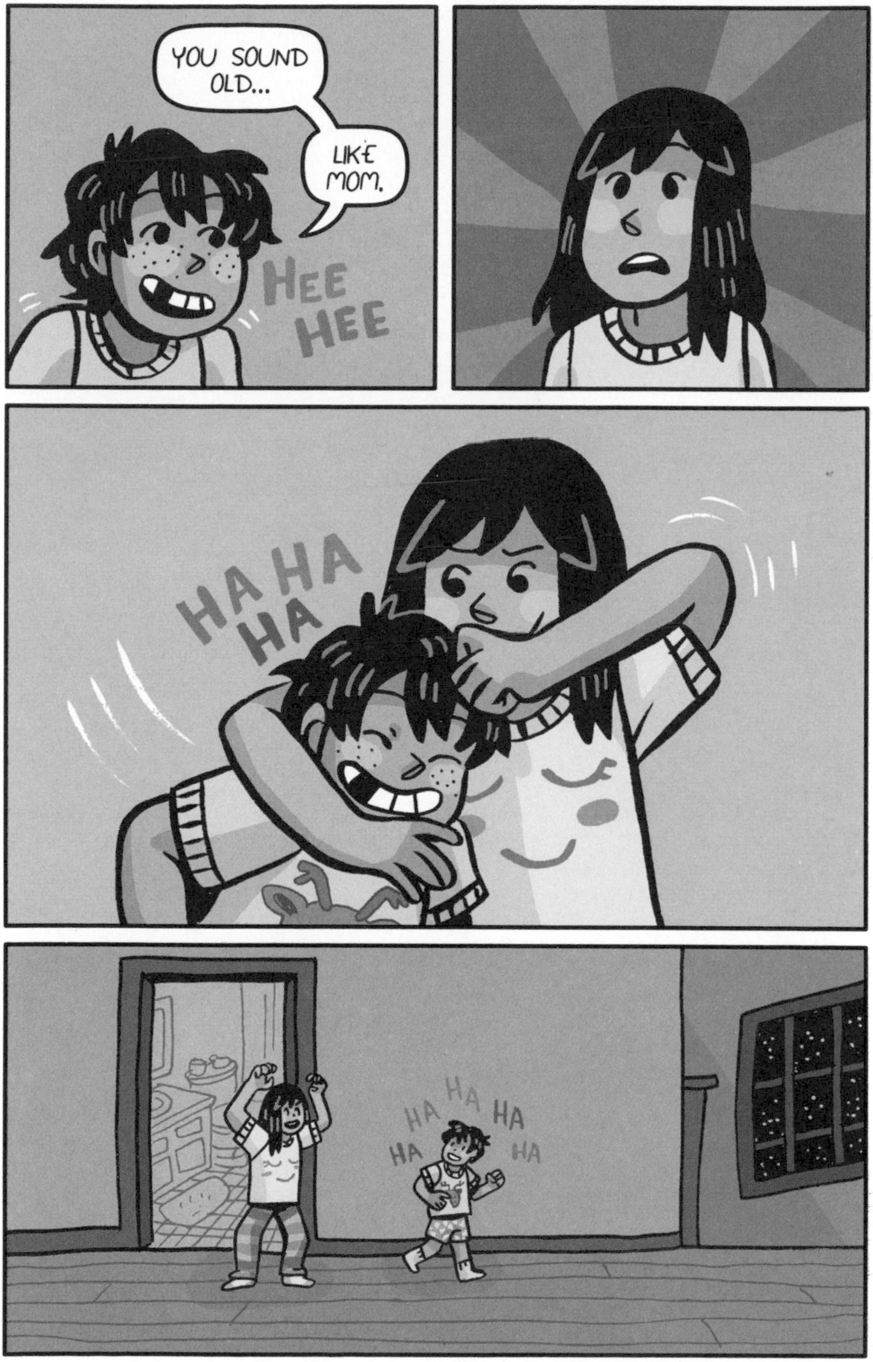
YOU SOUND OLD...
LIKE MOM.
HEE HEE
HA HA HA
HA HA HA HA HA HA

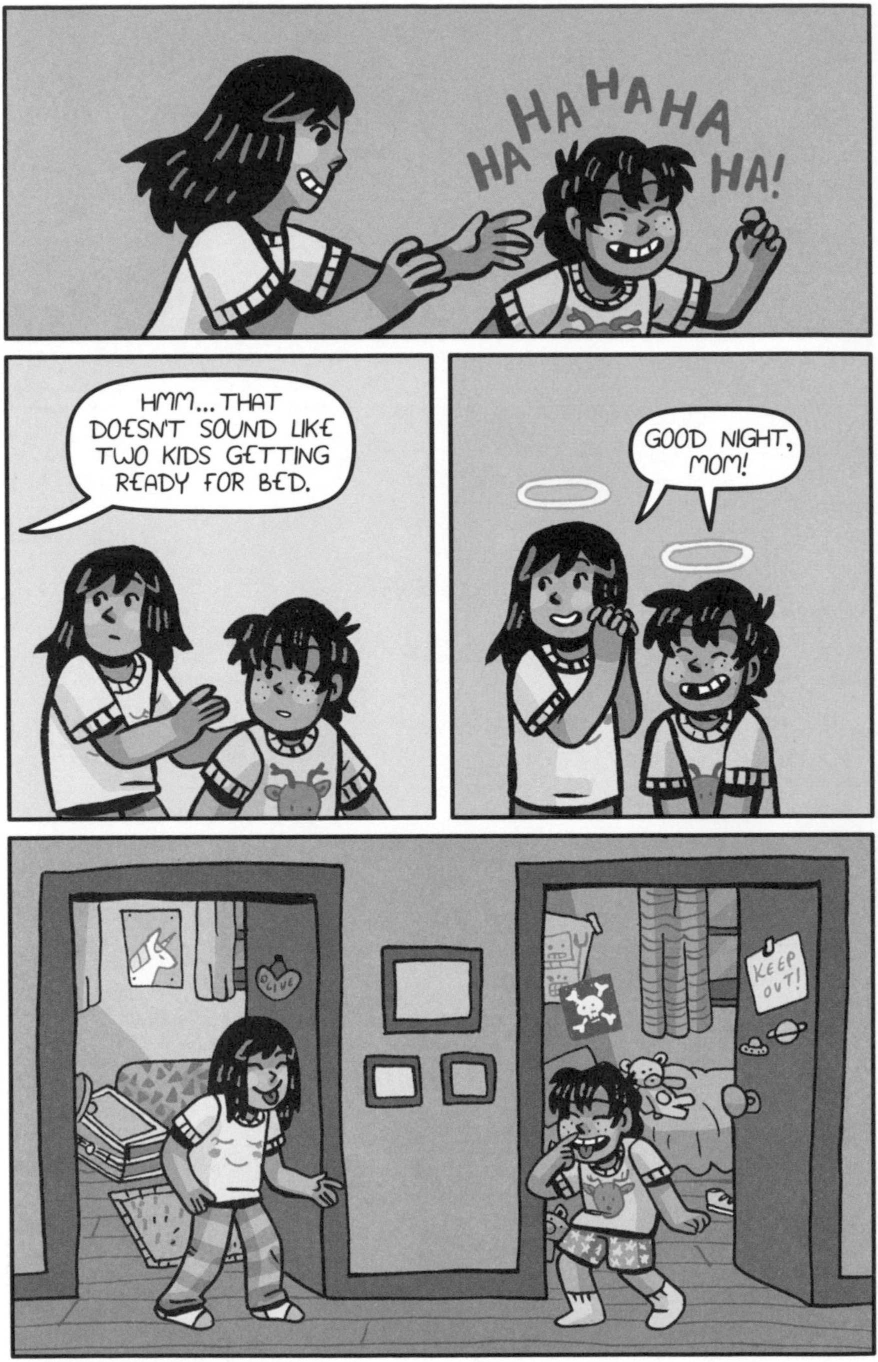
HA HA HA HA HA HA!
HMM... THAT DOESN'T SOUND LIKE TWO KIDS GETTING READY FOR BED.
GOOD NIGHT, MOM!
OLIVE
KEEP OUT!

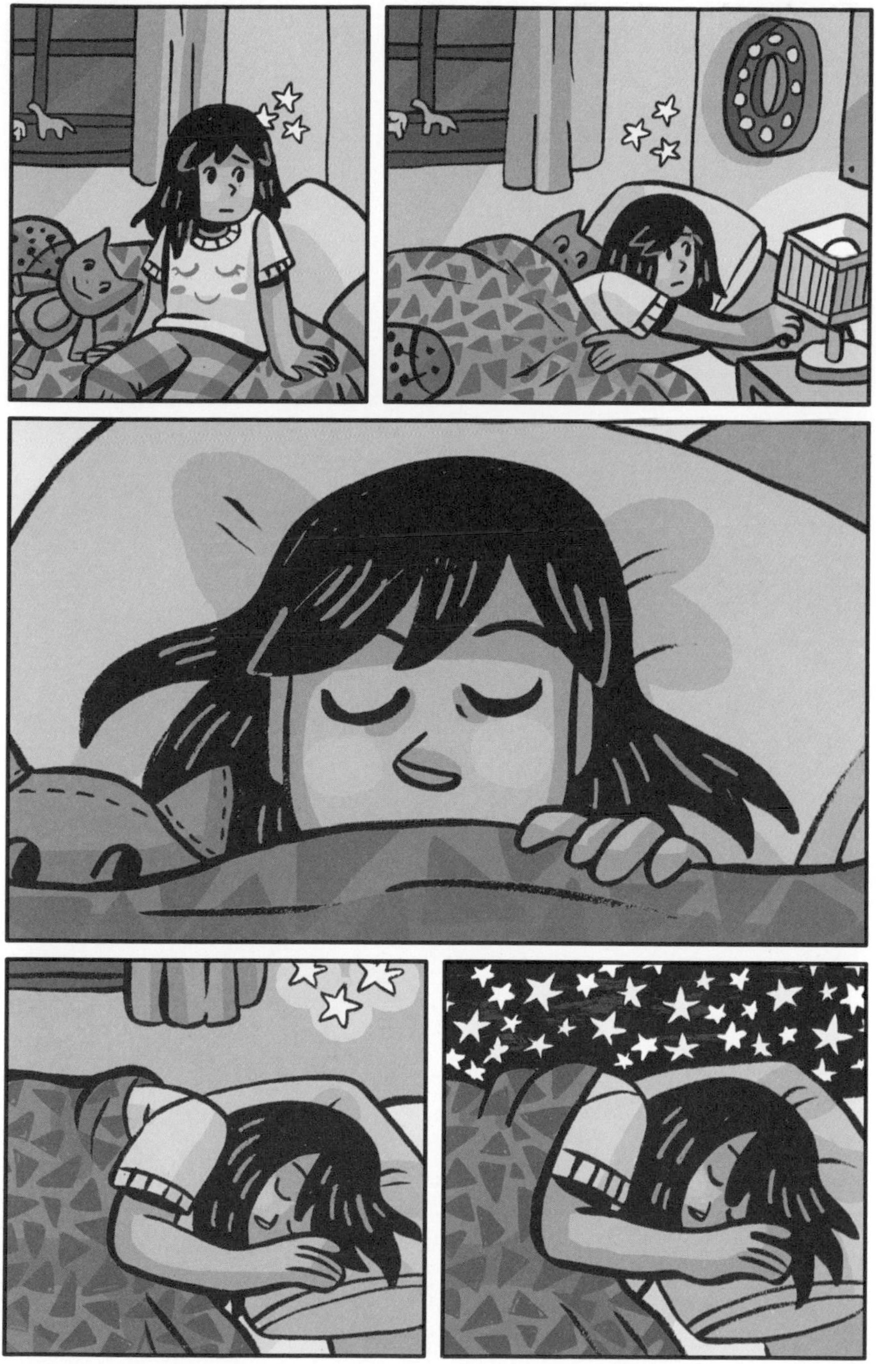

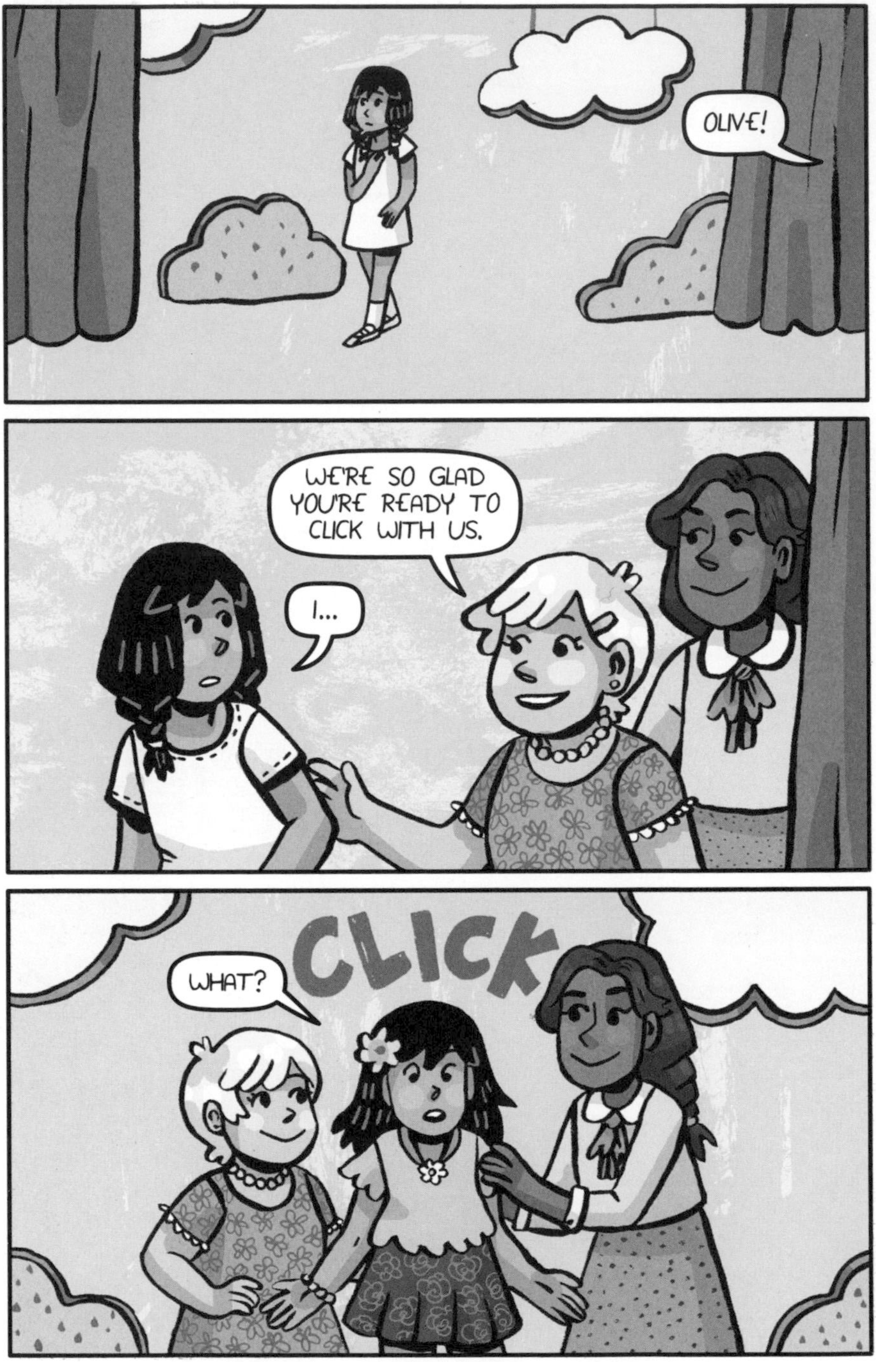
OLIVE!
WE'RE SO GLAD YOU'RE READY TO CLICK WITH US.
I...
CLICK
WHAT?

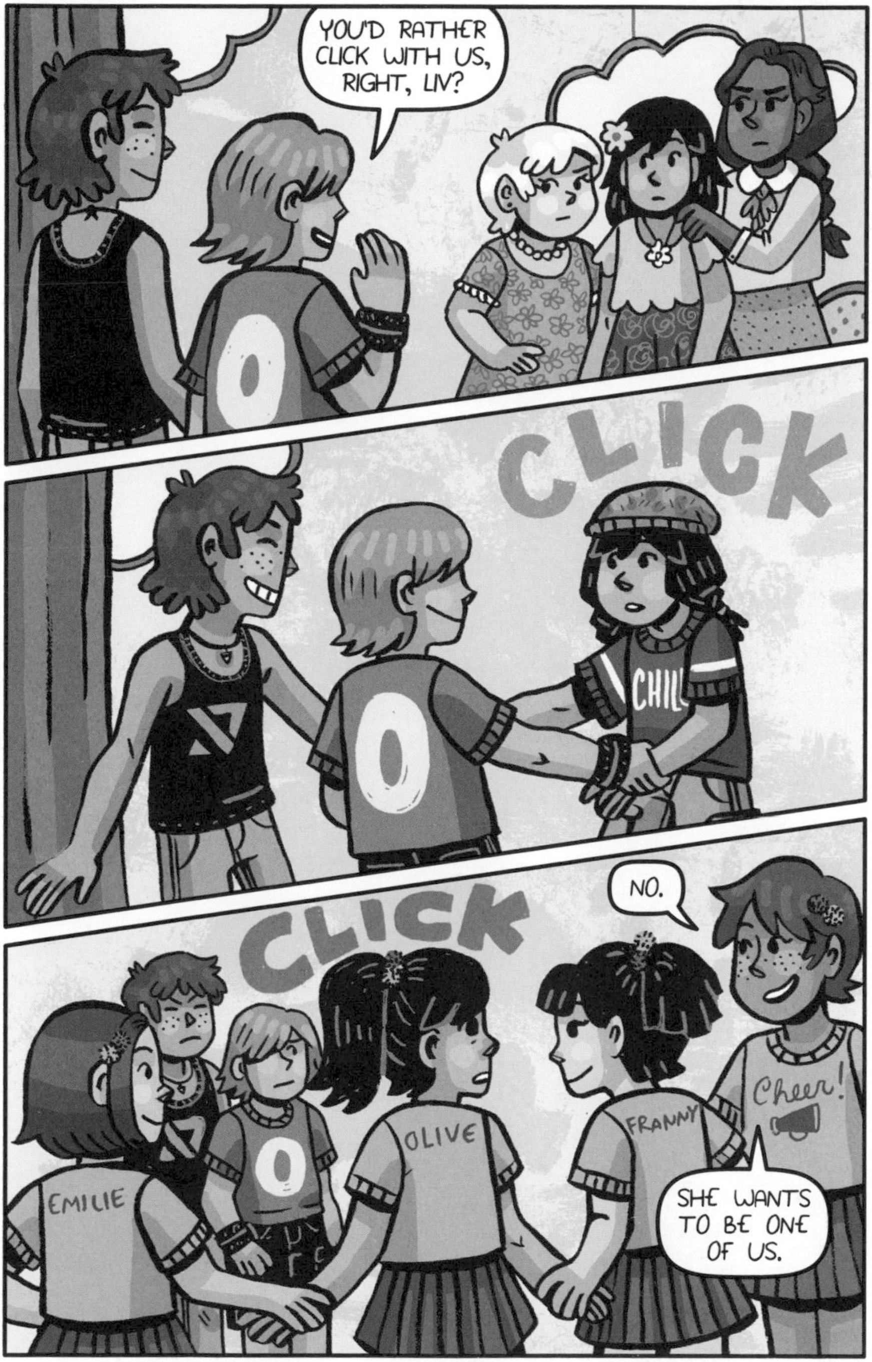
YOU'D RATHER CLICK WITH US, RIGHT, LIV?
CLICK
CHILL
CLICK
NO.
EMILIE
OLIVE
FRANNY
Cheer!
SHE WANTS TO BE ONE OF US.

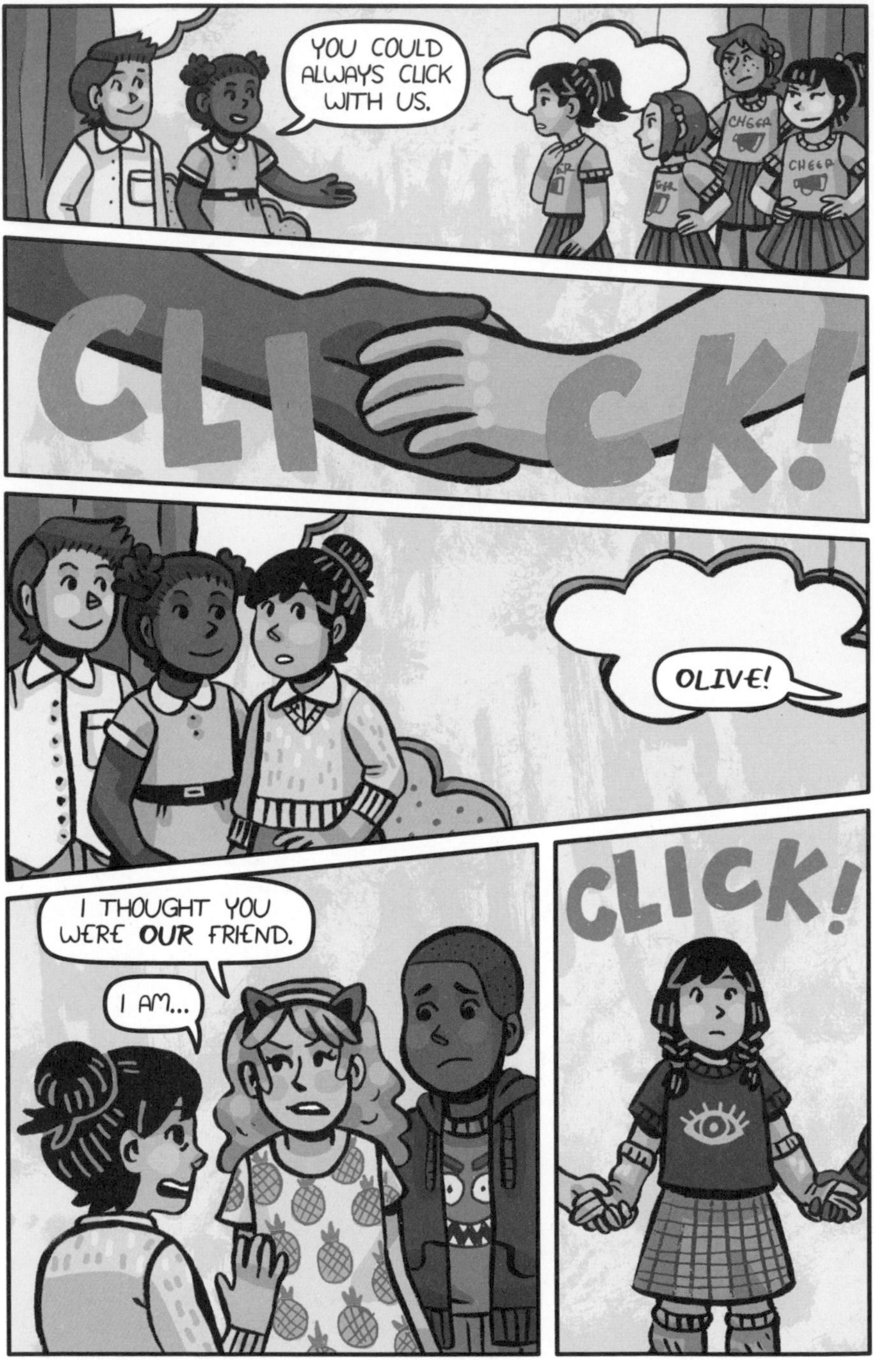

YOU COULD ALWAYS CLICK WITH US.
CLICK!
OLIVE!
I THOUGHT YOU WERE **OUR** FRIEND.
I AM...
CLICK!

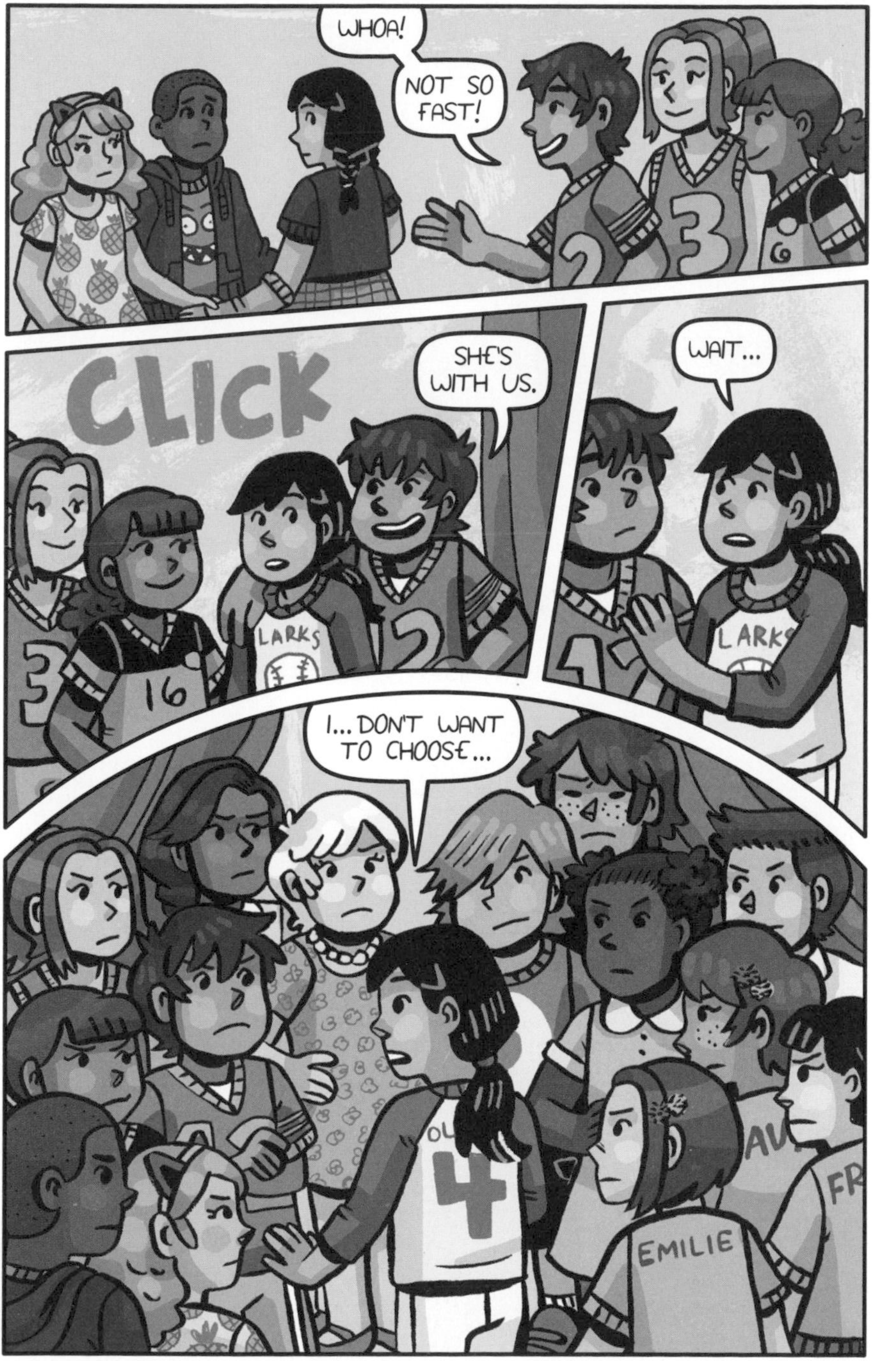
WHOA!
NOT SO FAST!
CLICK
SHE'S WITH US.
WAIT...
LARKS
16
LARKS
I... DON'T WANT TO CHOOSE...
EMILIE

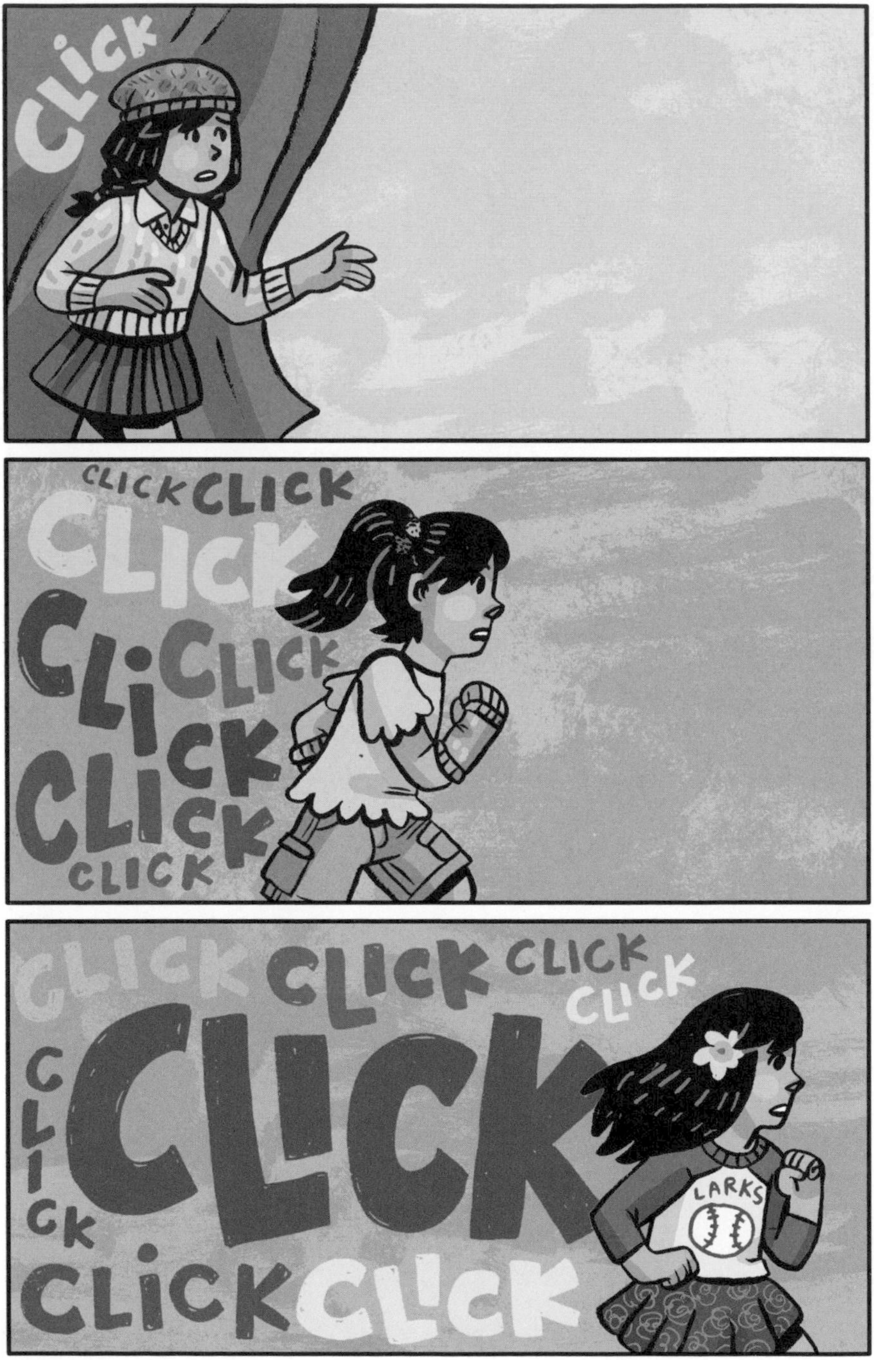
CLICK
CLICK CLICK
CLICK
CLICK
CLICK
CLICK
CLICK
CLICK
CLICK CLICK CLICK
CLICK
CLICK
CLICK
LARKS
CLICK CLICK

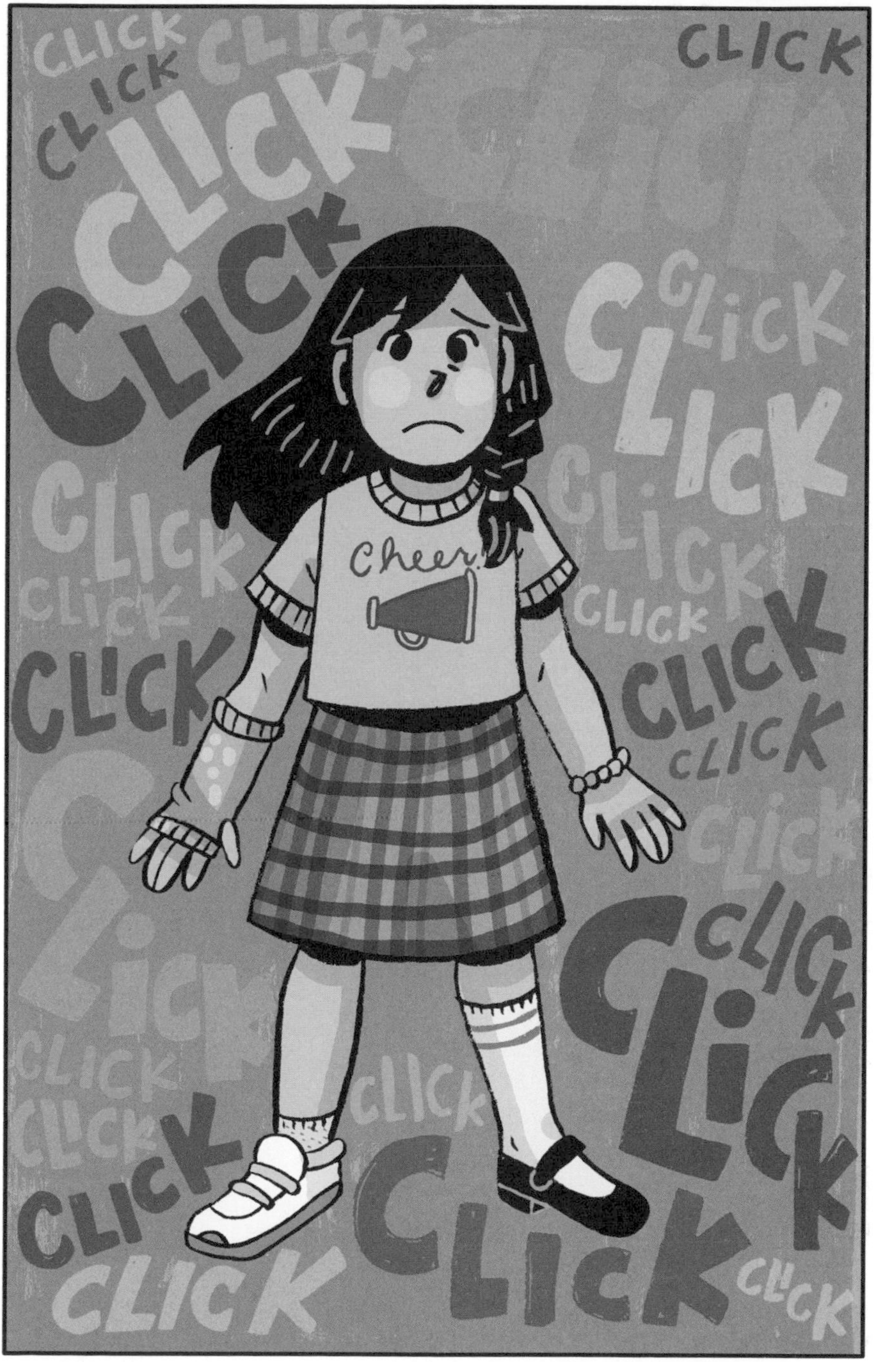
CLICK
CLICK
CLICK
CLICK
CLICK
CLICK
CLICK
Cheer!
CLICK
CLICK
CLICK
CLICK
CLICK

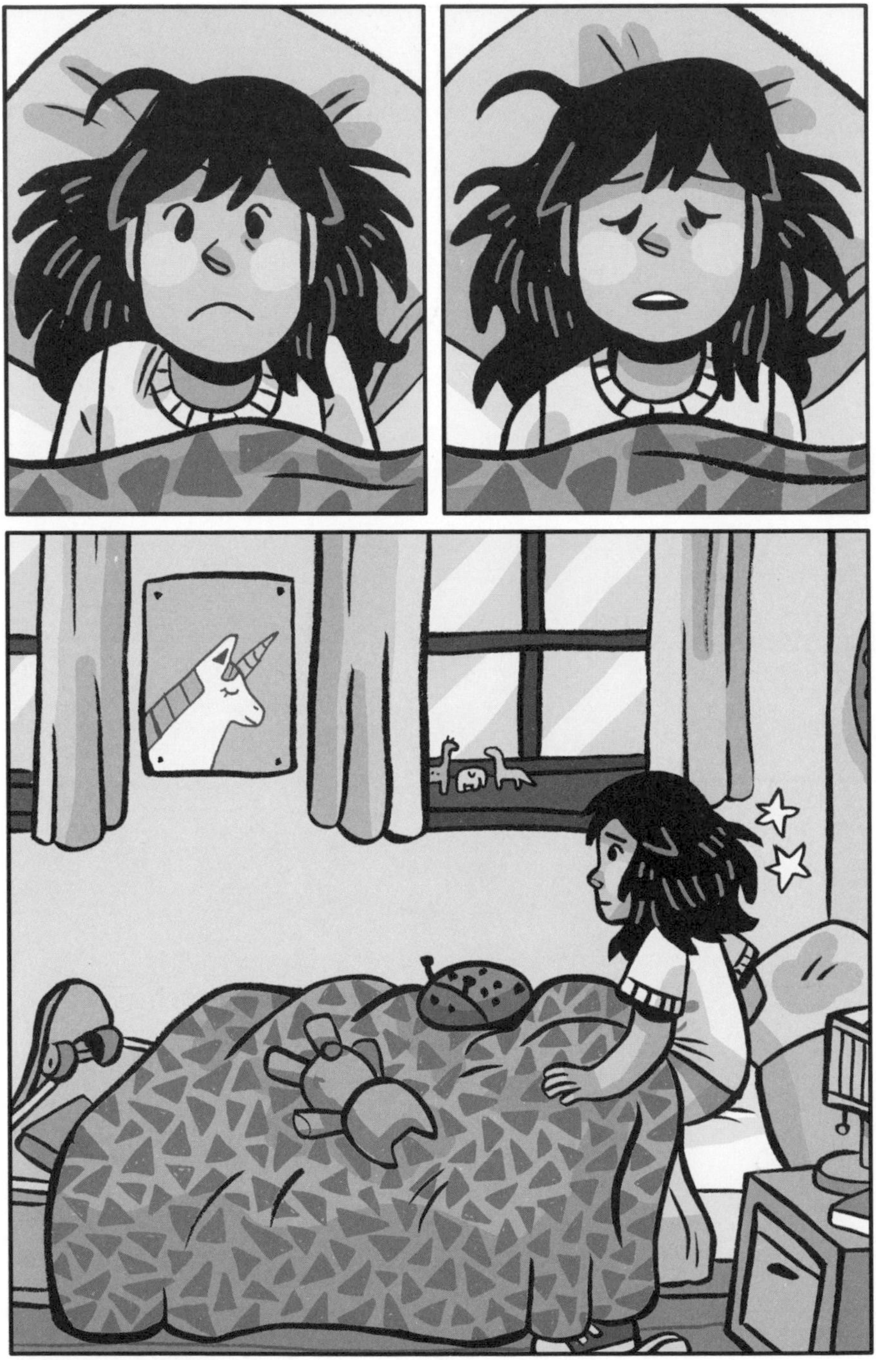

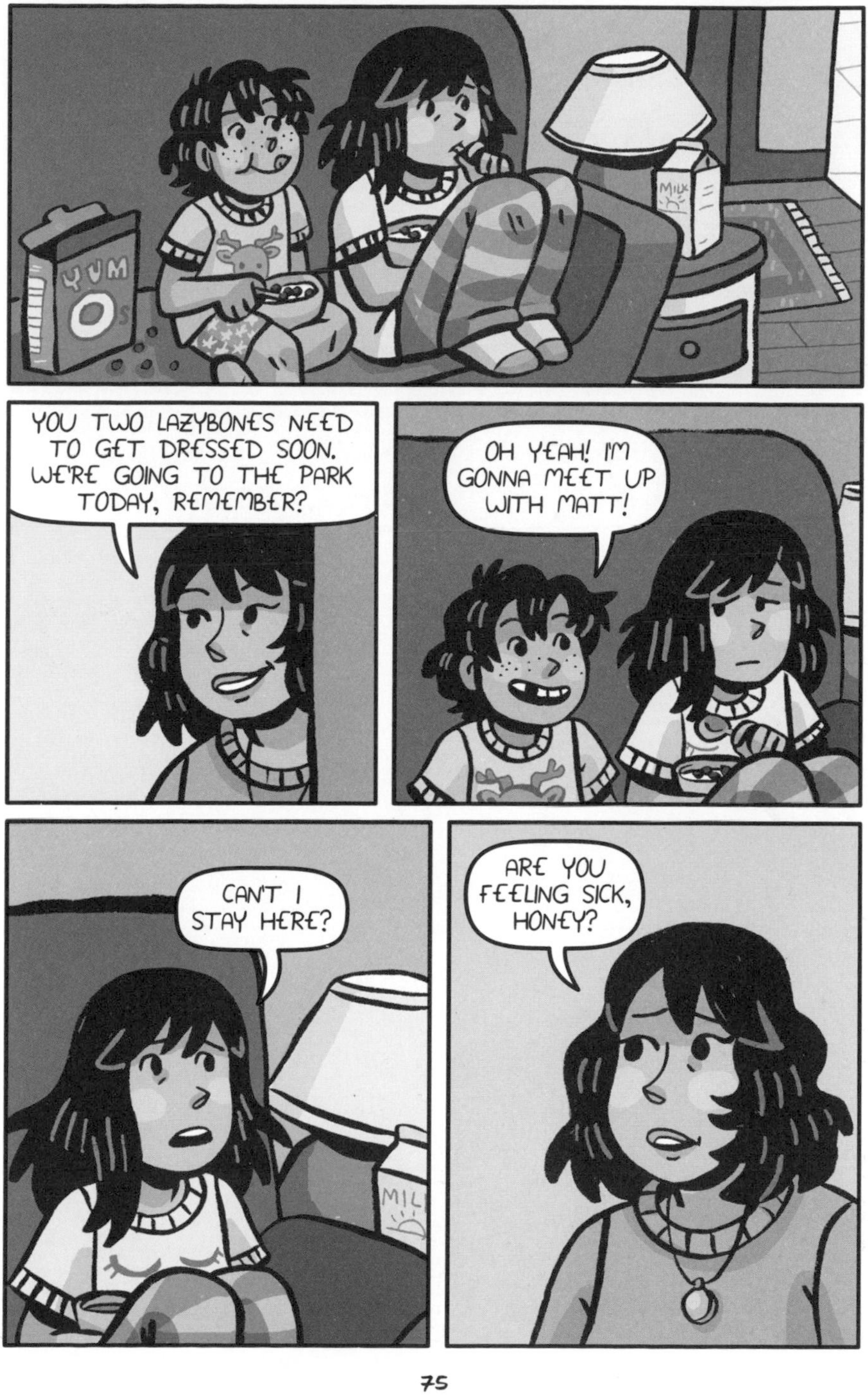
YUM Os
MILK
YOU TWO LAZYBONES NEED TO GET DRESSED SOON. WE'RE GOING TO THE PARK TODAY, REMEMBER?
OH YEAH! I'M GONNA MEET UP WITH MATT!
CAN'T I STAY HERE?
ARE YOU FEELING SICK, HONEY?

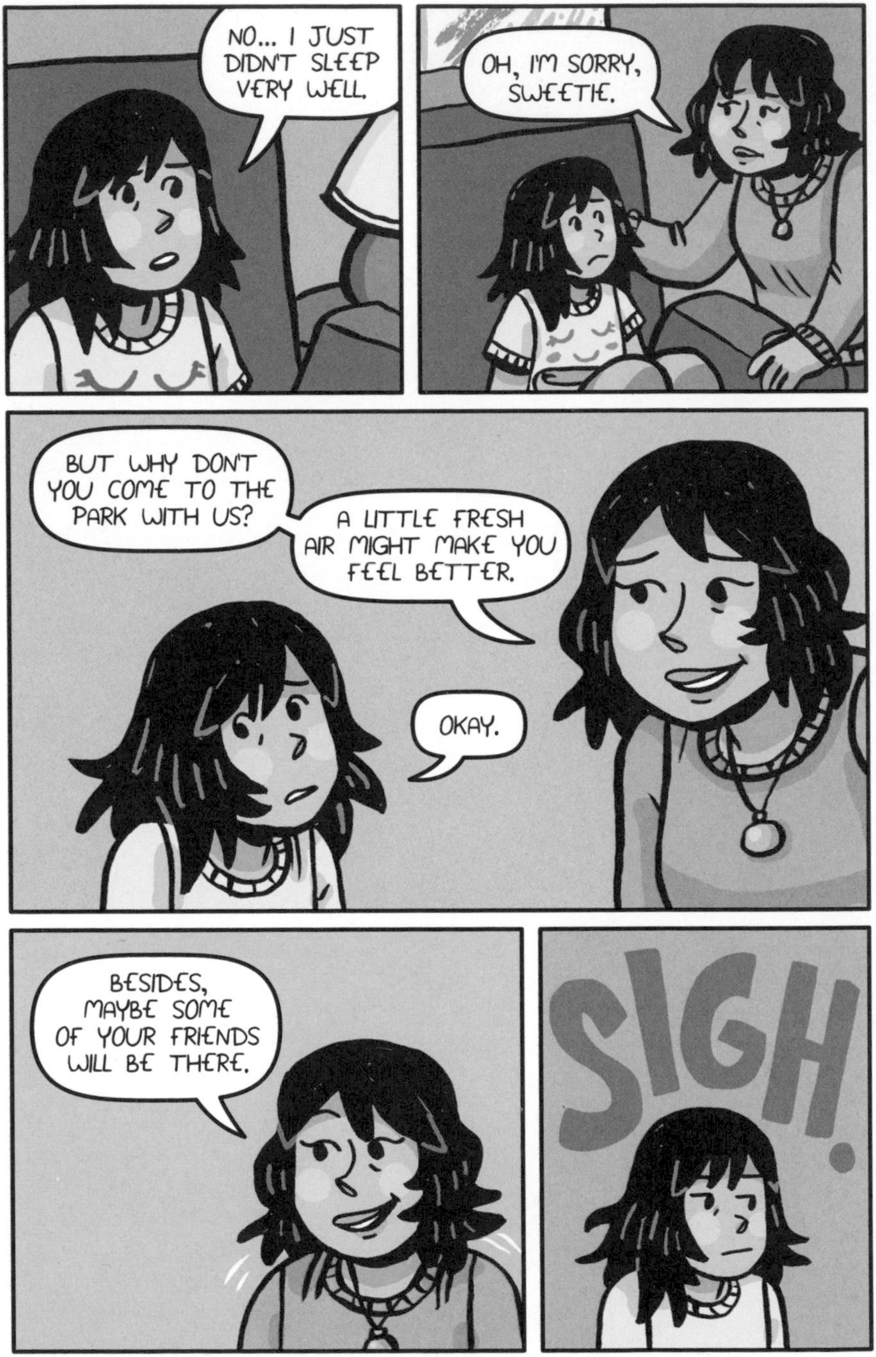
NO... I JUST DIDN'T SLEEP VERY WELL.
OH, I'M SORRY, SWEETIE.
BUT WHY DON'T YOU COME TO THE PARK WITH US?
A LITTLE FRESH AIR MIGHT MAKE YOU FEEL BETTER.
OKAY.
BESIDES, MAYBE SOME OF YOUR FRIENDS WILL BE THERE.
SIGH.

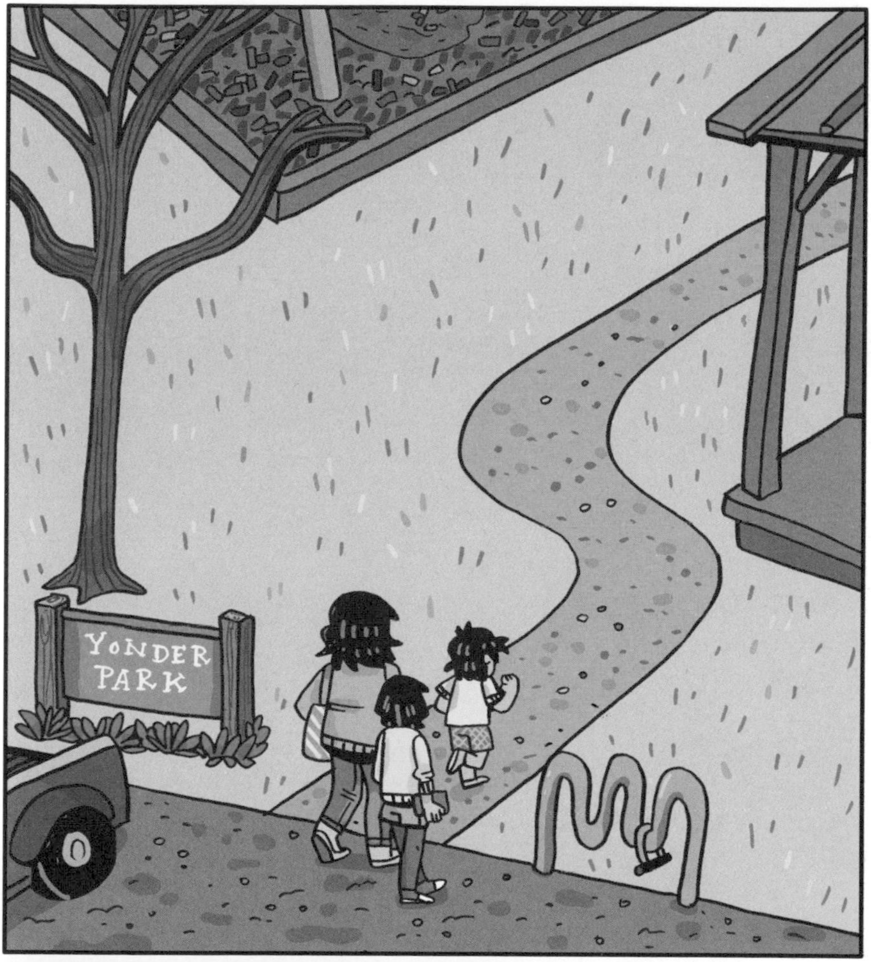
YONDER PARK
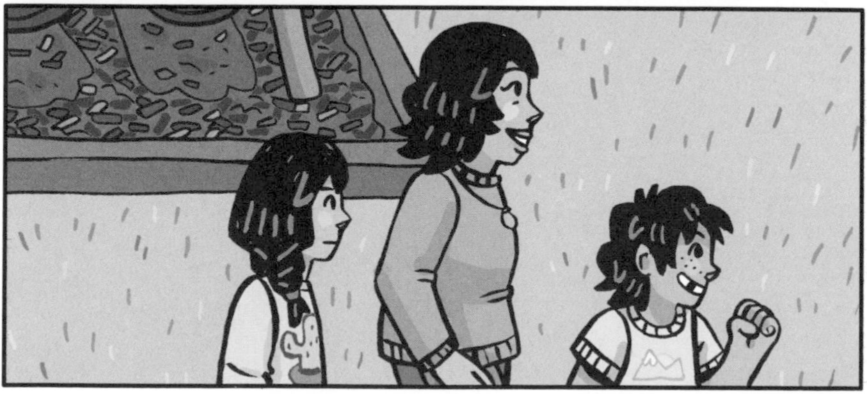

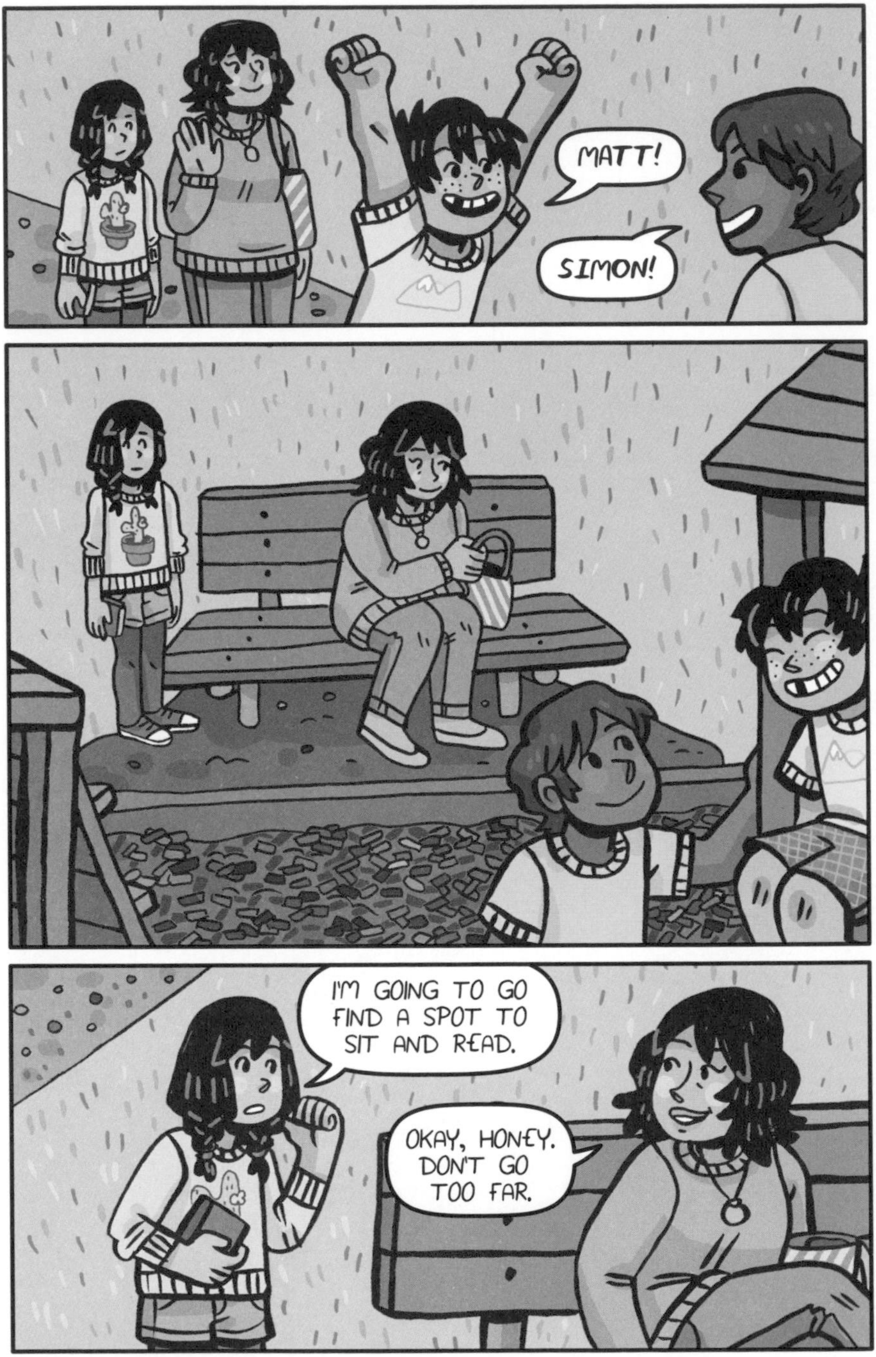
MATT!
SIMON!
I'M GOING TO GO FIND A SPOT TO SIT AND READ.
OKAY, HONEY. DON'T GO TOO FAR.

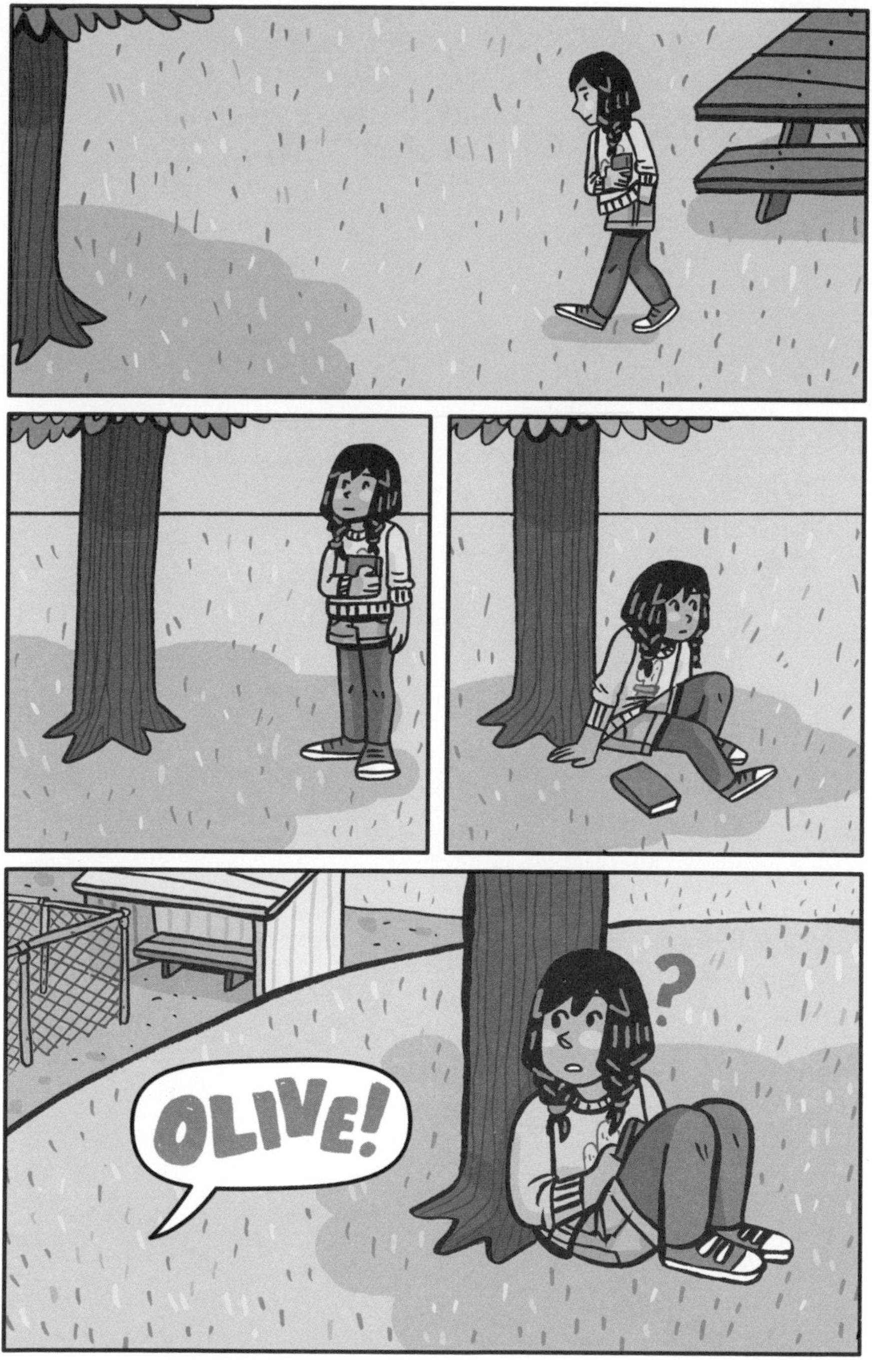
?
OLIVE!

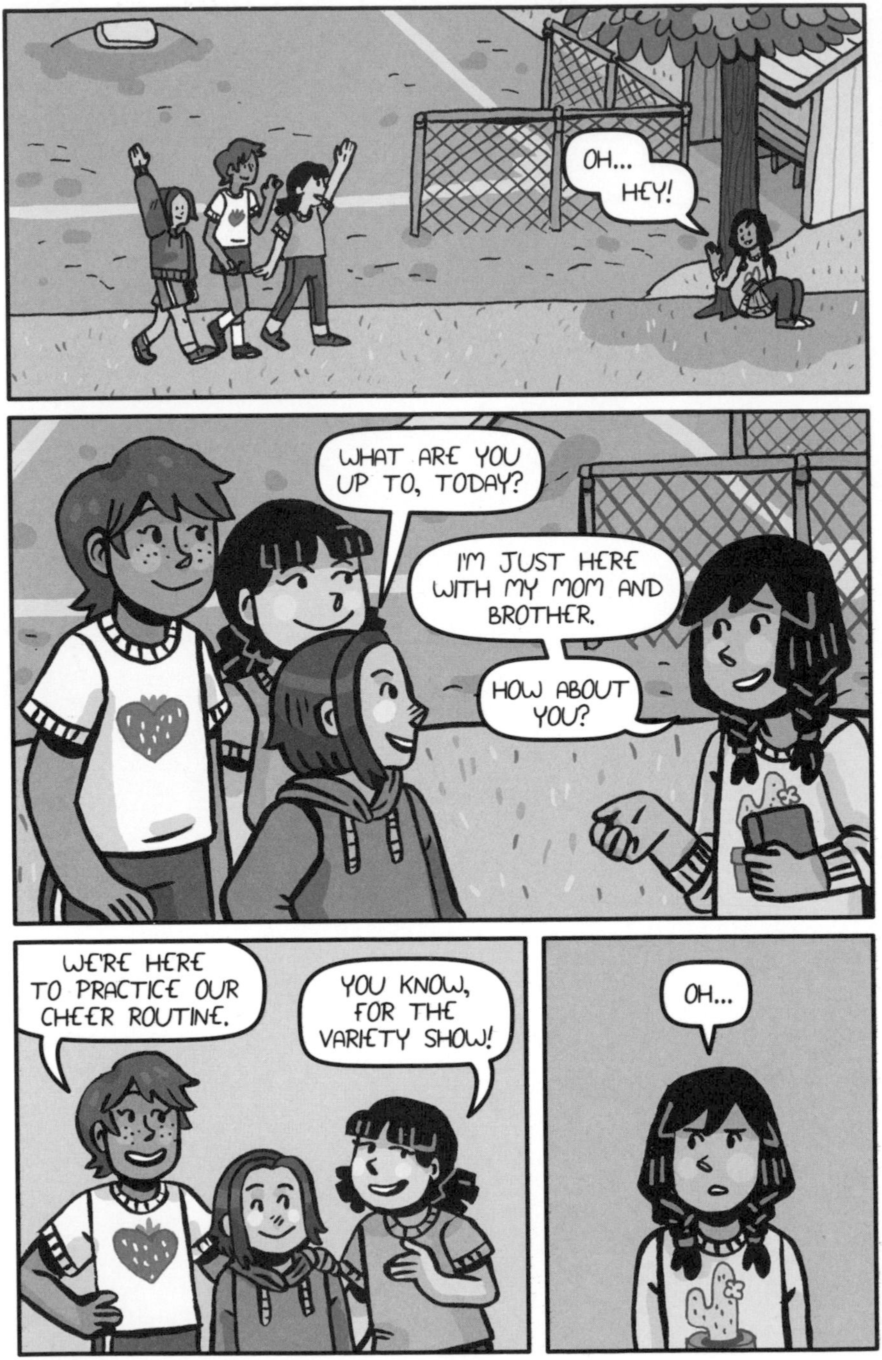
OH... HEY!
WHAT ARE YOU UP TO, TODAY?
I'M JUST HERE WITH MY MOM AND BROTHER.
HOW ABOUT YOU?
WE'RE HERE TO PRACTICE OUR CHEER ROUTINE.
YOU KNOW, FOR THE VARIETY SHOW!
OH...

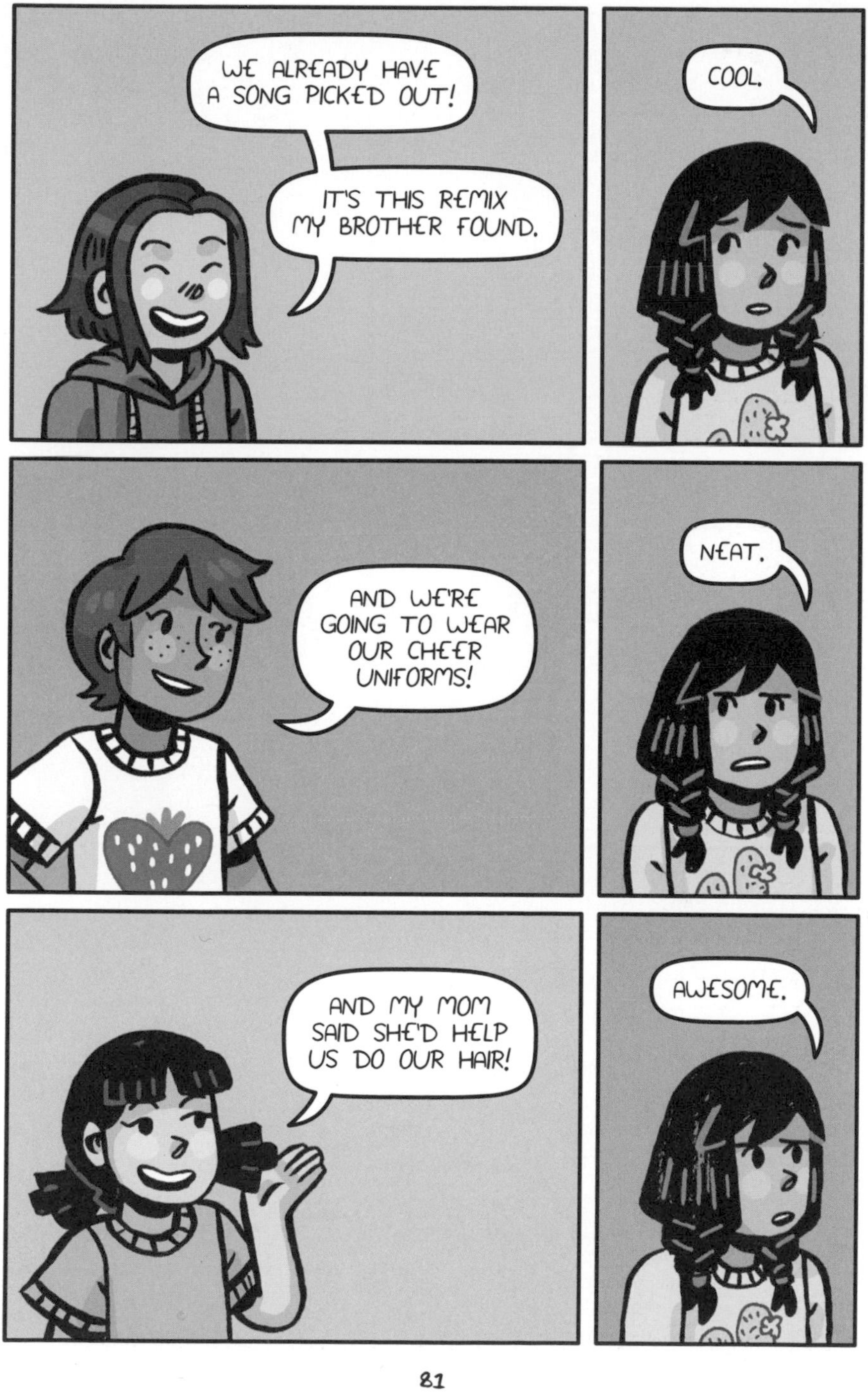
WE ALREADY HAVE A SONG PICKED OUT!
IT'S THIS REMIX MY BROTHER FOUND.
COOL.
AND WE'RE GOING TO WEAR OUR CHEER UNIFORMS!
NEAT.
AND MY MOM SAID SHE'D HELP US DO OUR HAIR!
AWESOME.

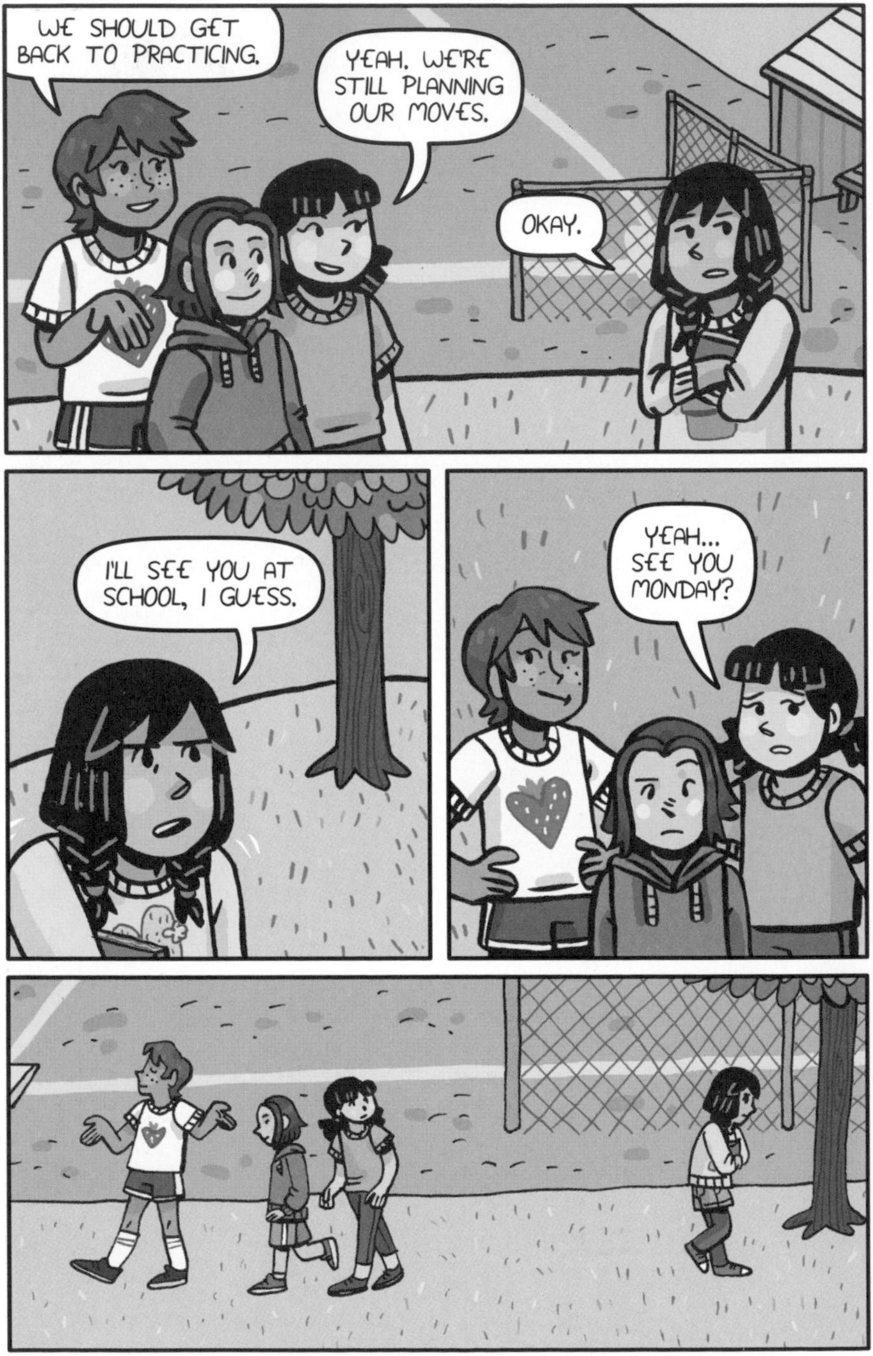
WE SHOULD GET BACK TO PRACTICING.
YEAH. WE'RE STILL PLANNING OUR MOVES.
OKAY.
I'LL SEE YOU AT SCHOOL, I GUESS.
YEAH... SEE YOU MONDAY?

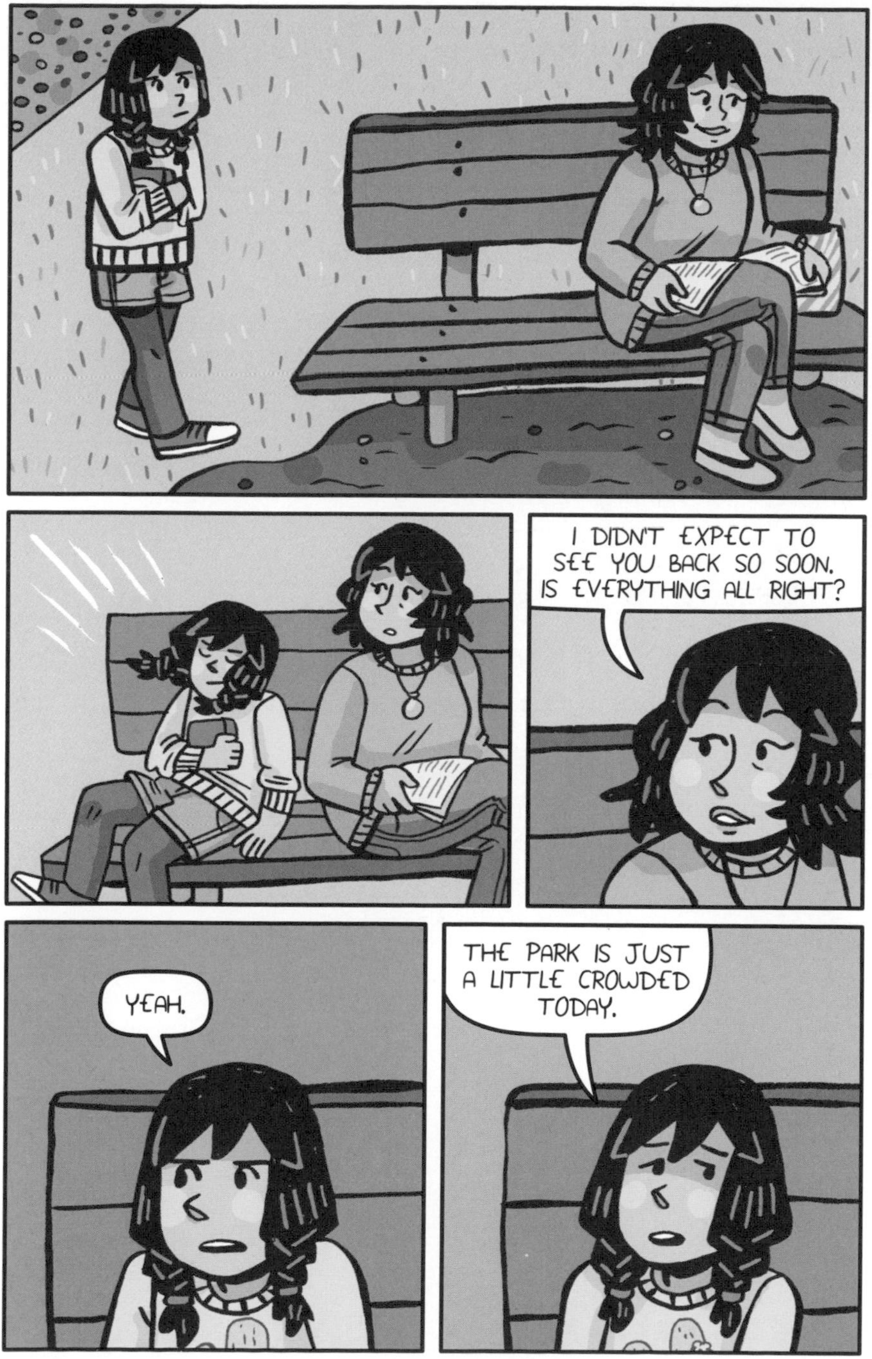
I DIDN'T EXPECT TO SEE YOU BACK SO SOON. IS EVERYTHING ALL RIGHT?
YEAH.
THE PARK IS JUST A LITTLE CROWDED TODAY.

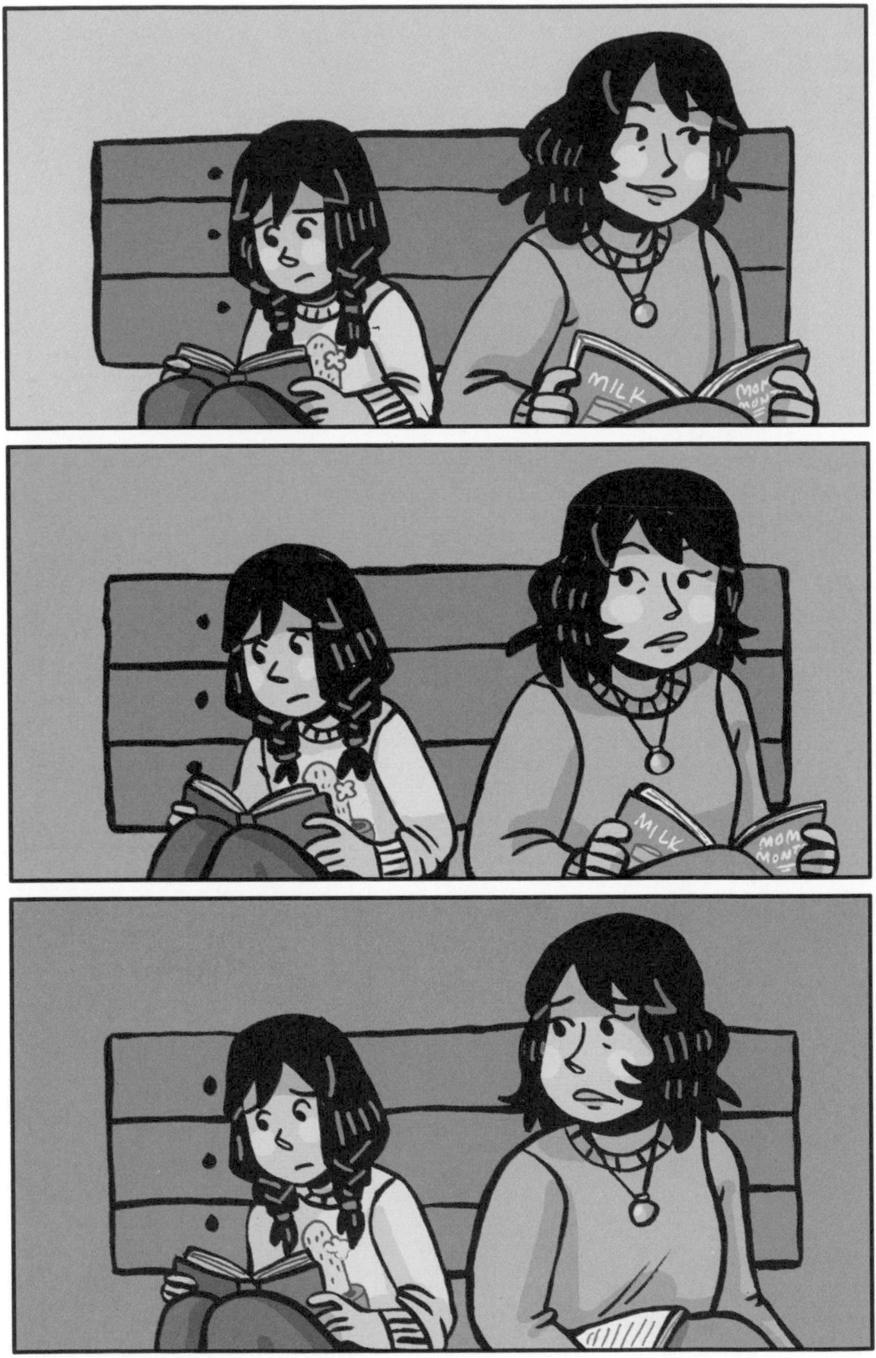
MILK
MOM

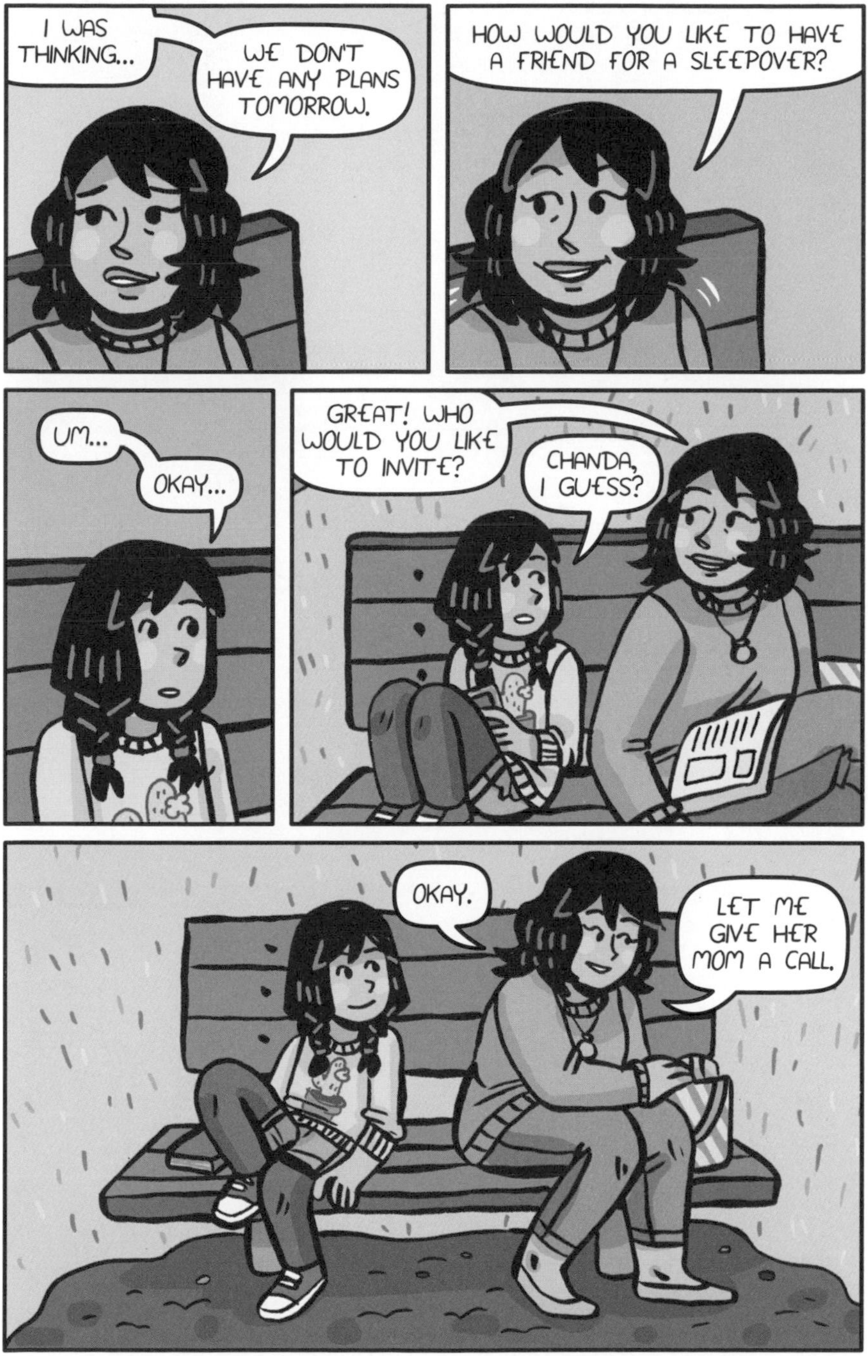
I WAS THINKING...
WE DON'T HAVE ANY PLANS TOMORROW.
HOW WOULD YOU LIKE TO HAVE A FRIEND FOR A SLEEPOVER?
UM...
OKAY...
GREAT! WHO WOULD YOU LIKE TO INVITE?
CHANDA, I GUESS?
OKAY.
LET ME GIVE HER MOM A CALL.

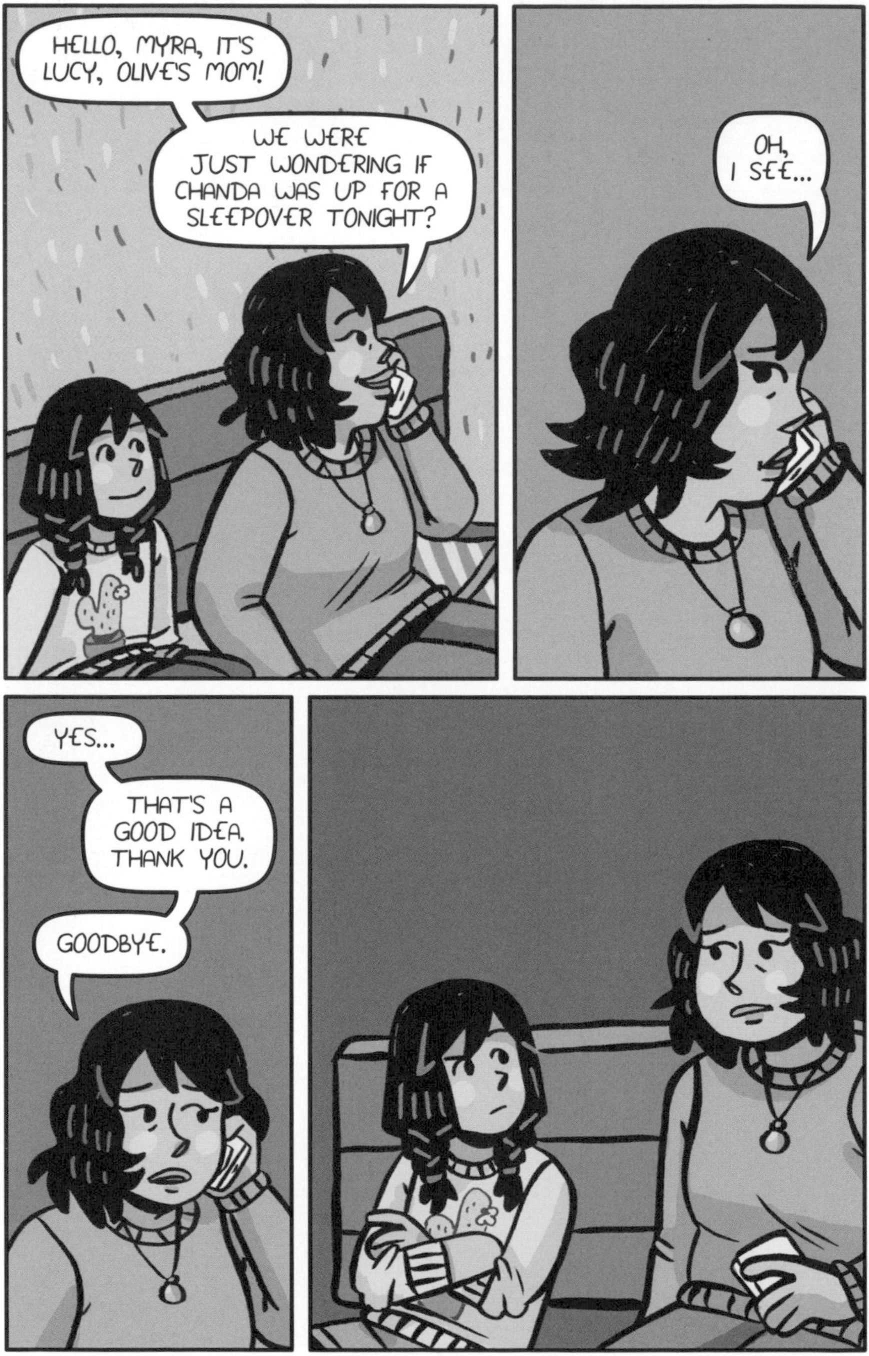
HELLO, MYRA, IT'S LUCY, OLIVE'S MOM!
WE WERE JUST WONDERING IF CHANDA WAS UP FOR A SLEEPOVER TONIGHT?
OH, I SEE...
YES...
THAT'S A GOOD IDEA. THANK YOU.
GOODBYE.

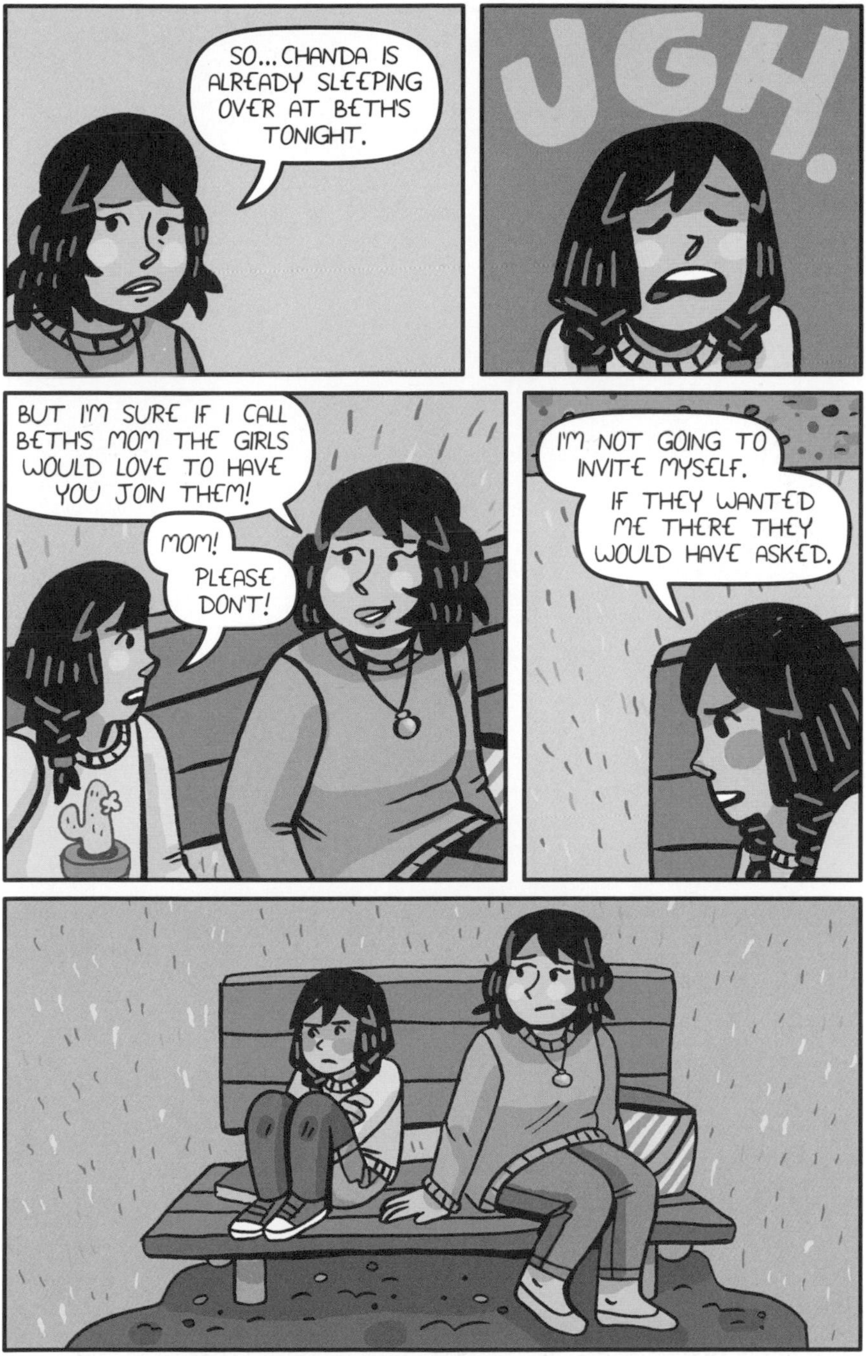
SO... CHANDA IS ALREADY SLEEPING OVER AT BETH'S TONIGHT.
UGH!
BUT I'M SURE IF I CALL BETH'S MOM THE GIRLS WOULD LOVE TO HAVE YOU JOIN THEM!
MOM! PLEASE DON'T!
I'M NOT GOING TO INVITE MYSELF.
IF THEY WANTED ME THERE THEY WOULD HAVE ASKED.

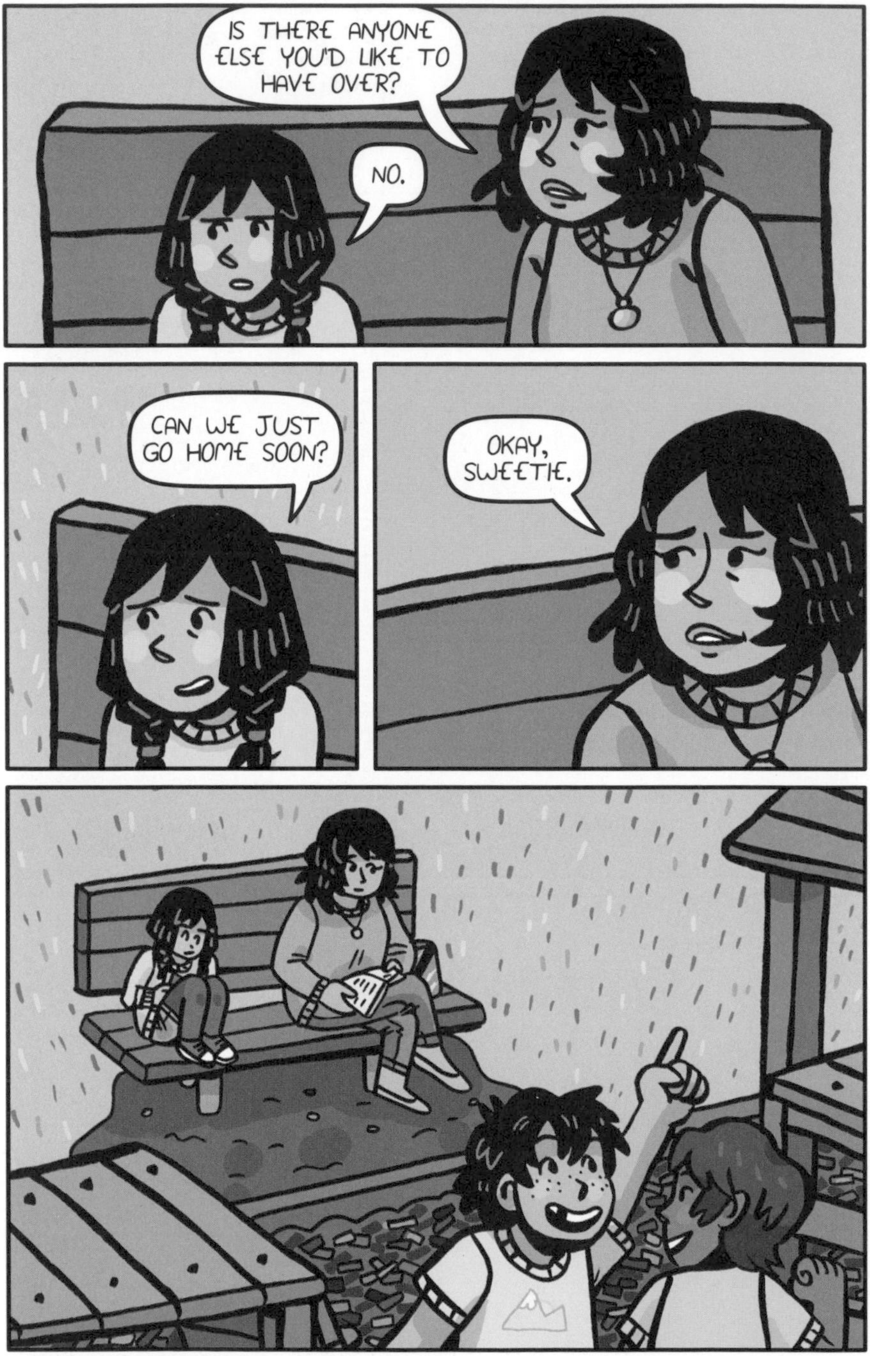
IS THERE ANYONE ELSE YOU'D LIKE TO HAVE OVER?
NO.
CAN WE JUST GO HOME SOON?
OKAY, SWEETIE.

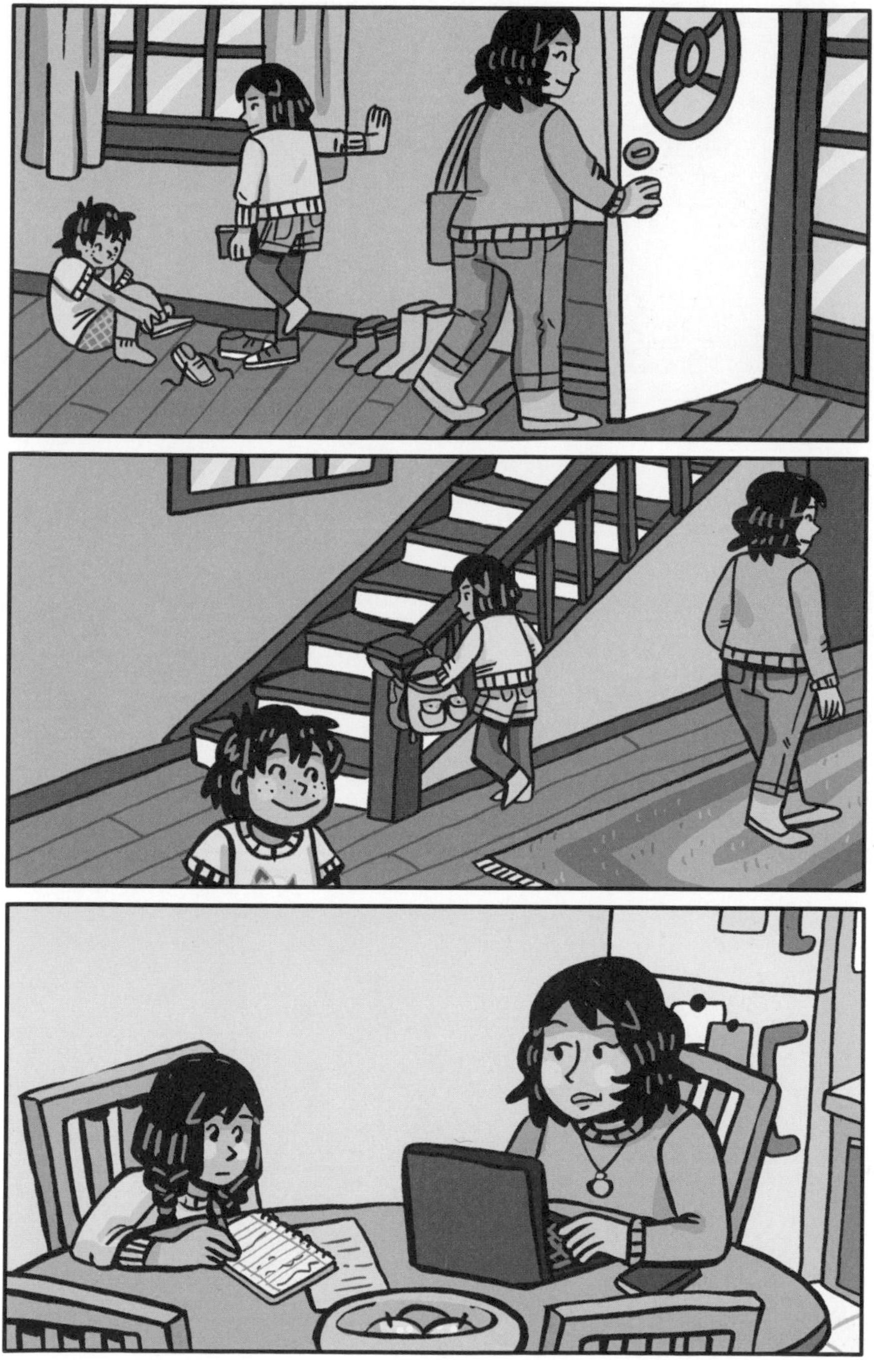

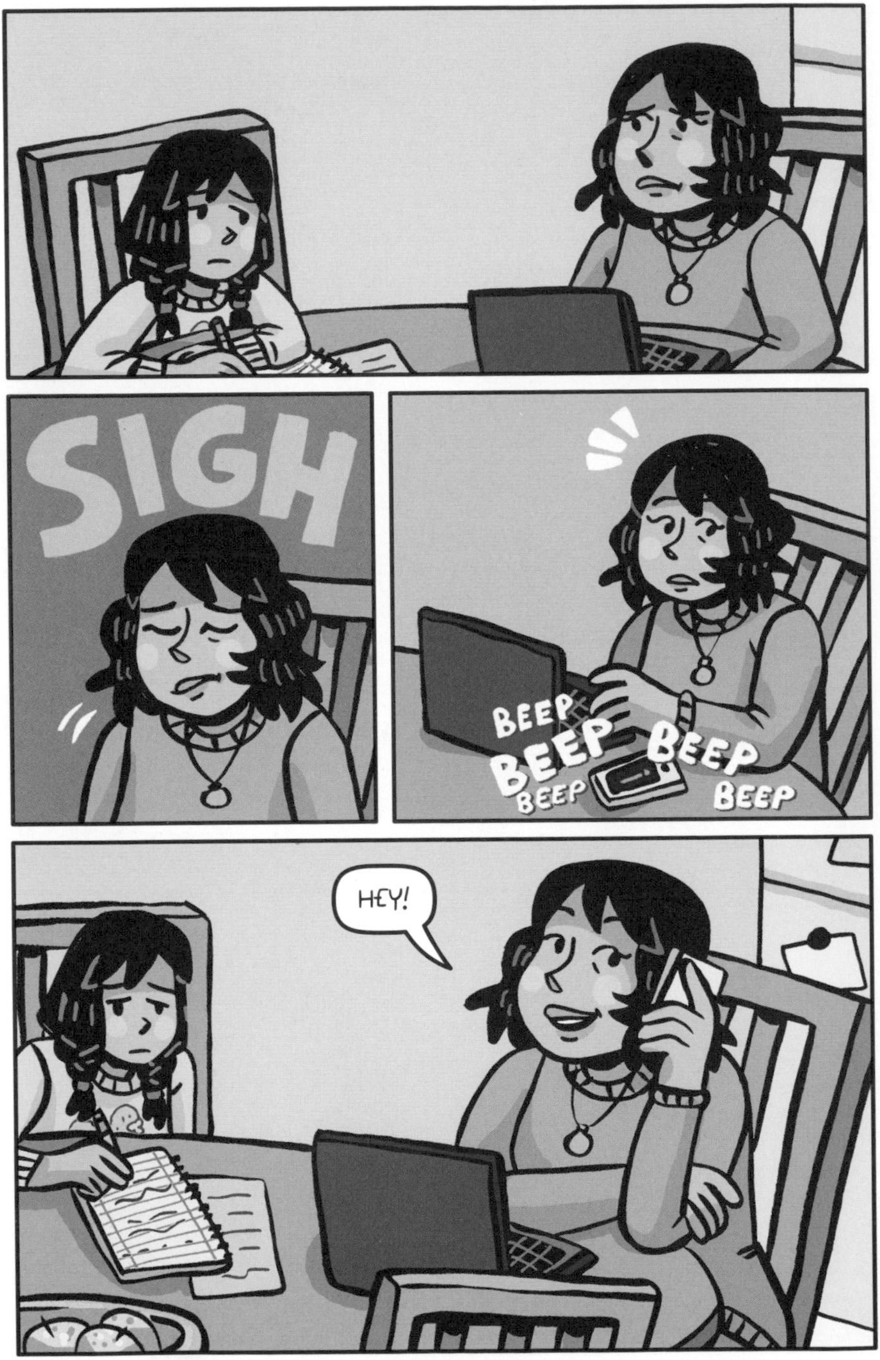
SIGH
BEEP
BEEP
BEEP
BEEP
BEEP
BEEP
HEY!

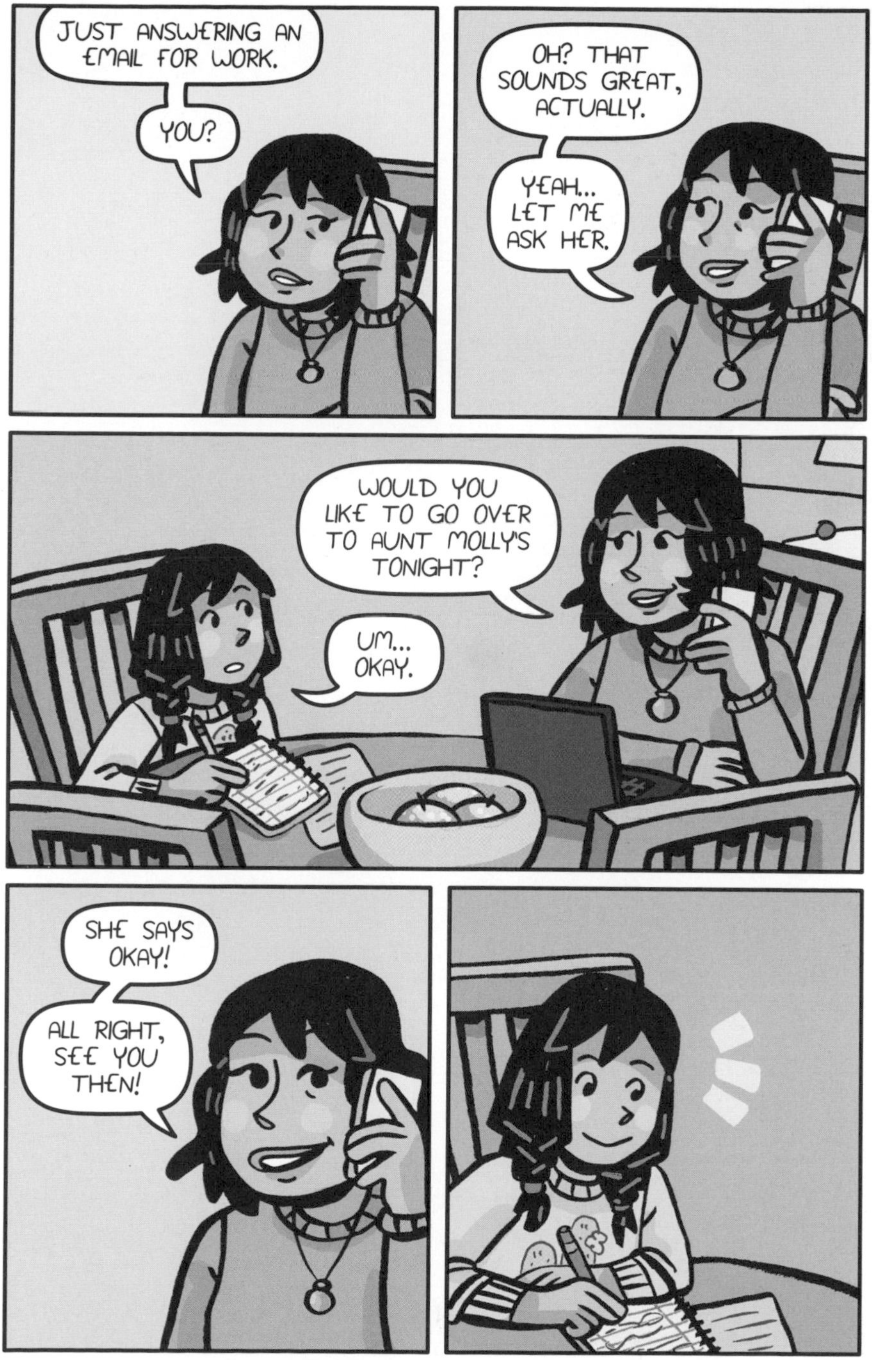
JUST ANSWERING AN EMAIL FOR WORK.
YOU?
OH? THAT SOUNDS GREAT, ACTUALLY.
YEAH... LET ME ASK HER.
WOULD YOU LIKE TO GO OVER TO AUNT MOLLY'S TONIGHT?
UM... OKAY.
SHE SAYS OKAY!
ALL RIGHT, SEE YOU THEN!

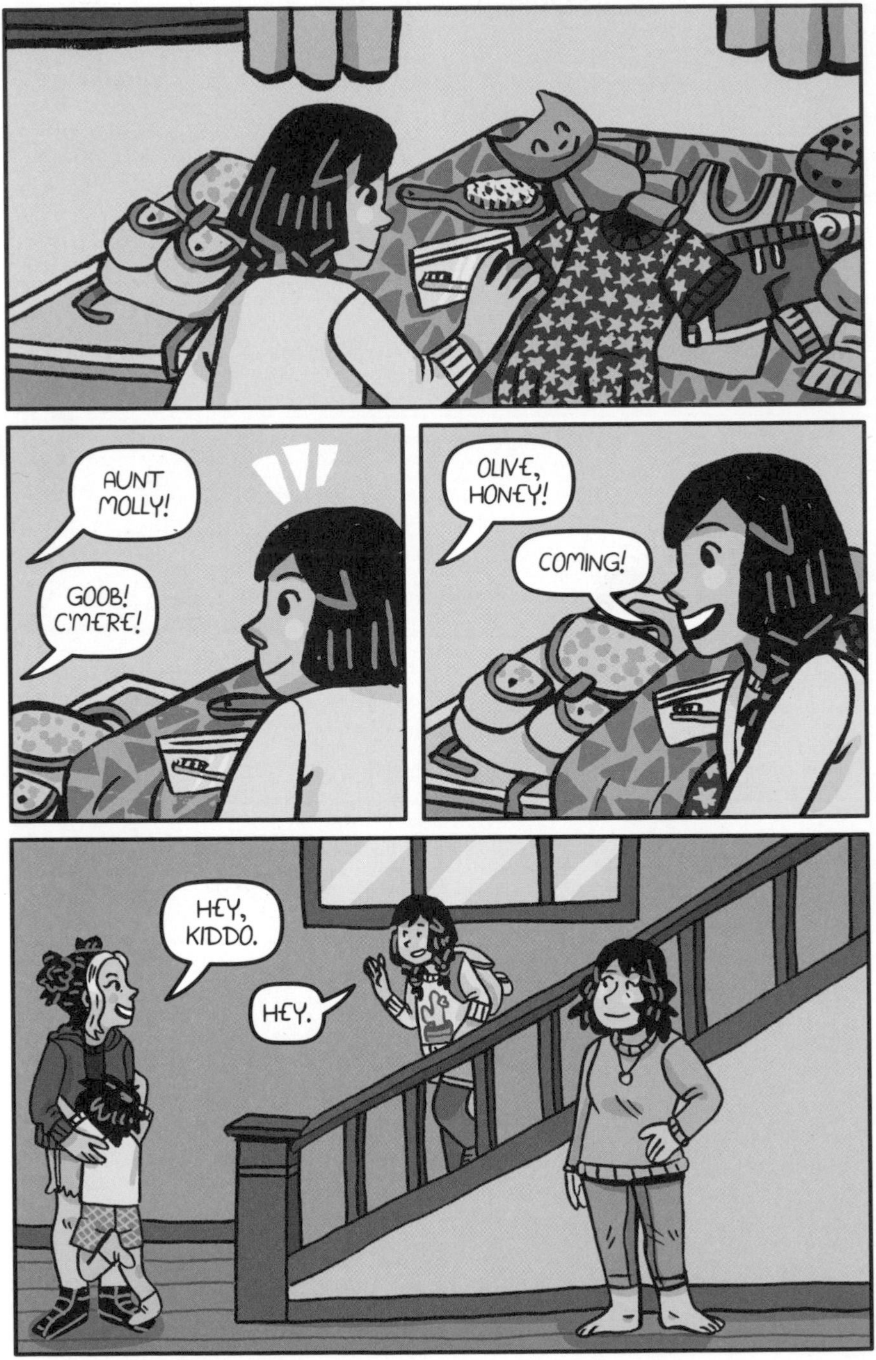
AUNT MOLLY!
GOOB! C'MERE!
OLIVE, HONEY!
COMING!
HEY, KIDDO.
HEY.

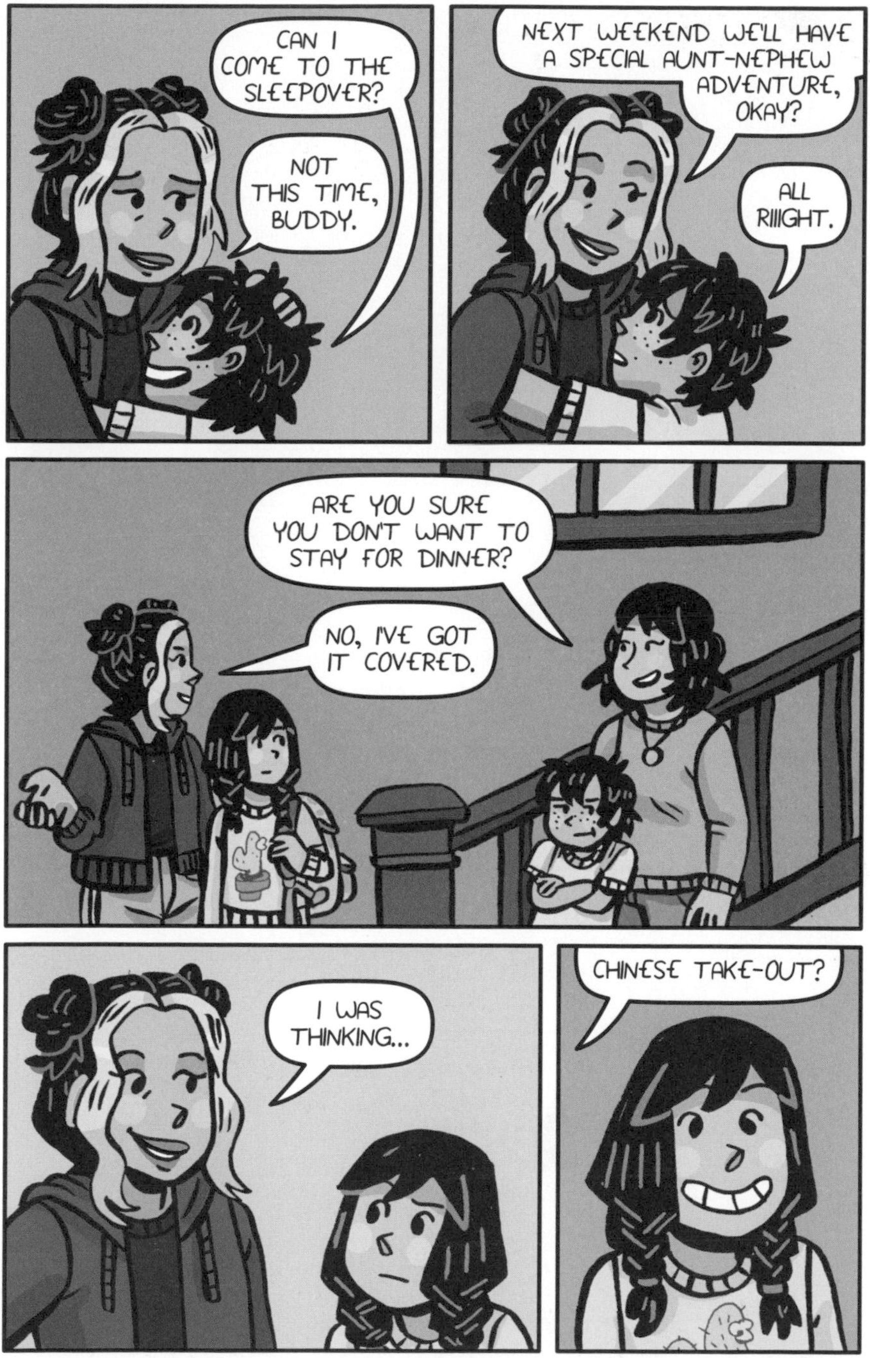
CAN I COME TO THE SLEEPOVER?
NOT THIS TIME, BUDDY.
NEXT WEEKEND WE'LL HAVE A SPECIAL AUNT-NEPHEW ADVENTURE, OKAY?
ALL RIIIGHT.
ARE YOU SURE YOU DON'T WANT TO STAY FOR DINNER?
NO, I'VE GOT IT COVERED.
I WAS THINKING...
CHINESE TAKE-OUT?

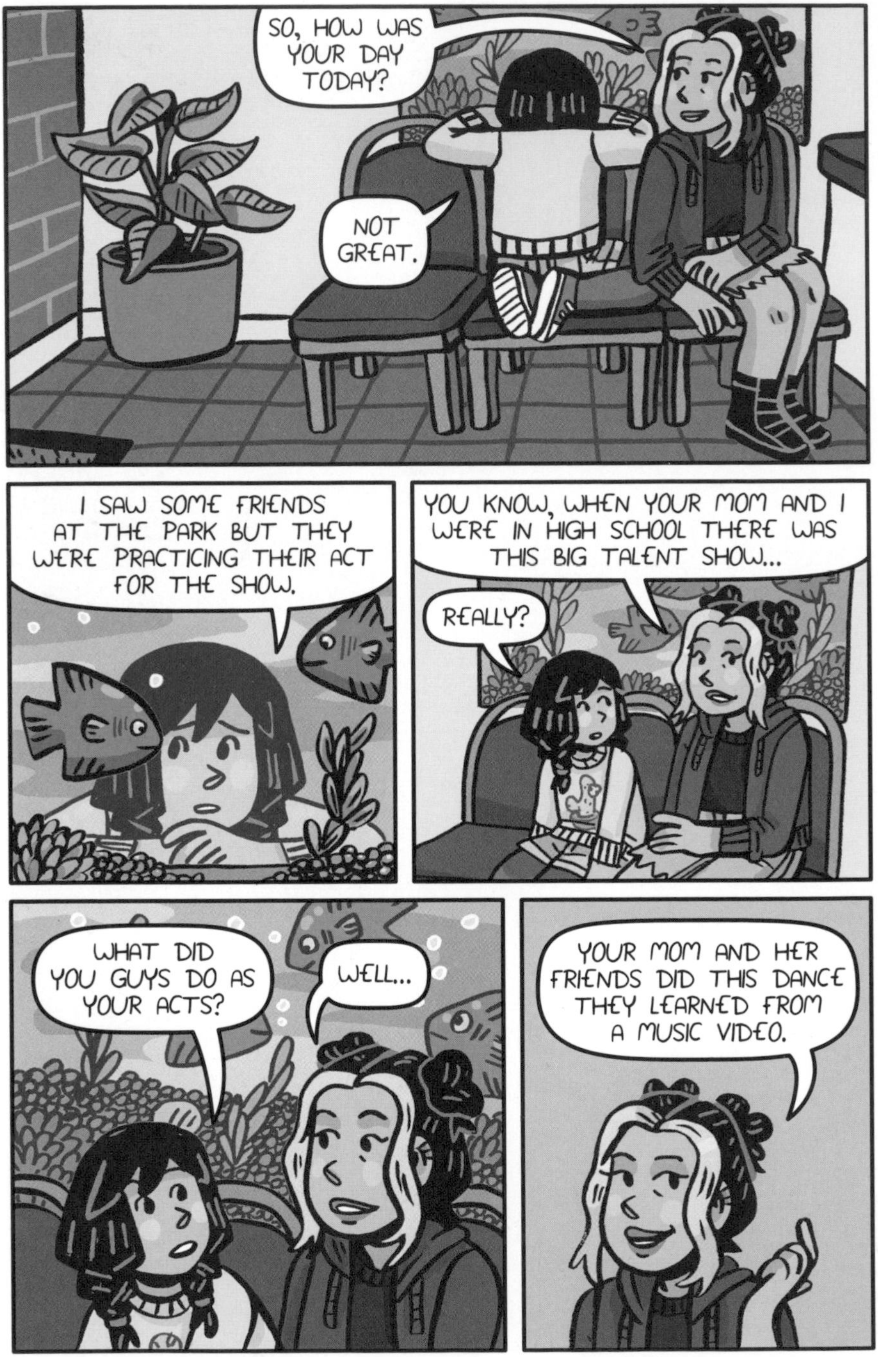
SO, HOW WAS YOUR DAY TODAY?
NOT GREAT.
I SAW SOME FRIENDS AT THE PARK BUT THEY WERE PRACTICING THEIR ACT FOR THE SHOW.
YOU KNOW, WHEN YOUR MOM AND I WERE IN HIGH SCHOOL THERE WAS THIS BIG TALENT SHOW...
REALLY?
WHAT DID YOU GUYS DO AS YOUR ACTS?
WELL...
YOUR MOM AND HER FRIENDS DID THIS DANCE THEY LEARNED FROM A MUSIC VIDEO.

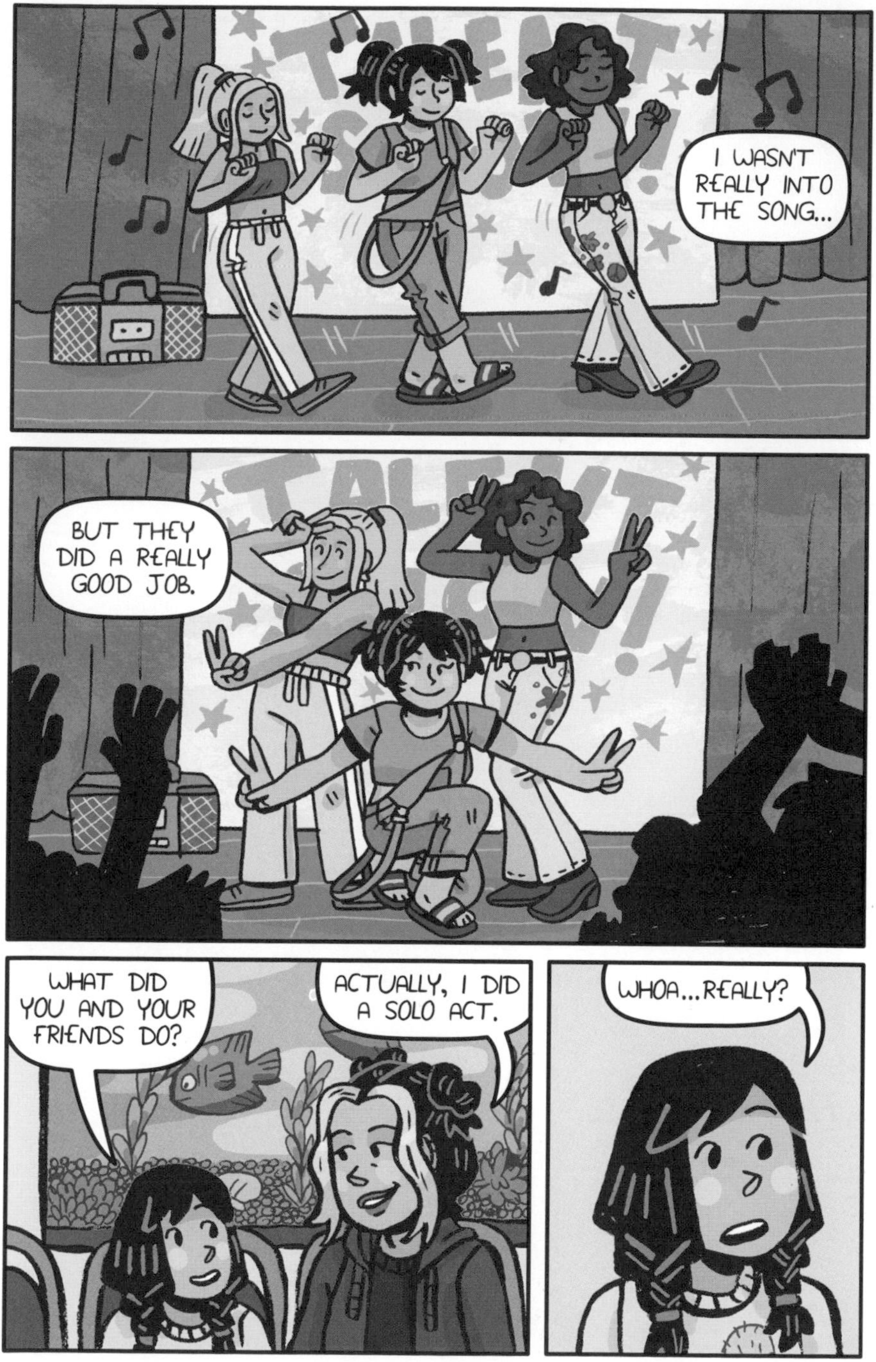
TALENT SHOW!
I WASN'T REALLY INTO THE SONG...
BUT THEY DID A REALLY GOOD JOB.
WHAT DID YOU AND YOUR FRIENDS DO?
ACTUALLY, I DID A SOLO ACT.
WHOA...REALLY?

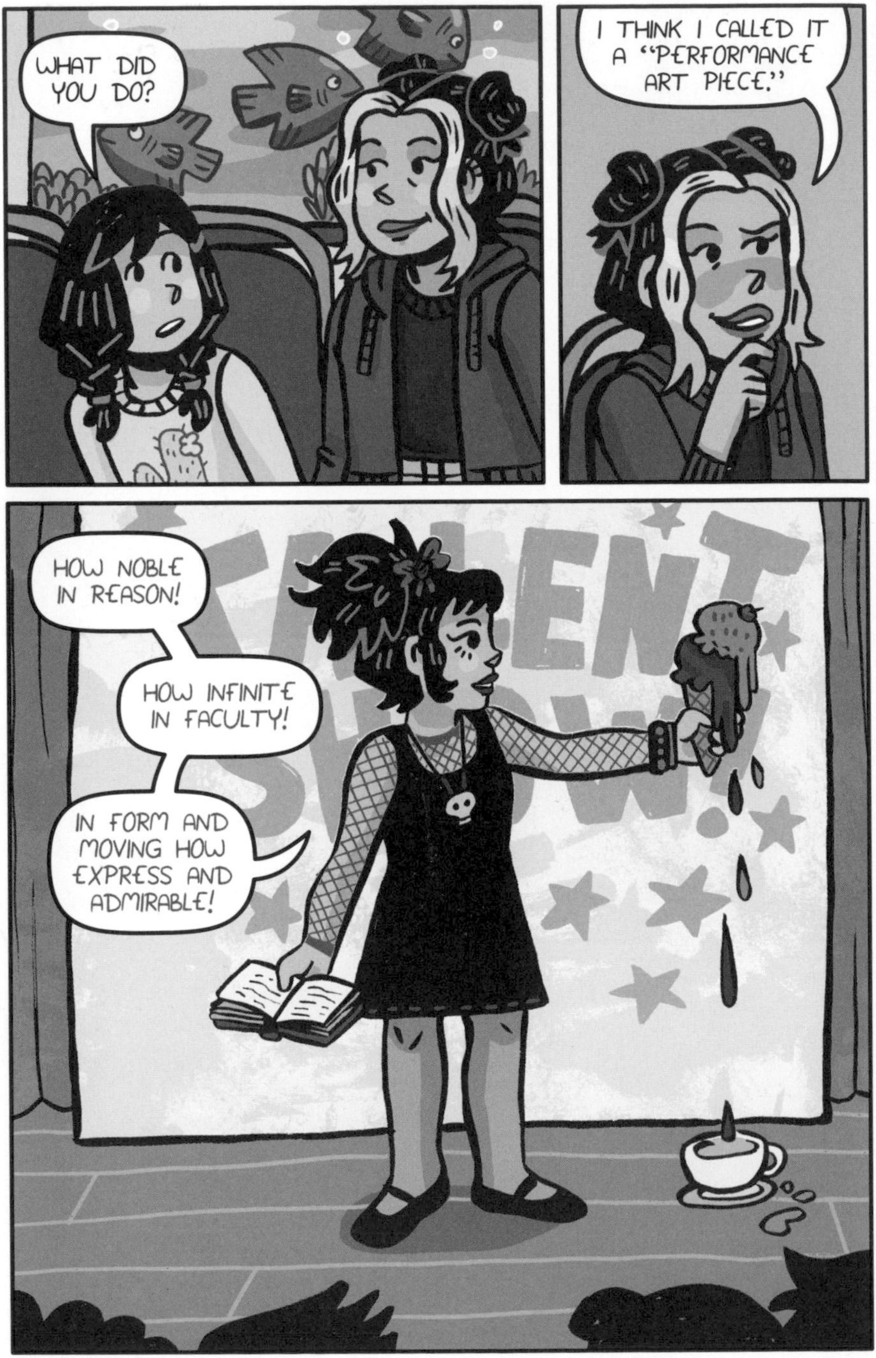
WHAT DID YOU DO?
I THINK I CALLED IT A "PERFORMANCE ART PIECE."
HOW NOBLE IN REASON!
HOW INFINITE IN FACULTY!
IN FORM AND MOVING HOW EXPRESS AND ADMIRABLE!

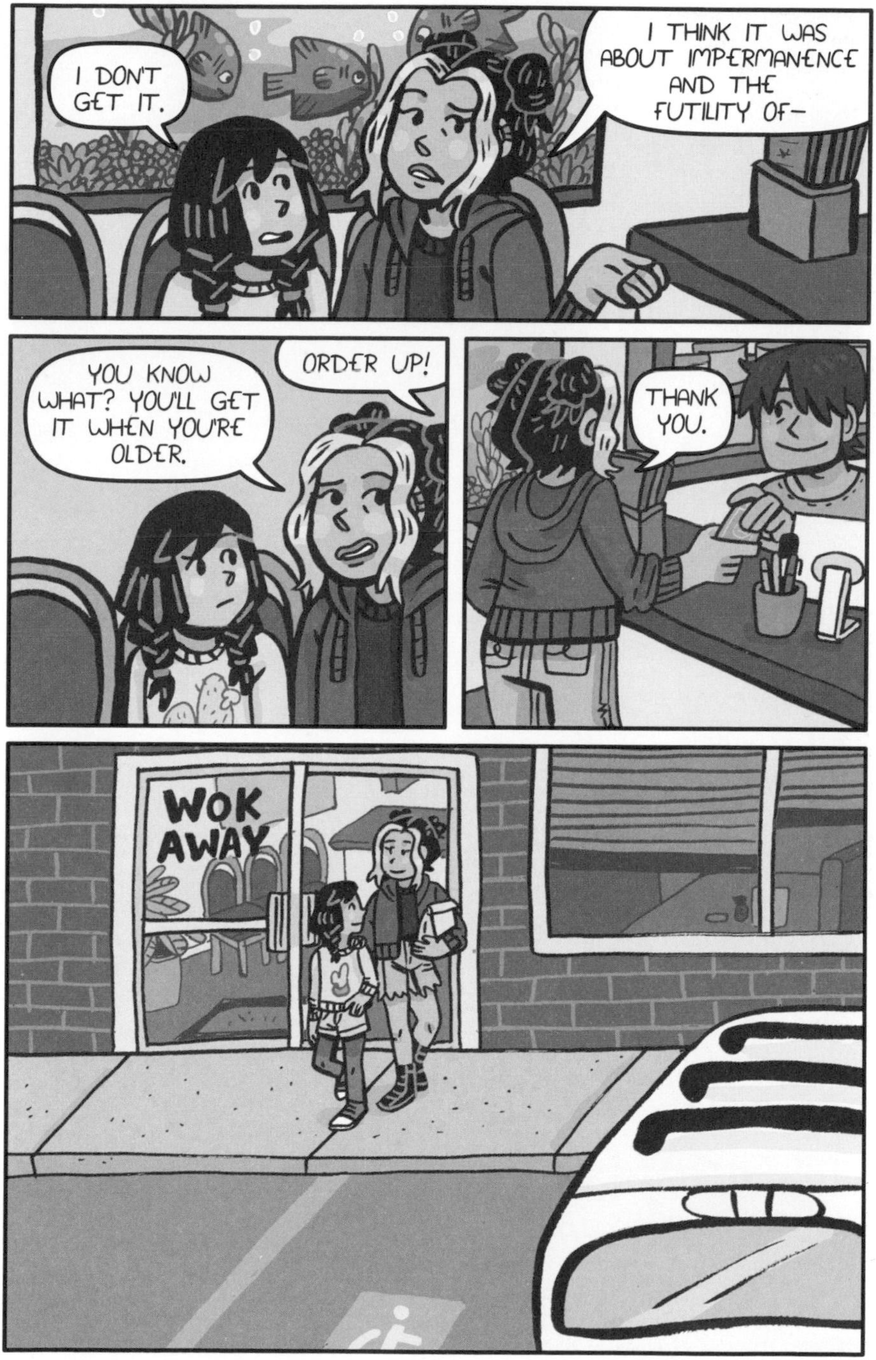
I DON'T GET IT.
I THINK IT WAS ABOUT IMPERMANENCE AND THE FUTILITY OF—
YOU KNOW WHAT? YOU'LL GET IT WHEN YOU'RE OLDER.
ORDER UP!
THANK YOU.
WOK AWAY

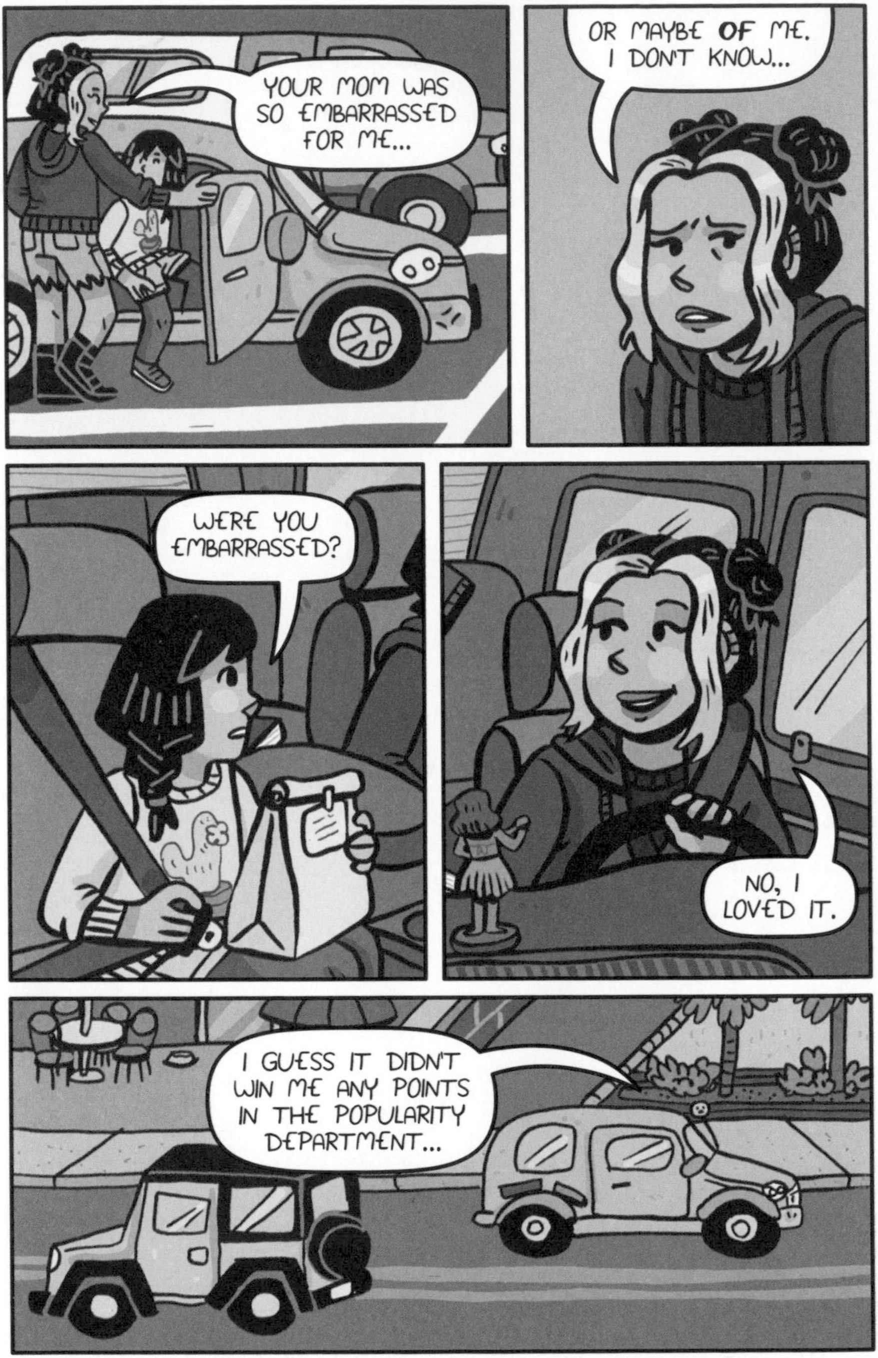
YOUR MOM WAS SO EMBARRASSED FOR ME...
OR MAYBE OF ME. I DON'T KNOW...
WERE YOU EMBARRASSED?
NO, I LOVED IT.
I GUESS IT DIDN'T WIN ME ANY POINTS IN THE POPULARITY DEPARTMENT...

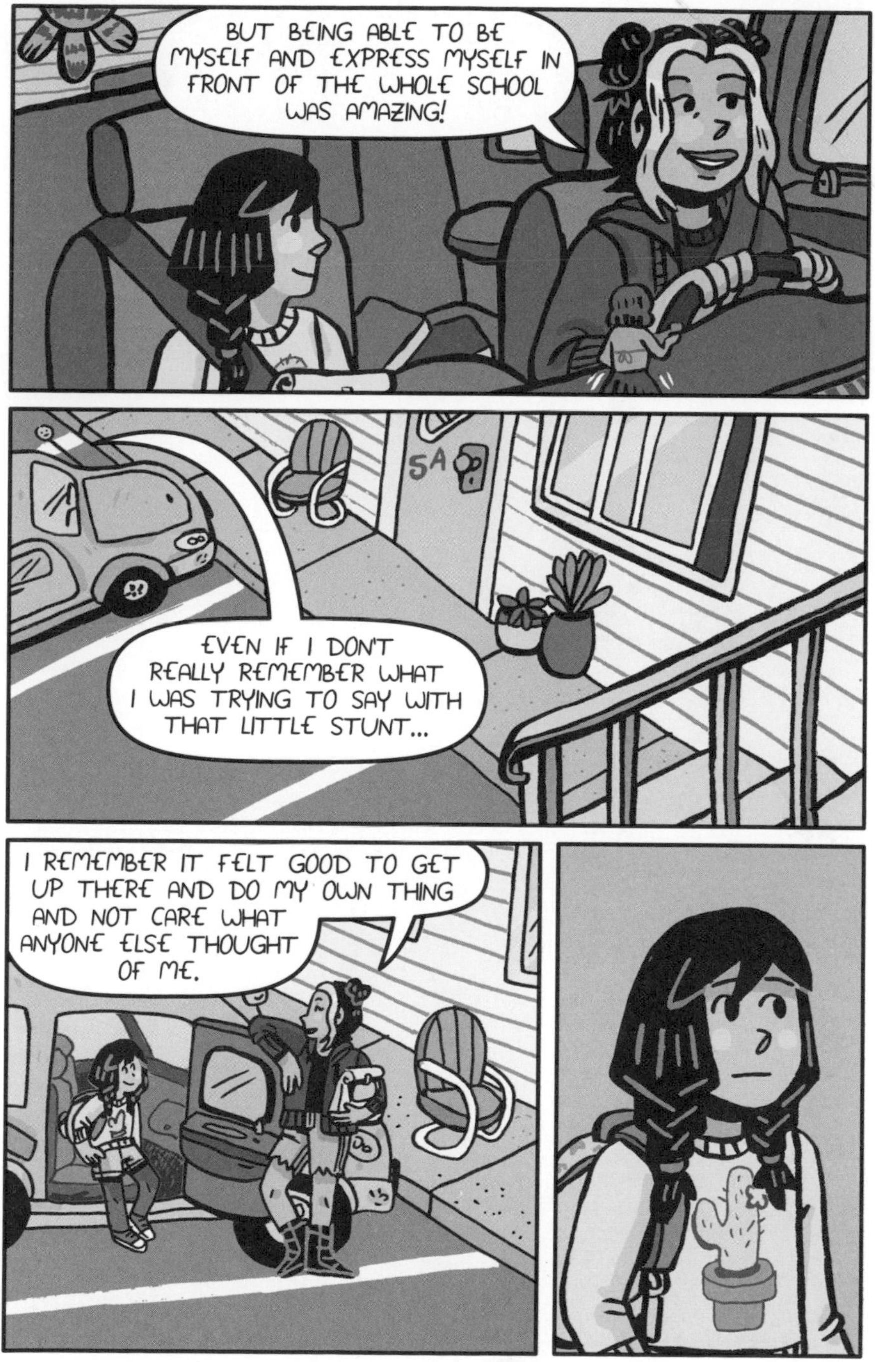
BUT BEING ABLE TO BE MYSELF AND EXPRESS MYSELF IN FRONT OF THE WHOLE SCHOOL WAS AMAZING!
5A
EVEN IF I DON'T REALLY REMEMBER WHAT I WAS TRYING TO SAY WITH THAT LITTLE STUNT...
I REMEMBER IT FELT GOOD TO GET UP THERE AND DO MY OWN THING AND NOT CARE WHAT ANYONE ELSE THOUGHT OF ME.

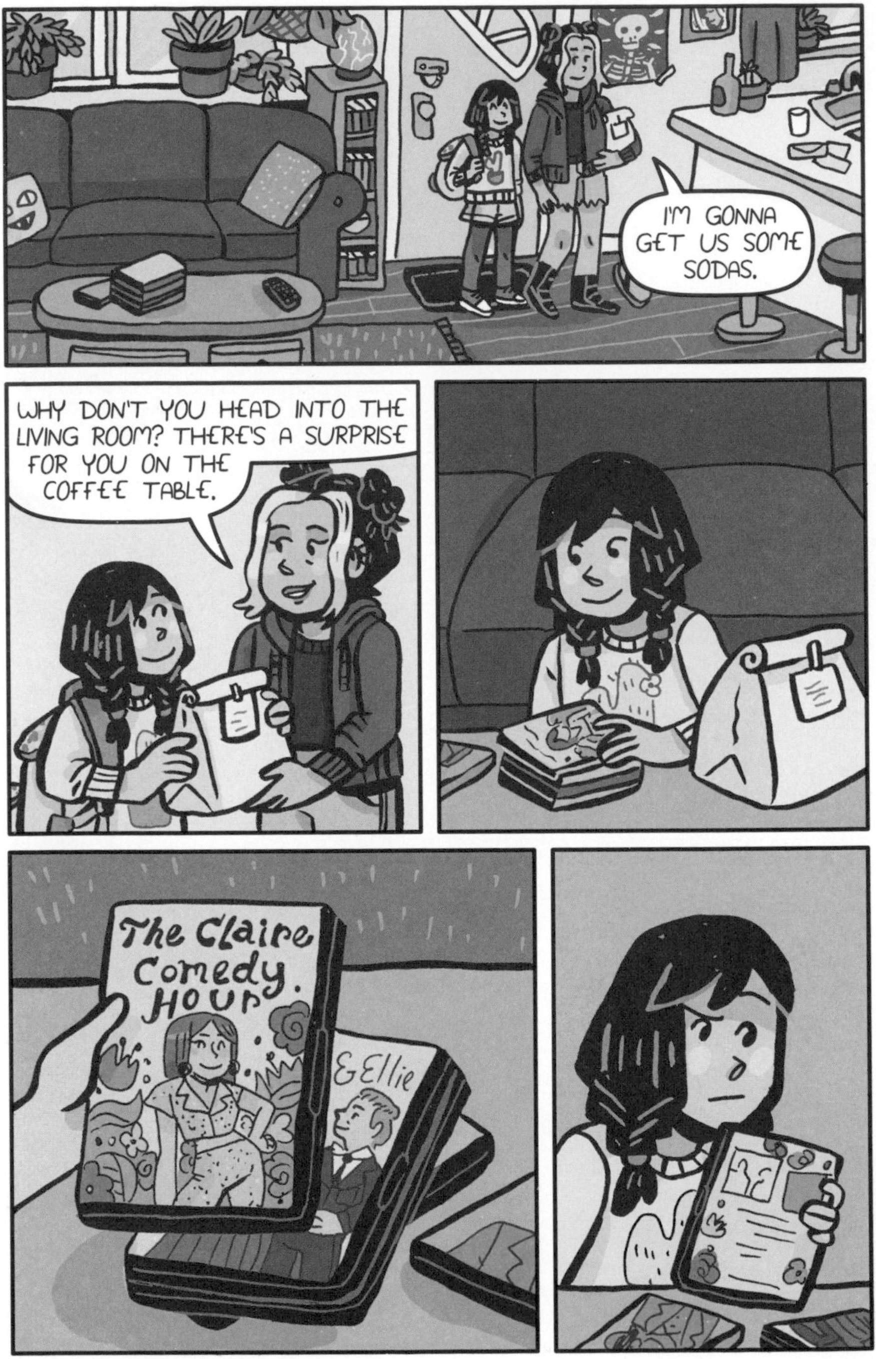
I'M GONNA GET US SOME SODAS.
WHY DON'T YOU HEAD INTO THE LIVING ROOM? THERE'S A SURPRISE FOR YOU ON THE COFFEE TABLE.
The Claire Comedy Hour
&Ellie

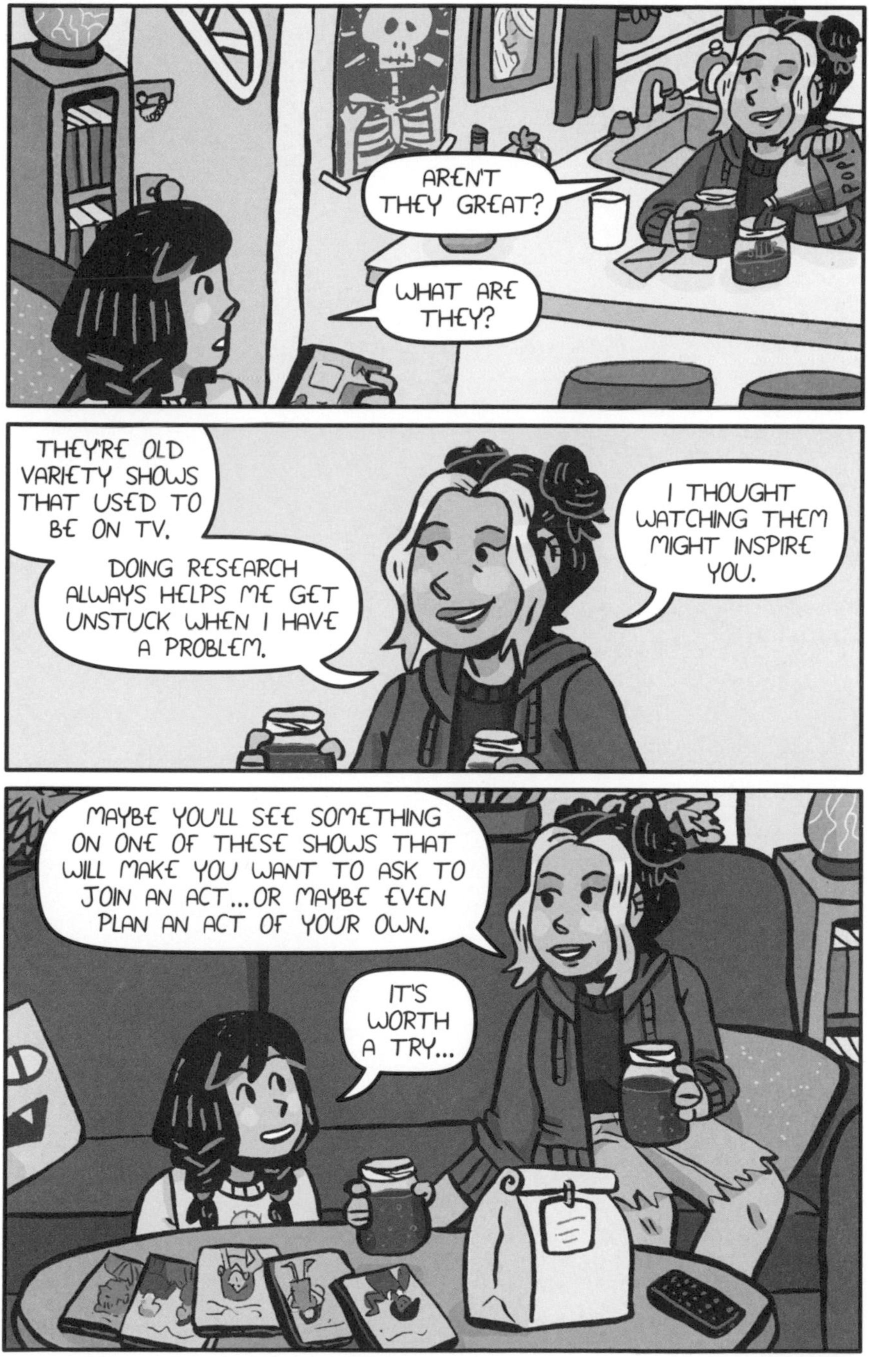
AREN'T THEY GREAT?
WHAT ARE THEY?
THEY'RE OLD VARIETY SHOWS THAT USED TO BE ON TV.
DOING RESEARCH ALWAYS HELPS ME GET UNSTUCK WHEN I HAVE A PROBLEM.
I THOUGHT WATCHING THEM MIGHT INSPIRE YOU.
MAYBE YOU'LL SEE SOMETHING ON ONE OF THESE SHOWS THAT WILL MAKE YOU WANT TO ASK TO JOIN AN ACT...OR MAYBE EVEN PLAN AN ACT OF YOUR OWN.
IT'S WORTH A TRY...

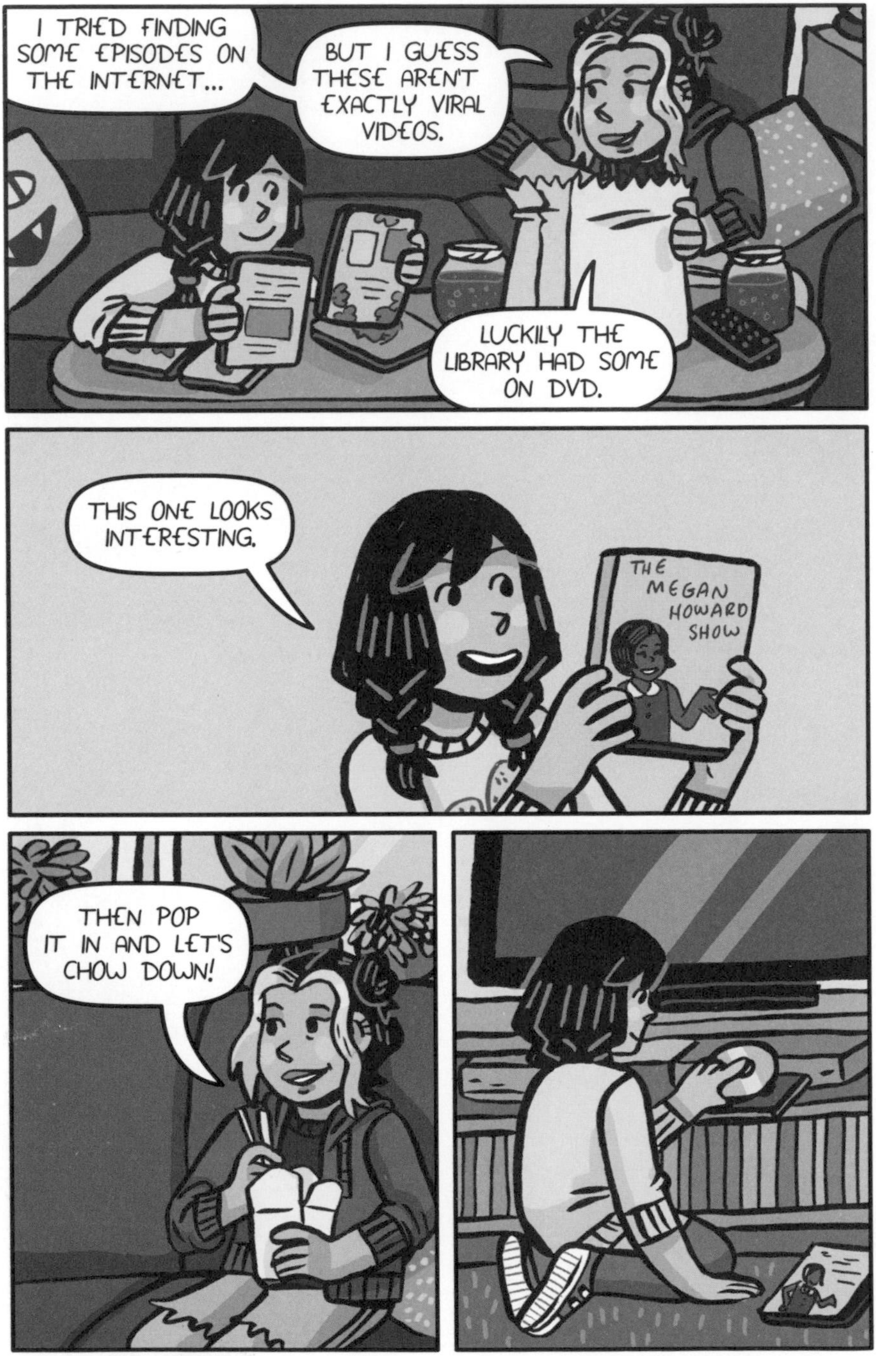
I TRIED FINDING SOME EPISODES ON THE INTERNET...
BUT I GUESS THESE AREN'T EXACTLY VIRAL VIDEOS.
LUCKILY THE LIBRARY HAD SOME ON DVD.
THIS ONE LOOKS INTERESTING.
THE MEGAN HOWARD SHOW
THEN POP IT IN AND LET'S CHOW DOWN!

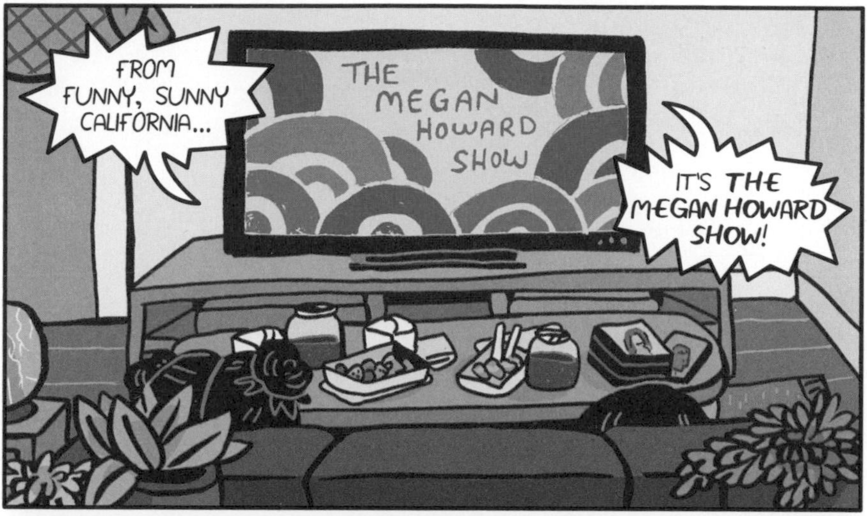
FROM FUNNY, SUNNY CALIFORNIA...
THE MEGAN HOWARD SHOW
IT'S THE MEGAN HOWARD SHOW!

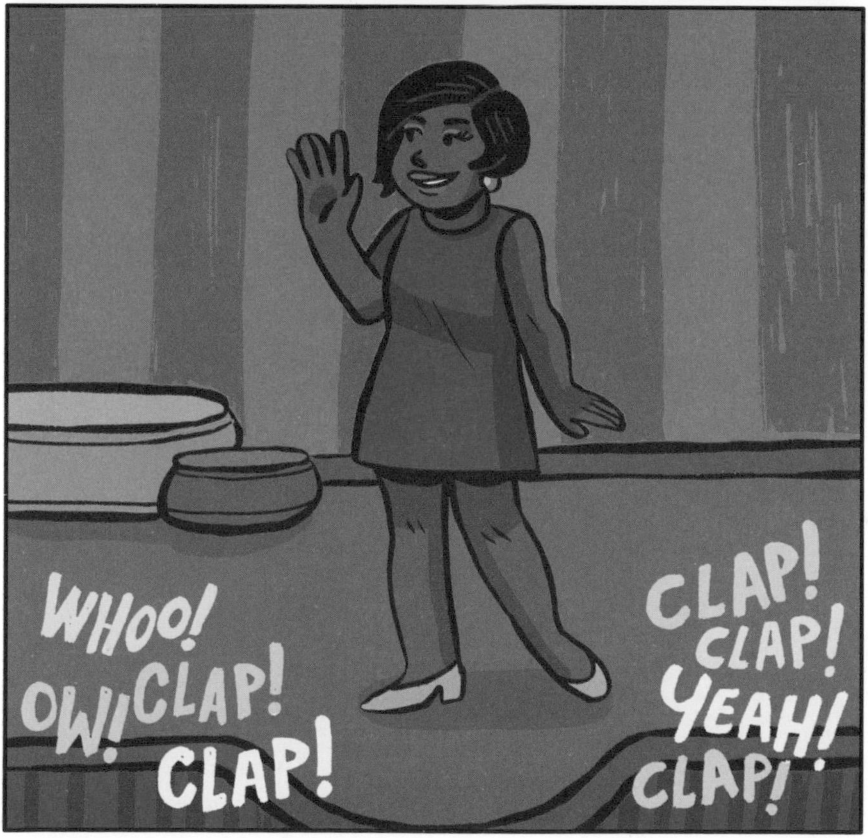
WHOO! OW! CLAP! CLAP!
CLAP! CLAP! YEAH! CLAP!

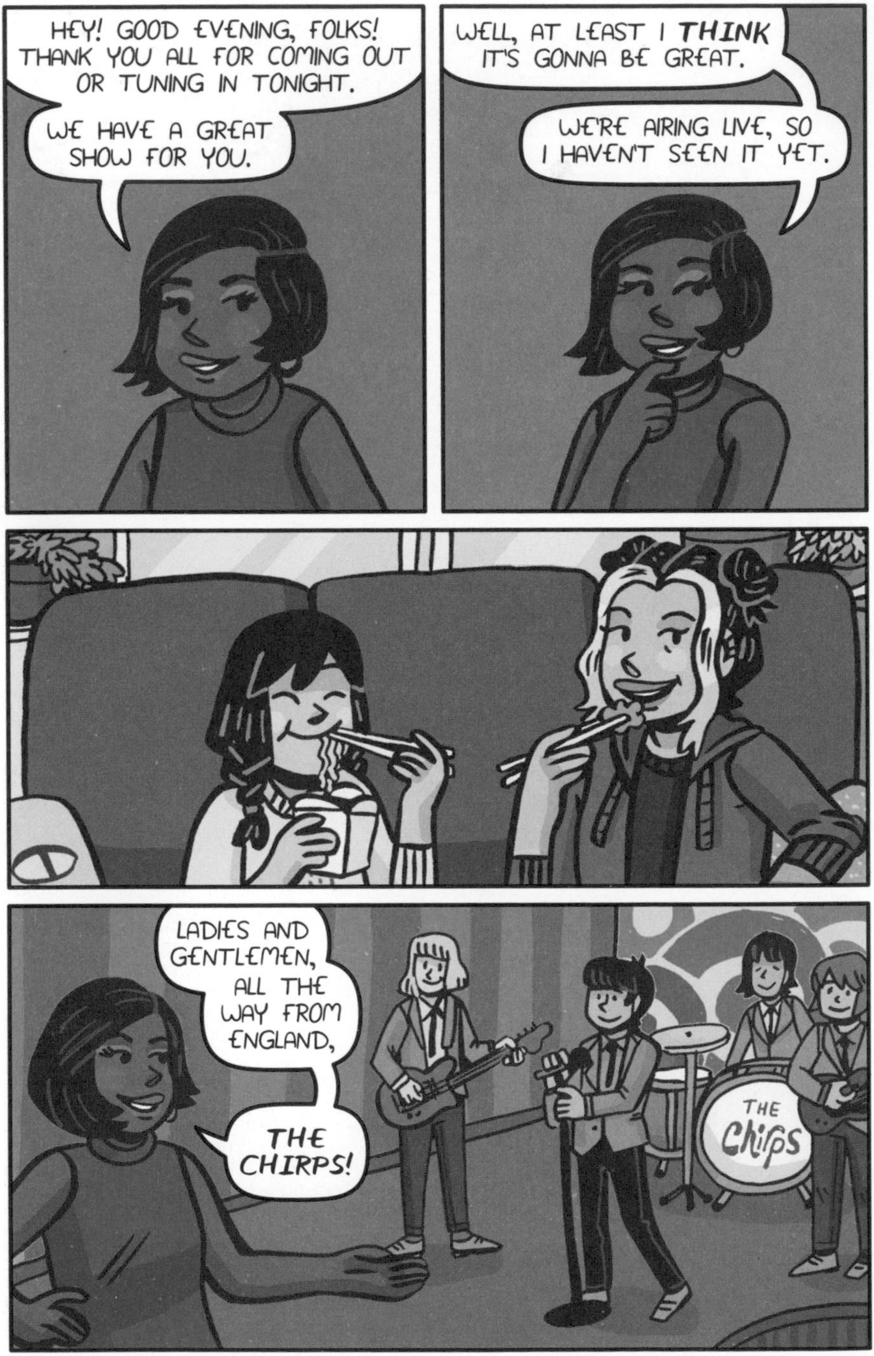
HEY! GOOD EVENING, FOLKS! THANK YOU ALL FOR COMING OUT OR TUNING IN TONIGHT.
WE HAVE A GREAT SHOW FOR YOU.
WELL, AT LEAST I **THINK** IT'S GONNA BE GREAT.
WE'RE AIRING LIVE, SO I HAVEN'T SEEN IT YET.
LADIES AND GENTLEMEN, ALL THE WAY FROM ENGLAND,
THE CHIRPS!
THE Chirps

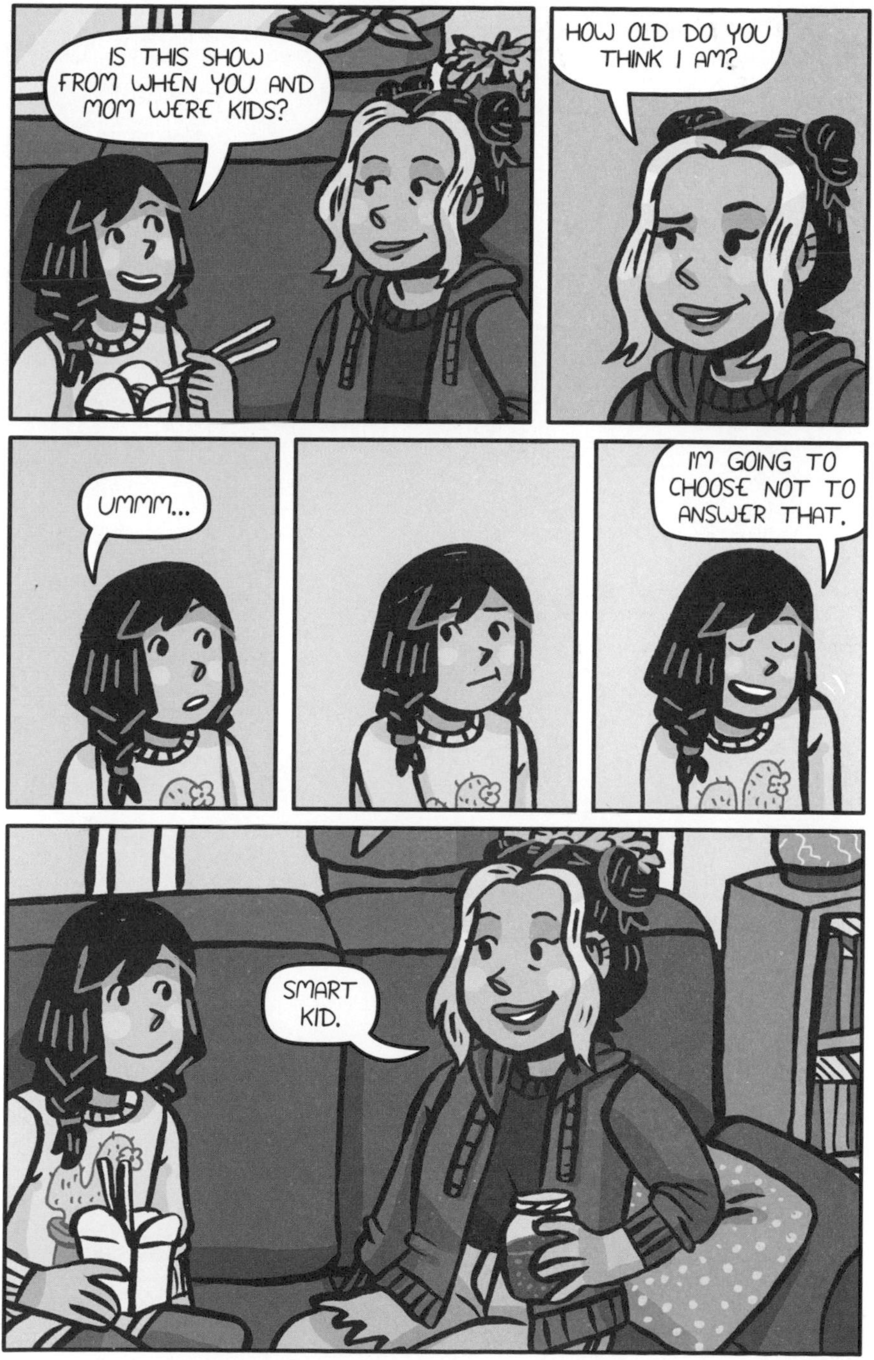
IS THIS SHOW FROM WHEN YOU AND MOM WERE KIDS?
HOW OLD DO YOU THINK I AM?
UMMM...
I'M GOING TO CHOOSE NOT TO ANSWER THAT.
SMART KID.

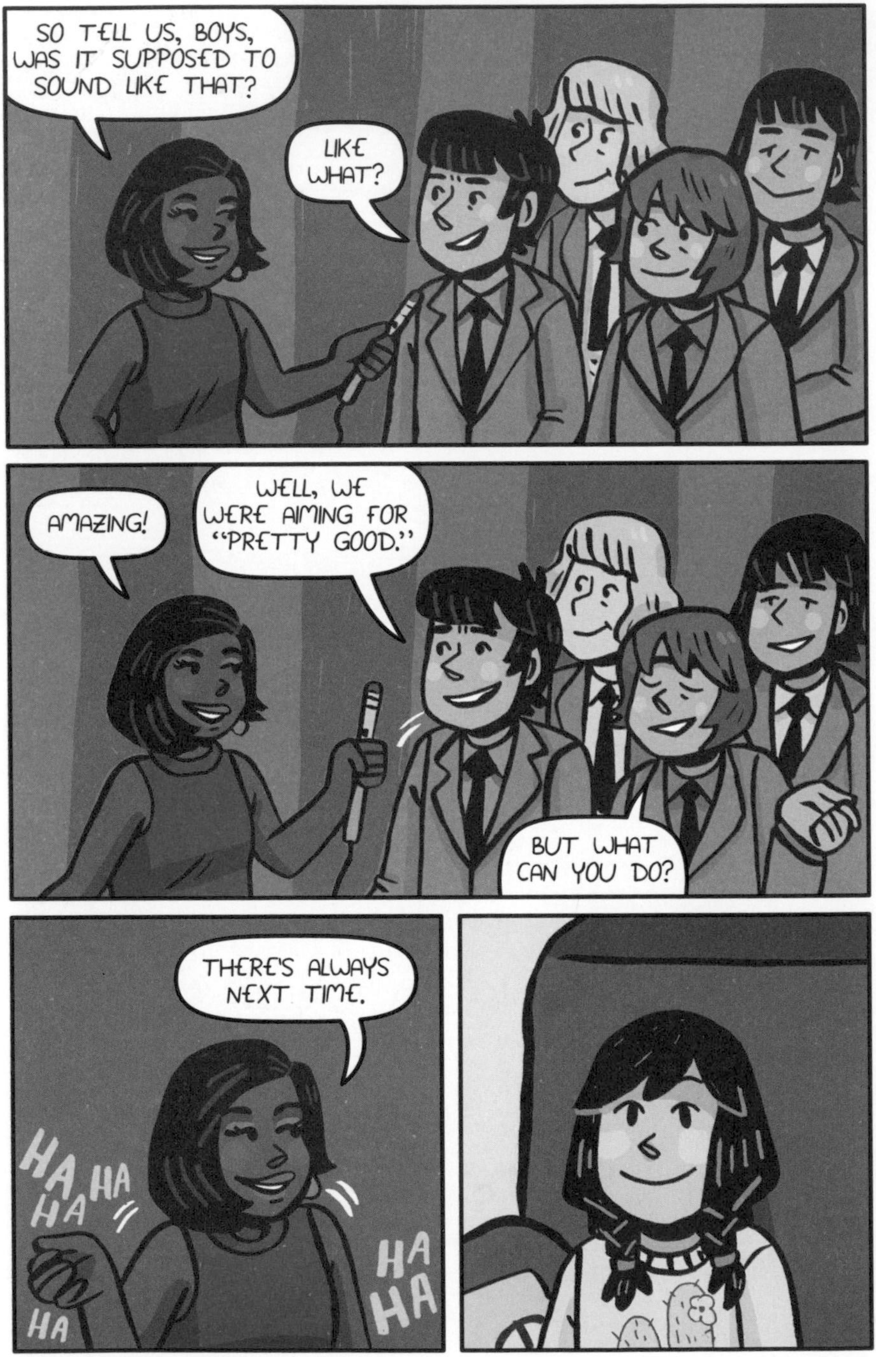
SO TELL US, BOYS, WAS IT SUPPOSED TO SOUND LIKE THAT?
LIKE WHAT?
AMAZING!
WELL, WE WERE AIMING FOR "PRETTY GOOD."
BUT WHAT CAN YOU DO?
THERE'S ALWAYS NEXT TIME.
HA HA HA HA
HA HA
HA

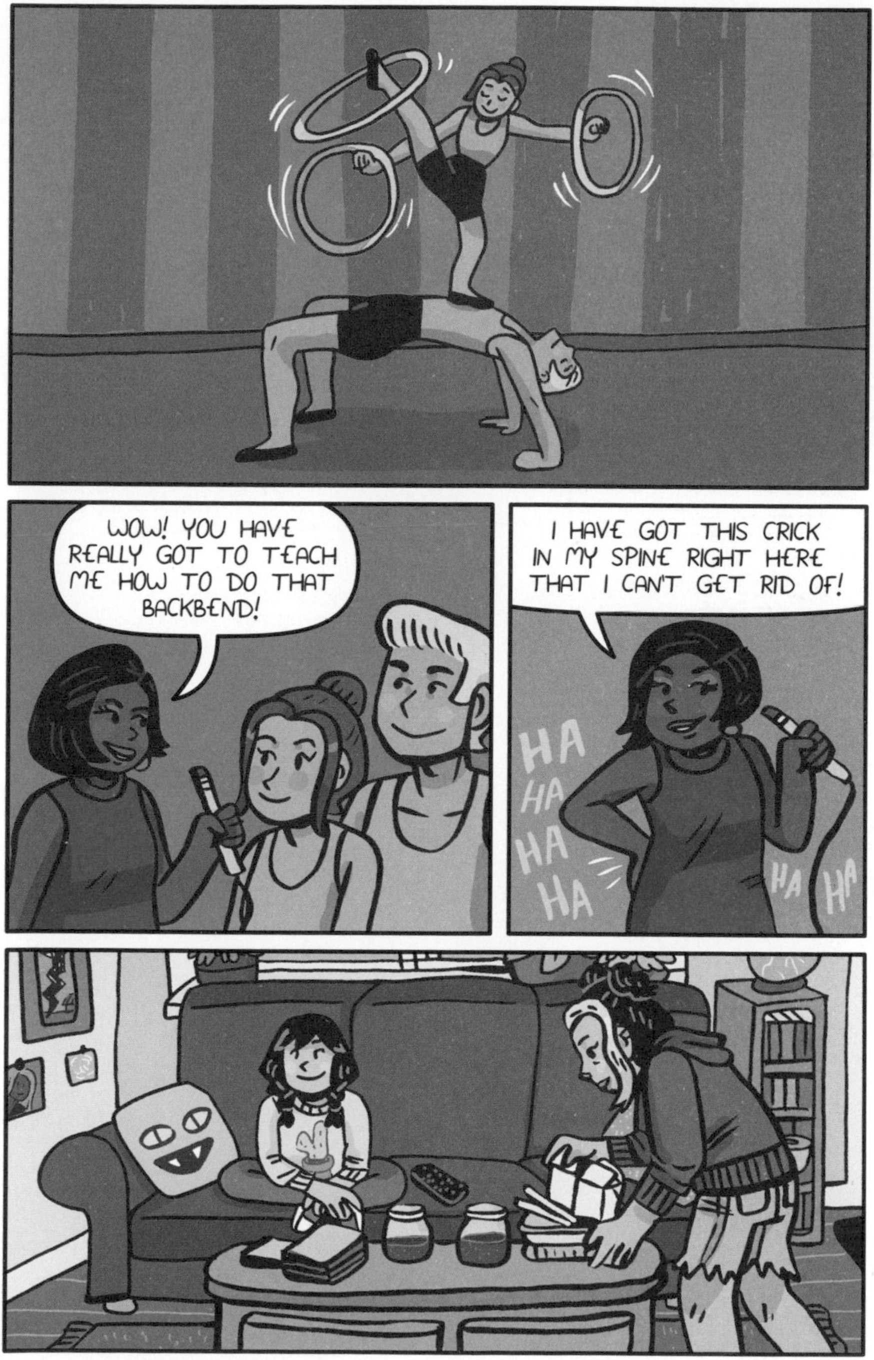
WOW! YOU HAVE REALLY GOT TO TEACH ME HOW TO DO THAT BACKBEND!
I HAVE GOT THIS CRICK IN MY SPINE RIGHT HERE THAT I CAN'T GET RID OF!
HA HA HA HA
HA HA

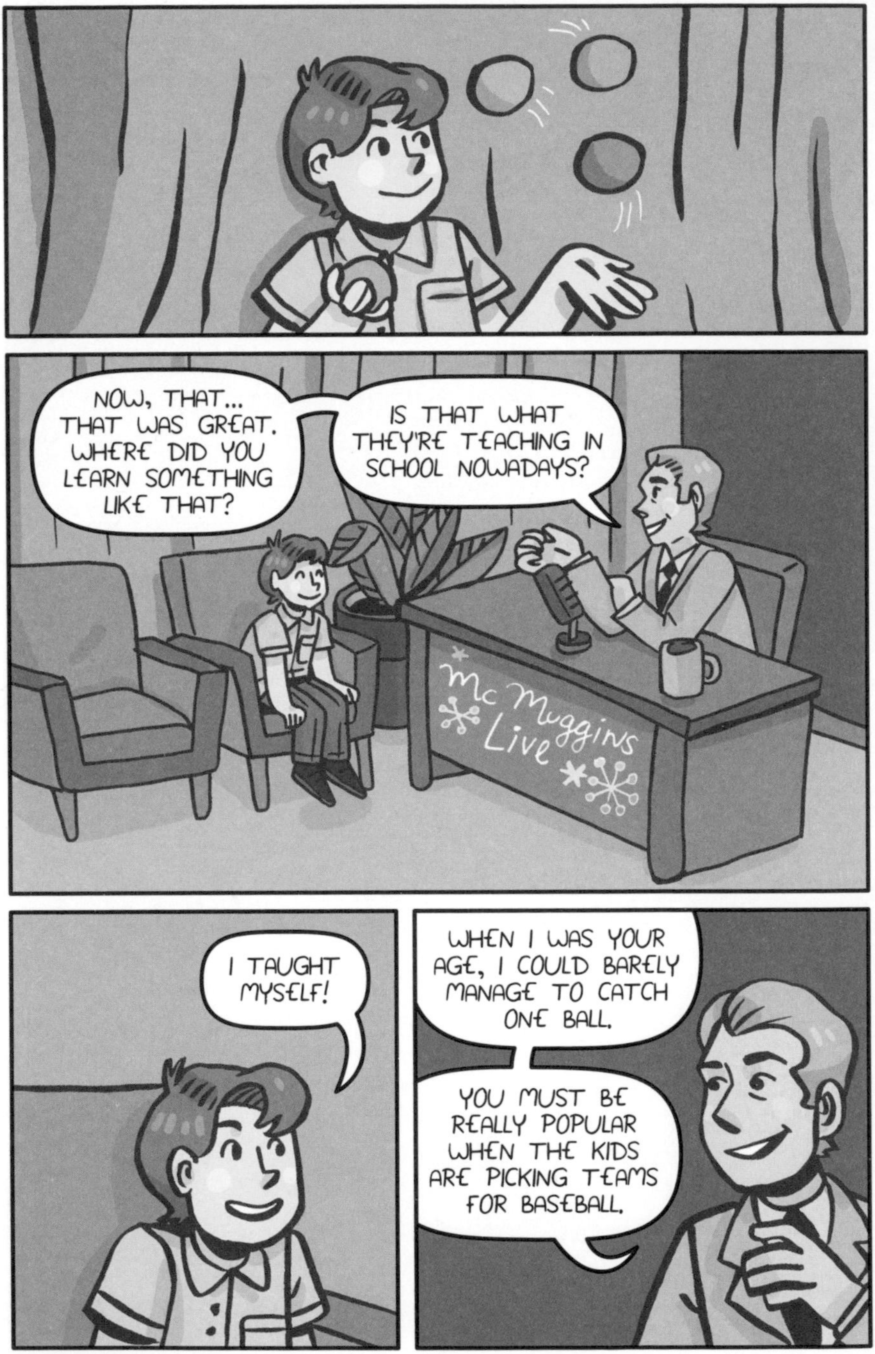
NOW, THAT... THAT WAS GREAT. WHERE DID YOU LEARN SOMETHING LIKE THAT?
IS THAT WHAT THEY'RE TEACHING IN SCHOOL NOWADAYS?
McMuggins Live
I TAUGHT MYSELF!
WHEN I WAS YOUR AGE, I COULD BARELY MANAGE TO CATCH ONE BALL.
YOU MUST BE REALLY POPULAR WHEN THE KIDS ARE PICKING TEAMS FOR BASEBALL.

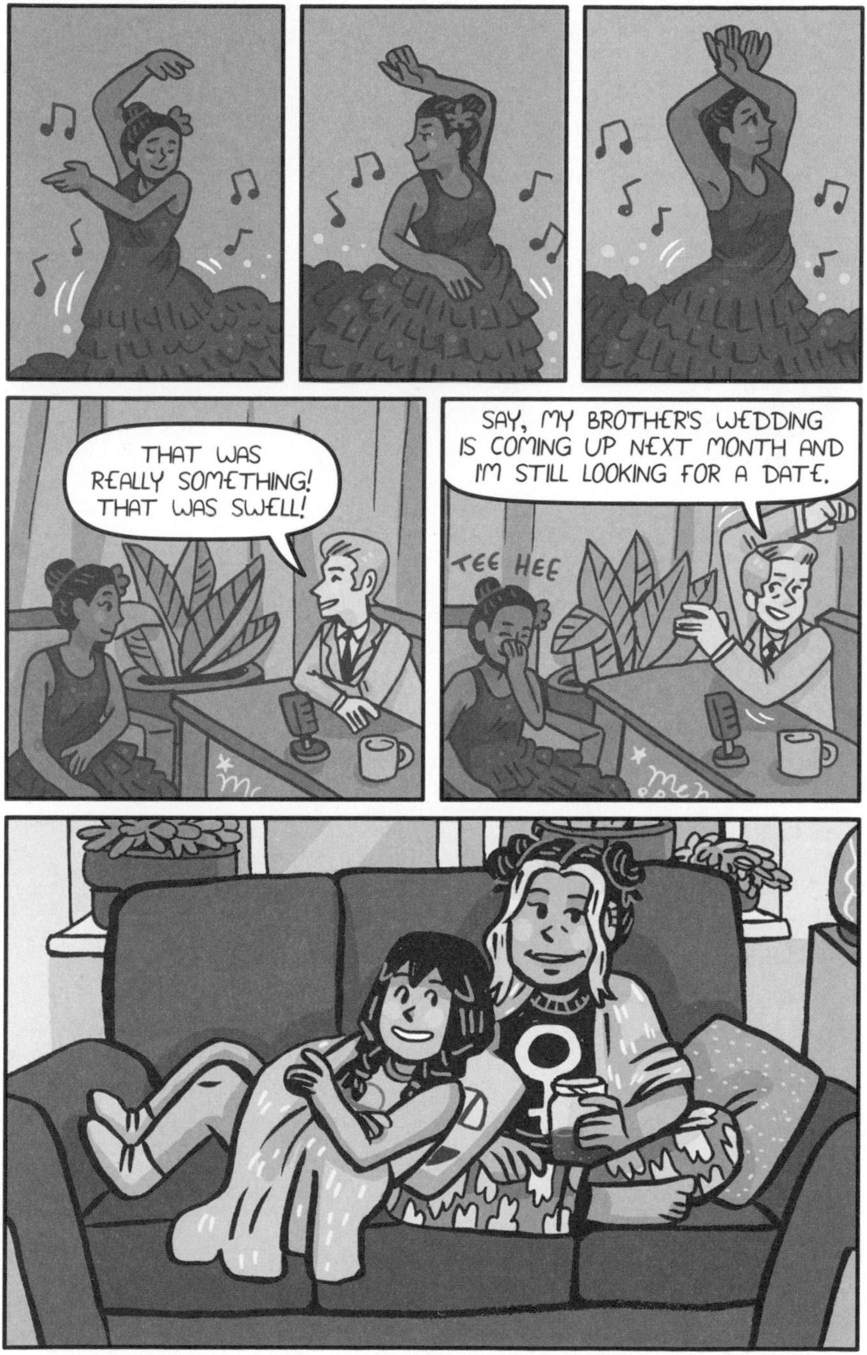
THAT WAS REALLY SOMETHING! THAT WAS SWELL!
SAY, MY BROTHER'S WEDDING IS COMING UP NEXT MONTH AND I'M STILL LOOKING FOR A DATE.
TEE HEE

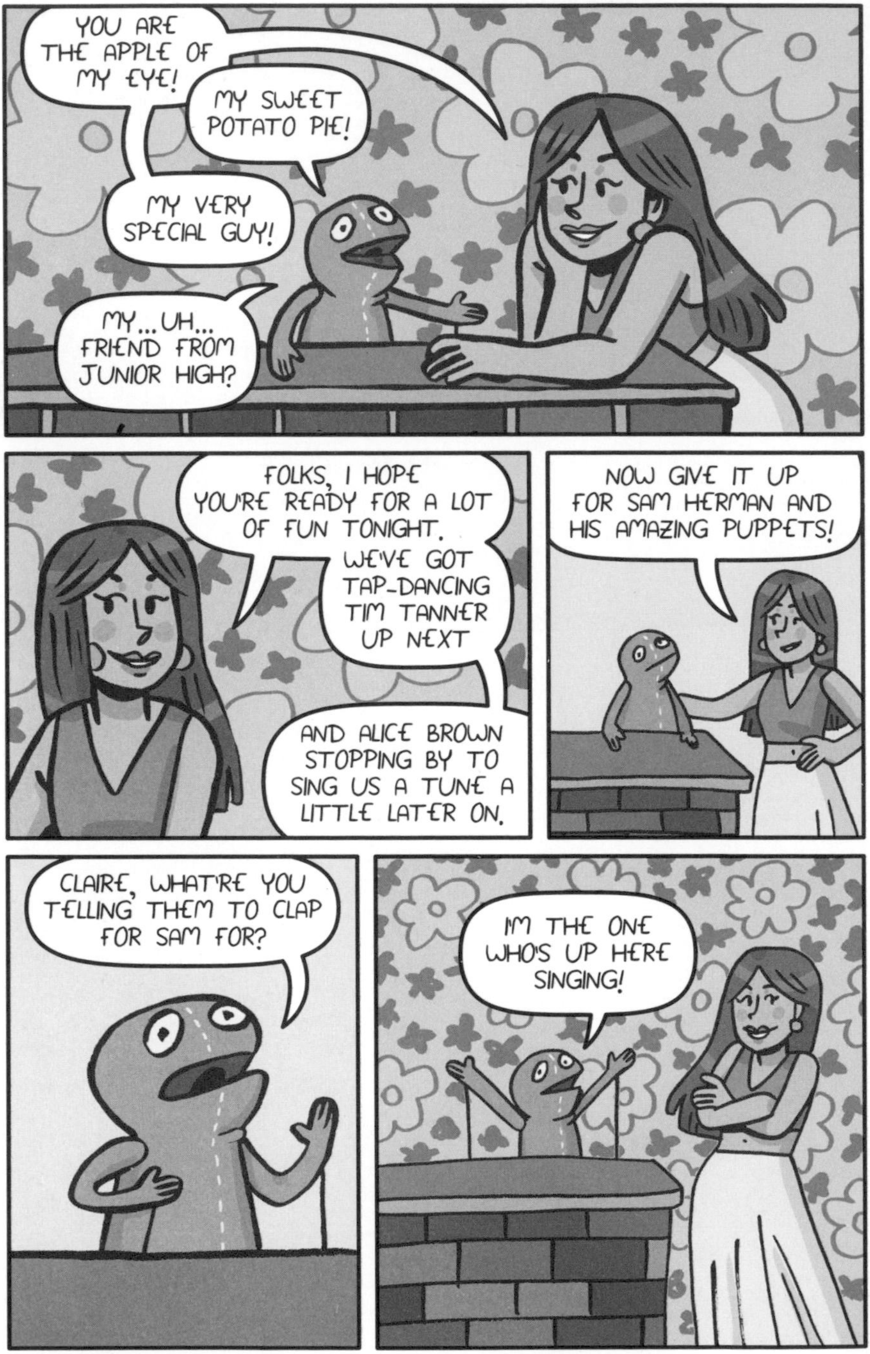
YOU ARE THE APPLE OF MY EYE!
MY SWEET POTATO PIE!
MY VERY SPECIAL GUY!
MY...UH... FRIEND FROM JUNIOR HIGH?
FOLKS, I HOPE YOU'RE READY FOR A LOT OF FUN TONIGHT.
WE'VE GOT TAP-DANCING TIM TANNER UP NEXT
AND ALICE BROWN STOPPING BY TO SING US A TUNE A LITTLE LATER ON.
NOW GIVE IT UP FOR SAM HERMAN AND HIS AMAZING PUPPETS!
CLAIRE, WHAT'RE YOU TELLING THEM TO CLAP FOR SAM FOR?
I'M THE ONE WHO'S UP HERE SINGING!

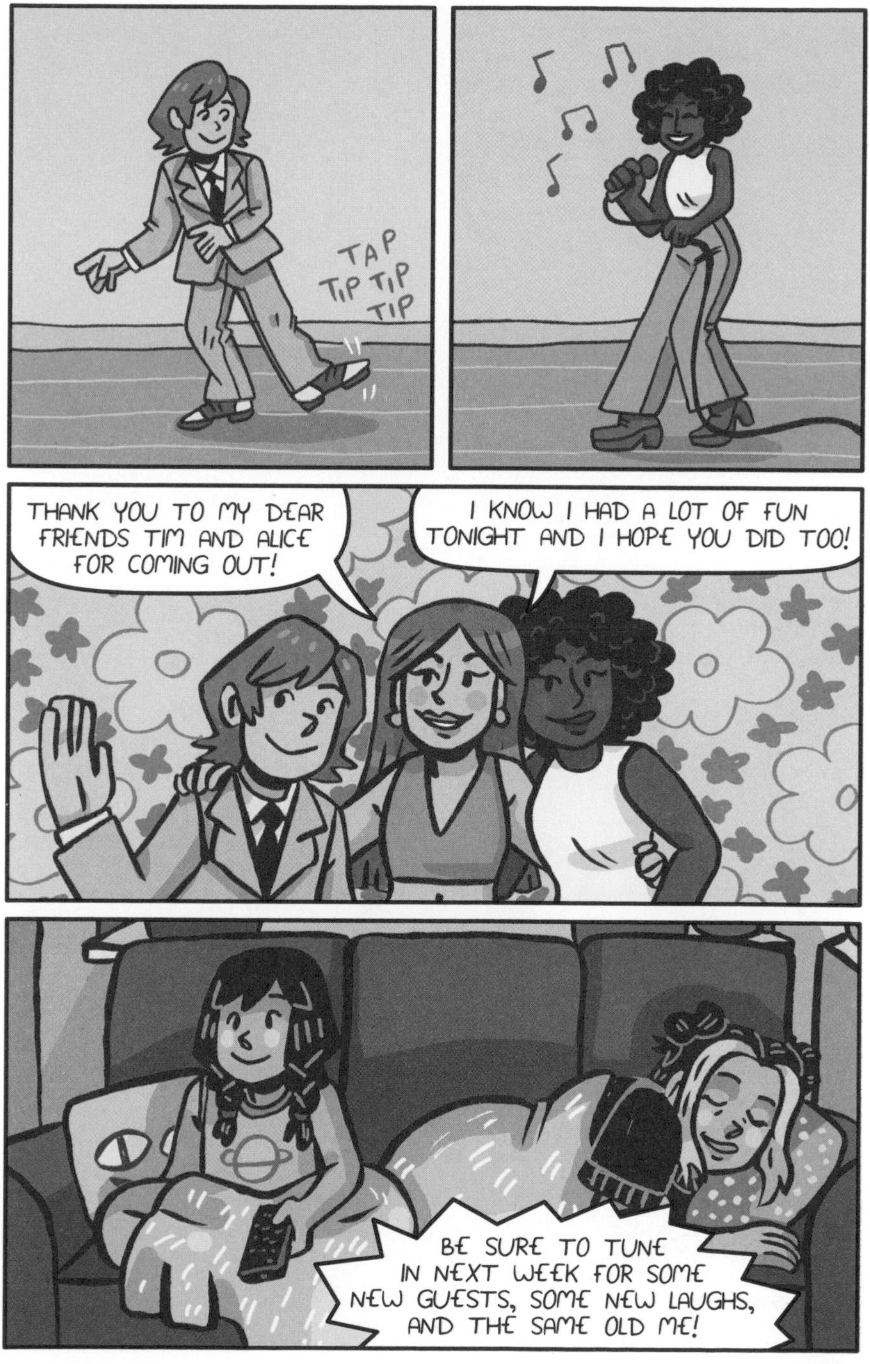
TAP
TIP TIP
TIP
THANK YOU TO MY DEAR FRIENDS TIM AND ALICE FOR COMING OUT!
I KNOW I HAD A LOT OF FUN TONIGHT AND I HOPE YOU DID TOO!
BE SURE TO TUNE IN NEXT WEEK FOR SOME NEW GUESTS, SOME NEW LAUGHS, AND THE SAME OLD ME!

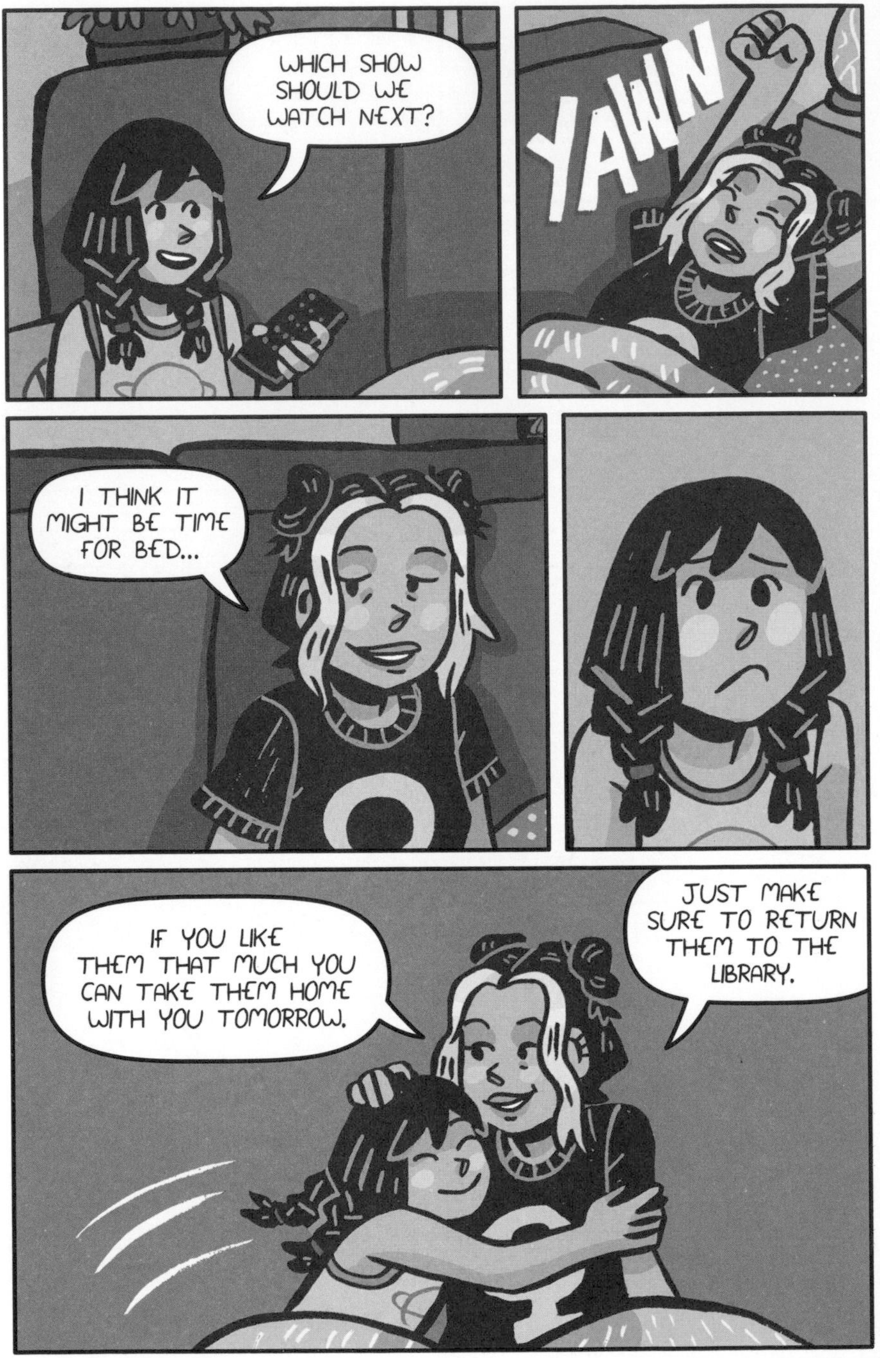
WHICH SHOW SHOULD WE WATCH NEXT?
YAWN
I THINK IT MIGHT BE TIME FOR BED...
IF YOU LIKE THEM THAT MUCH YOU CAN TAKE THEM HOME WITH YOU TOMORROW.
JUST MAKE SURE TO RETURN THEM TO THE LIBRARY.

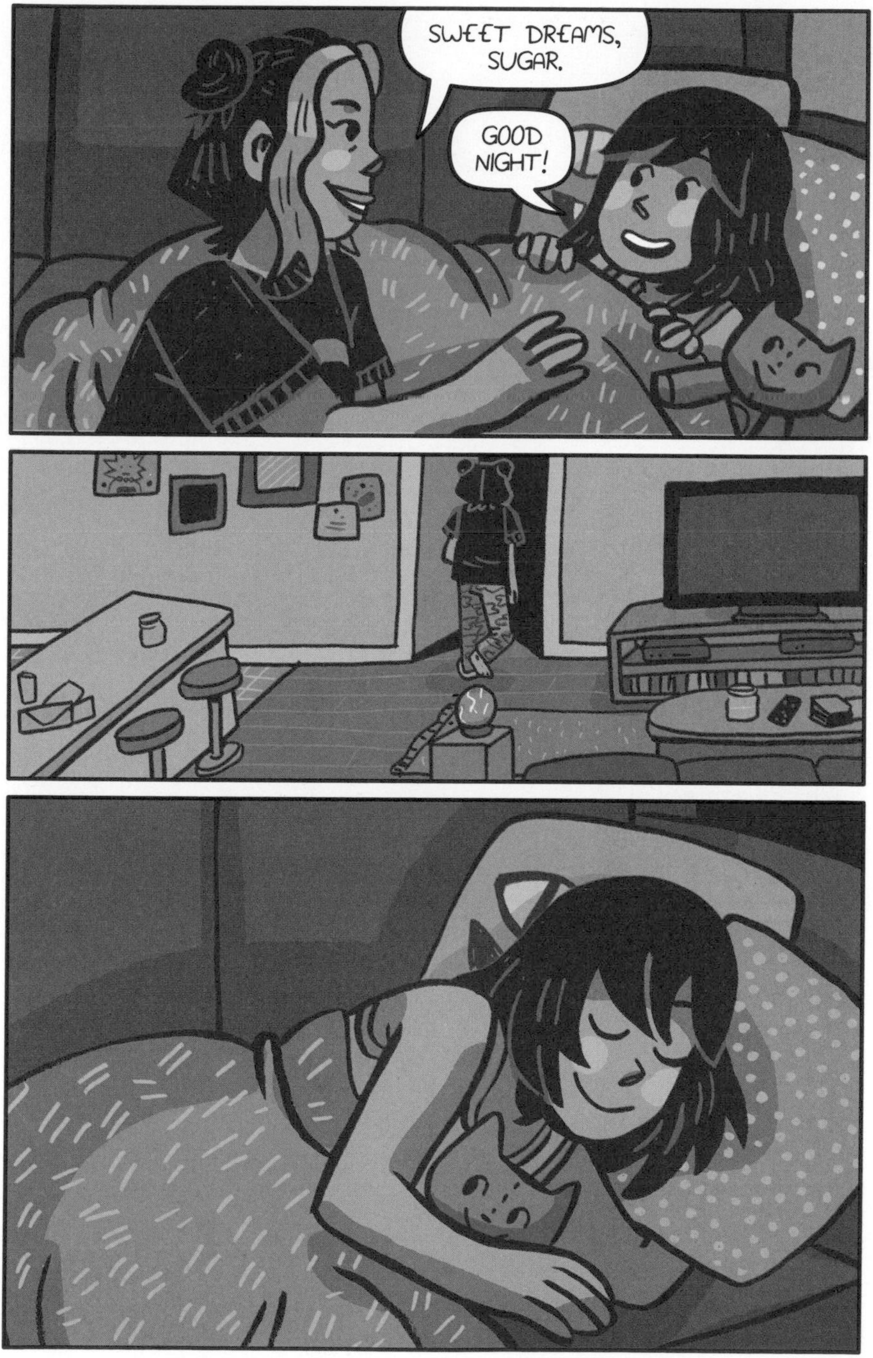
SWEET DREAMS, SUGAR.
GOOD NIGHT!

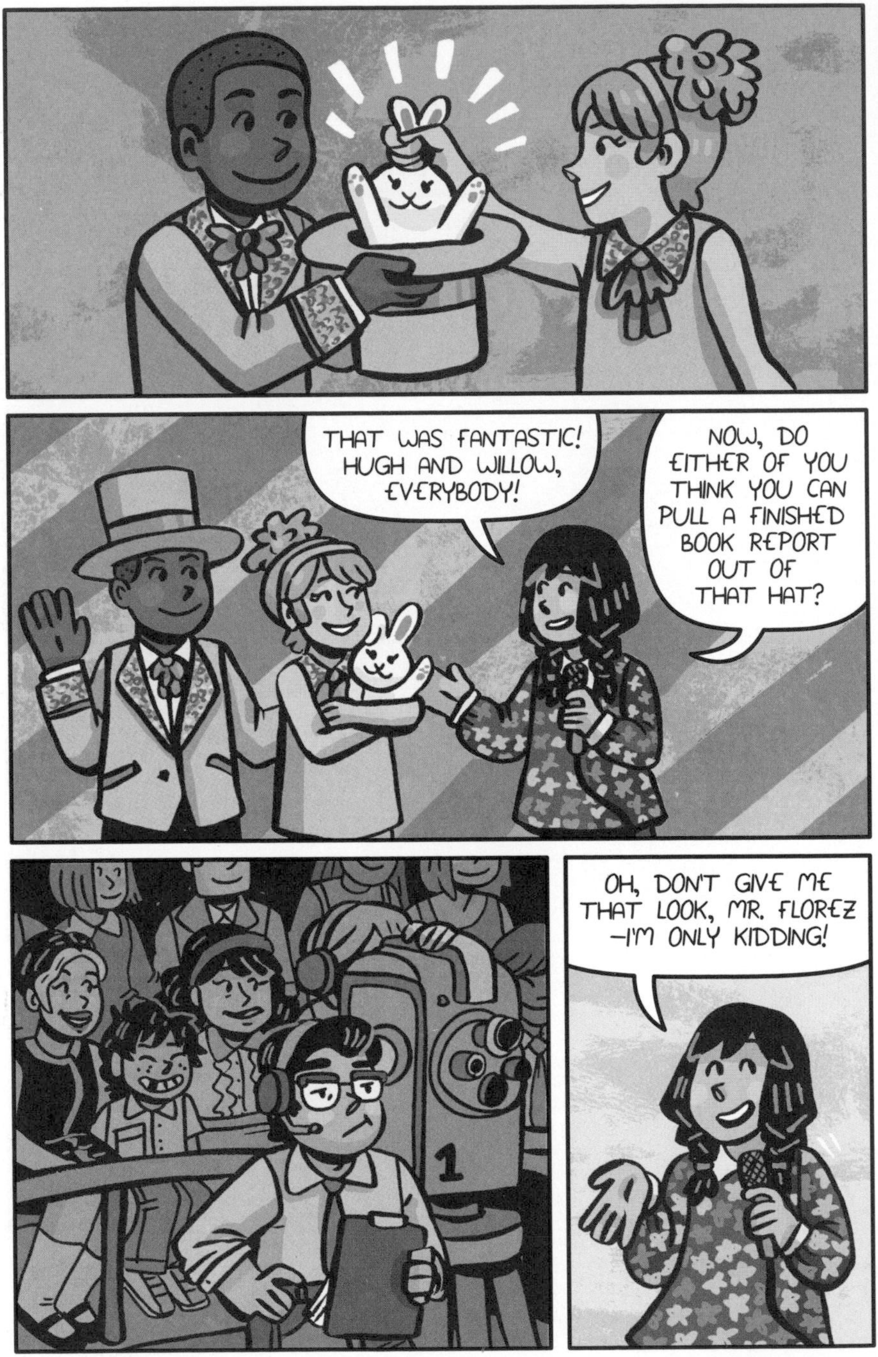
THAT WAS FANTASTIC! HUGH AND WILLOW, EVERYBODY!
NOW, DO EITHER OF YOU THINK YOU CAN PULL A FINISHED BOOK REPORT OUT OF THAT HAT?
1
OH, DON'T GIVE ME THAT LOOK, MR. FLOREZ —I'M ONLY KIDDING!

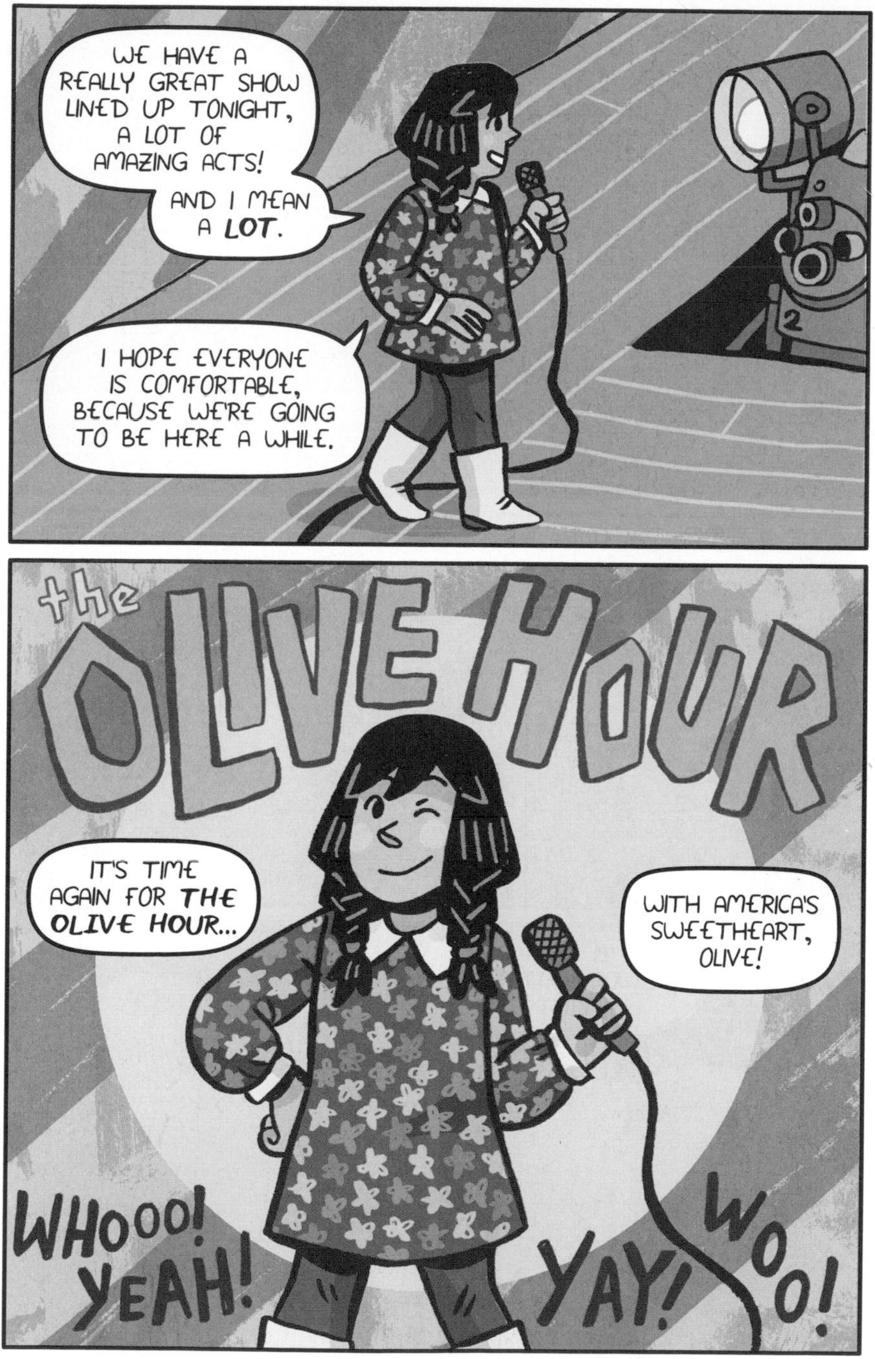
WE HAVE A REALLY GREAT SHOW LINED UP TONIGHT, A LOT OF AMAZING ACTS!
AND I MEAN A **LOT**.
I HOPE EVERYONE IS COMFORTABLE, BECAUSE WE'RE GOING TO BE HERE A WHILE.
2
the OLIVE HOUR
IT'S TIME AGAIN FOR **THE OLIVE HOUR**...
WITH AMERICA'S SWEETHEART, OLIVE!
WHOOO!
YEAH!
YAY!
WOO!

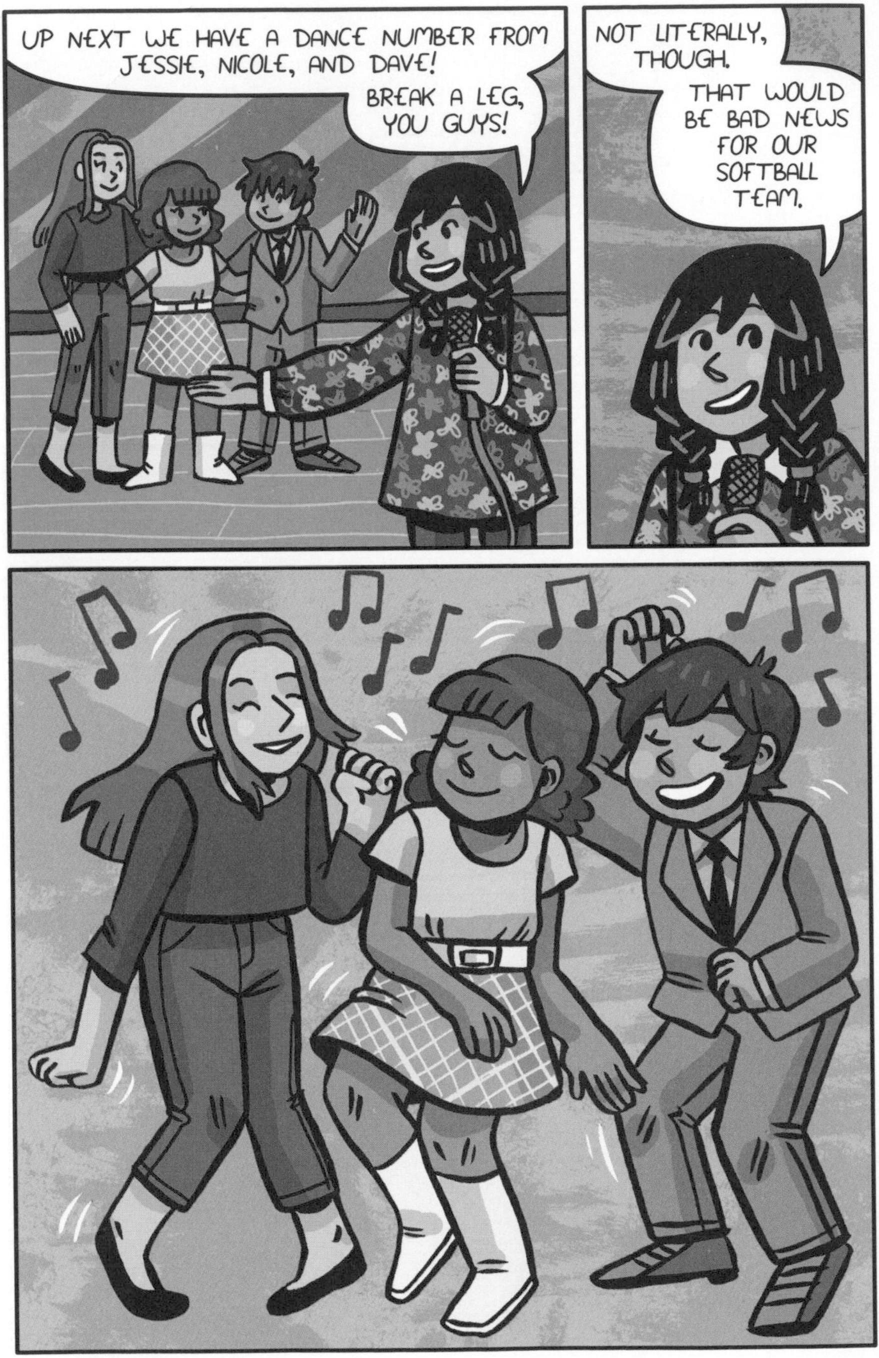
UP NEXT WE HAVE A DANCE NUMBER FROM JESSIE, NICOLE, AND DAVE!
BREAK A LEG, YOU GUYS!
NOT LITERALLY, THOUGH.
THAT WOULD BE BAD NEWS FOR OUR SOFTBALL TEAM.

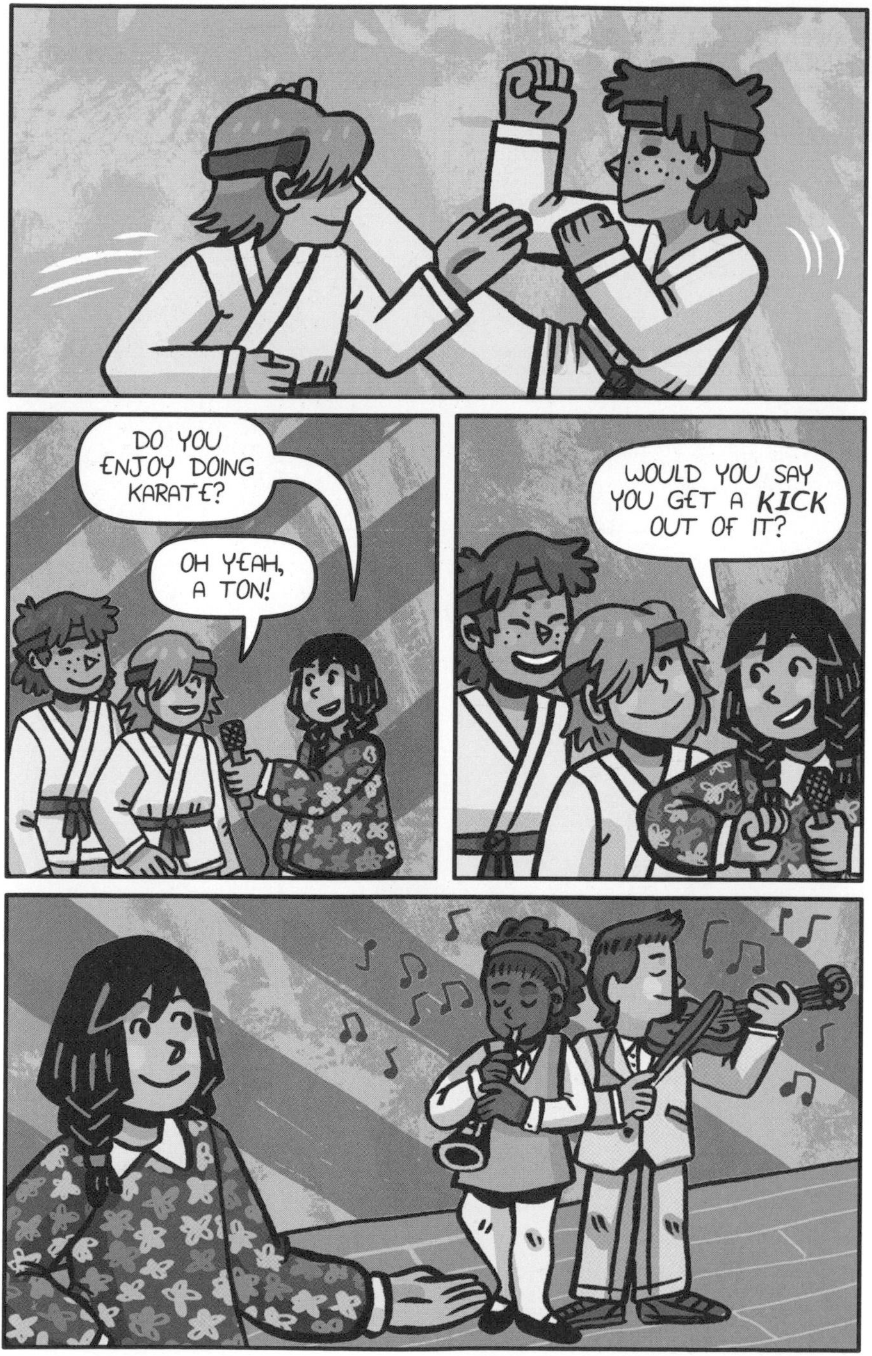
DO YOU ENJOY DOING KARATE?
OH YEAH, A TON!
WOULD YOU SAY YOU GET A **KICK** OUT OF IT?

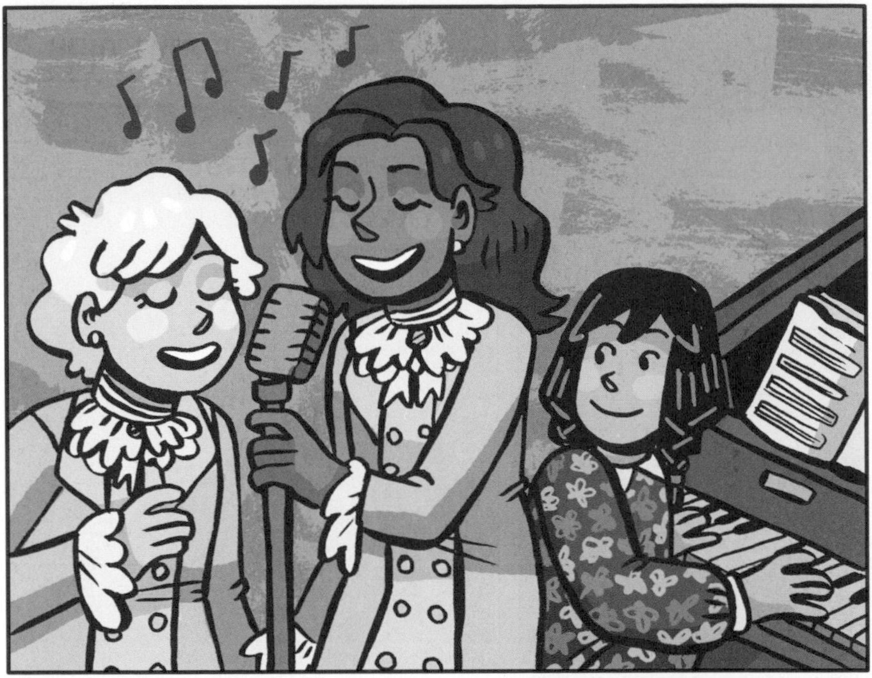

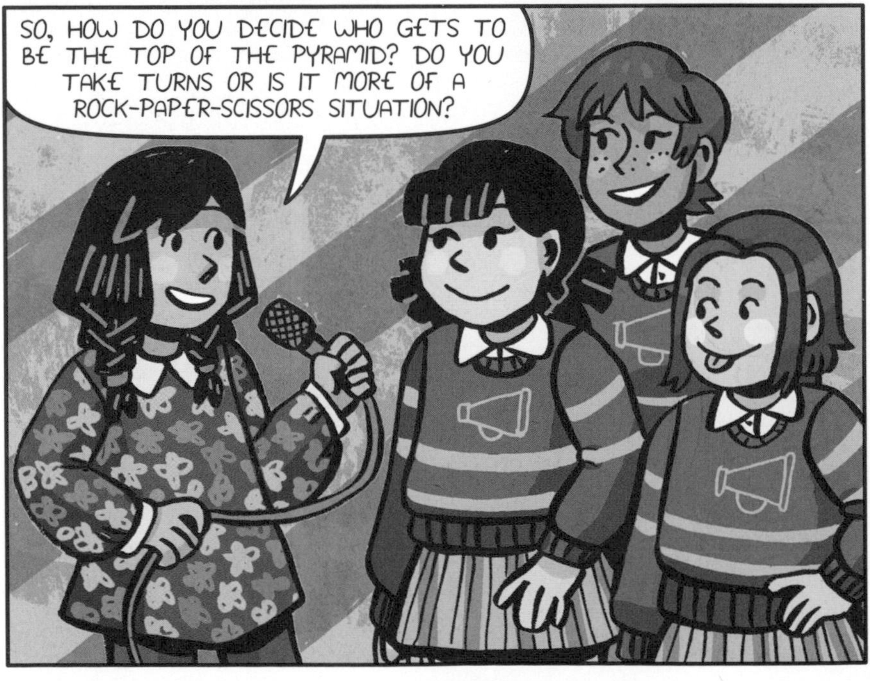
SO, HOW DO YOU DECIDE WHO GETS TO BE THE TOP OF THE PYRAMID? DO YOU TAKE TURNS OR IS IT MORE OF A ROCK-PAPER-SCISSORS SITUATION?

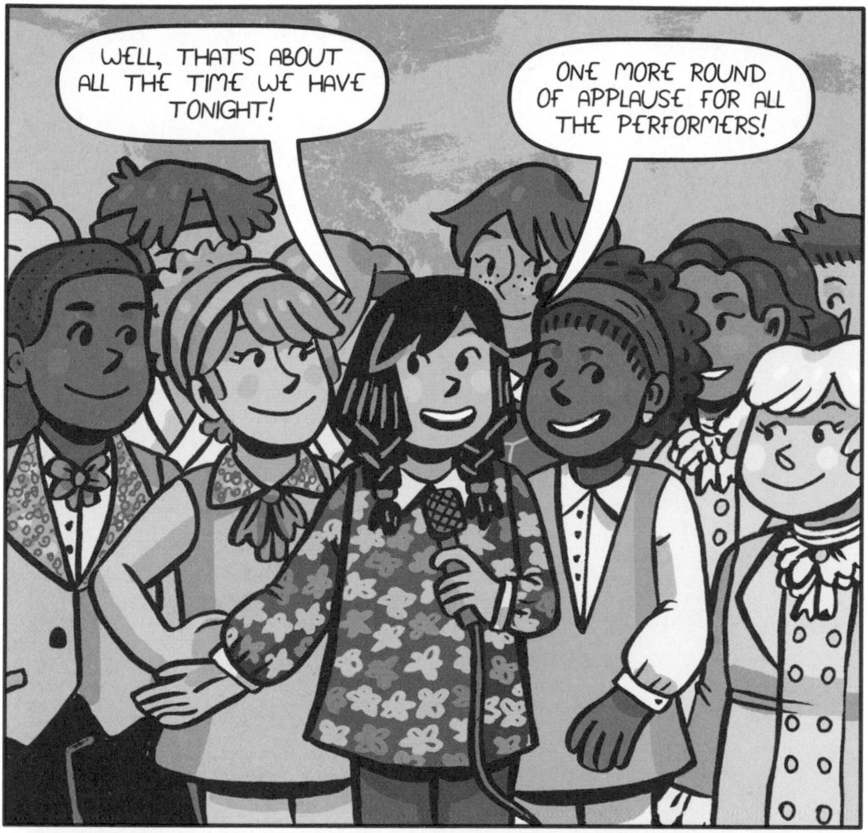
WELL, THAT'S ABOUT ALL THE TIME WE HAVE TONIGHT!
ONE MORE ROUND OF APPLAUSE FOR ALL THE PERFORMERS!

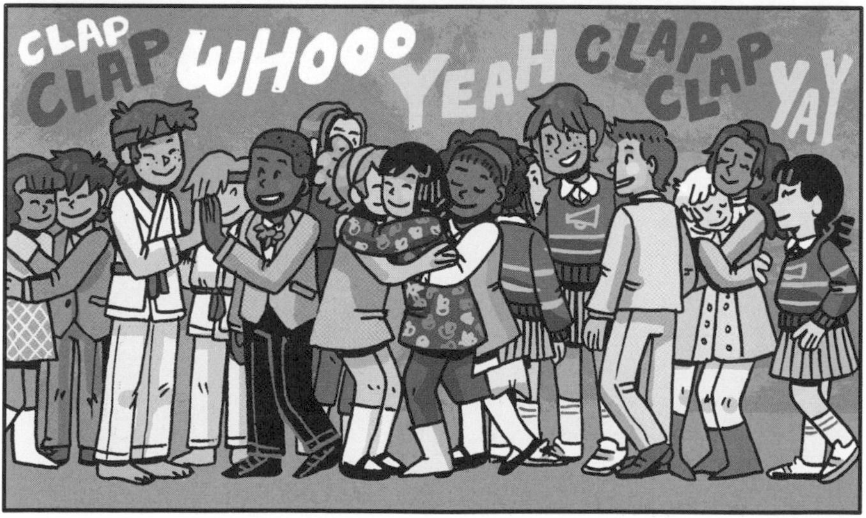
CLAP CLAP
WHOOO
YEAH
CLAP CLAP
YAY

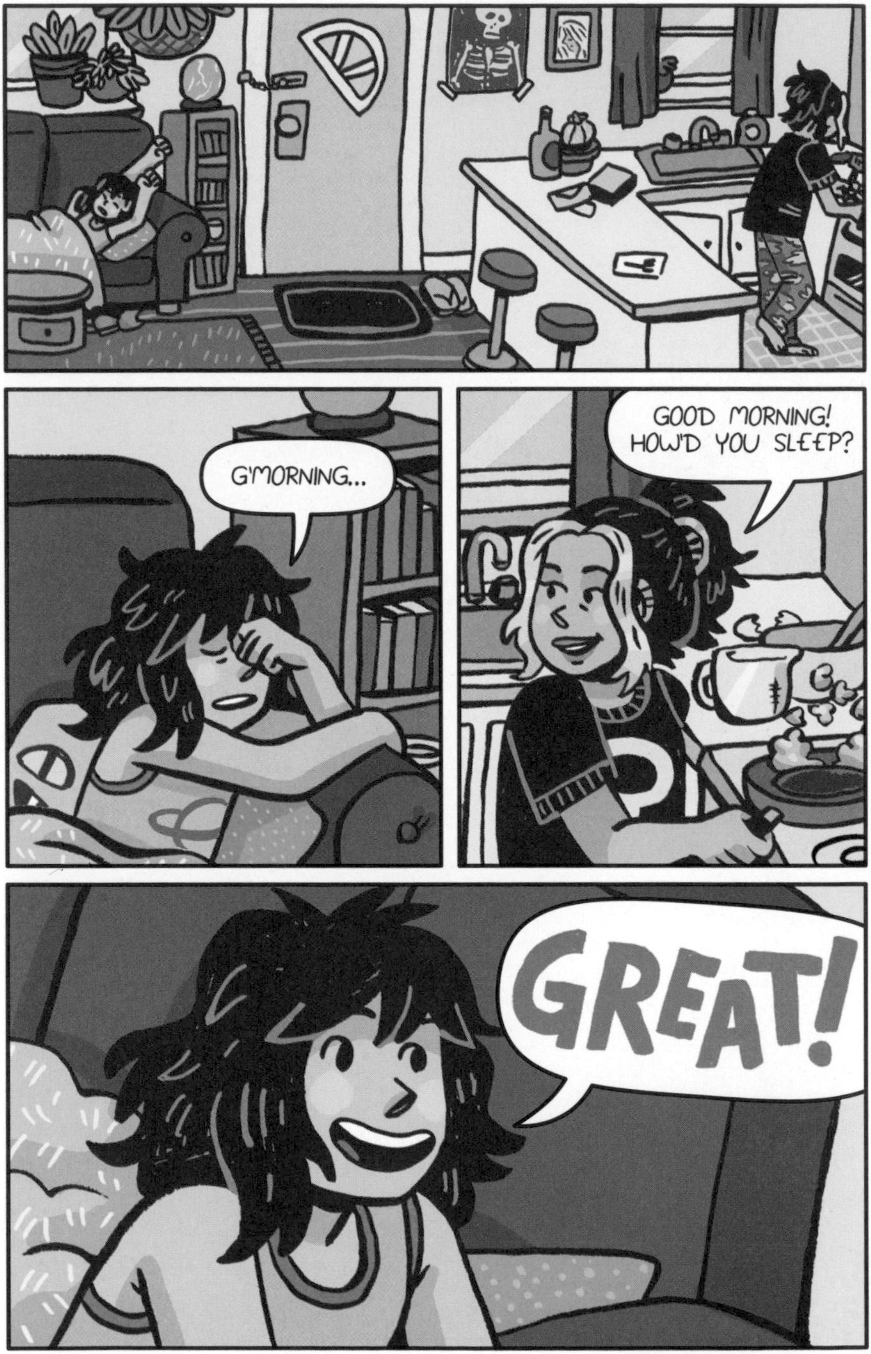
G'MORNING...
GOOD MORNING! HOW'D YOU SLEEP?
GREAT!

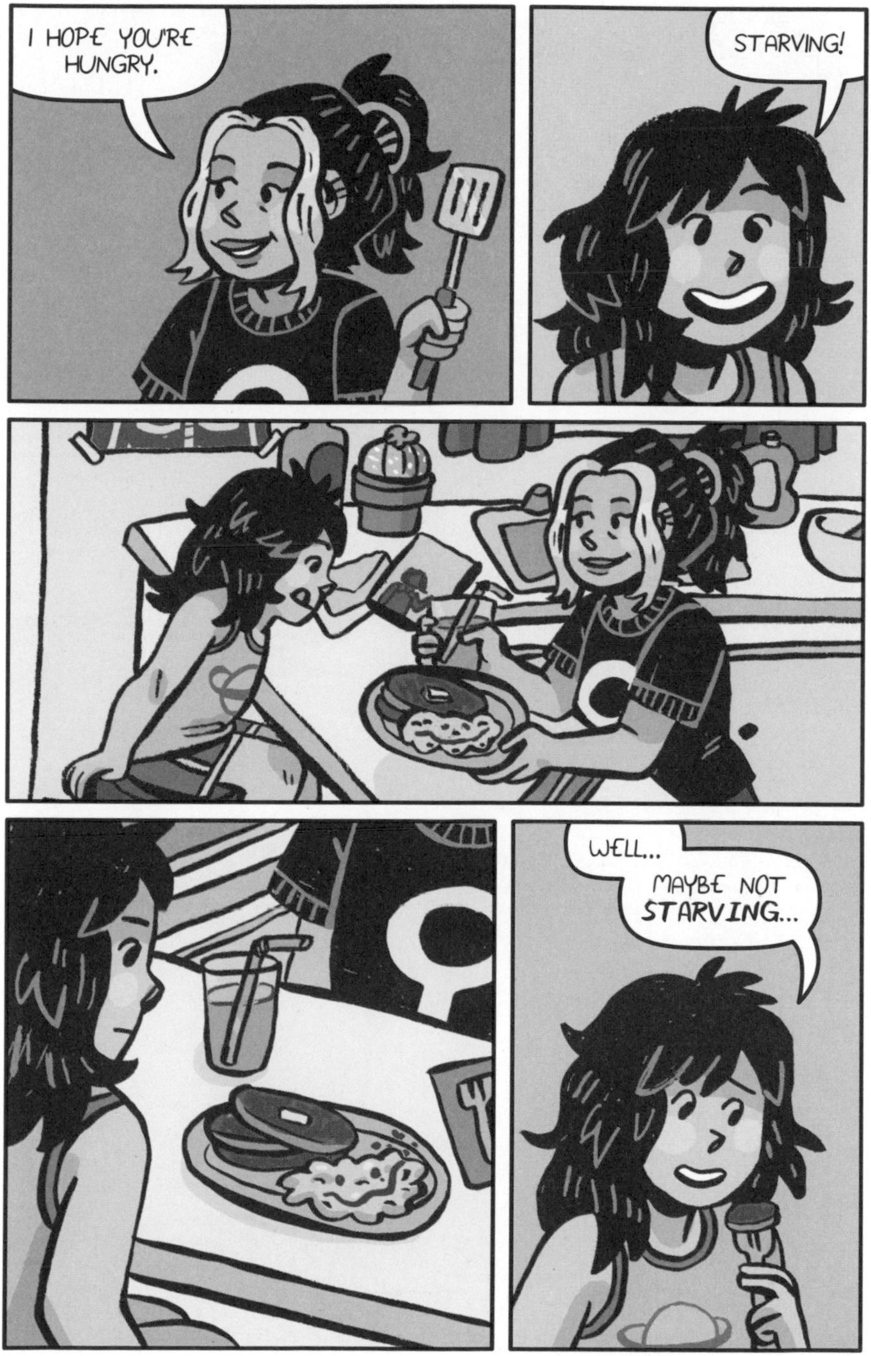
I HOPE YOU'RE HUNGRY.
STARVING!
WELL...
MAYBE NOT STARVING...

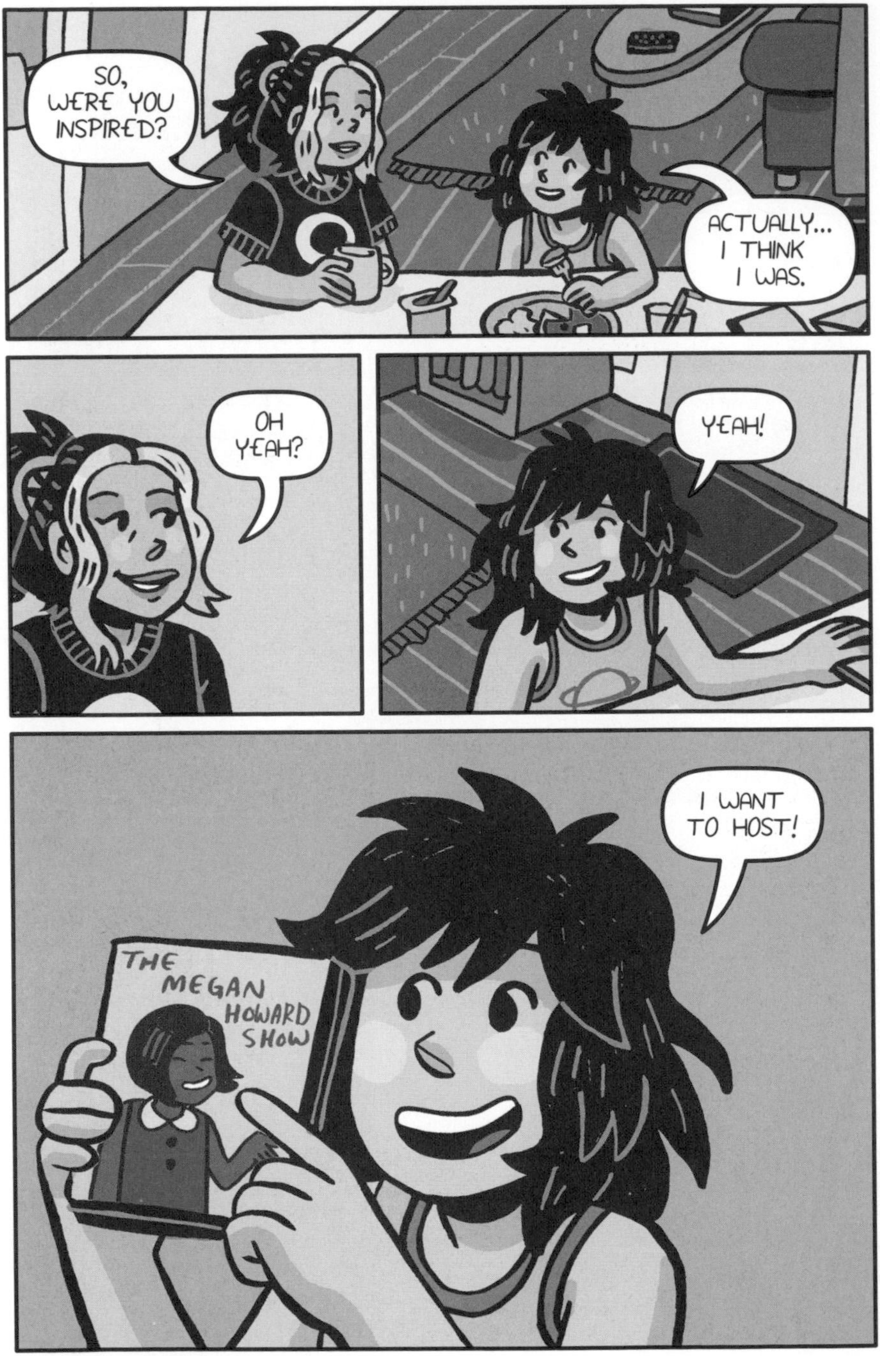
SO, WERE YOU INSPIRED?
ACTUALLY... I THINK I WAS.
OH YEAH?
YEAH!
I WANT TO HOST!
THE MEGAN HOWARD SHOW

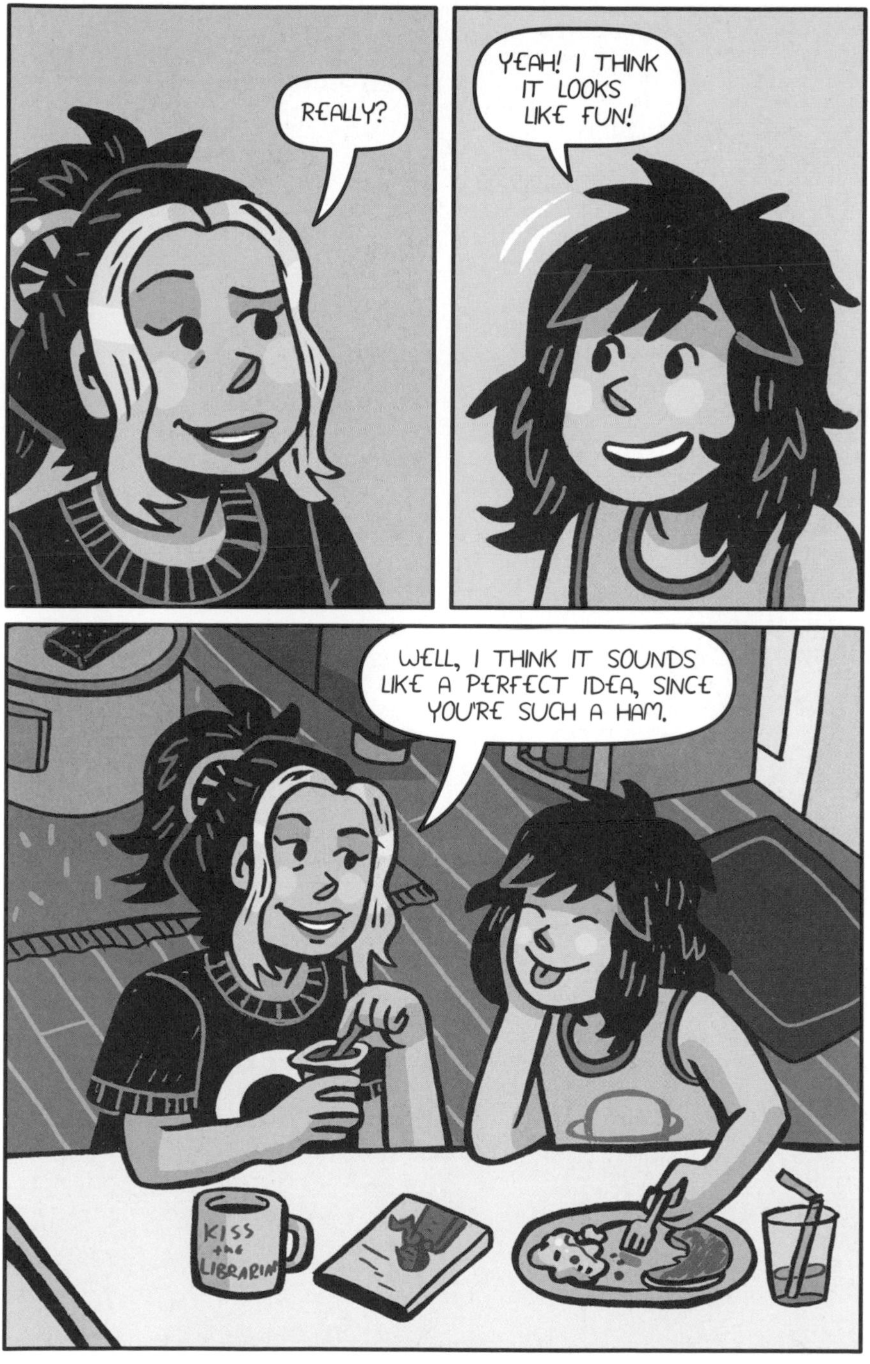
REALLY?
YEAH! I THINK IT LOOKS LIKE FUN!
WELL, I THINK IT SOUNDS LIKE A PERFECT IDEA, SINCE YOU'RE SUCH A HAM.
KISS the LIBRARIAN

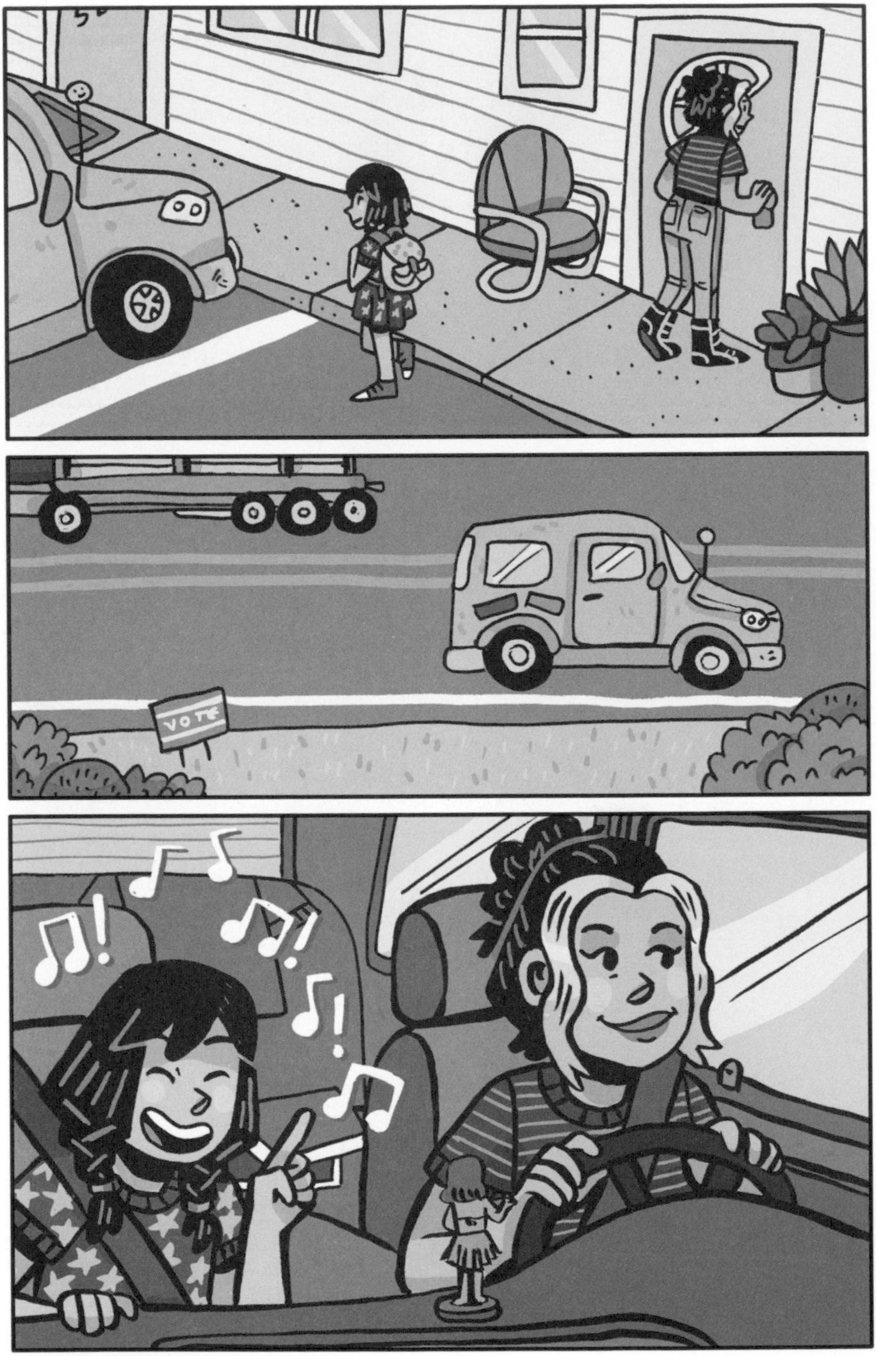
VOTE

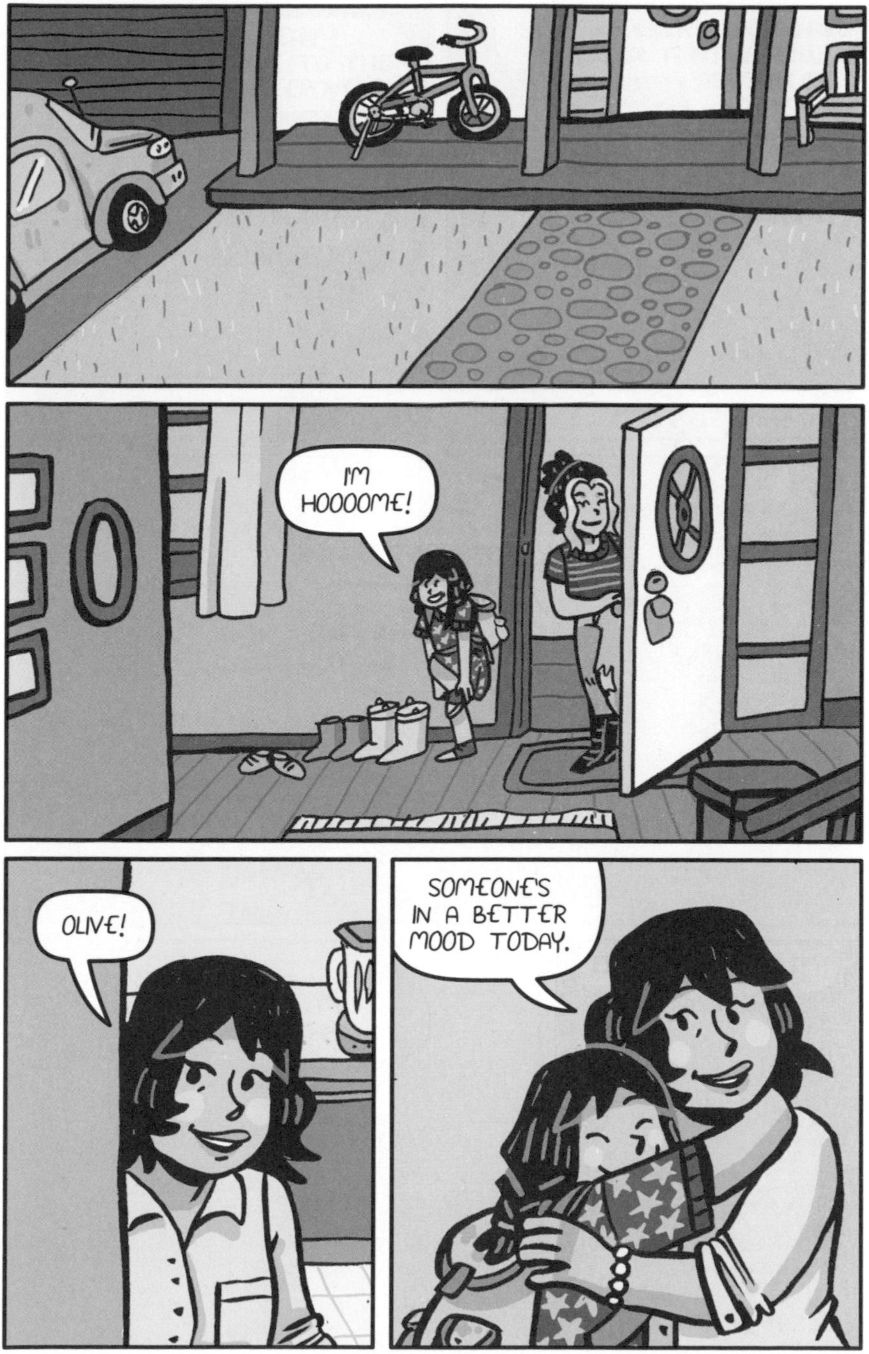

I'M HOOOOME!
OLIVE!
SOMEONE'S IN A BETTER MOOD TODAY.

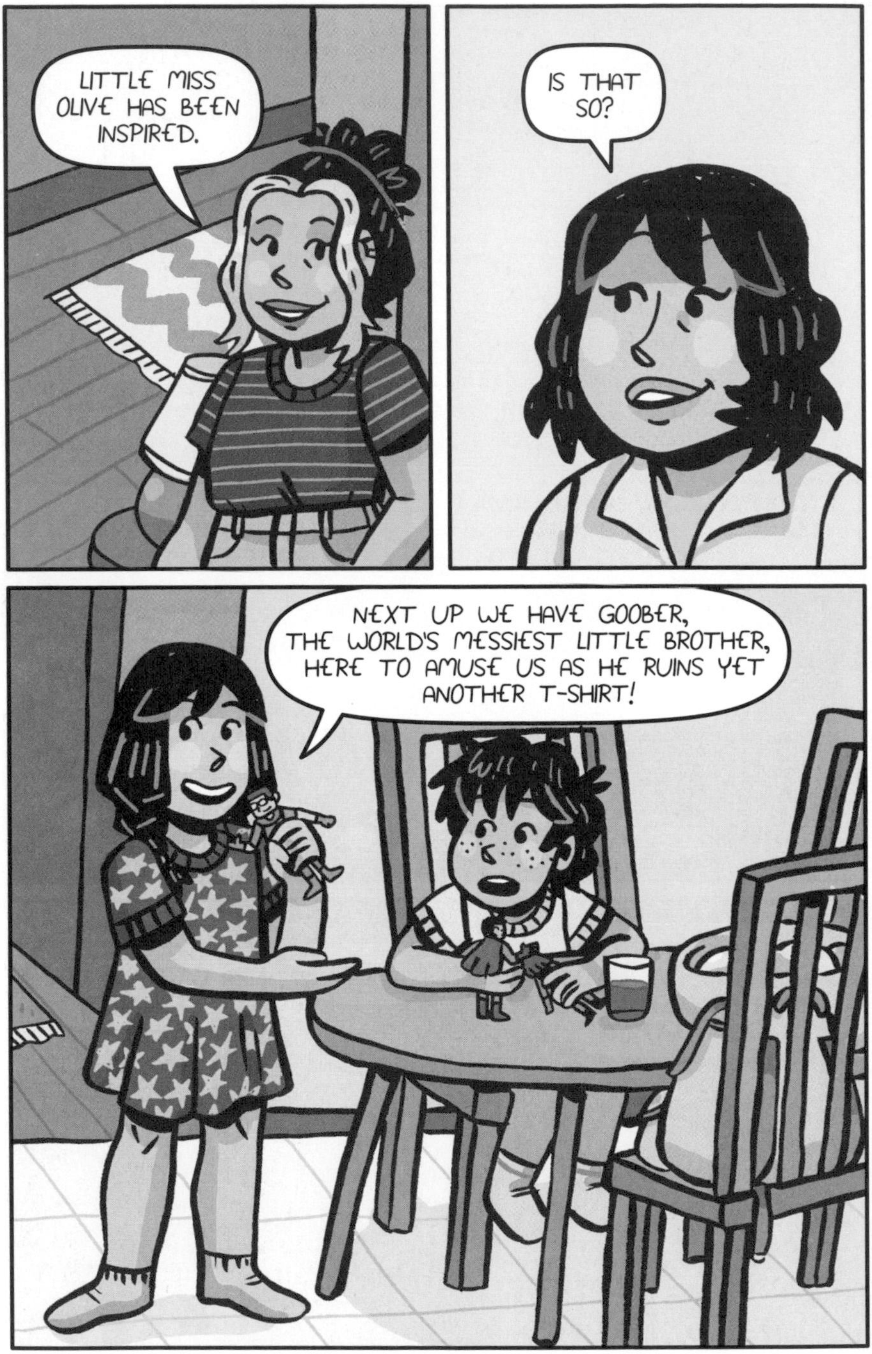
LITTLE MISS OLIVE HAS BEEN INSPIRED.
IS THAT SO?
NEXT UP WE HAVE GOOBER, THE WORLD'S MESSIEST LITTLE BROTHER, HERE TO AMUSE US AS HE RUINS YET ANOTHER T-SHIRT!

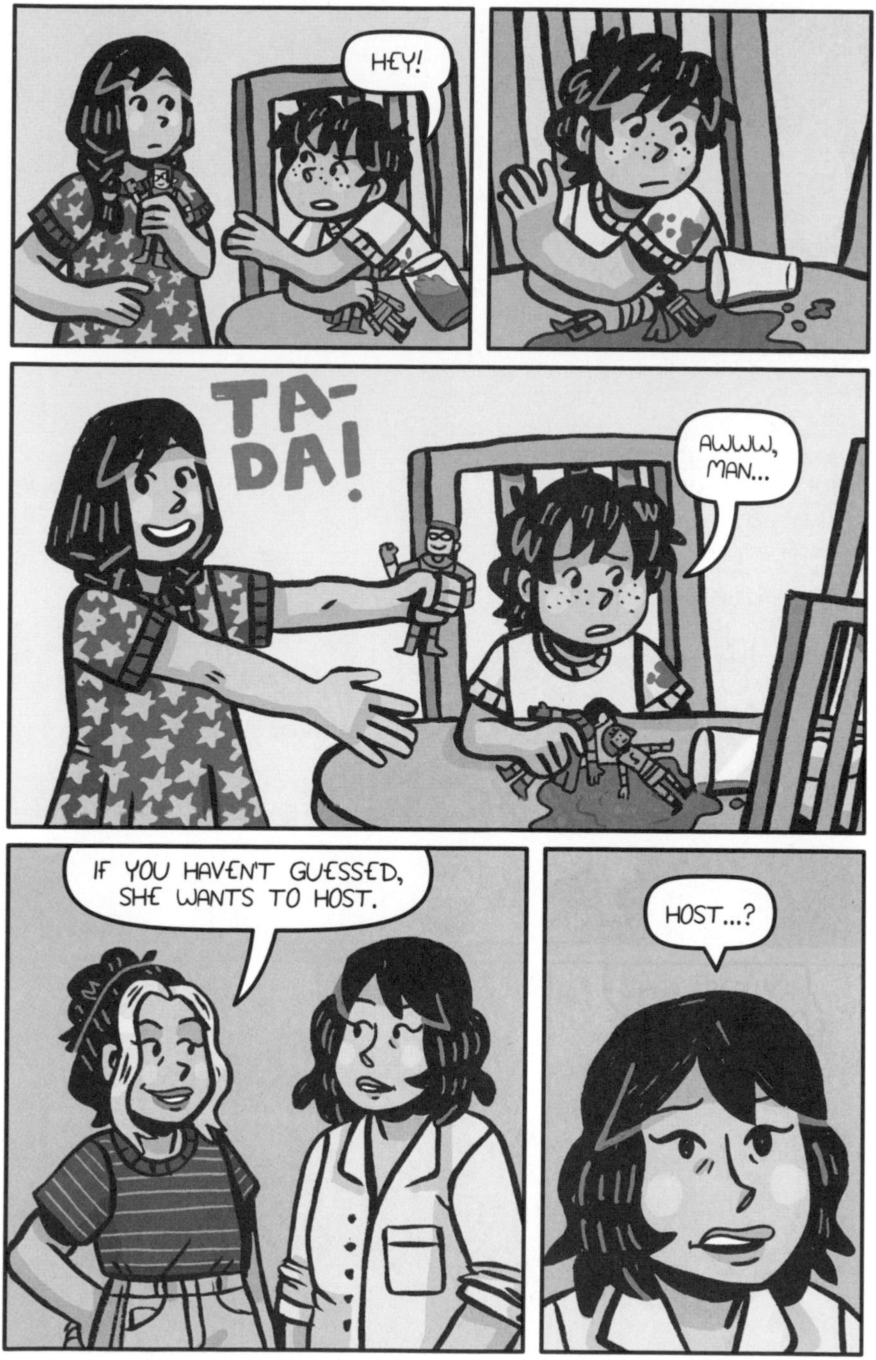
HEY!
TA-DA!
AWWW, MAN...
IF YOU HAVEN'T GUESSED, SHE WANTS TO HOST.
HOST...?

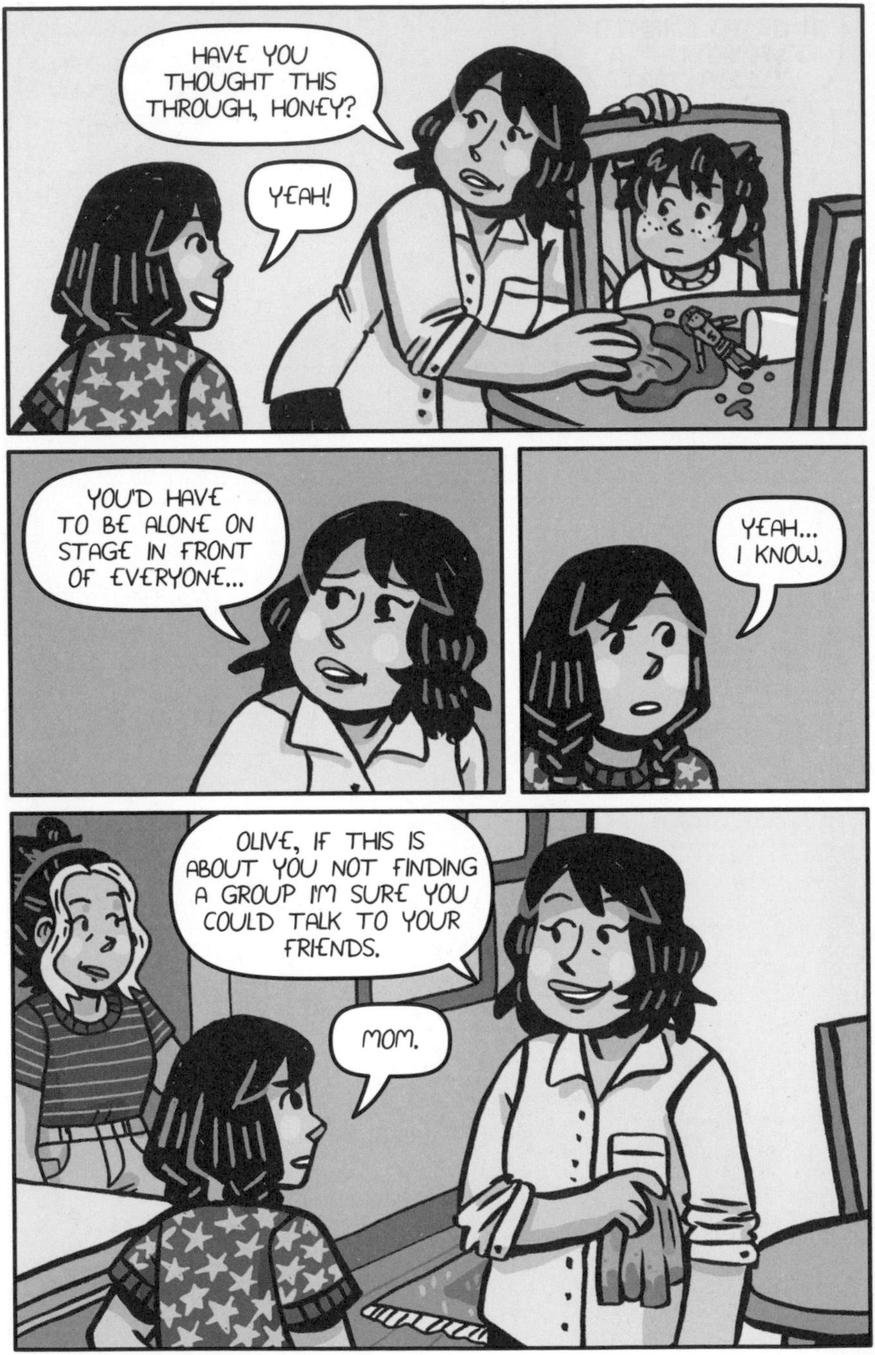
HAVE YOU THOUGHT THIS THROUGH, HONEY?
YEAH!
YOU'D HAVE TO BE ALONE ON STAGE IN FRONT OF EVERYONE...
YEAH... I KNOW.
OLIVE, IF THIS IS ABOUT YOU NOT FINDING A GROUP I'M SURE YOU COULD TALK TO YOUR FRIENDS.
MOM.

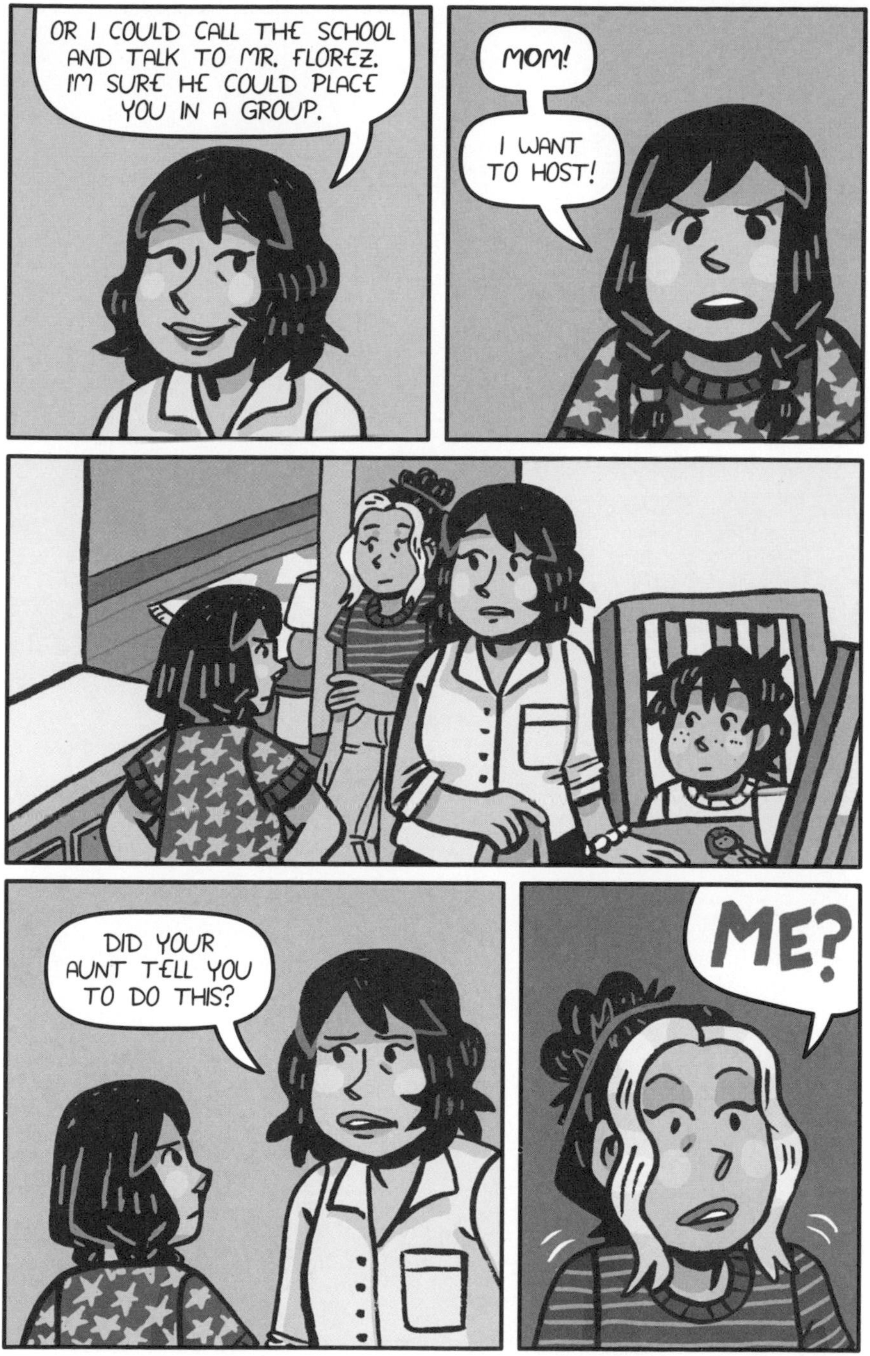
OR I COULD CALL THE SCHOOL AND TALK TO MR. FLOREZ. I'M SURE HE COULD PLACE YOU IN A GROUP.
MOM!
I WANT TO HOST!
DID YOUR AUNT TELL YOU TO DO THIS?
ME?

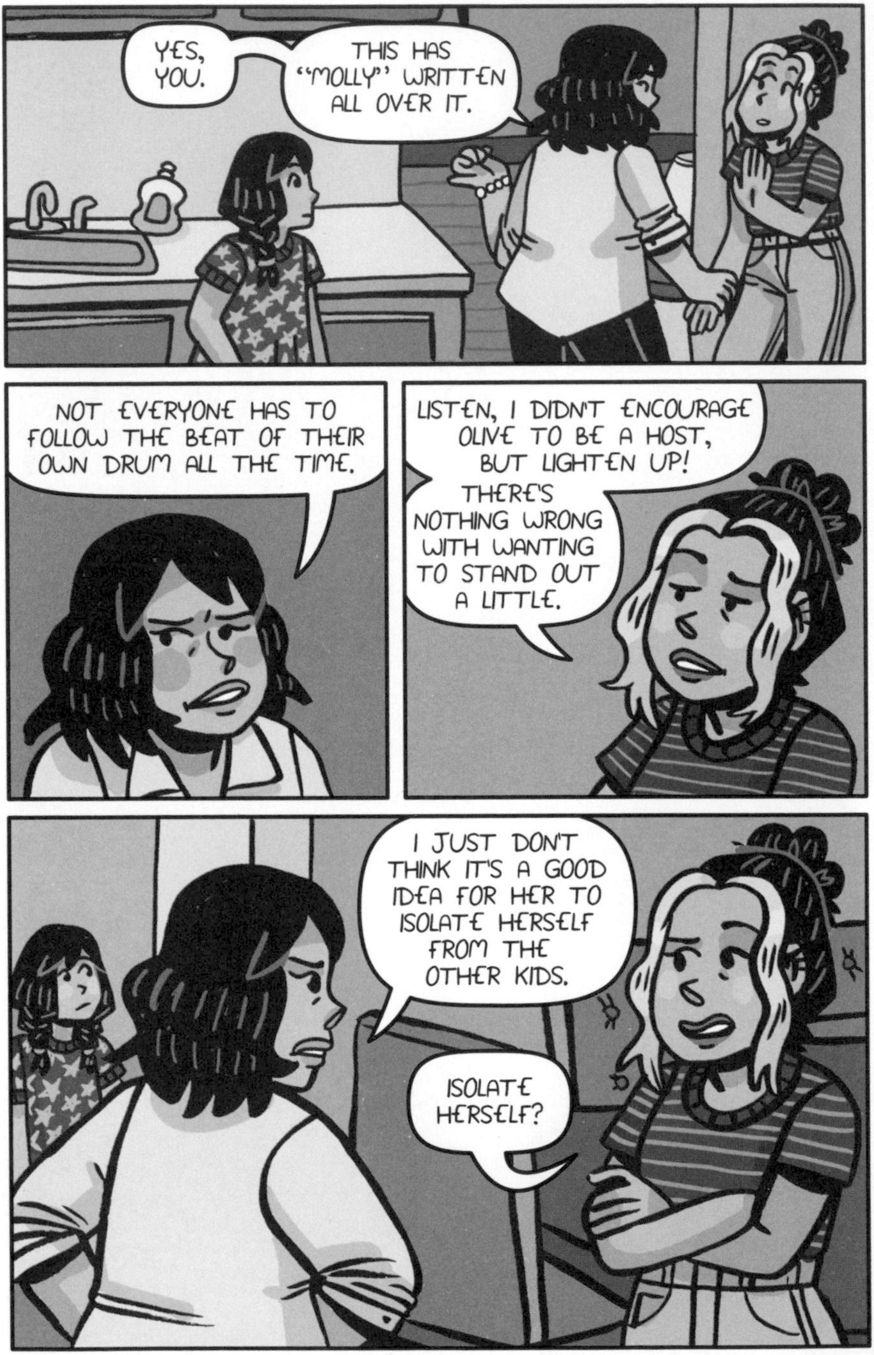
YES, YOU.
THIS HAS "MOLLY" WRITTEN ALL OVER IT.
NOT EVERYONE HAS TO FOLLOW THE BEAT OF THEIR OWN DRUM ALL THE TIME.
LISTEN, I DIDN'T ENCOURAGE OLIVE TO BE A HOST, BUT LIGHTEN UP!
THERE'S NOTHING WRONG WITH WANTING TO STAND OUT A LITTLE.
I JUST DON'T THINK IT'S A GOOD IDEA FOR HER TO ISOLATE HERSELF FROM THE OTHER KIDS.
ISOLATE HERSELF?

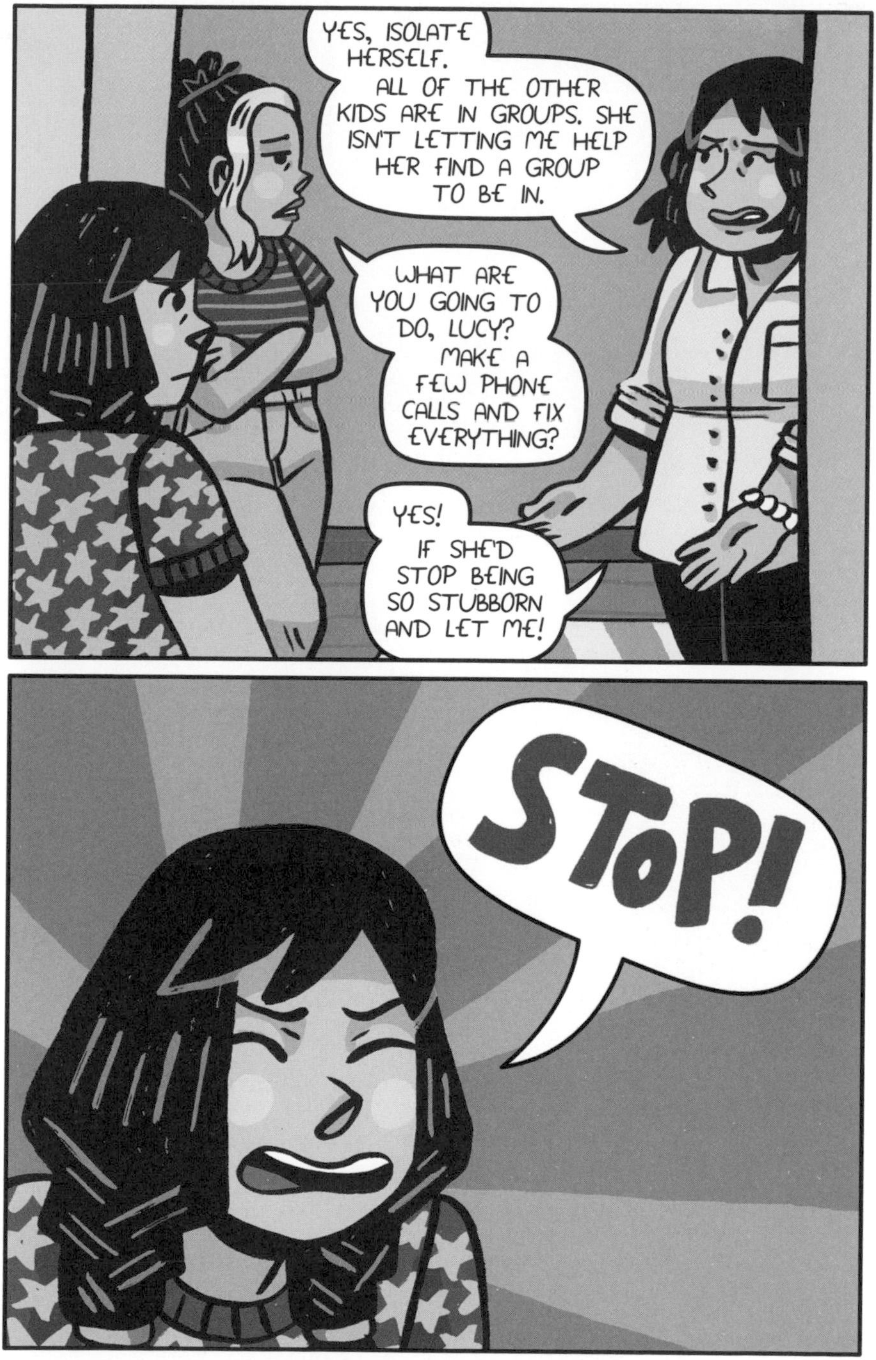
YES, ISOLATE HERSELF. ALL OF THE OTHER KIDS ARE IN GROUPS. SHE ISN'T LETTING ME HELP HER FIND A GROUP TO BE IN.
WHAT ARE YOU GOING TO DO, LUCY? MAKE A FEW PHONE CALLS AND FIX EVERYTHING?
YES! IF SHE'D STOP BEING SO STUBBORN AND LET ME!
STOP!

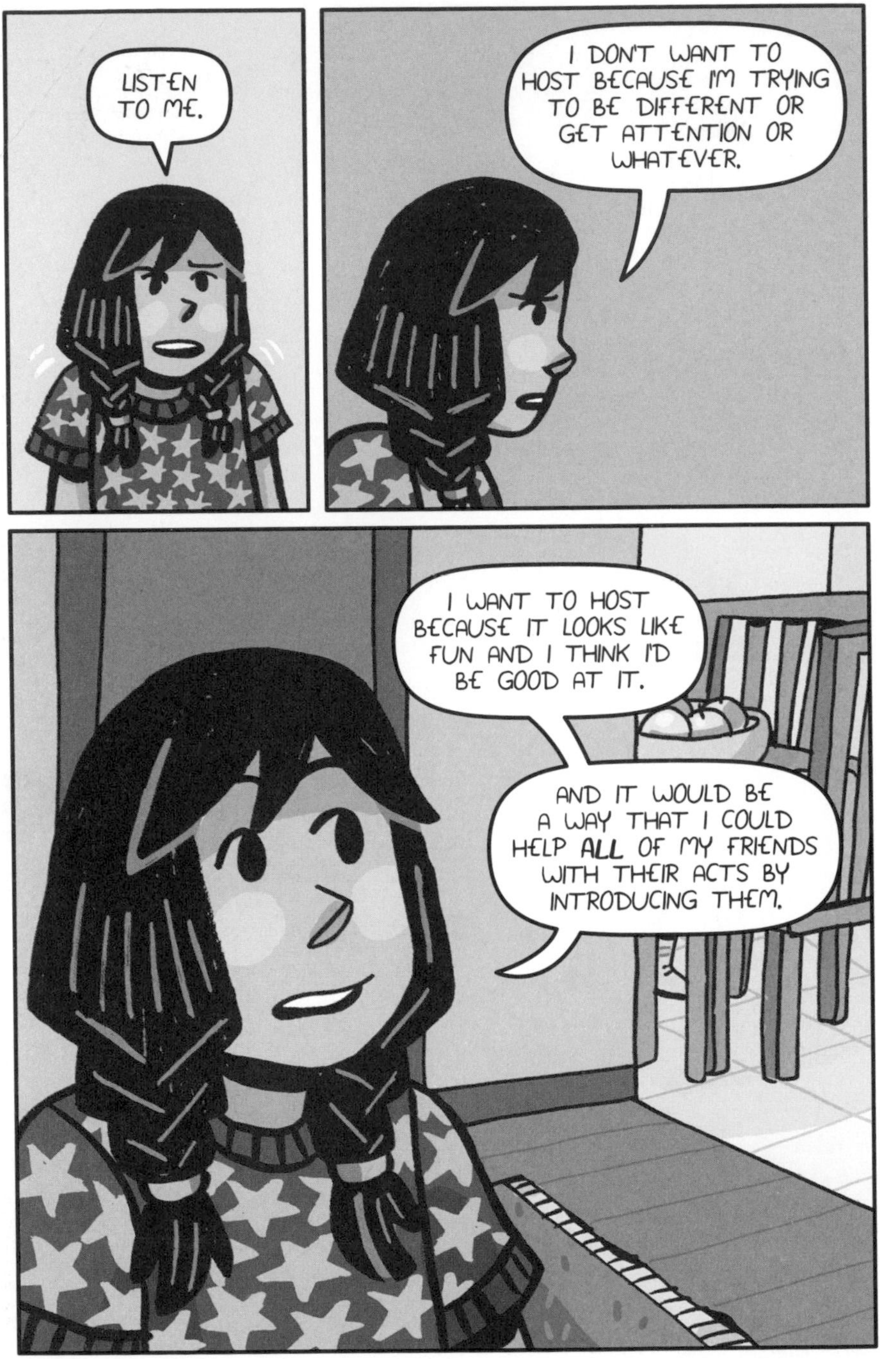
LISTEN TO ME.
I DON'T WANT TO HOST BECAUSE I'M TRYING TO BE DIFFERENT OR GET ATTENTION OR WHATEVER.
I WANT TO HOST BECAUSE IT LOOKS LIKE FUN AND I THINK I'D BE GOOD AT IT.
AND IT WOULD BE A WAY THAT I COULD HELP ALL OF MY FRIENDS WITH THEIR ACTS BY INTRODUCING THEM.

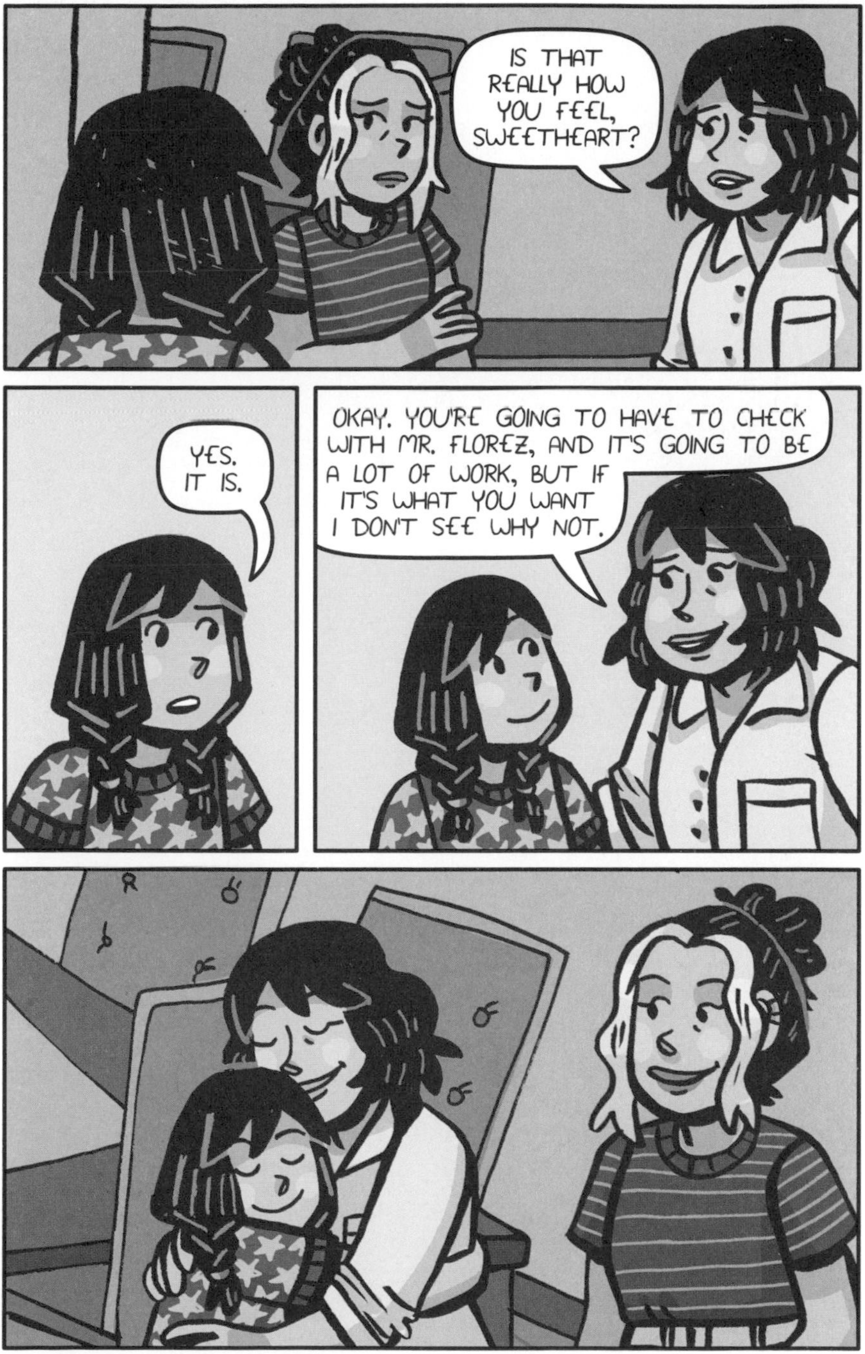
IS THAT REALLY HOW YOU FEEL, SWEETHEART?
YES. IT IS.
OKAY. YOU'RE GOING TO HAVE TO CHECK WITH MR. FLOREZ, AND IT'S GOING TO BE A LOT OF WORK, BUT IF IT'S WHAT YOU WANT I DON'T SEE WHY NOT.

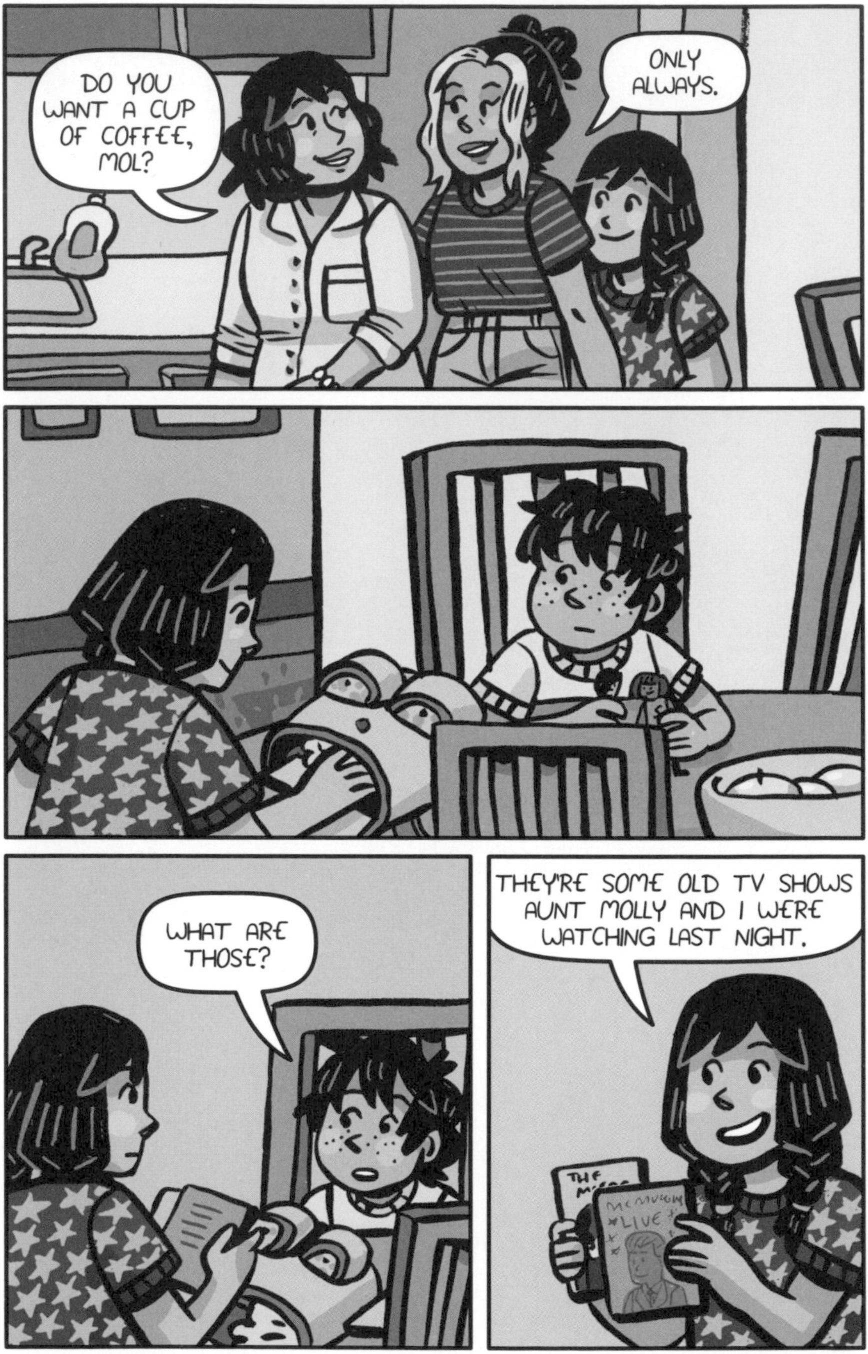
DO YOU WANT A CUP OF COFFEE, MOL?
ONLY ALWAYS.
WHAT ARE THOSE?
THEY'RE SOME OLD TV SHOWS AUNT MOLLY AND I WERE WATCHING LAST NIGHT.

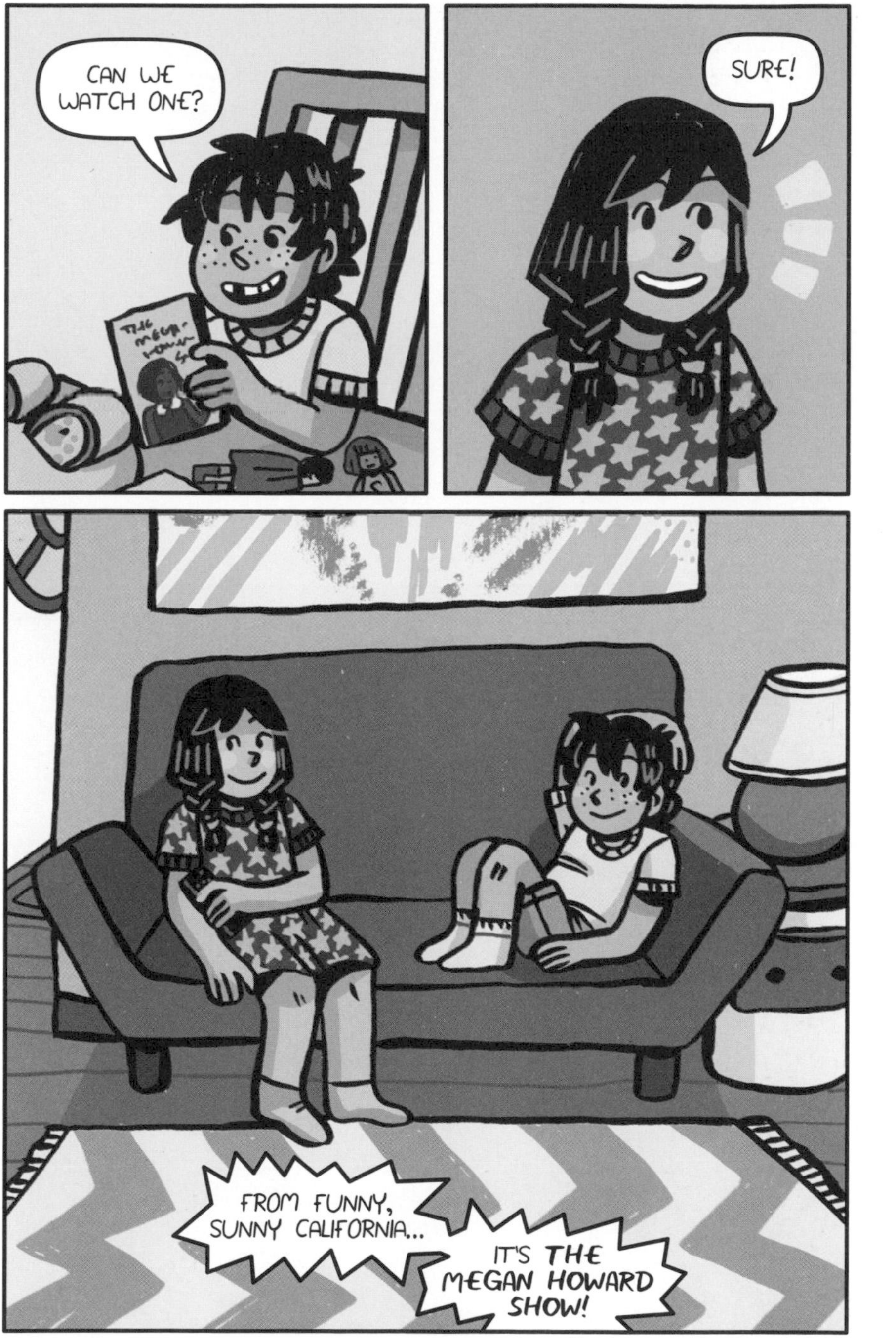
CAN WE WATCH ONE?
SURE!
FROM FUNNY, SUNNY CALIFORNIA...
IT'S THE MEGAN HOWARD SHOW!

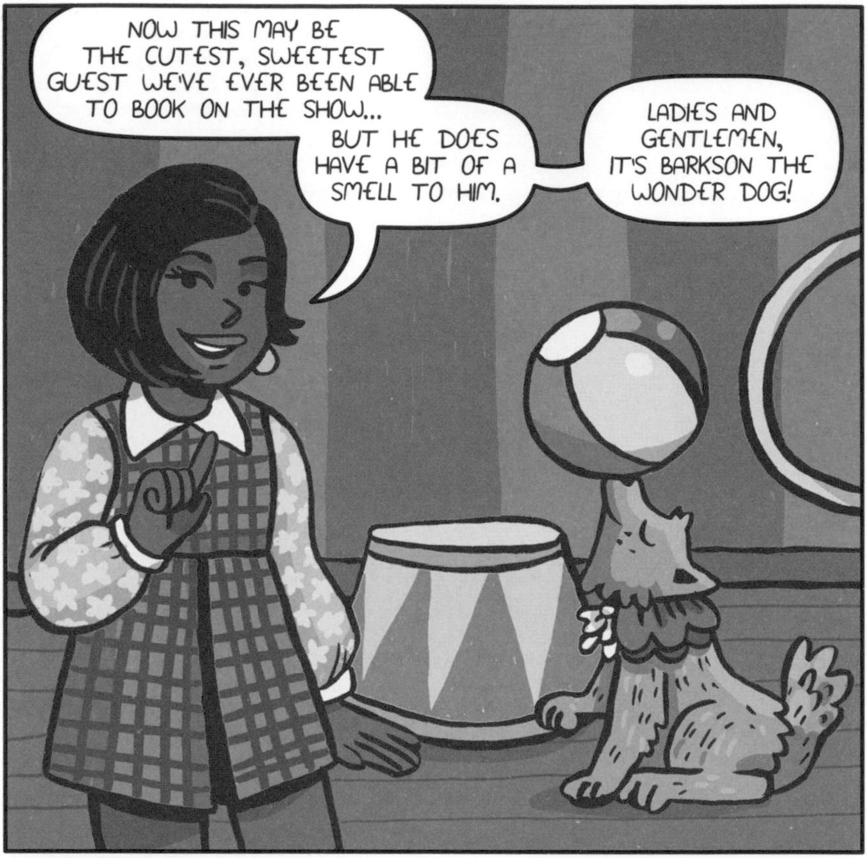
NOW THIS MAY BE THE CUTEST, SWEETEST GUEST WE'VE EVER BEEN ABLE TO BOOK ON THE SHOW...
BUT HE DOES HAVE A BIT OF A SMELL TO HIM.
LADIES AND GENTLEMEN, IT'S BARKSON THE WONDER DOG!

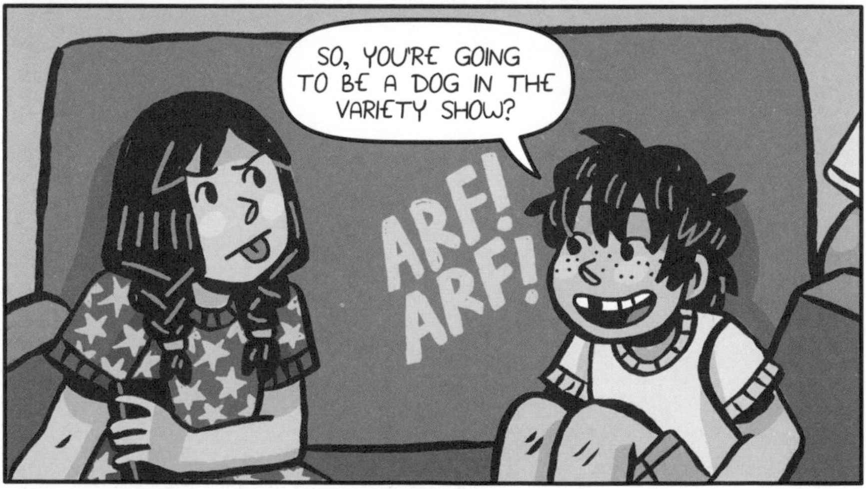
SO, YOU'RE GOING TO BE A DOG IN THE VARIETY SHOW?
ARF! ARF!

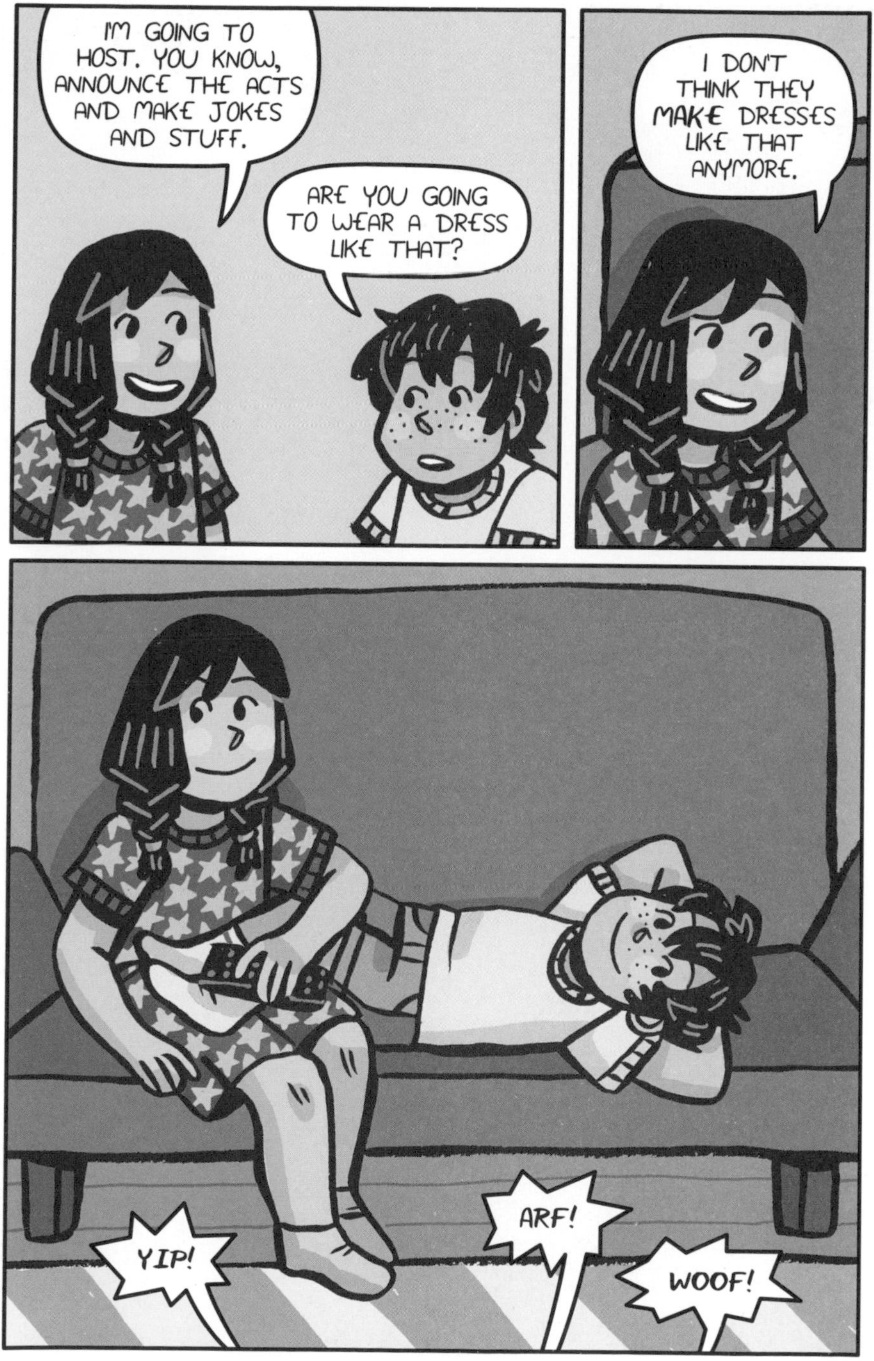
I'M GOING TO HOST. YOU KNOW, ANNOUNCE THE ACTS AND MAKE JOKES AND STUFF.
ARE YOU GOING TO WEAR A DRESS LIKE THAT?
I DON'T THINK THEY MAKE DRESSES LIKE THAT ANYMORE.
YIP!
ARF!
WOOF!

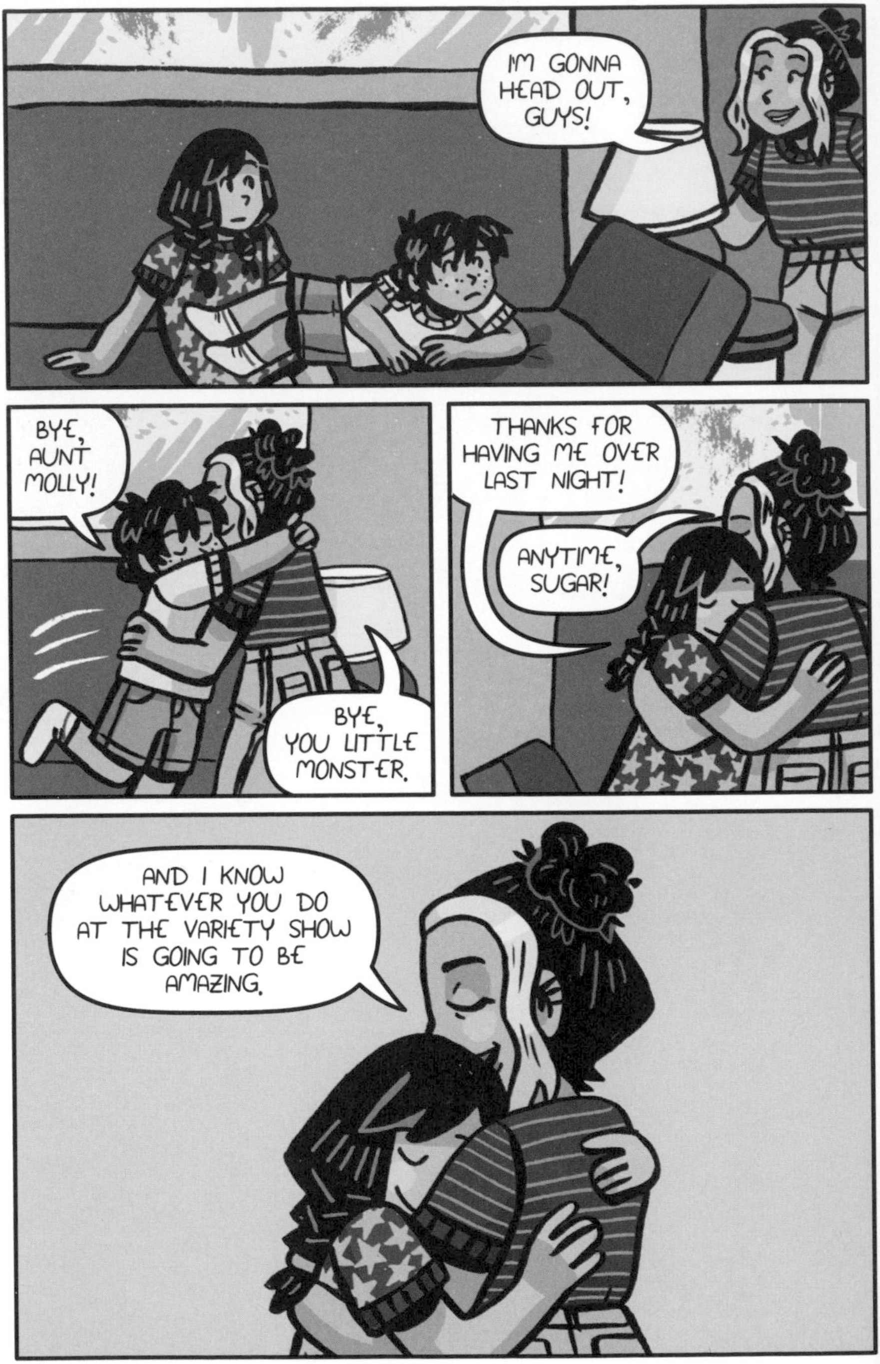
I'M GONNA HEAD OUT, GUYS!
BYE, AUNT MOLLY!
BYE, YOU LITTLE MONSTER.
THANKS FOR HAVING ME OVER LAST NIGHT!
ANYTIME, SUGAR!
AND I KNOW WHATEVER YOU DO AT THE VARIETY SHOW IS GOING TO BE AMAZING.

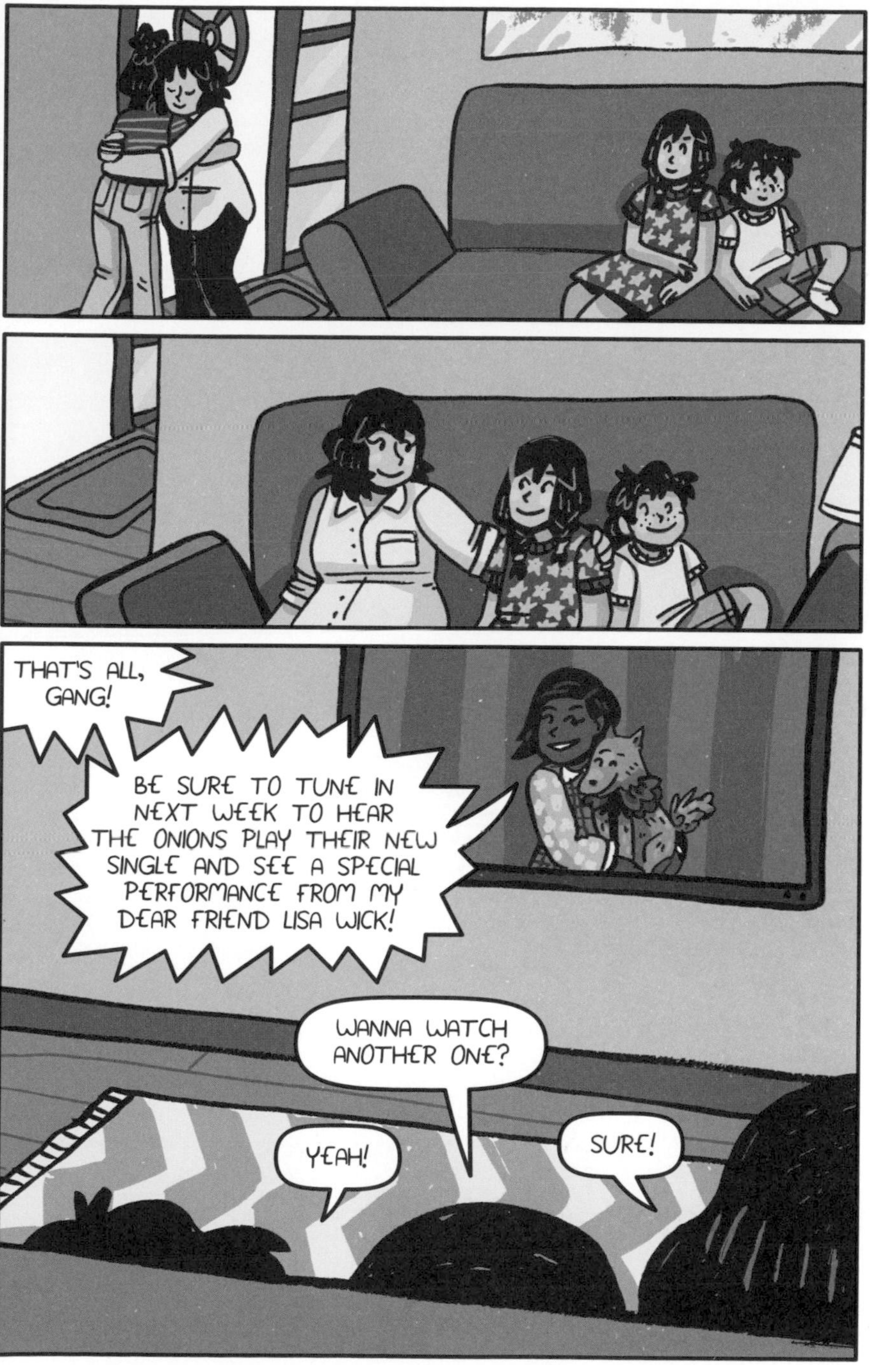
THAT'S ALL, GANG!
BE SURE TO TUNE IN NEXT WEEK TO HEAR THE ONIONS PLAY THEIR NEW SINGLE AND SEE A SPECIAL PERFORMANCE FROM MY DEAR FRIEND LISA WICK!
WANNA WATCH ANOTHER ONE?
YEAH!
SURE!

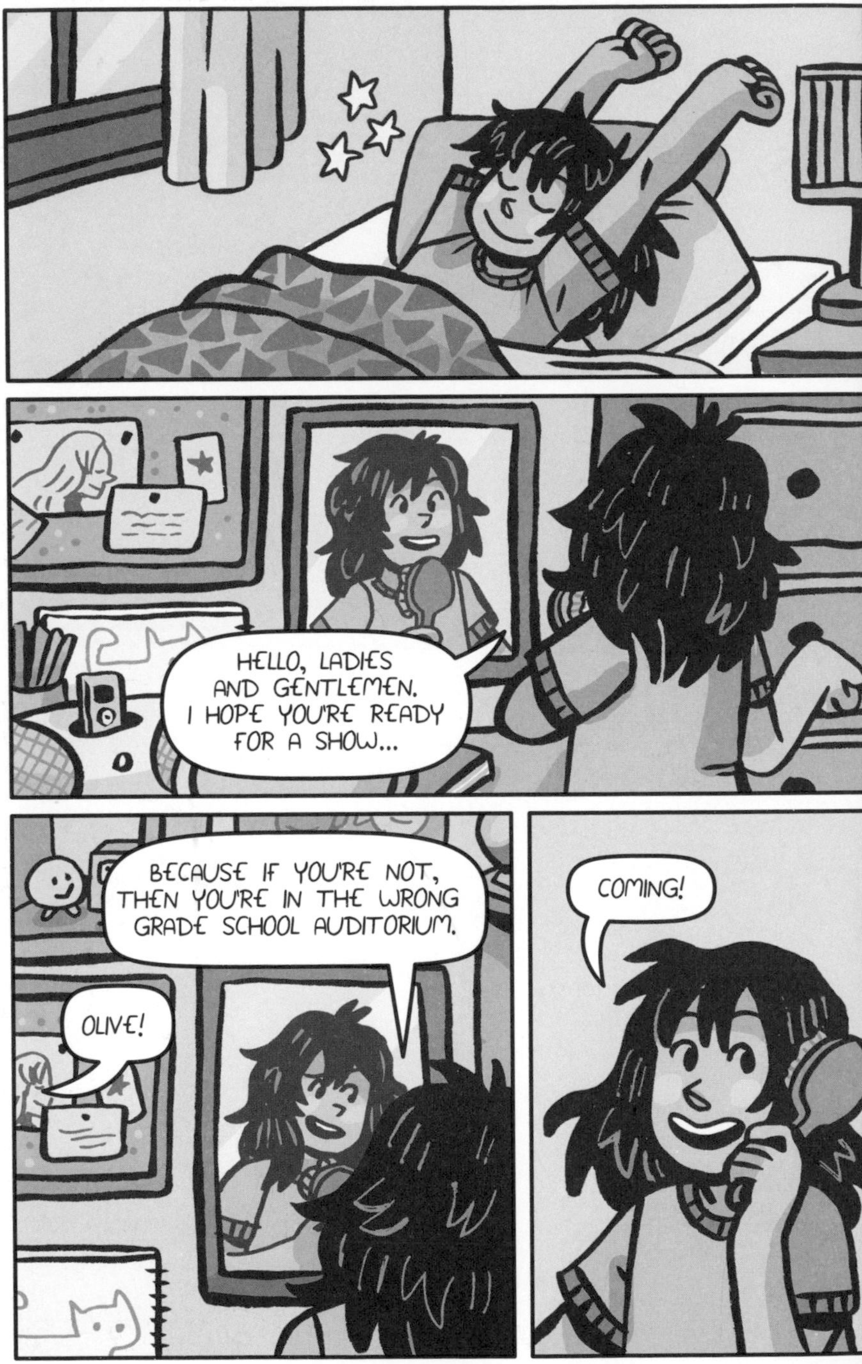
HELLO, LADIES AND GENTLEMEN. I HOPE YOU'RE READY FOR A SHOW...
BECAUSE IF YOU'RE NOT, THEN YOU'RE IN THE WRONG GRADE SCHOOL AUDITORIUM.
OLIVE!
COMING!

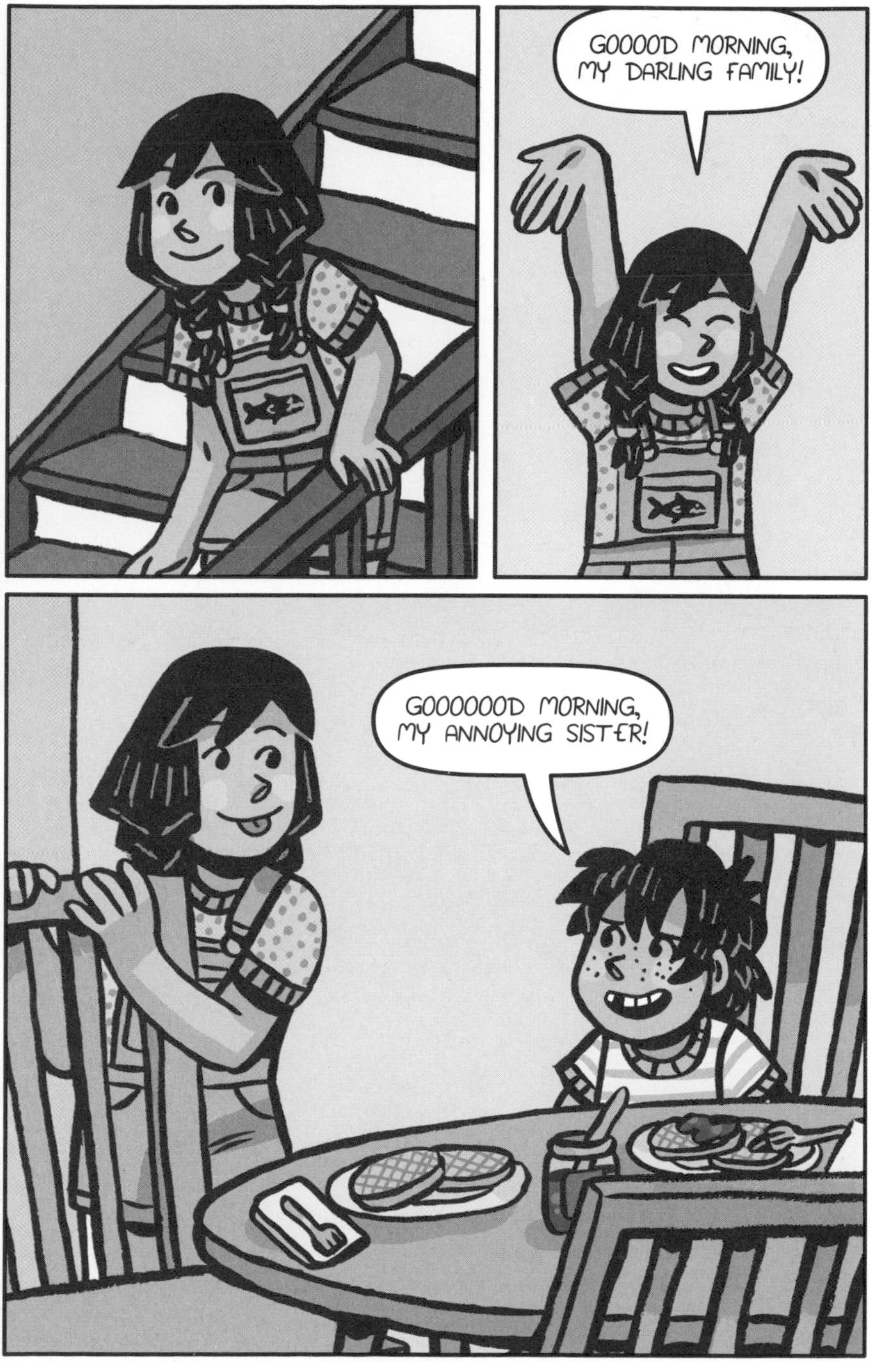
GOOOOD MORNING, MY DARLING FAMILY!
GOOOOOOD MORNING, MY ANNOYING SISTER!

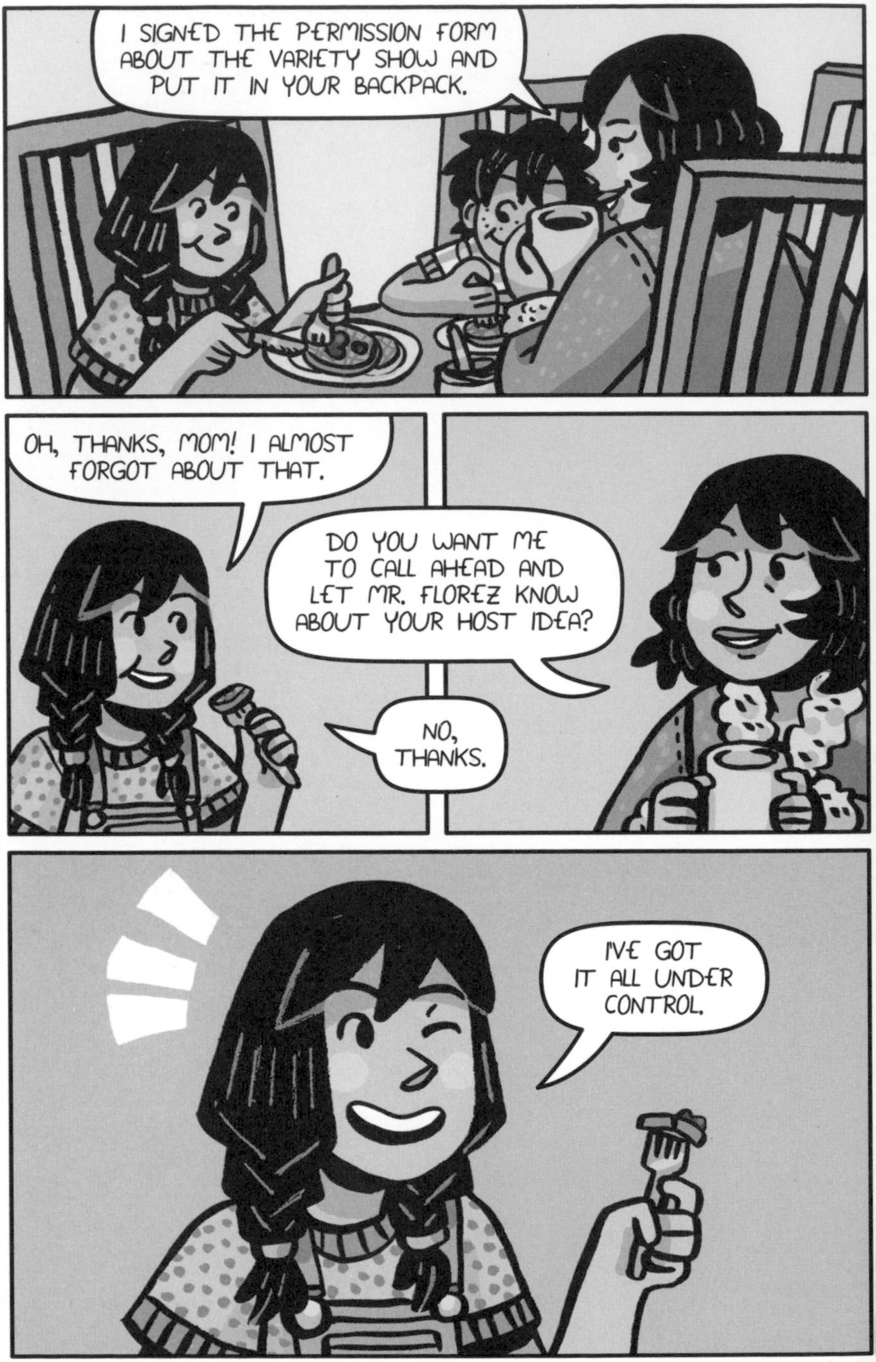
I SIGNED THE PERMISSION FORM ABOUT THE VARIETY SHOW AND PUT IT IN YOUR BACKPACK.
OH, THANKS, MOM! I ALMOST FORGOT ABOUT THAT.
DO YOU WANT ME TO CALL AHEAD AND LET MR. FLOREZ KNOW ABOUT YOUR HOST IDEA?
NO, THANKS.
I'VE GOT IT ALL UNDER CONTROL.

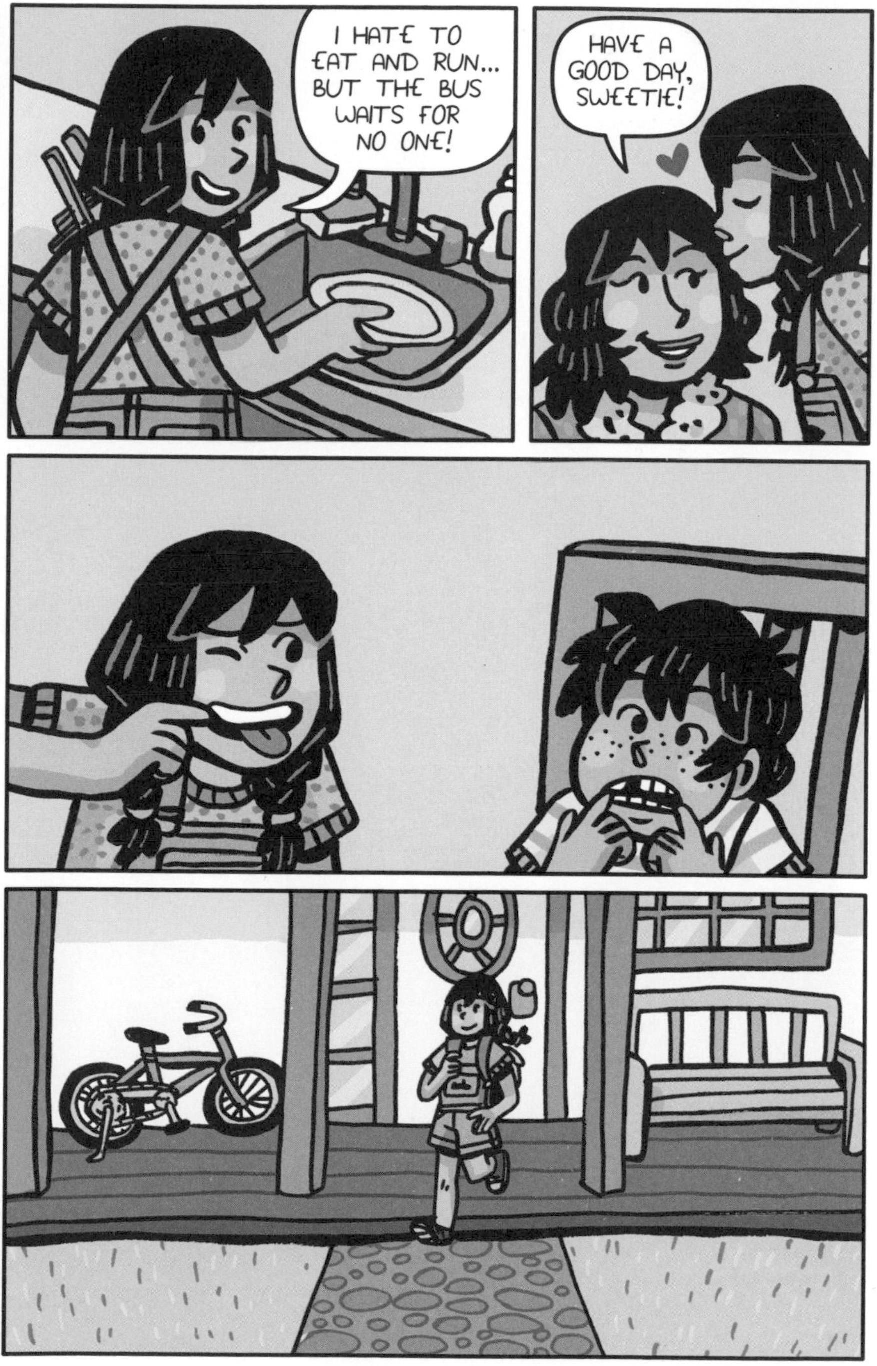
I HATE TO EAT AND RUN... BUT THE BUS WAITS FOR NO ONE!
HAVE A GOOD DAY, SWEETIE!

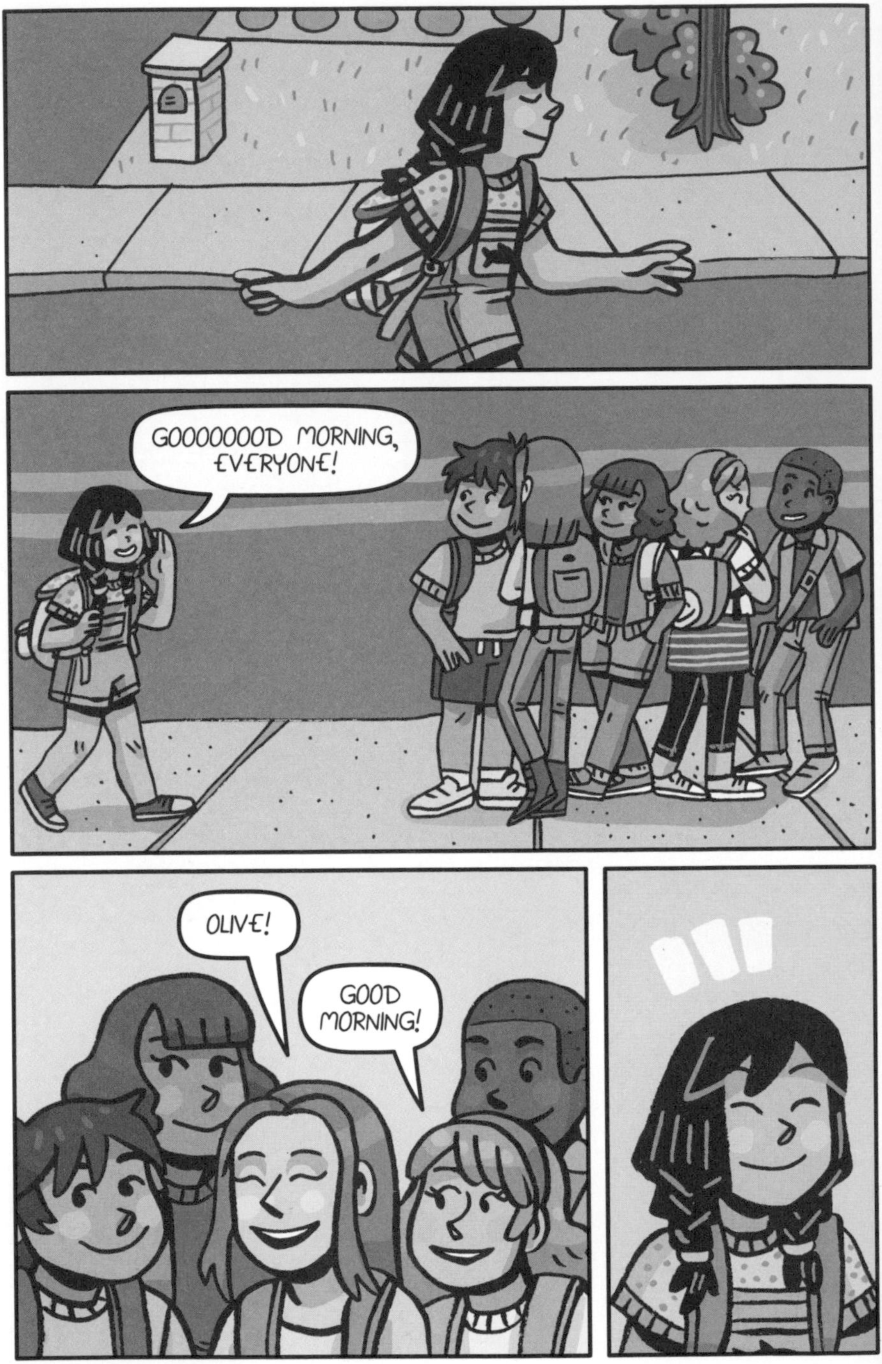
GOOOOOOOD MORNING, EVERYONE!
OLIVE!
GOOD MORNING!

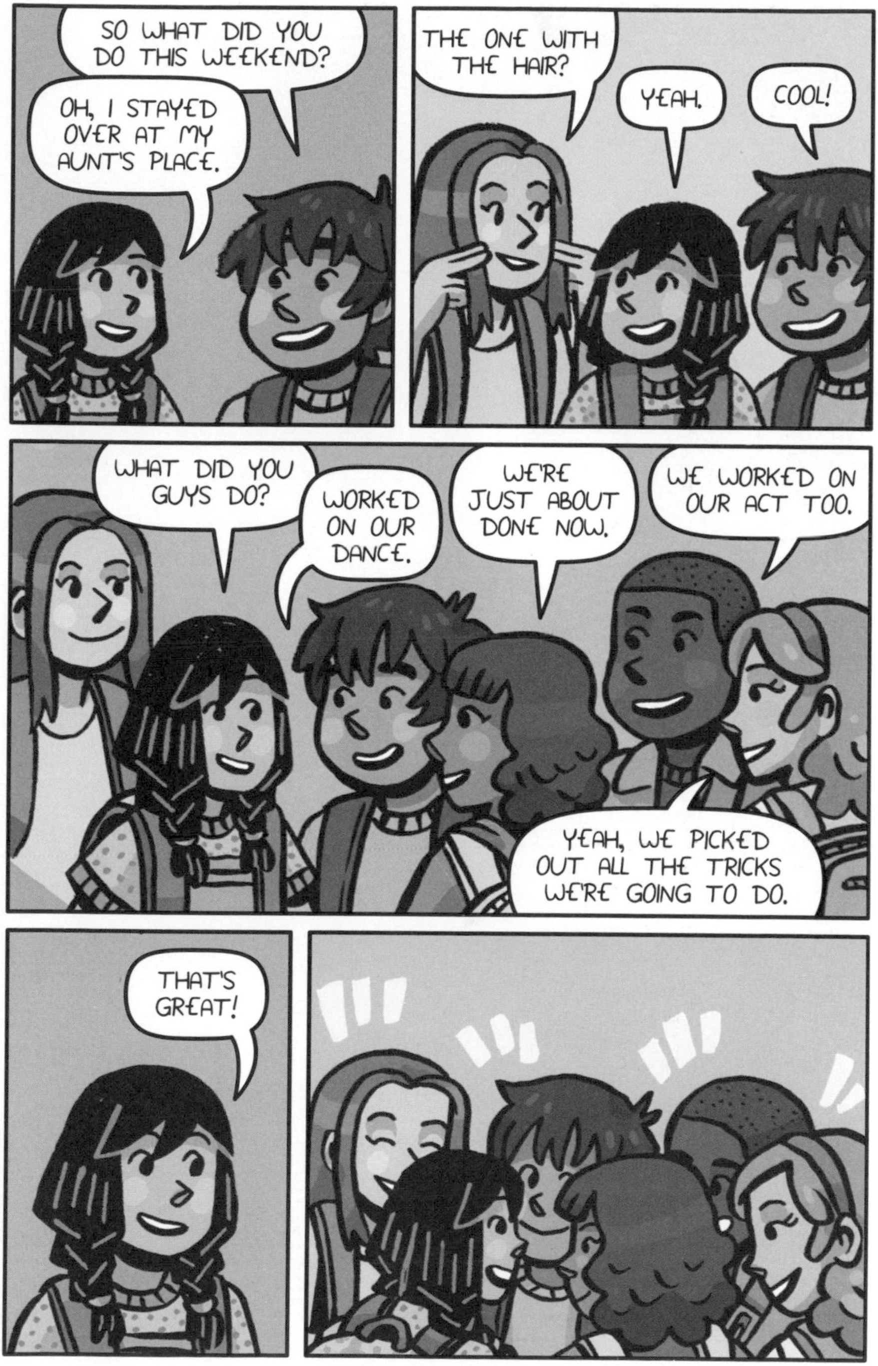
SO WHAT DID YOU DO THIS WEEKEND?
OH, I STAYED OVER AT MY AUNT'S PLACE.
THE ONE WITH THE HAIR?
YEAH.
COOL!
WHAT DID YOU GUYS DO?
WORKED ON OUR DANCE.
WE'RE JUST ABOUT DONE NOW.
WE WORKED ON OUR ACT TOO.
YEAH, WE PICKED OUT ALL THE TRICKS WE'RE GOING TO DO.
THAT'S GREAT!

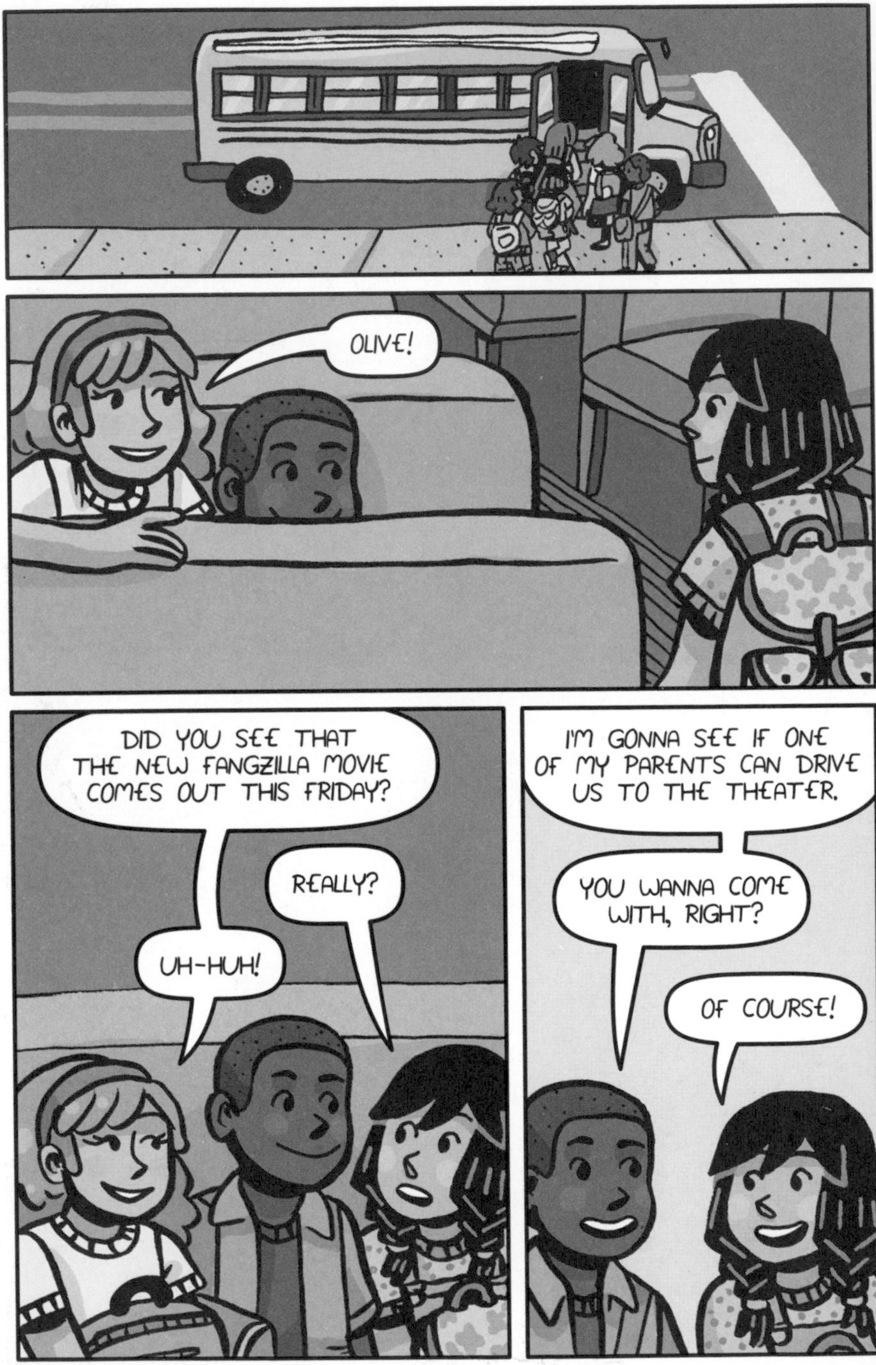
OLIVE!
DID YOU SEE THAT THE NEW FANGZILLA MOVIE COMES OUT THIS FRIDAY?
REALLY?
UH-HUH!
I'M GONNA SEE IF ONE OF MY PARENTS CAN DRIVE US TO THE THEATER.
YOU WANNA COME WITH, RIGHT?
OF COURSE!

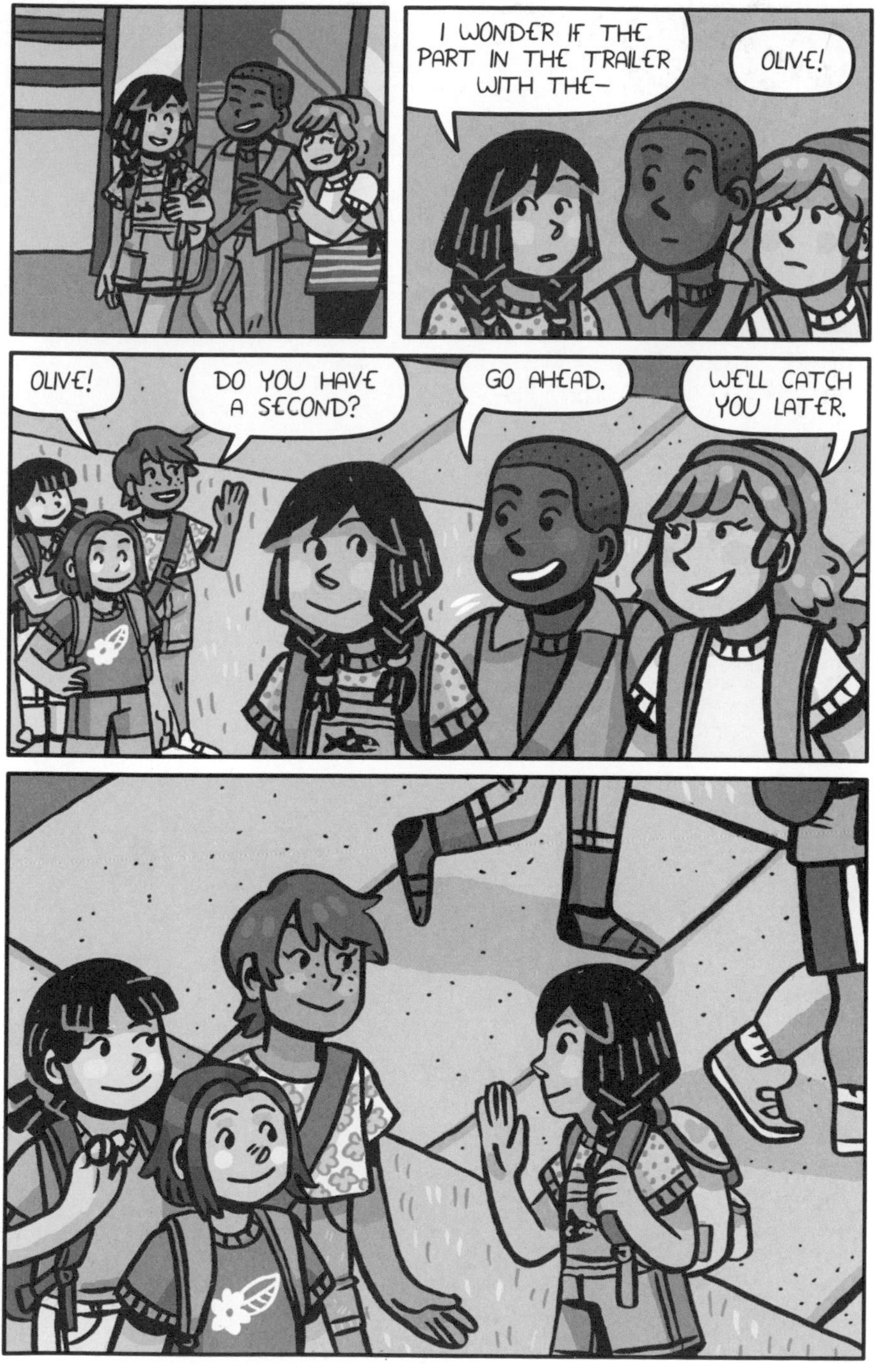
I WONDER IF THE PART IN THE TRAILER WITH THE–
OLIVE!
OLIVE!
DO YOU HAVE A SECOND?
GO AHEAD.
WE'LL CATCH YOU LATER.

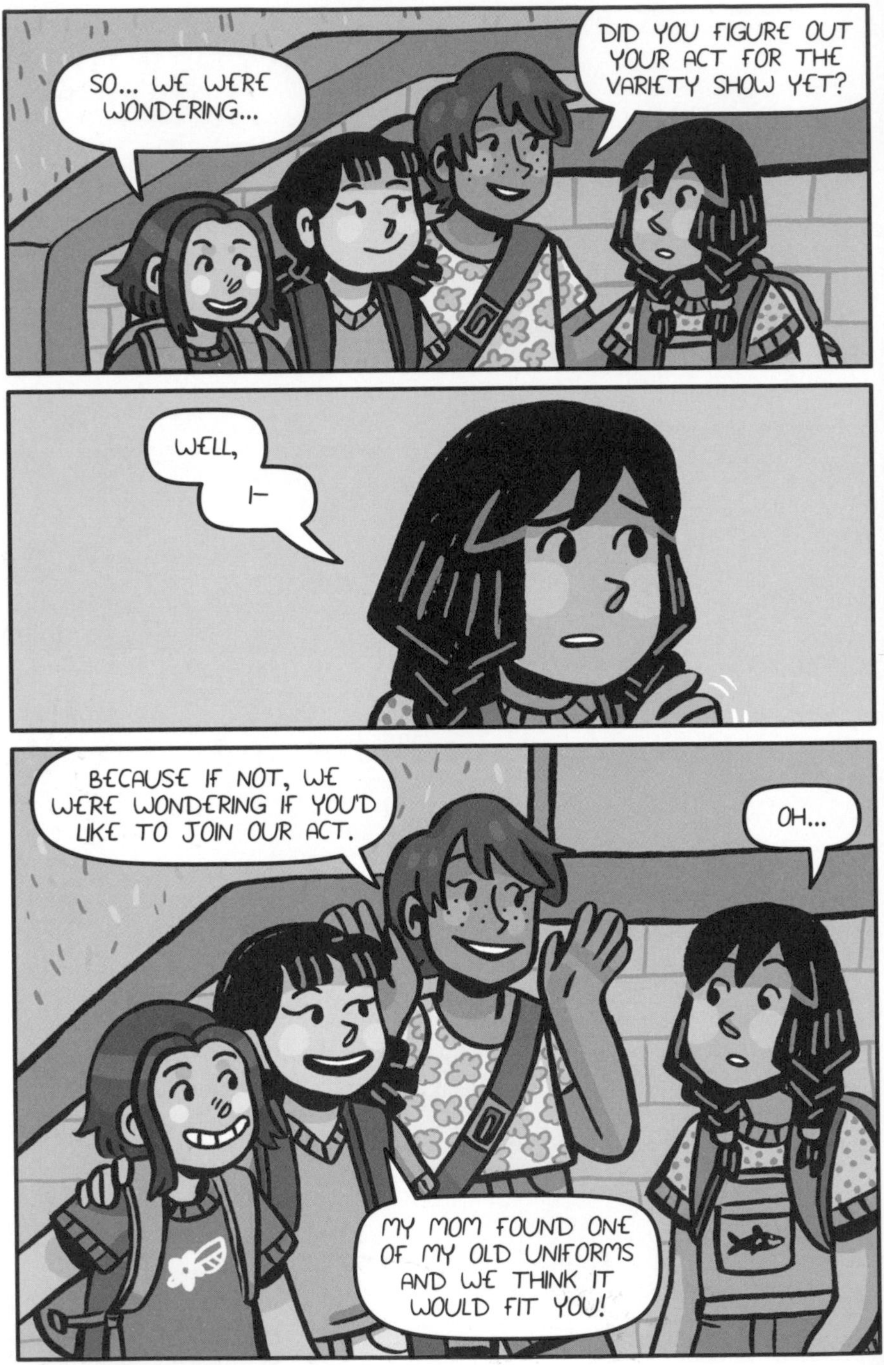
SO... WE WERE WONDERING...
DID YOU FIGURE OUT YOUR ACT FOR THE VARIETY SHOW YET?
WELL,
I–
BECAUSE IF NOT, WE WERE WONDERING IF YOU'D LIKE TO JOIN OUR ACT.
OH...
MY MOM FOUND ONE OF MY OLD UNIFORMS AND WE THINK IT WOULD FIT YOU!

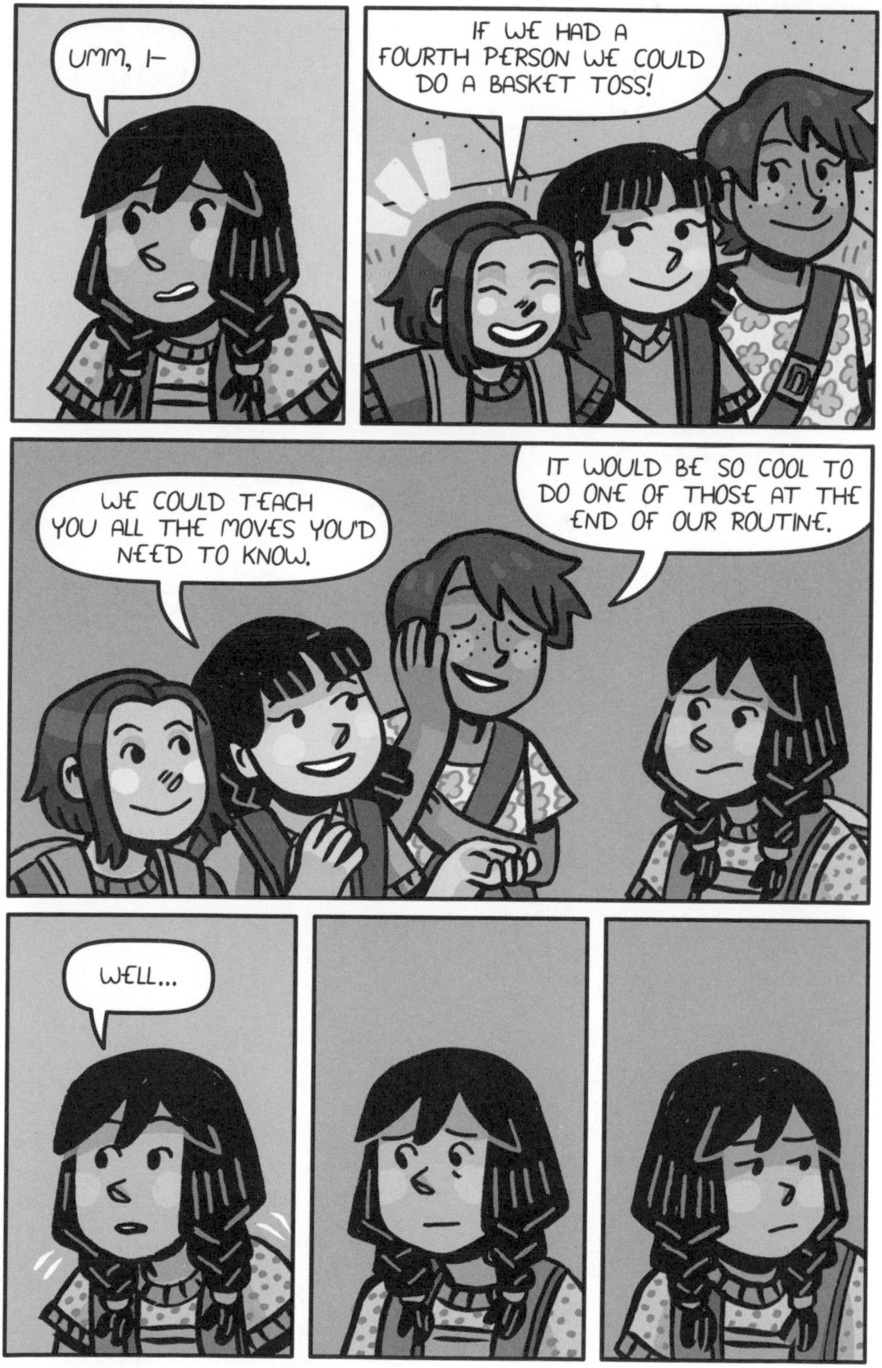
UMM, I—
IF WE HAD A FOURTH PERSON WE COULD DO A BASKET TOSS!
WE COULD TEACH YOU ALL THE MOVES YOU'D NEED TO KNOW.
IT WOULD BE SO COOL TO DO ONE OF THOSE AT THE END OF OUR ROUTINE.
WELL...

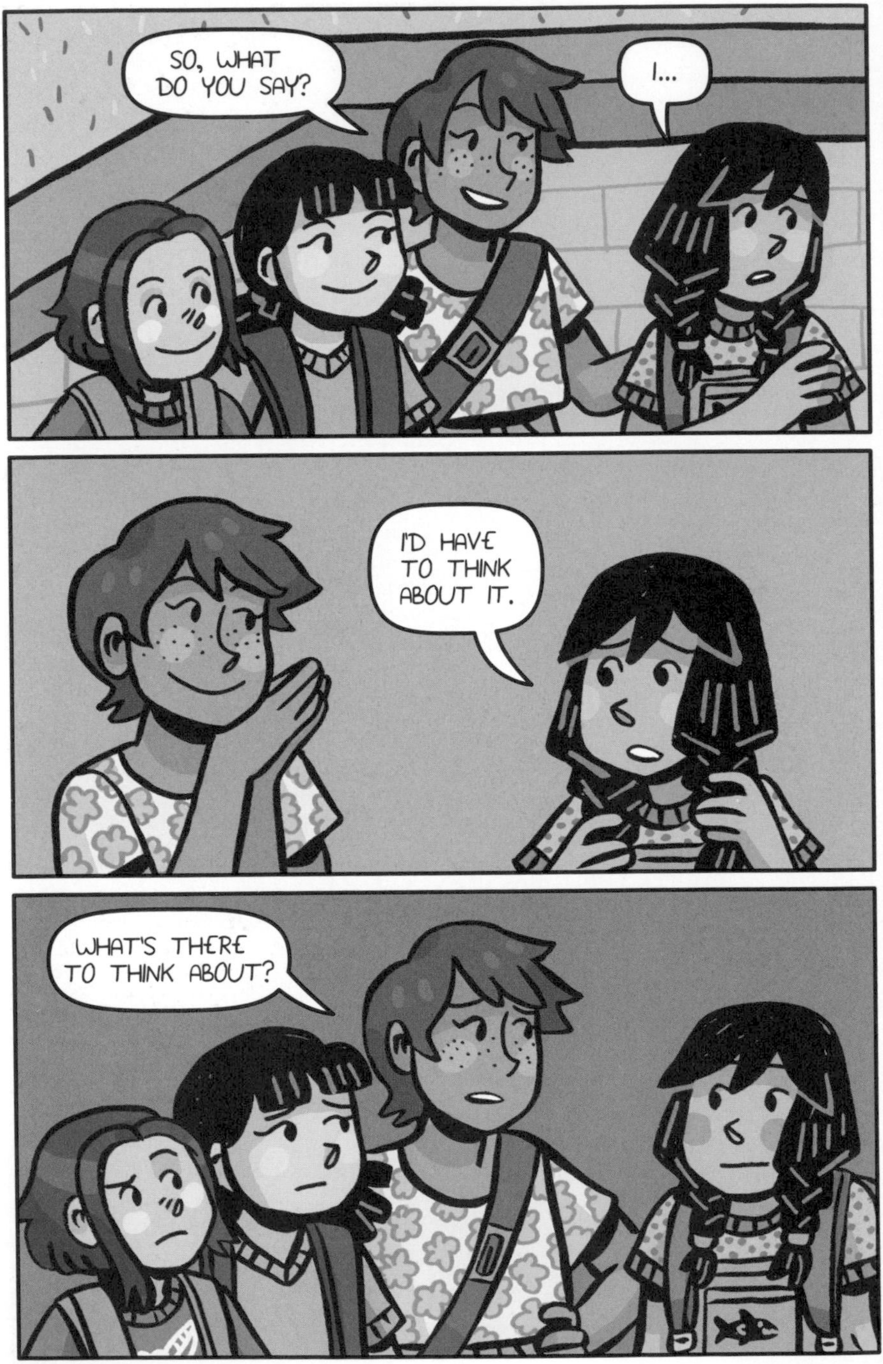
SO, WHAT DO YOU SAY?
I...
I'D HAVE TO THINK ABOUT IT.
WHAT'S THERE TO THINK ABOUT?

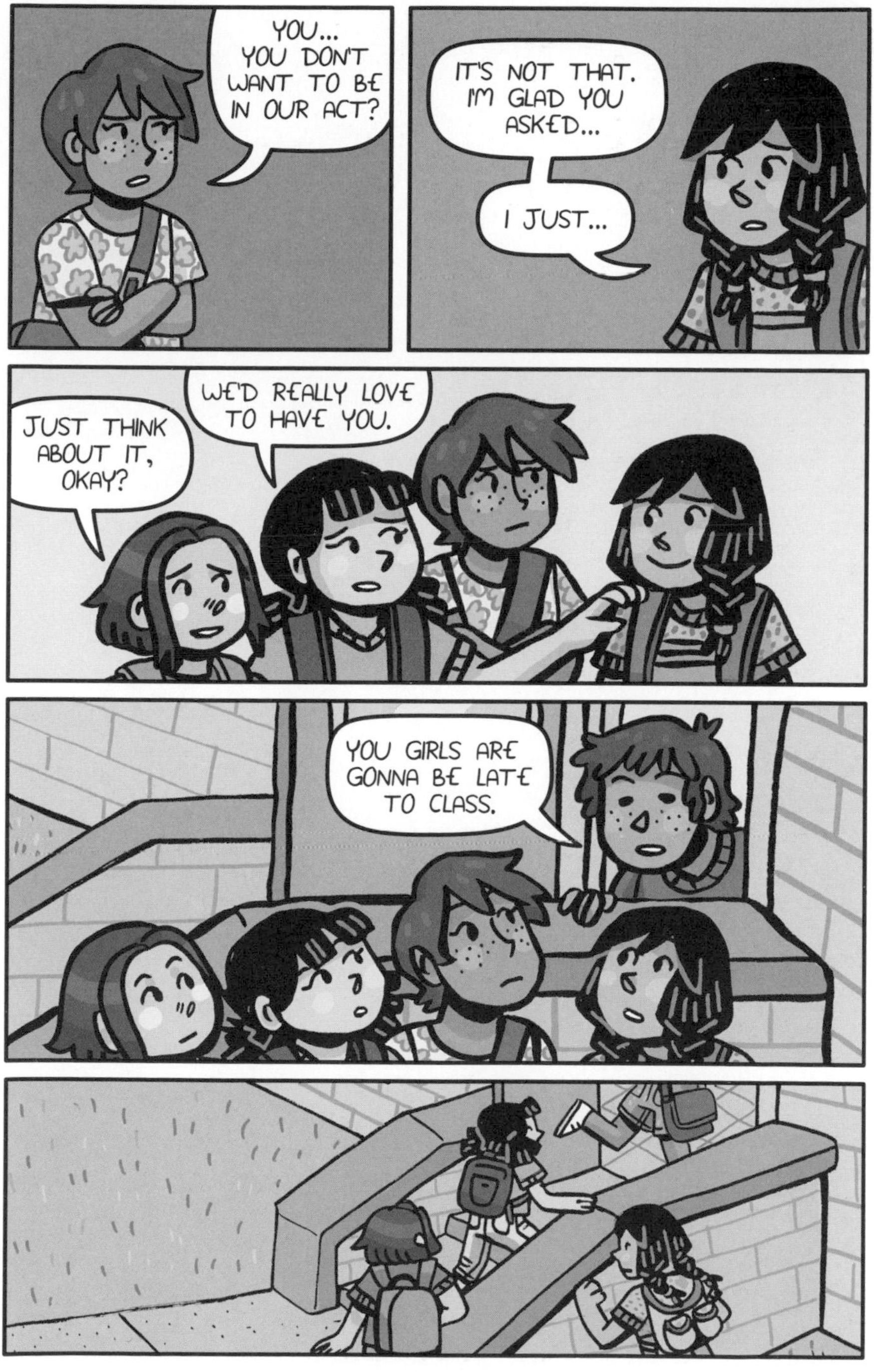
YOU... YOU DON'T WANT TO BE IN OUR ACT?
IT'S NOT THAT. I'M GLAD YOU ASKED...
I JUST...
JUST THINK ABOUT IT, OKAY?
WE'D REALLY LOVE TO HAVE YOU.
YOU GIRLS ARE GONNA BE LATE TO CLASS.

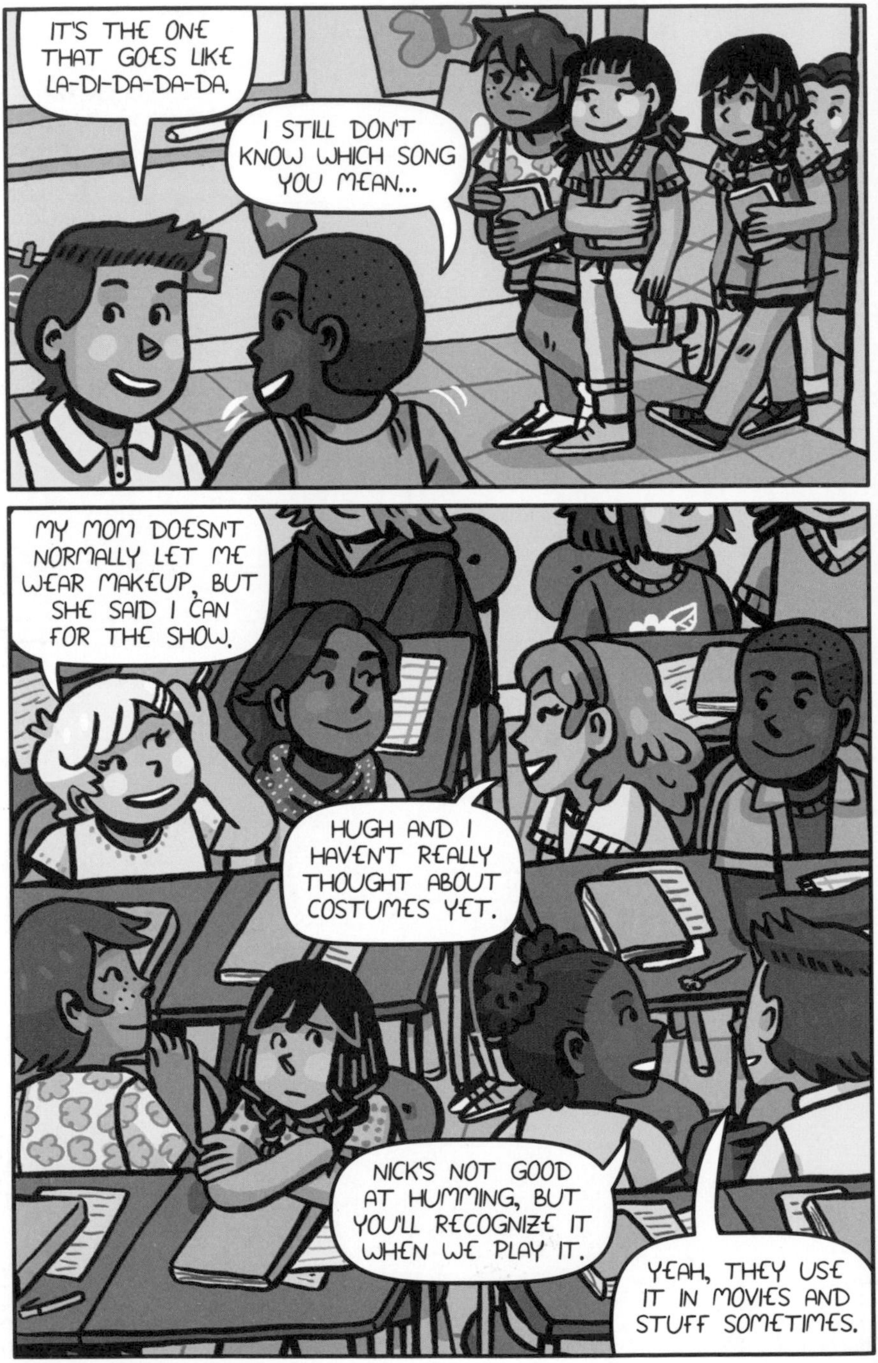
IT'S THE ONE THAT GOES LIKE LA-DI-DA-DA-DA.
I STILL DON'T KNOW WHICH SONG YOU MEAN...
MY MOM DOESN'T NORMALLY LET ME WEAR MAKEUP, BUT SHE SAID I CAN FOR THE SHOW.
HUGH AND I HAVEN'T REALLY THOUGHT ABOUT COSTUMES YET.
NICK'S NOT GOOD AT HUMMING, BUT YOU'LL RECOGNIZE IT WHEN WE PLAY IT.
YEAH, THEY USE IT IN MOVIES AND STUFF SOMETIMES.

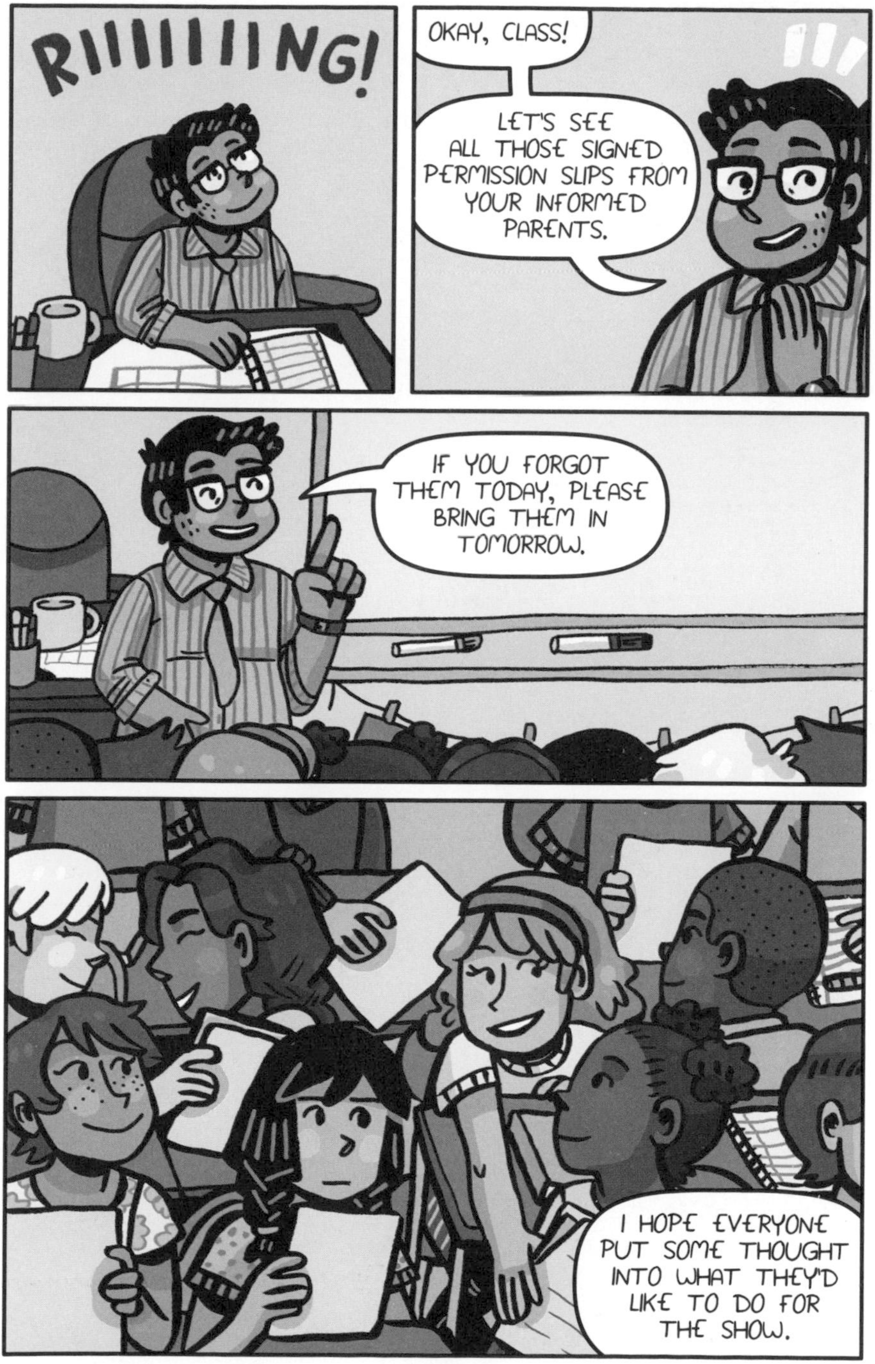
RIIIIIIING!
OKAY, CLASS!
LET'S SEE ALL THOSE SIGNED PERMISSION SLIPS FROM YOUR INFORMED PARENTS.
IF YOU FORGOT THEM TODAY, PLEASE BRING THEM IN TOMORROW.
I HOPE EVERYONE PUT SOME THOUGHT INTO WHAT THEY'D LIKE TO DO FOR THE SHOW.

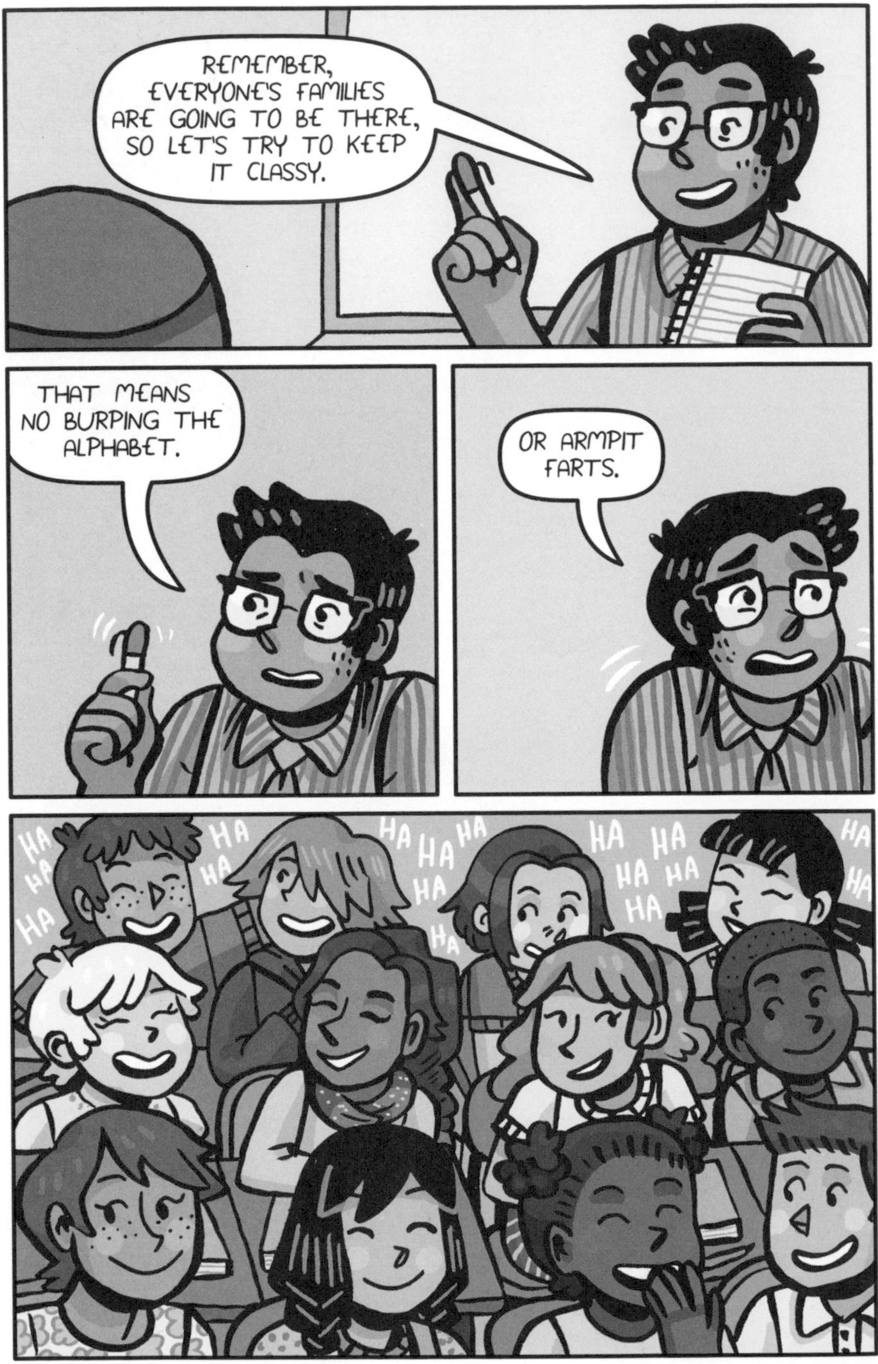
REMEMBER, EVERYONE'S FAMILIES ARE GOING TO BE THERE, SO LET'S TRY TO KEEP IT CLASSY.
THAT MEANS NO BURPING THE ALPHABET.
OR ARMPIT FARTS.

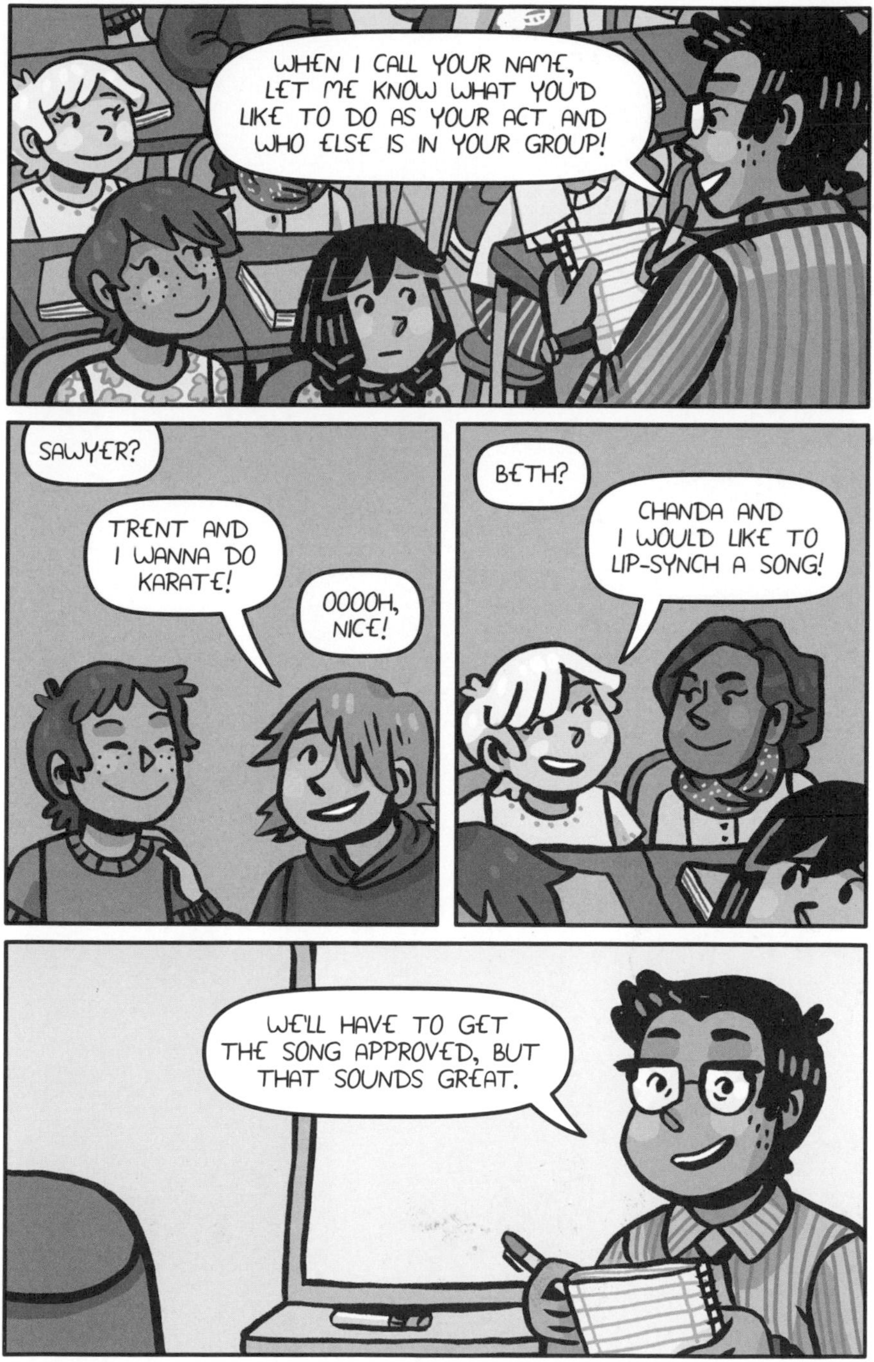
WHEN I CALL YOUR NAME, LET ME KNOW WHAT YOU'D LIKE TO DO AS YOUR ACT AND WHO ELSE IS IN YOUR GROUP!
SAWYER?
TRENT AND I WANNA DO KARATE!
OOOOH, NICE!
BETH?
CHANDA AND I WOULD LIKE TO LIP-SYNCH A SONG!
WE'LL HAVE TO GET THE SONG APPROVED, BUT THAT SOUNDS GREAT.

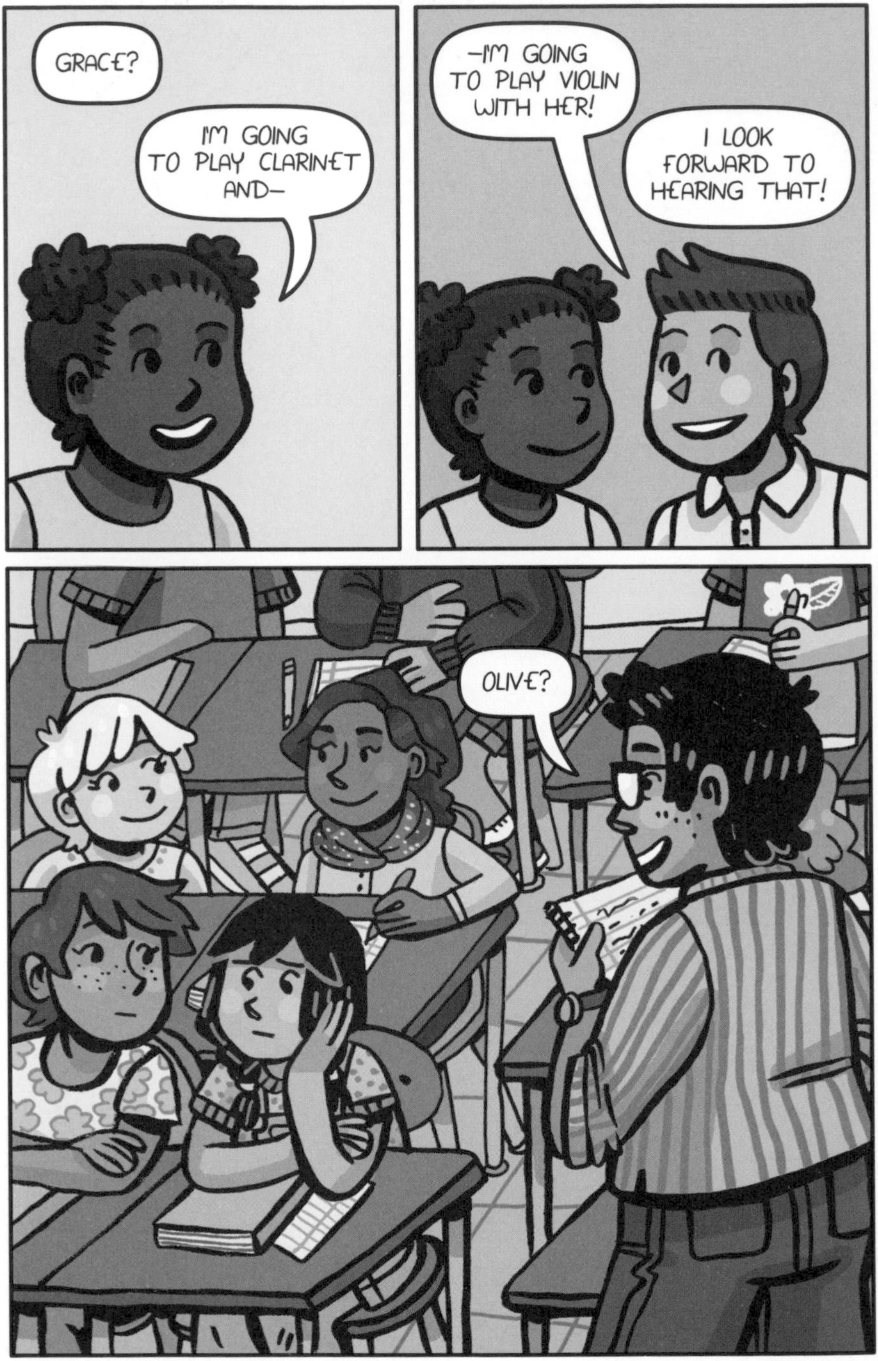
GRACE?
I'M GOING TO PLAY CLARINET AND—
—I'M GOING TO PLAY VIOLIN WITH HER!
I LOOK FORWARD TO HEARING THAT!
OLIVE?

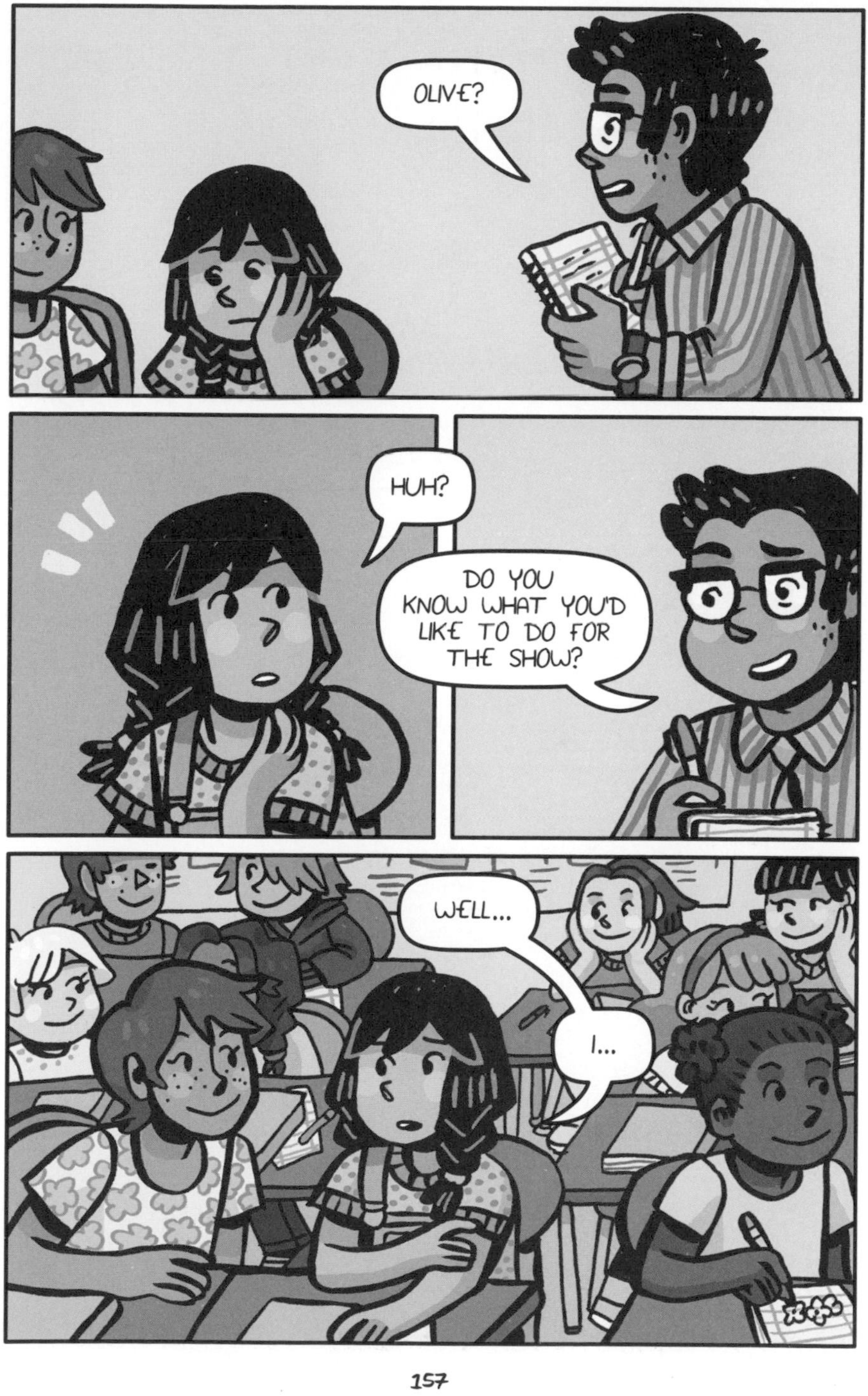
OLIVE?
HUH?
DO YOU KNOW WHAT YOU'D LIKE TO DO FOR THE SHOW?
WELL...
I...

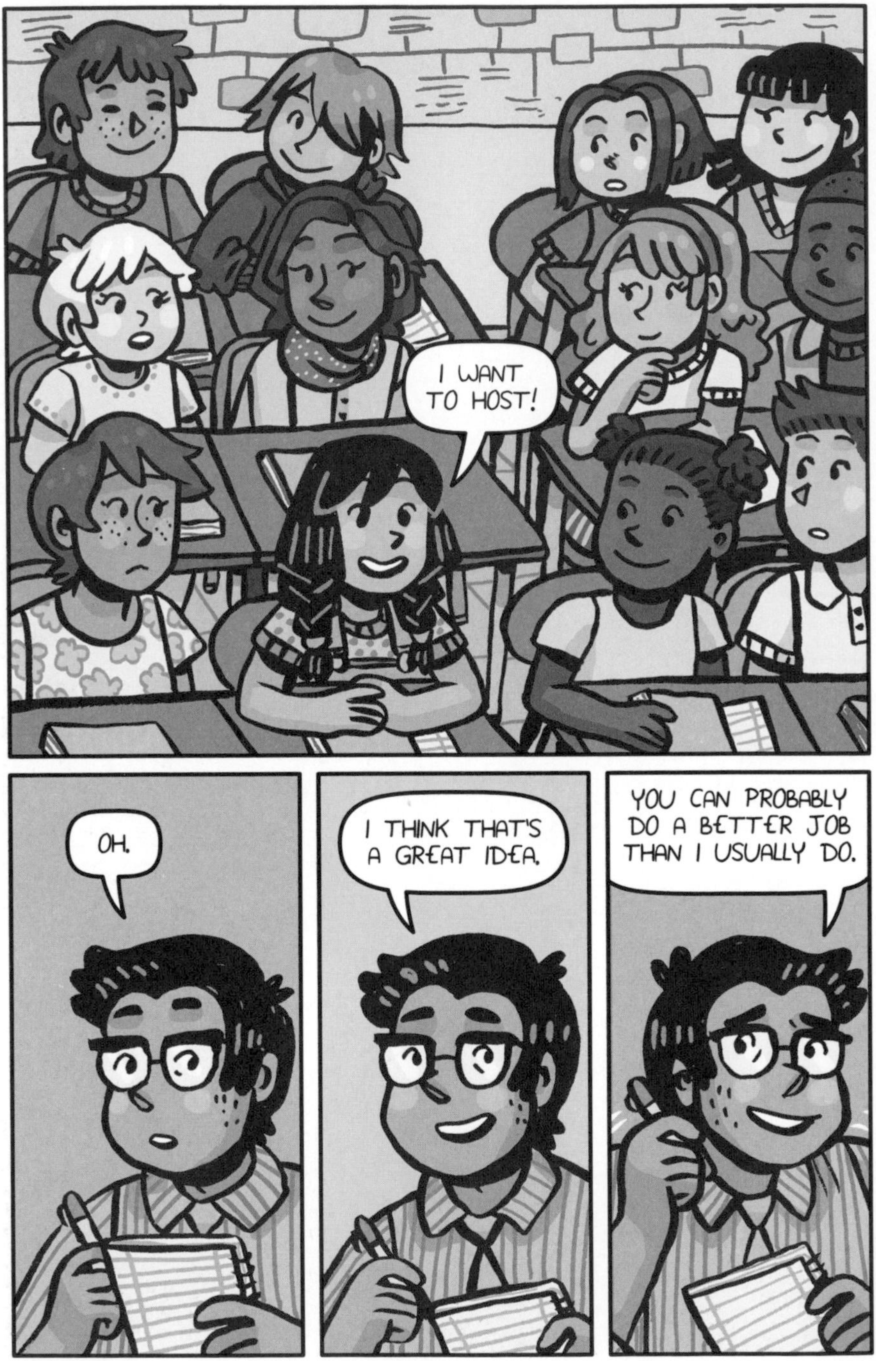
I WANT TO HOST!
OH.
I THINK THAT'S A GREAT IDEA.
YOU CAN PROBABLY DO A BETTER JOB THAN I USUALLY DO.

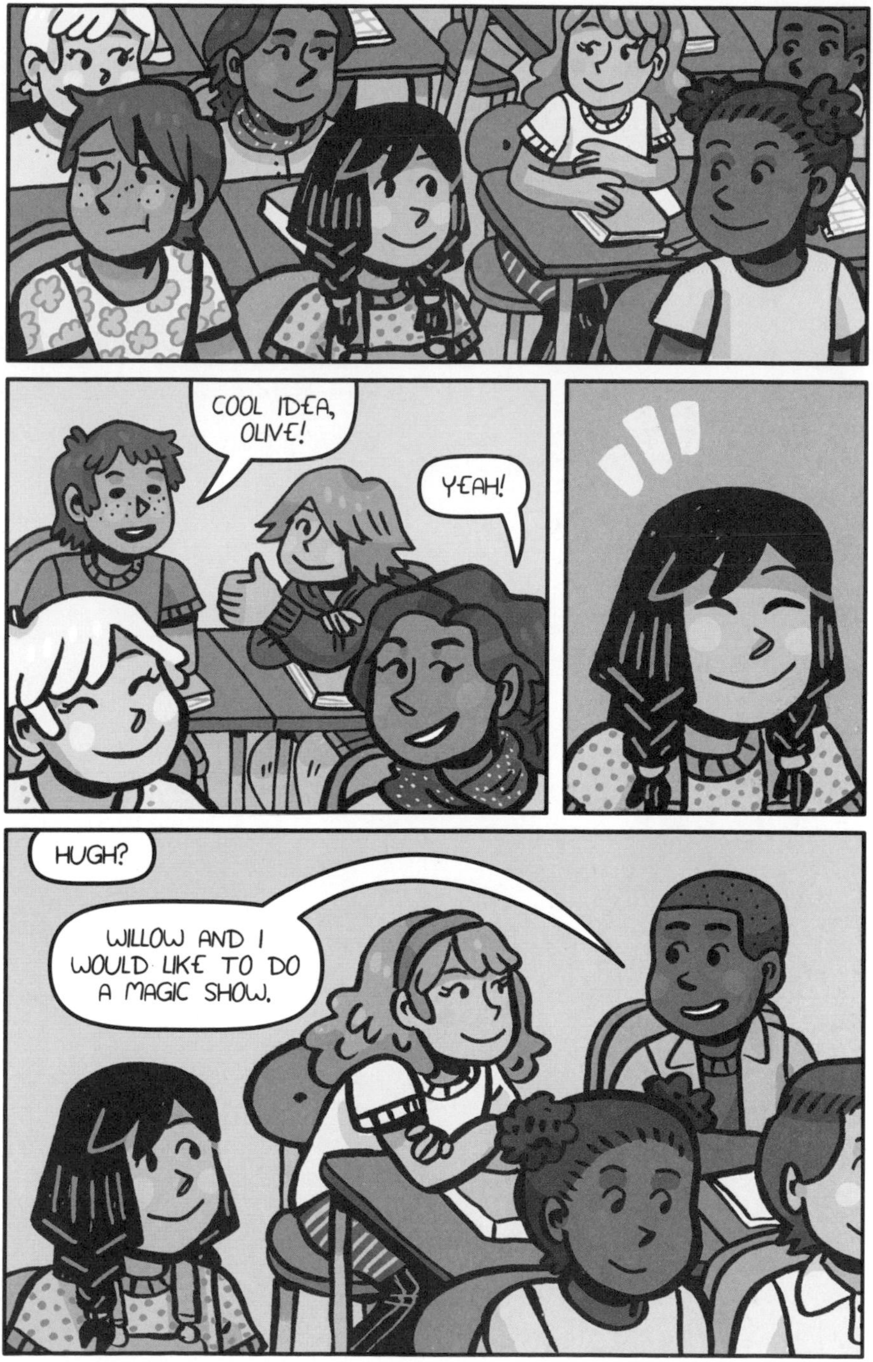
COOL IDEA, OLIVE!
YEAH!
HUGH?
WILLOW AND I WOULD LIKE TO DO A MAGIC SHOW.

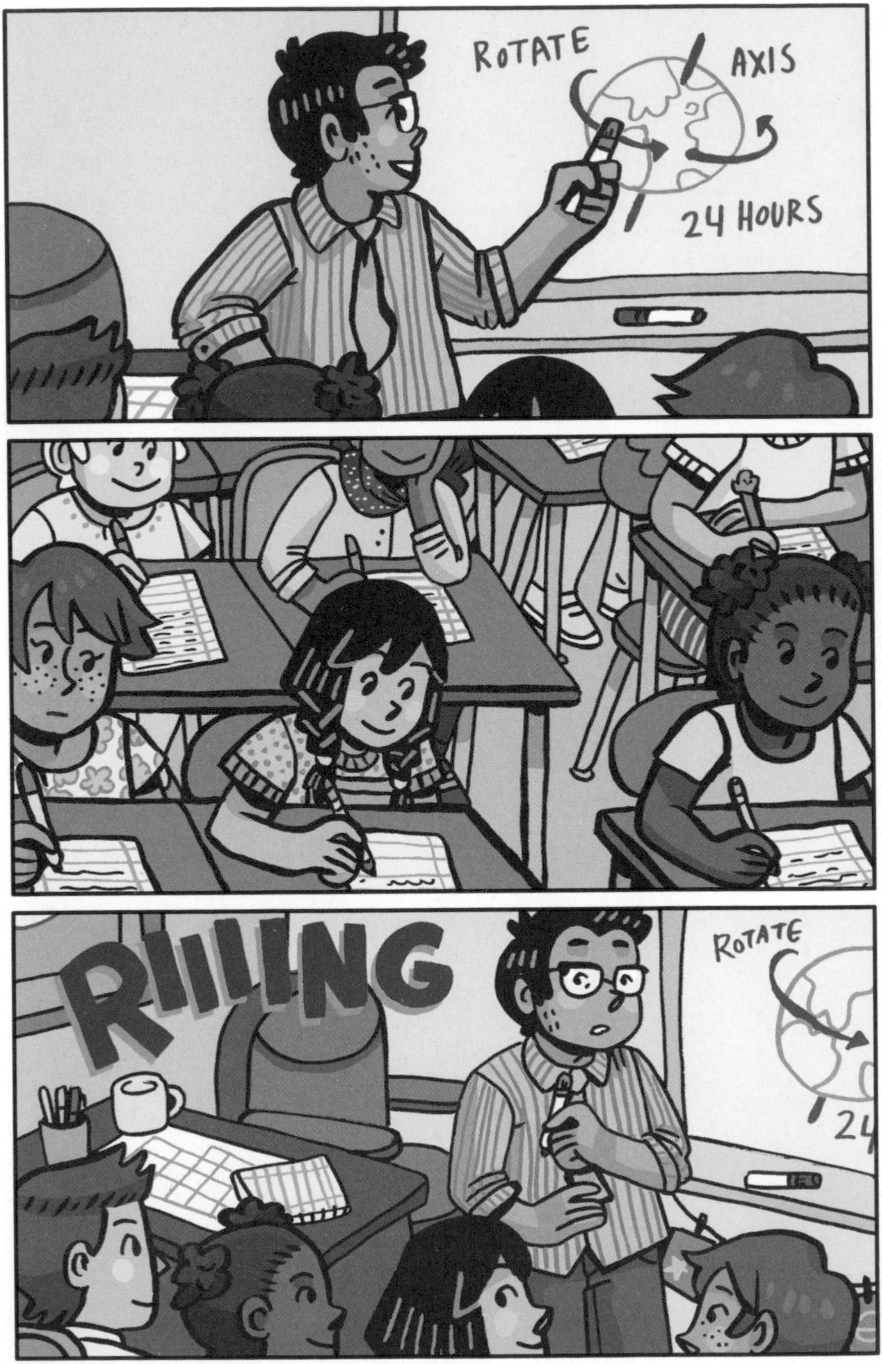
ROTATE
AXIS
24 HOURS
RIIIING
ROTATE
24

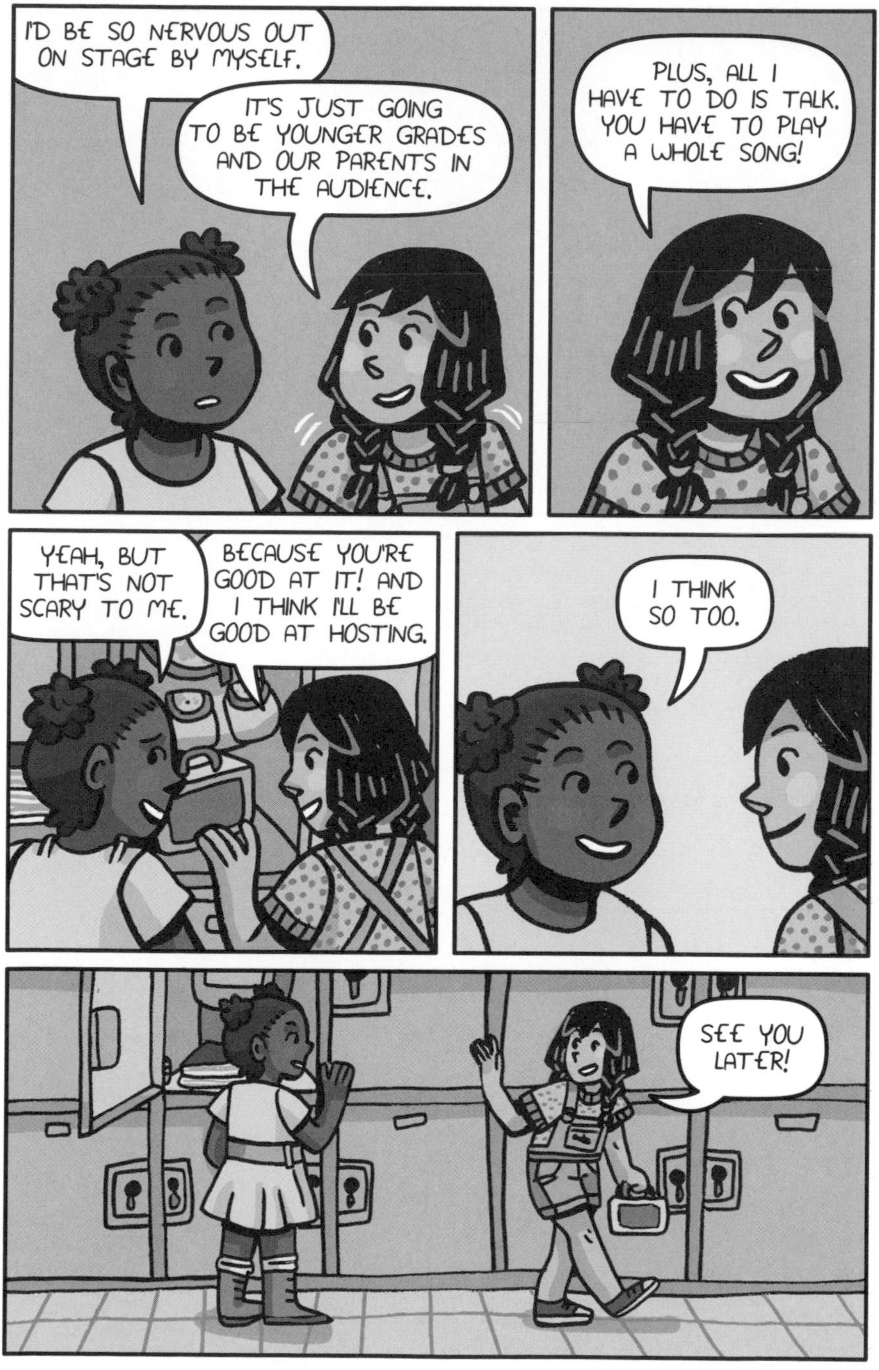
I'D BE SO NERVOUS OUT ON STAGE BY MYSELF.
IT'S JUST GOING TO BE YOUNGER GRADES AND OUR PARENTS IN THE AUDIENCE.
PLUS, ALL I HAVE TO DO IS TALK. YOU HAVE TO PLAY A WHOLE SONG!
YEAH, BUT THAT'S NOT SCARY TO ME.
BECAUSE YOU'RE GOOD AT IT! AND I THINK I'LL BE GOOD AT HOSTING.
I THINK SO TOO.
SEE YOU LATER!

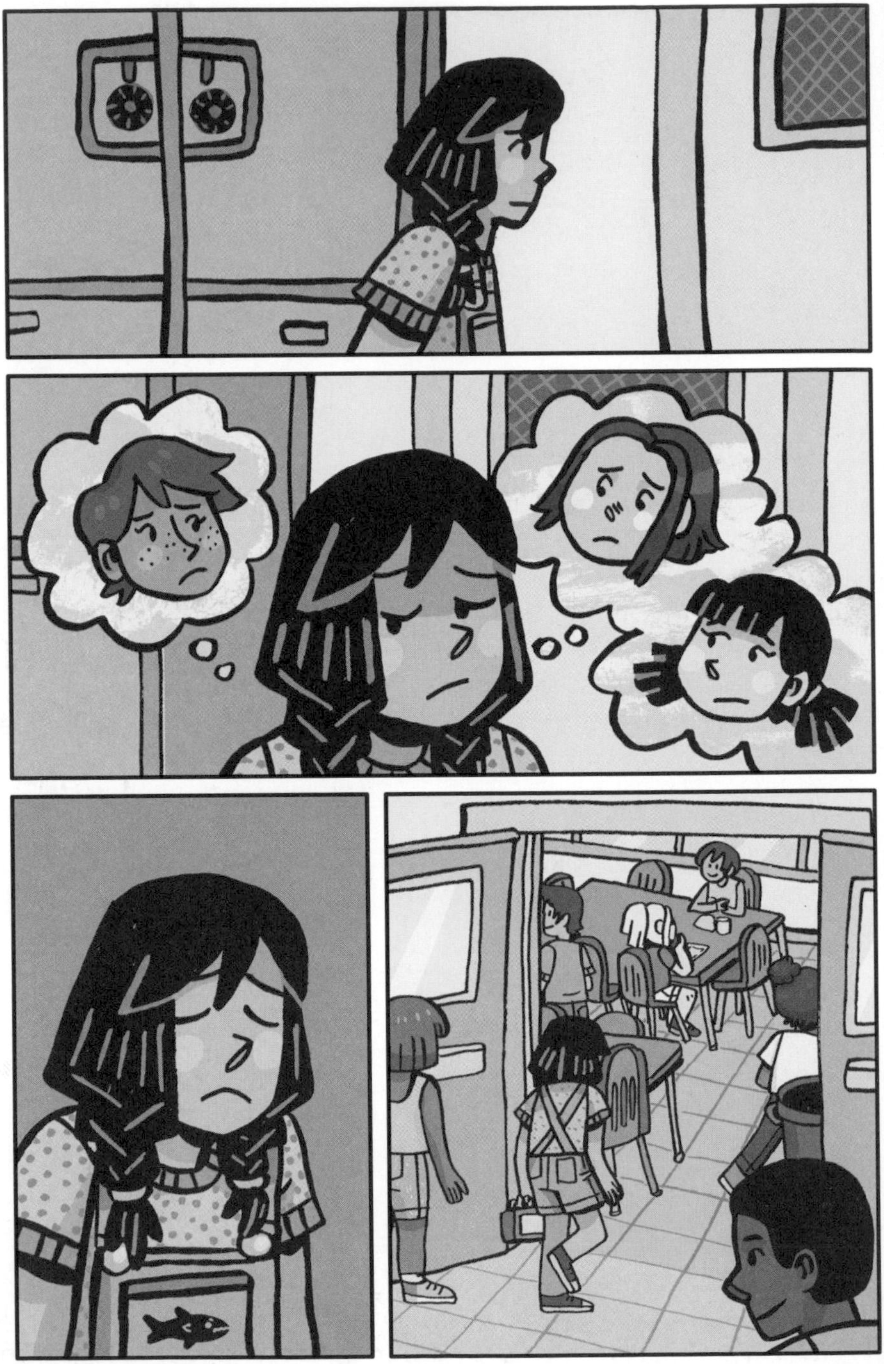

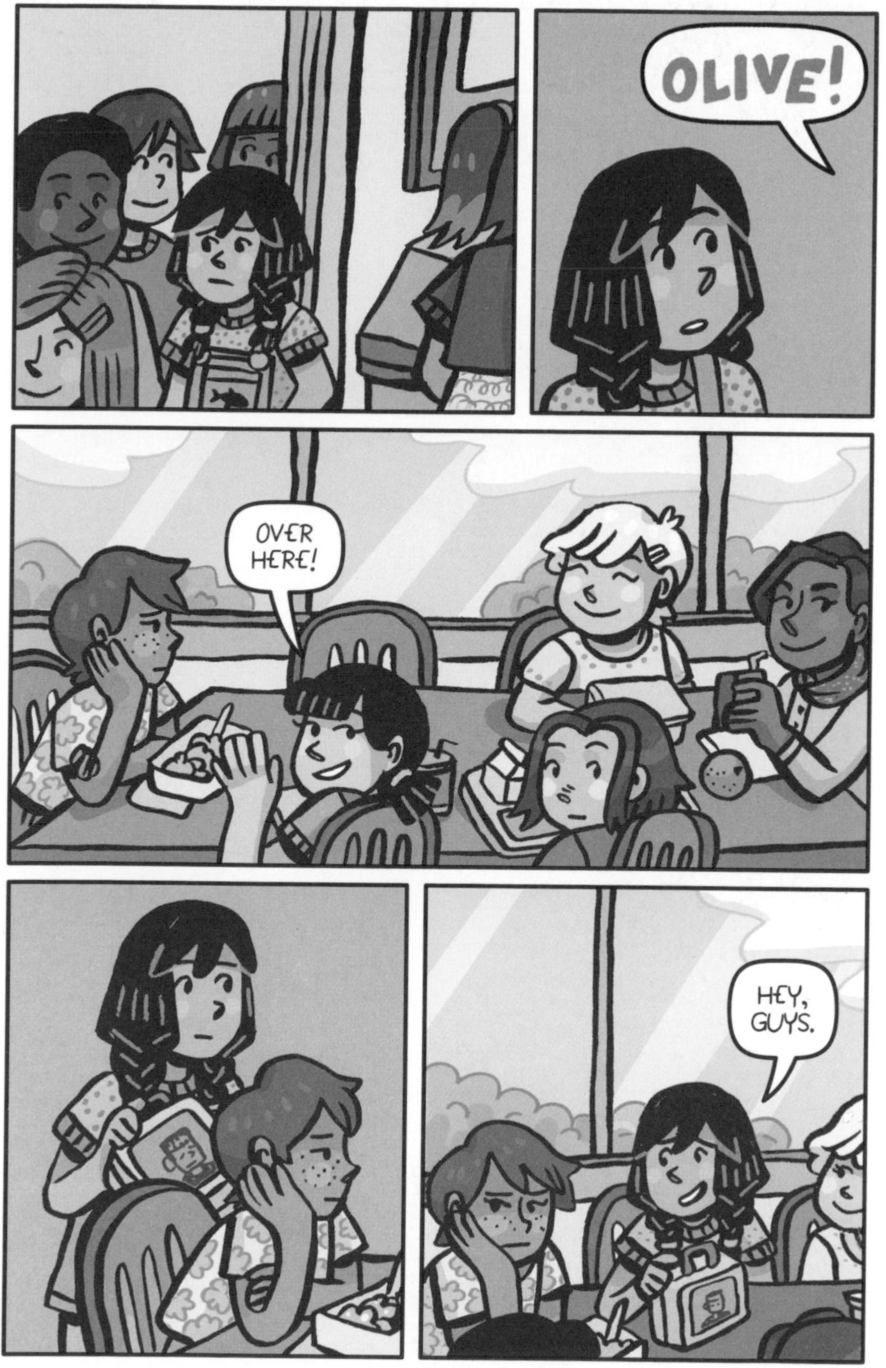
OLIVE!
OVER HERE!
HEY, GUYS.

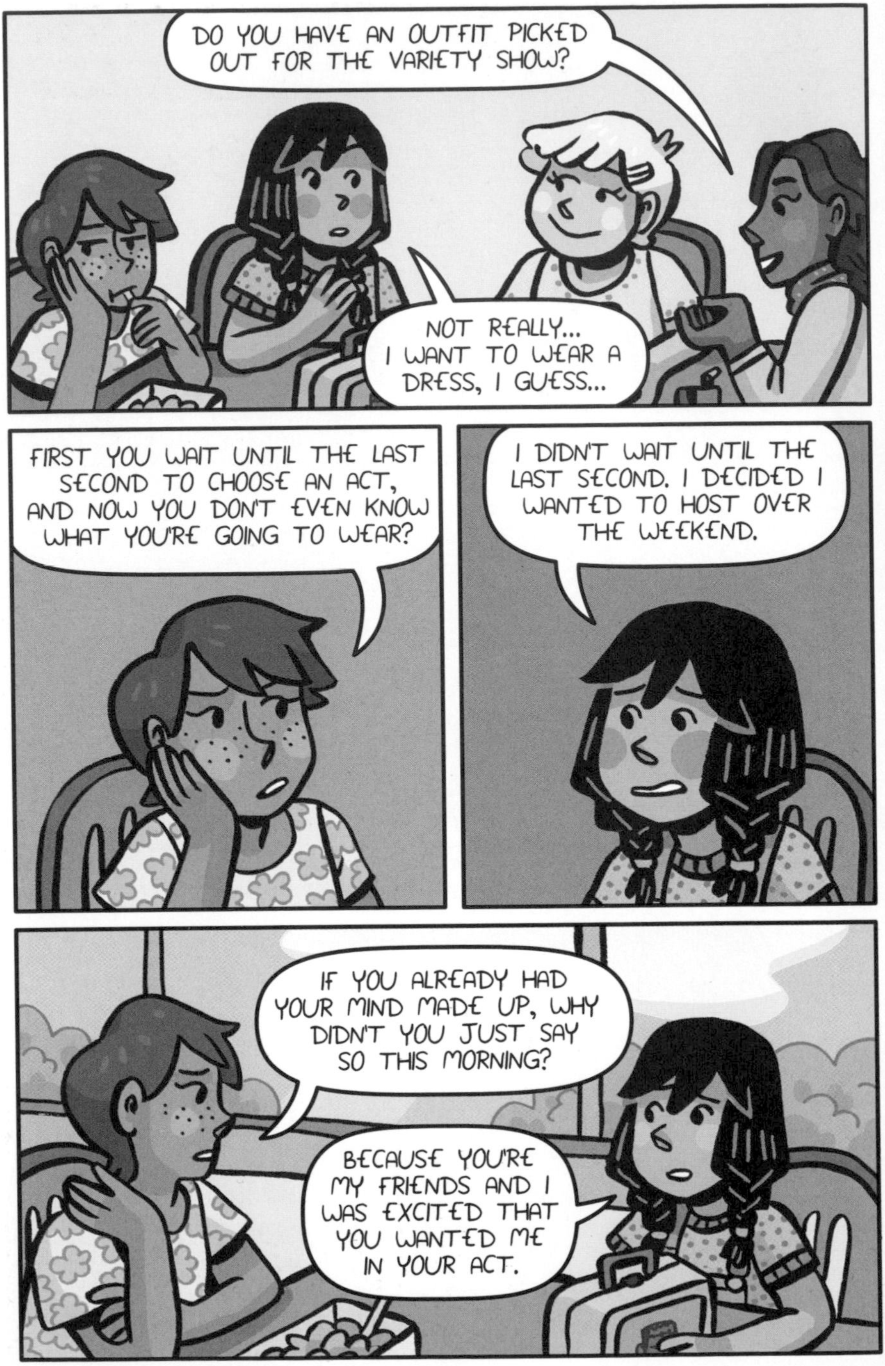
DO YOU HAVE AN OUTFIT PICKED OUT FOR THE VARIETY SHOW?
NOT REALLY... I WANT TO WEAR A DRESS, I GUESS...
FIRST YOU WAIT UNTIL THE LAST SECOND TO CHOOSE AN ACT, AND NOW YOU DON'T EVEN KNOW WHAT YOU'RE GOING TO WEAR?
I DIDN'T WAIT UNTIL THE LAST SECOND. I DECIDED I WANTED TO HOST OVER THE WEEKEND.
IF YOU ALREADY HAD YOUR MIND MADE UP, WHY DIDN'T YOU JUST SAY SO THIS MORNING?
BECAUSE YOU'RE MY FRIENDS AND I WAS EXCITED THAT YOU WANTED ME IN YOUR ACT.

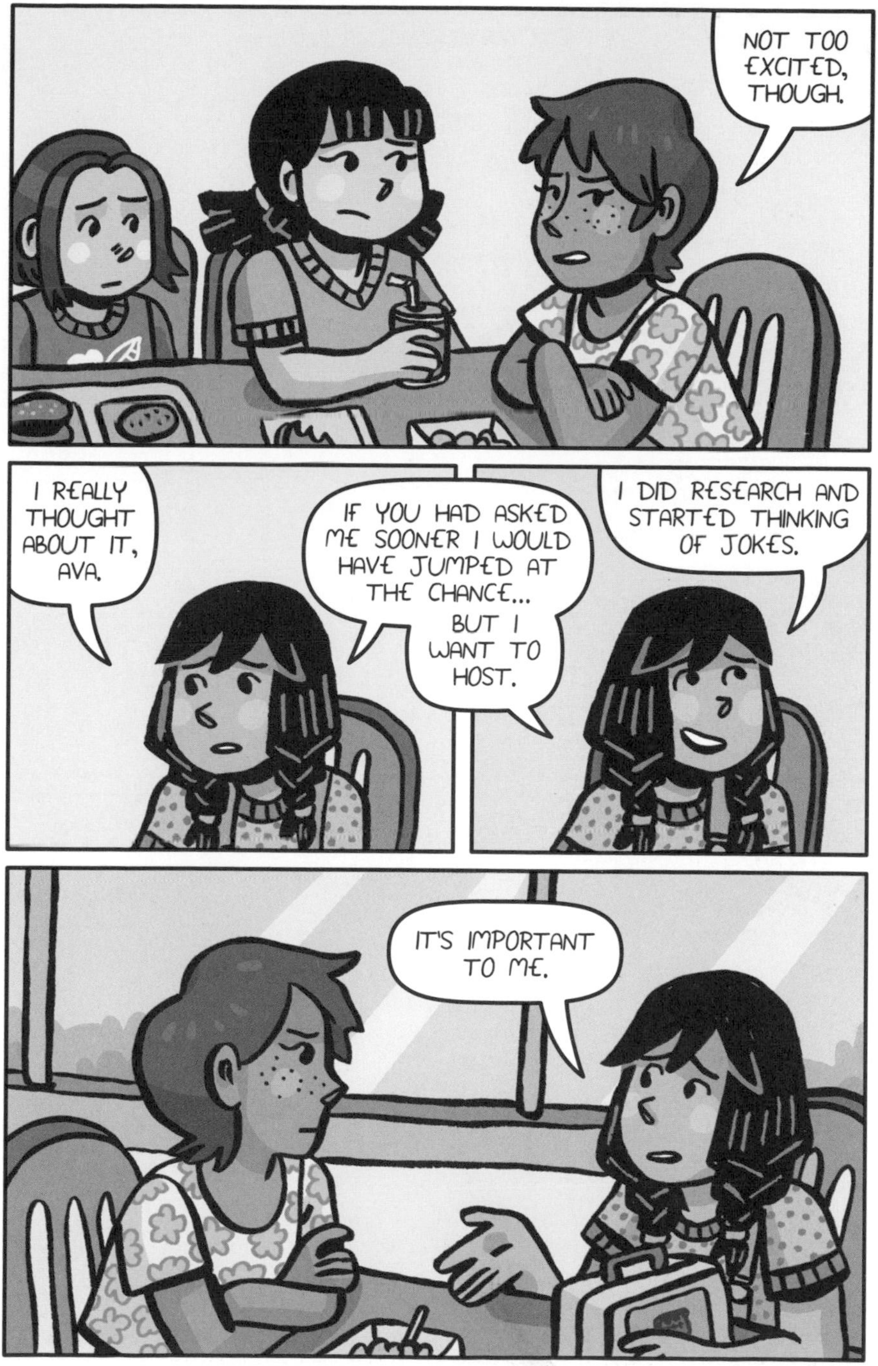
NOT TOO EXCITED, THOUGH.
I REALLY THOUGHT ABOUT IT, AVA.
IF YOU HAD ASKED ME SOONER I WOULD HAVE JUMPED AT THE CHANCE...
BUT I WANT TO HOST.
I DID RESEARCH AND STARTED THINKING OF JOKES.
IT'S IMPORTANT TO ME.

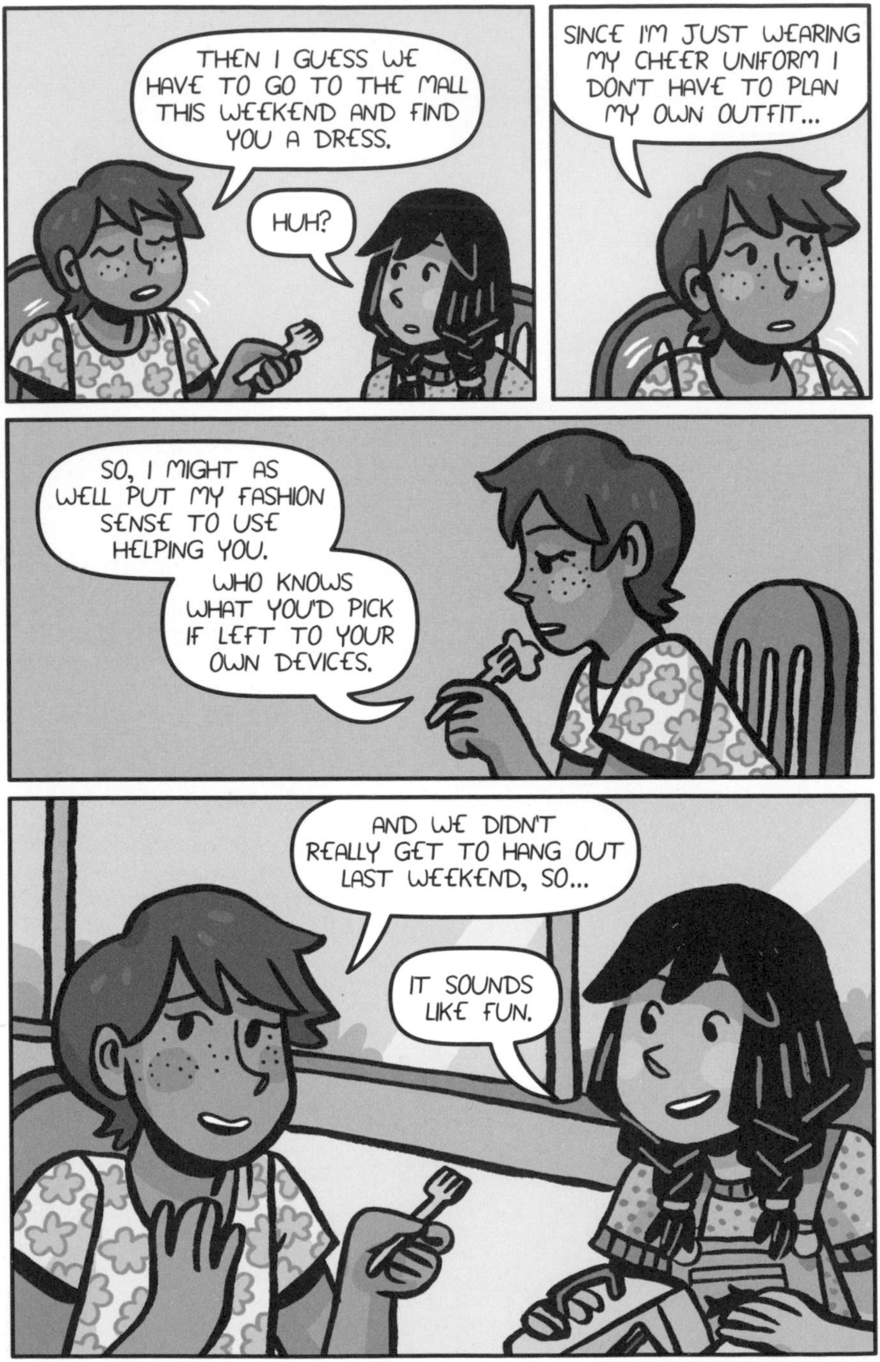
THEN I GUESS WE HAVE TO GO TO THE MALL THIS WEEKEND AND FIND YOU A DRESS.
HUH?
SINCE I'M JUST WEARING MY CHEER UNIFORM I DON'T HAVE TO PLAN MY OWN OUTFIT...
SO, I MIGHT AS WELL PUT MY FASHION SENSE TO USE HELPING YOU.
WHO KNOWS WHAT YOU'D PICK IF LEFT TO YOUR OWN DEVICES.
AND WE DIDN'T REALLY GET TO HANG OUT LAST WEEKEND, SO...
IT SOUNDS LIKE FUN.

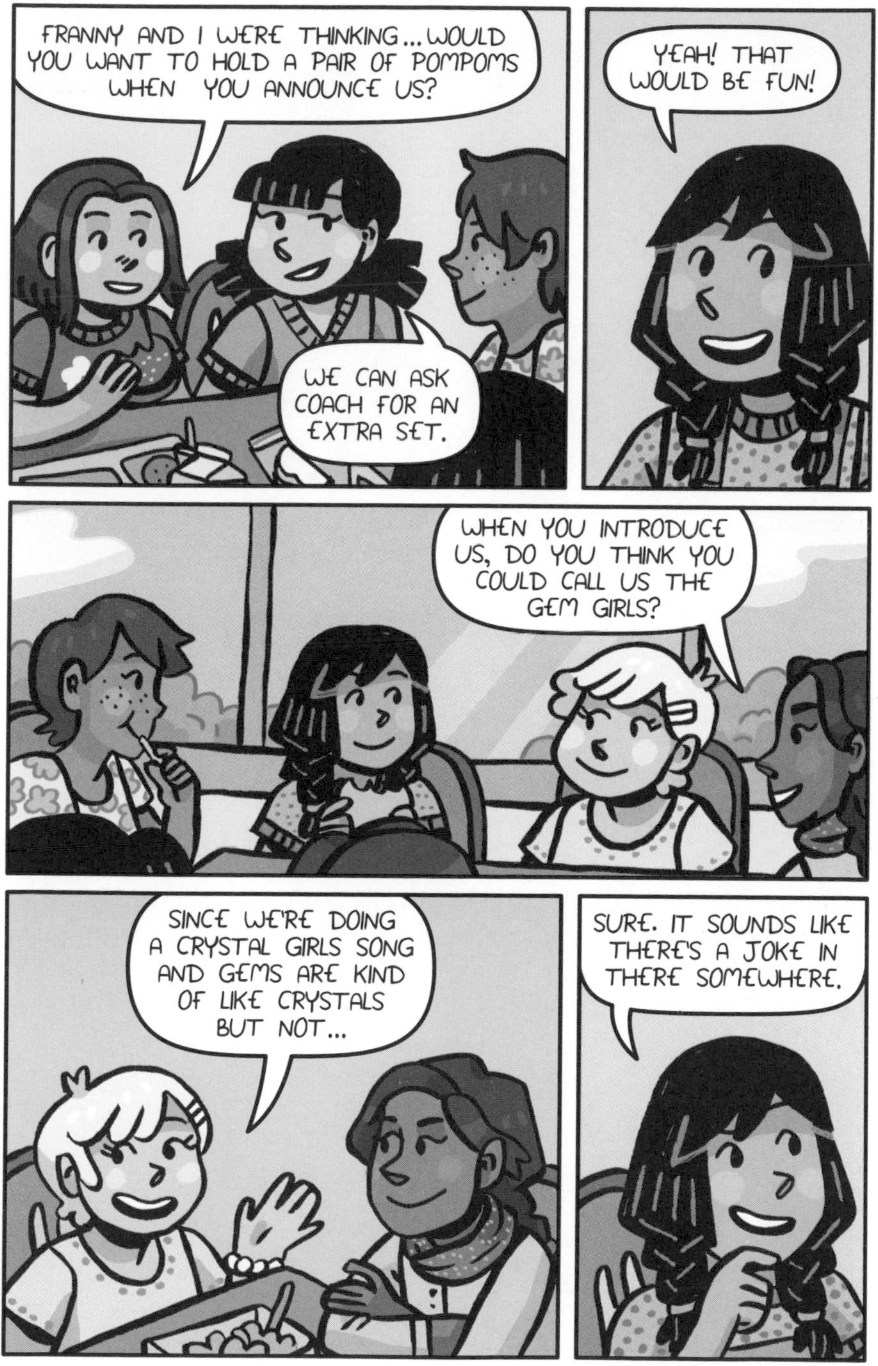
FRANNY AND I WERE THINKING... WOULD YOU WANT TO HOLD A PAIR OF POMPOMS WHEN YOU ANNOUNCE US?
WE CAN ASK COACH FOR AN EXTRA SET.
YEAH! THAT WOULD BE FUN!
WHEN YOU INTRODUCE US, DO YOU THINK YOU COULD CALL US THE GEM GIRLS?
SINCE WE'RE DOING A CRYSTAL GIRLS SONG AND GEMS ARE KIND OF LIKE CRYSTALS BUT NOT...
SURE. IT SOUNDS LIKE THERE'S A JOKE IN THERE SOMEWHERE.

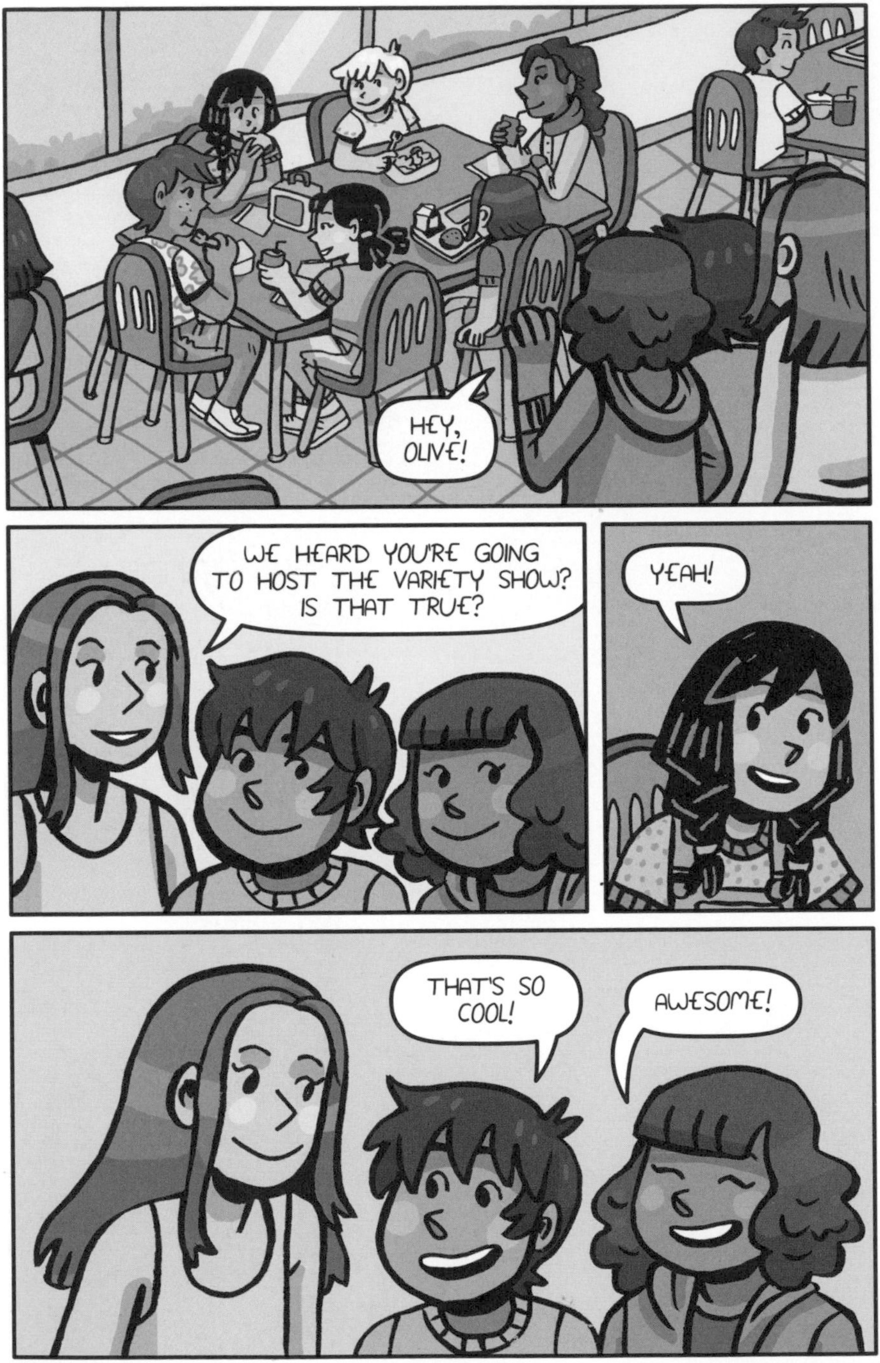
HEY, OLIVE!
WE HEARD YOU'RE GOING TO HOST THE VARIETY SHOW? IS THAT TRUE?
YEAH!
THAT'S SO COOL!
AWESOME!

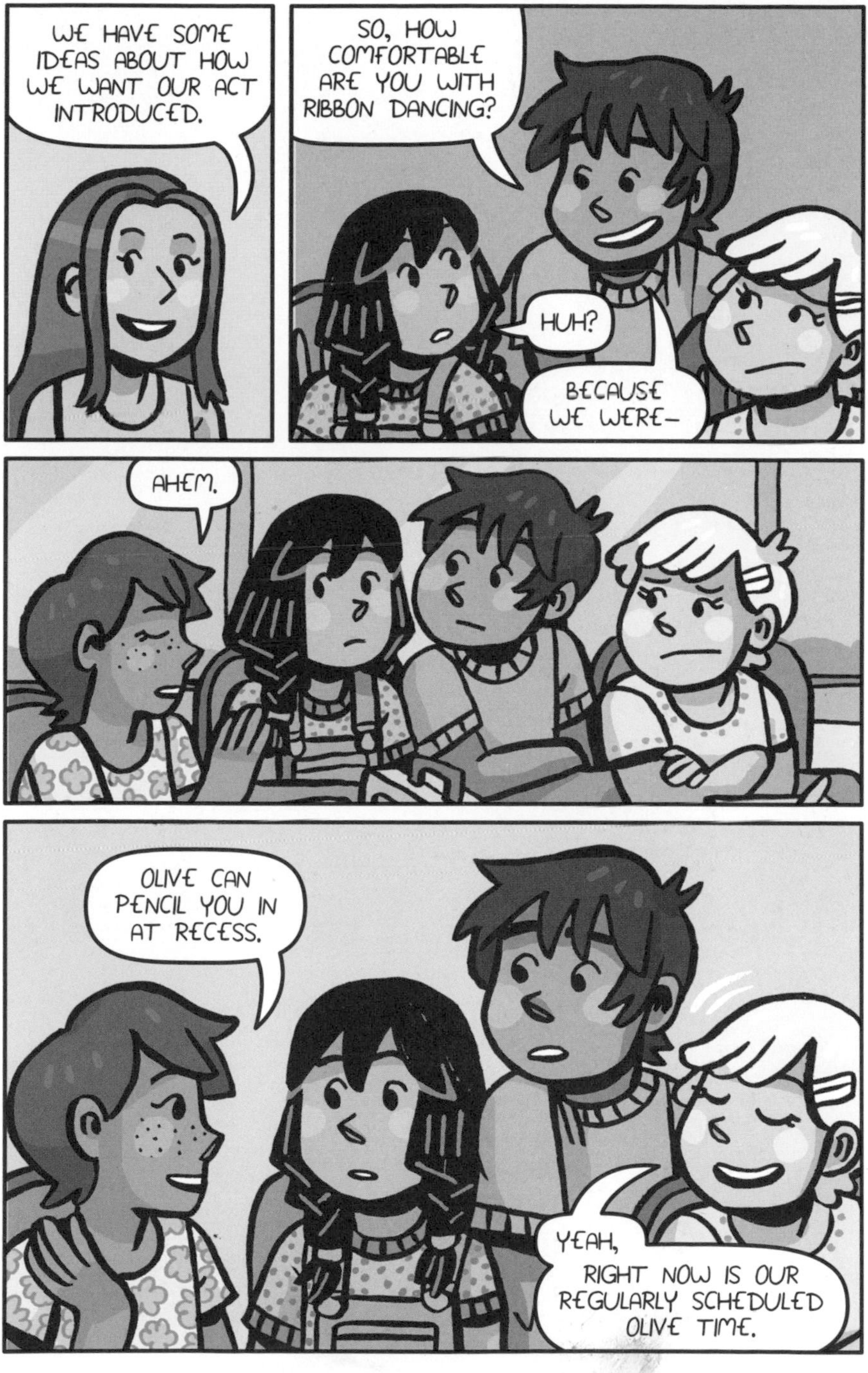
WE HAVE SOME IDEAS ABOUT HOW WE WANT OUR ACT INTRODUCED.
SO, HOW COMFORTABLE ARE YOU WITH RIBBON DANCING?
HUH?
BECAUSE WE WERE–
AHEM.
OLIVE CAN PENCIL YOU IN AT RECESS.
YEAH,
RIGHT NOW IS OUR REGULARLY SCHEDULED OLIVE TIME.

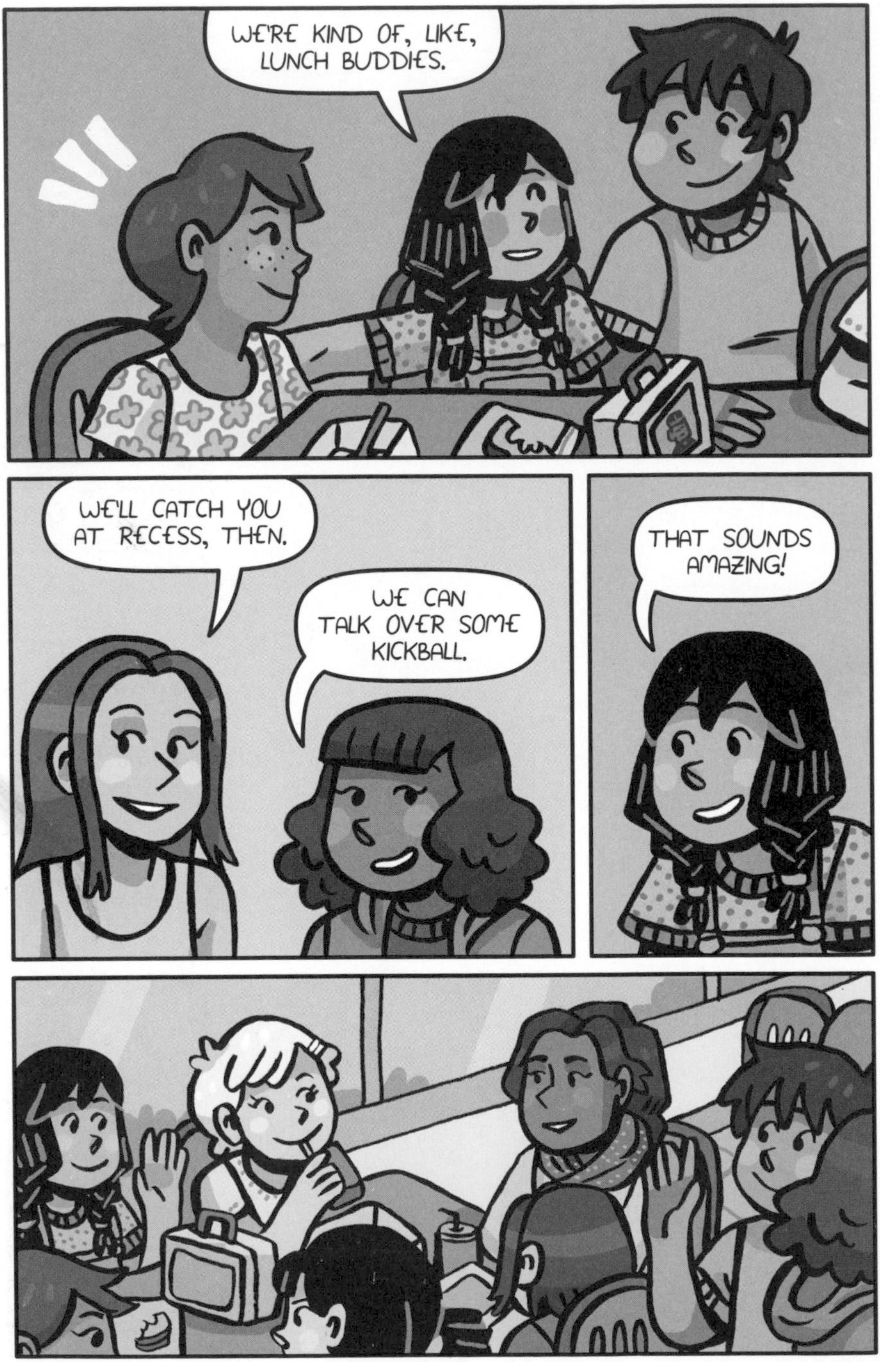
WE'RE KIND OF, LIKE, LUNCH BUDDIES.
WE'LL CATCH YOU AT RECESS, THEN.
WE CAN TALK OVER SOME KICKBALL.
THAT SOUNDS AMAZING!

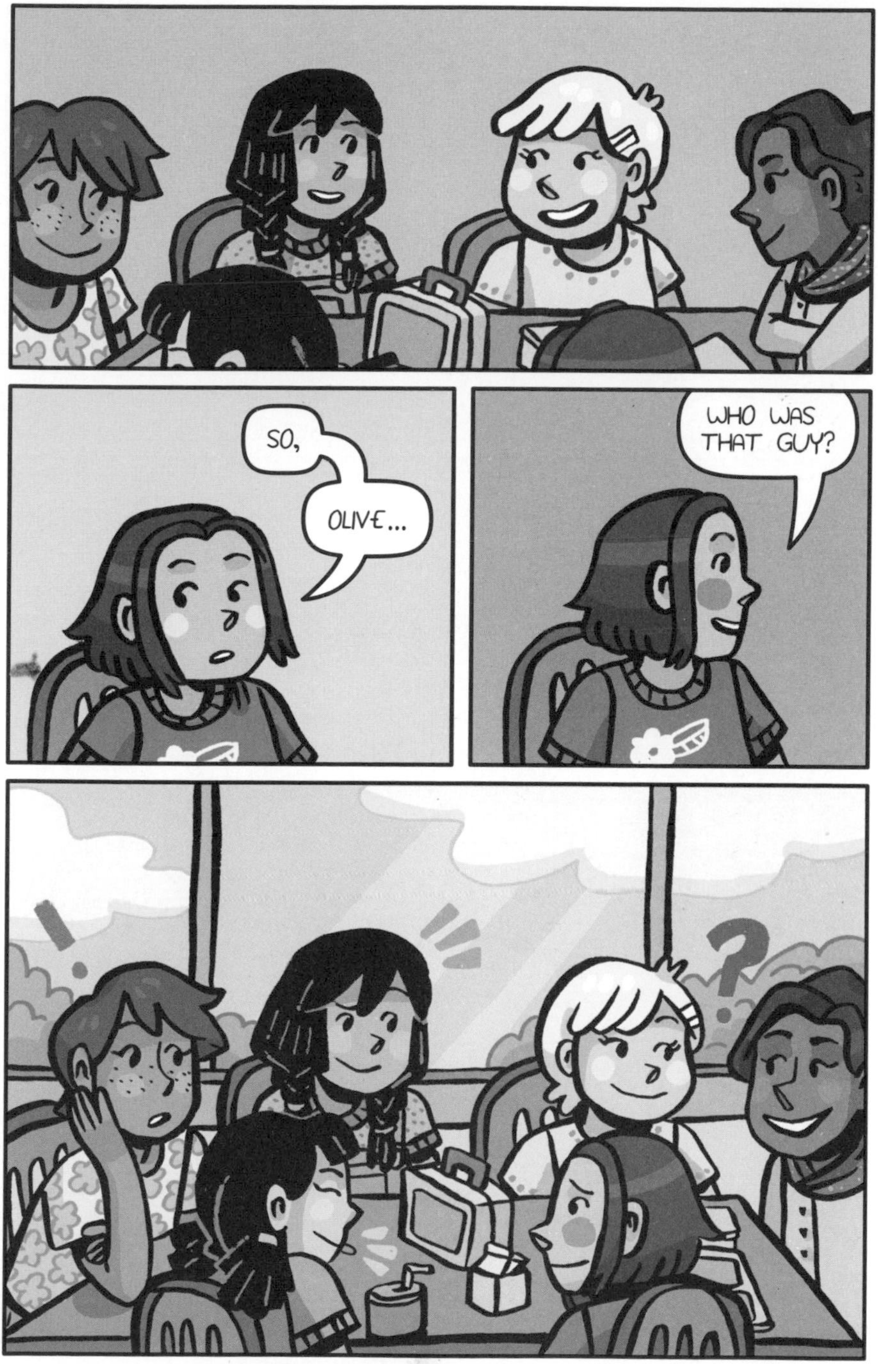
SO,
OLIVE...
WHO WAS THAT GUY?
!
?

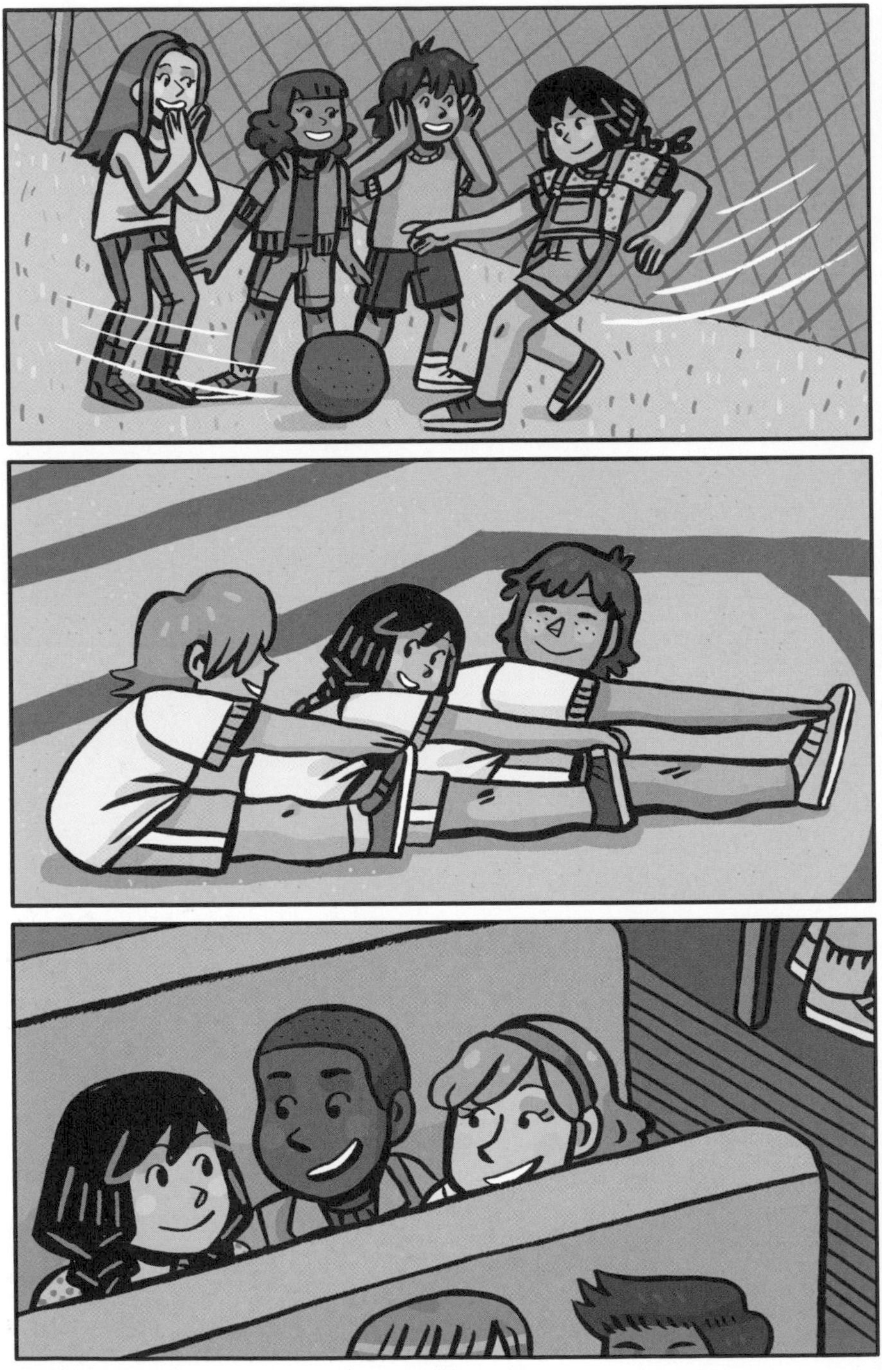

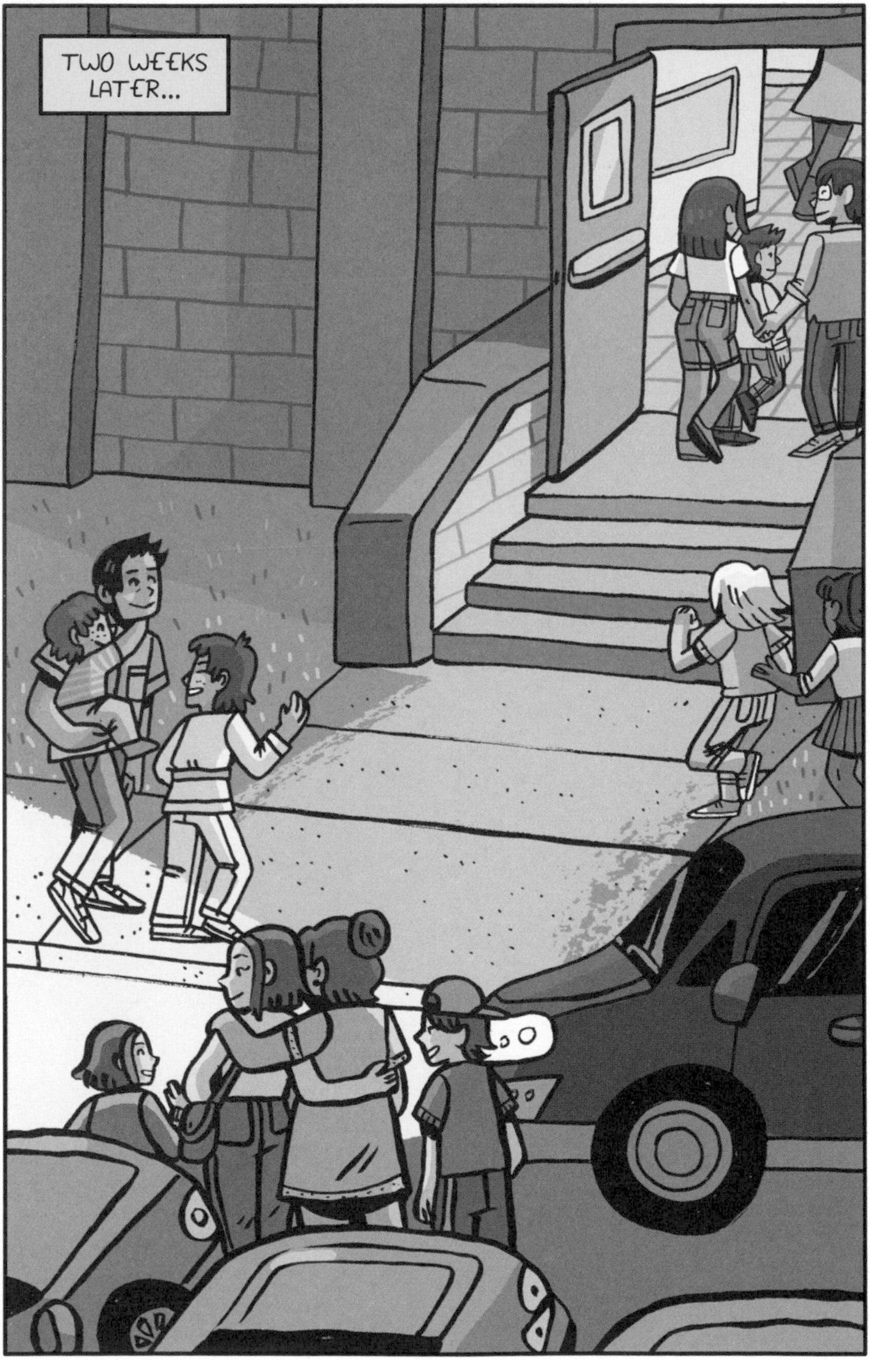
TWO WEEKS LATER...

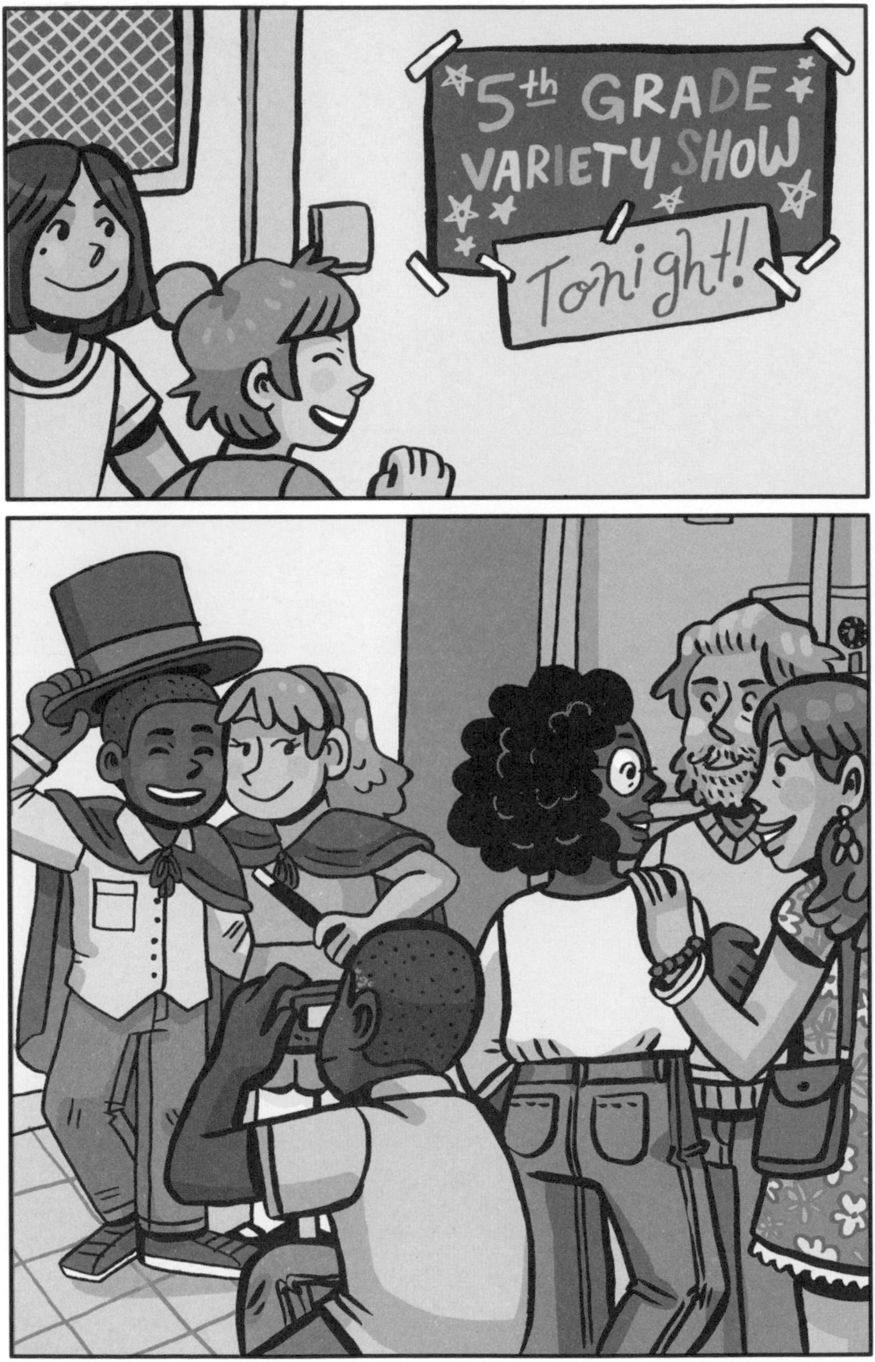
5th GRADE VARIETY SHOW
Tonight!

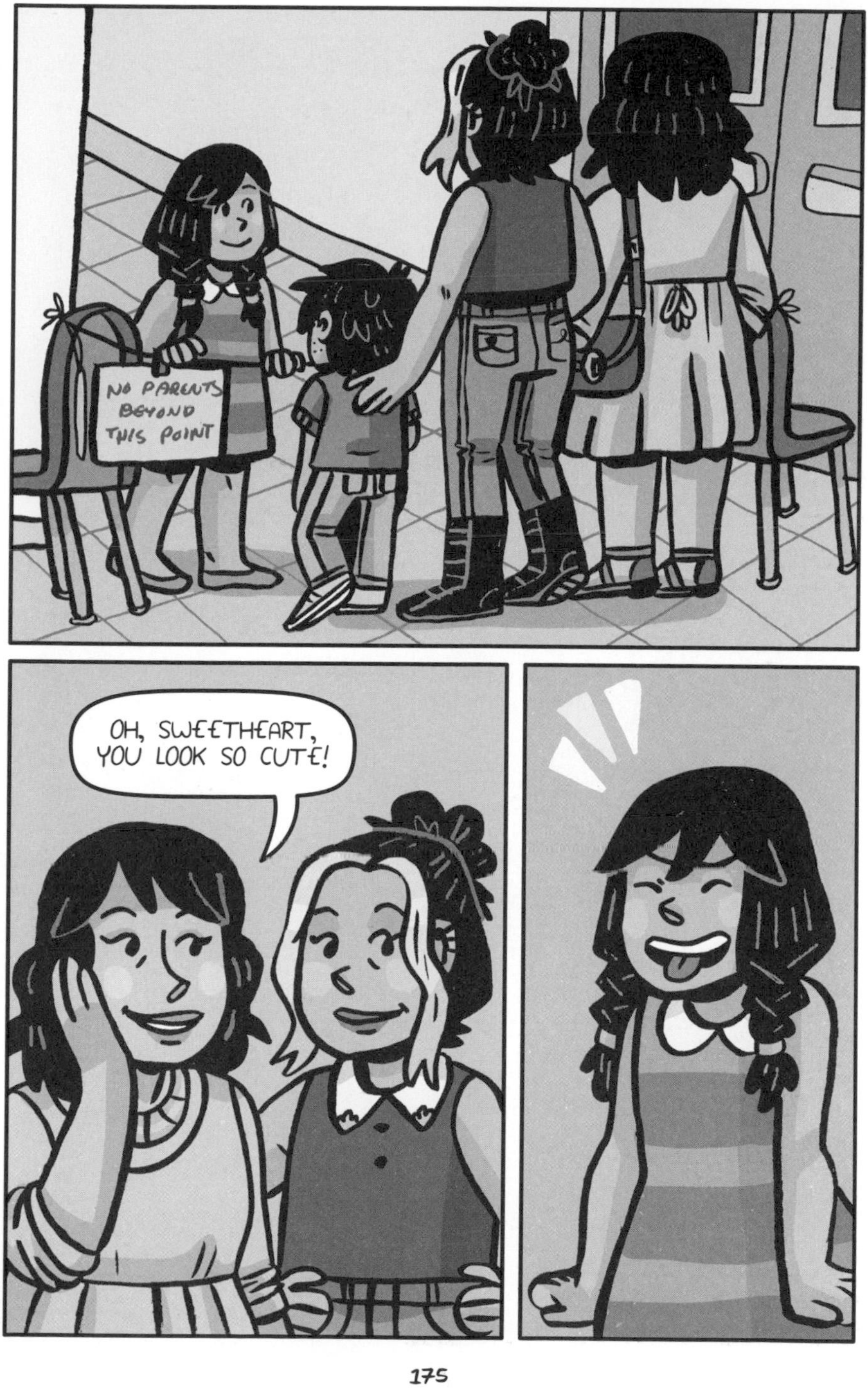
NO PARENTS BEYOND THIS POINT
OH, SWEETHEART, YOU LOOK SO CUTE!

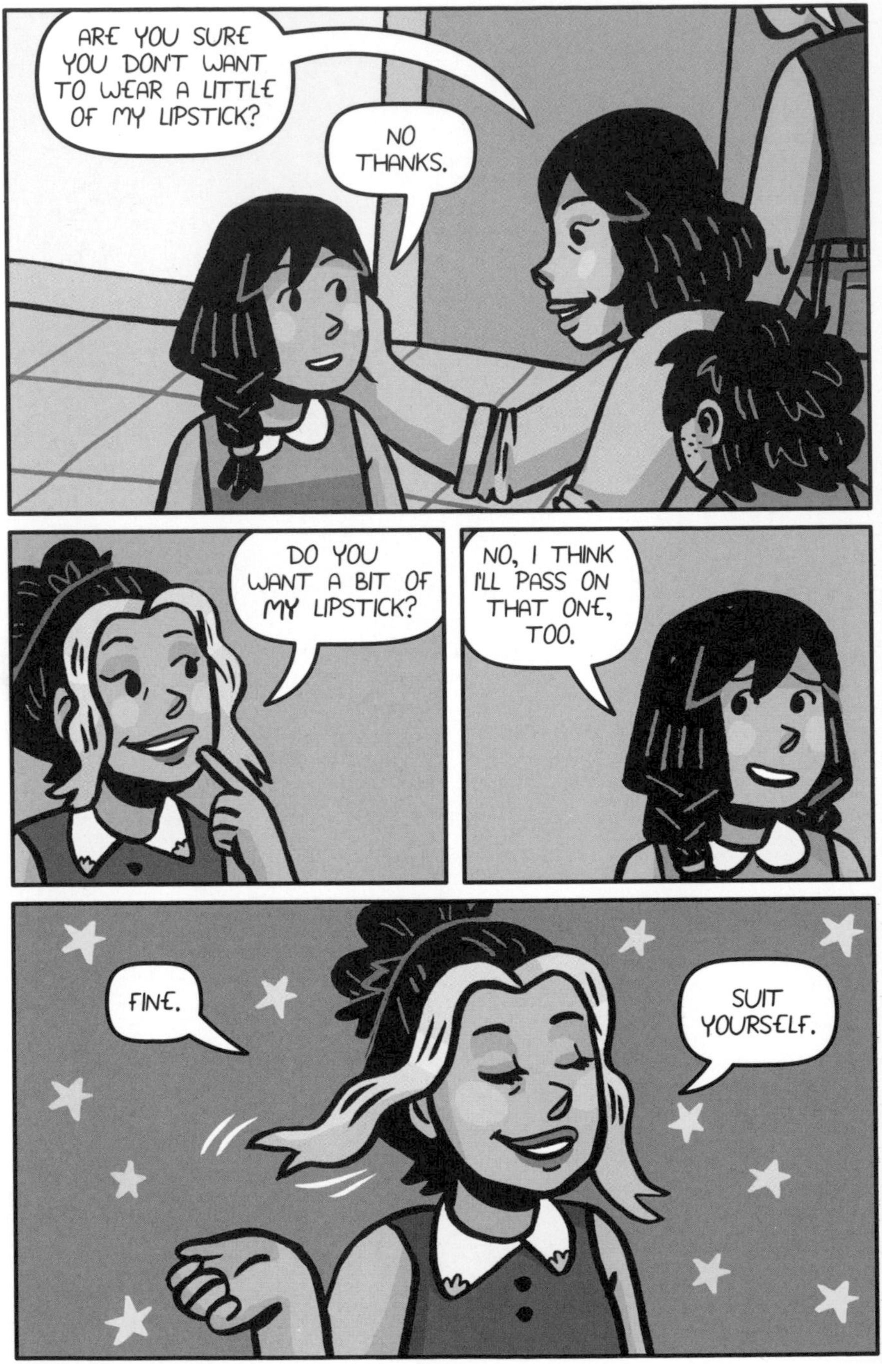
ARE YOU SURE YOU DON'T WANT TO WEAR A LITTLE OF MY LIPSTICK?
NO THANKS.
DO YOU WANT A BIT OF MY LIPSTICK?
NO, I THINK I'LL PASS ON THAT ONE, TOO.
FINE.
SUIT YOURSELF.

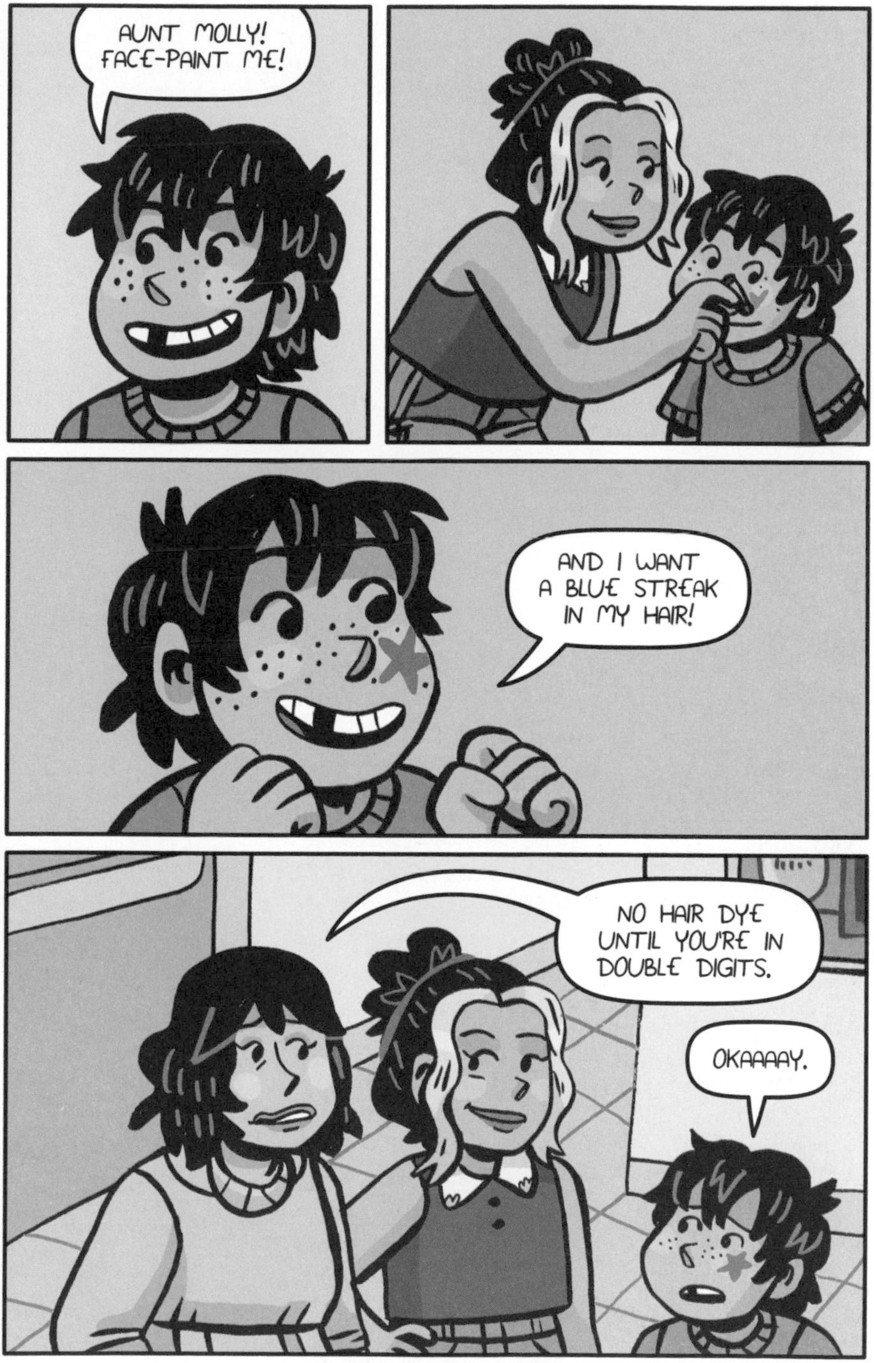
AUNT MOLLY! FACE-PAINT ME!
AND I WANT A BLUE STREAK IN MY HAIR!
NO HAIR DYE UNTIL YOU'RE IN DOUBLE DIGITS.
OKAAAAY.

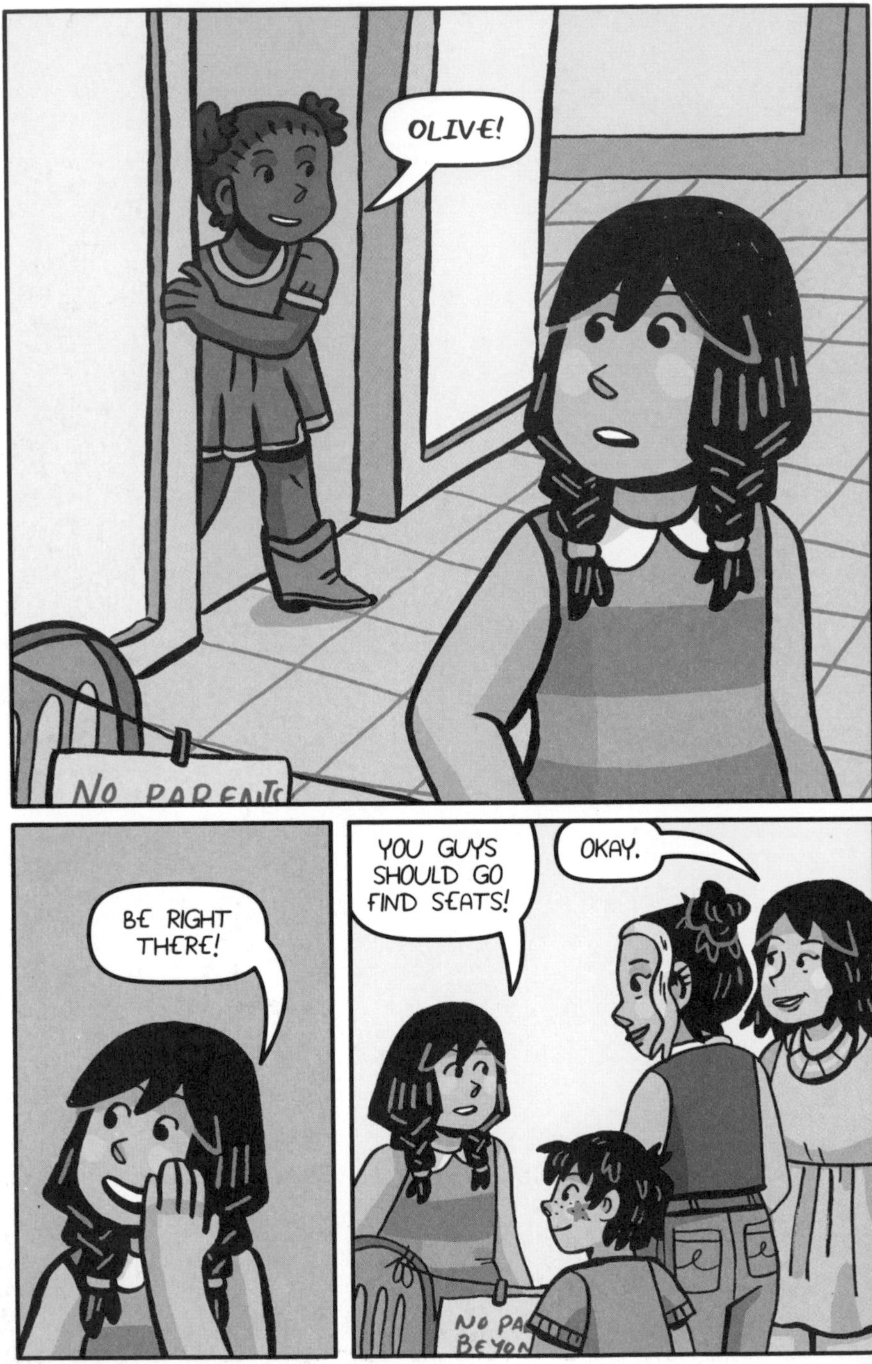
OLIVE!
NO PARENTS
BE RIGHT THERE!
YOU GUYS SHOULD GO FIND SEATS!
OKAY.

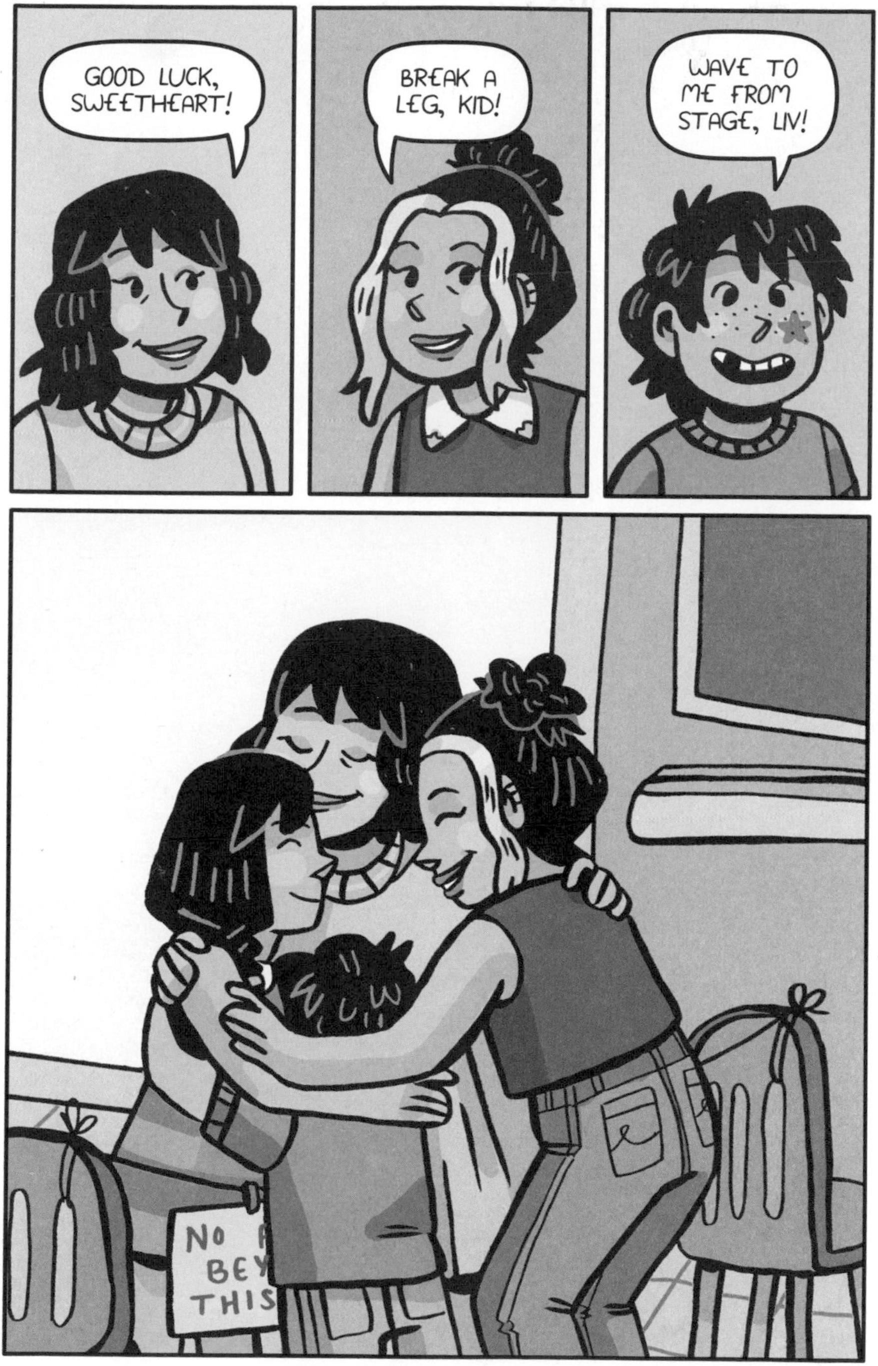
GOOD LUCK, SWEETHEART!
BREAK A LEG, KID!
WAVE TO ME FROM STAGE, LIV!
NO
BEY
THIS

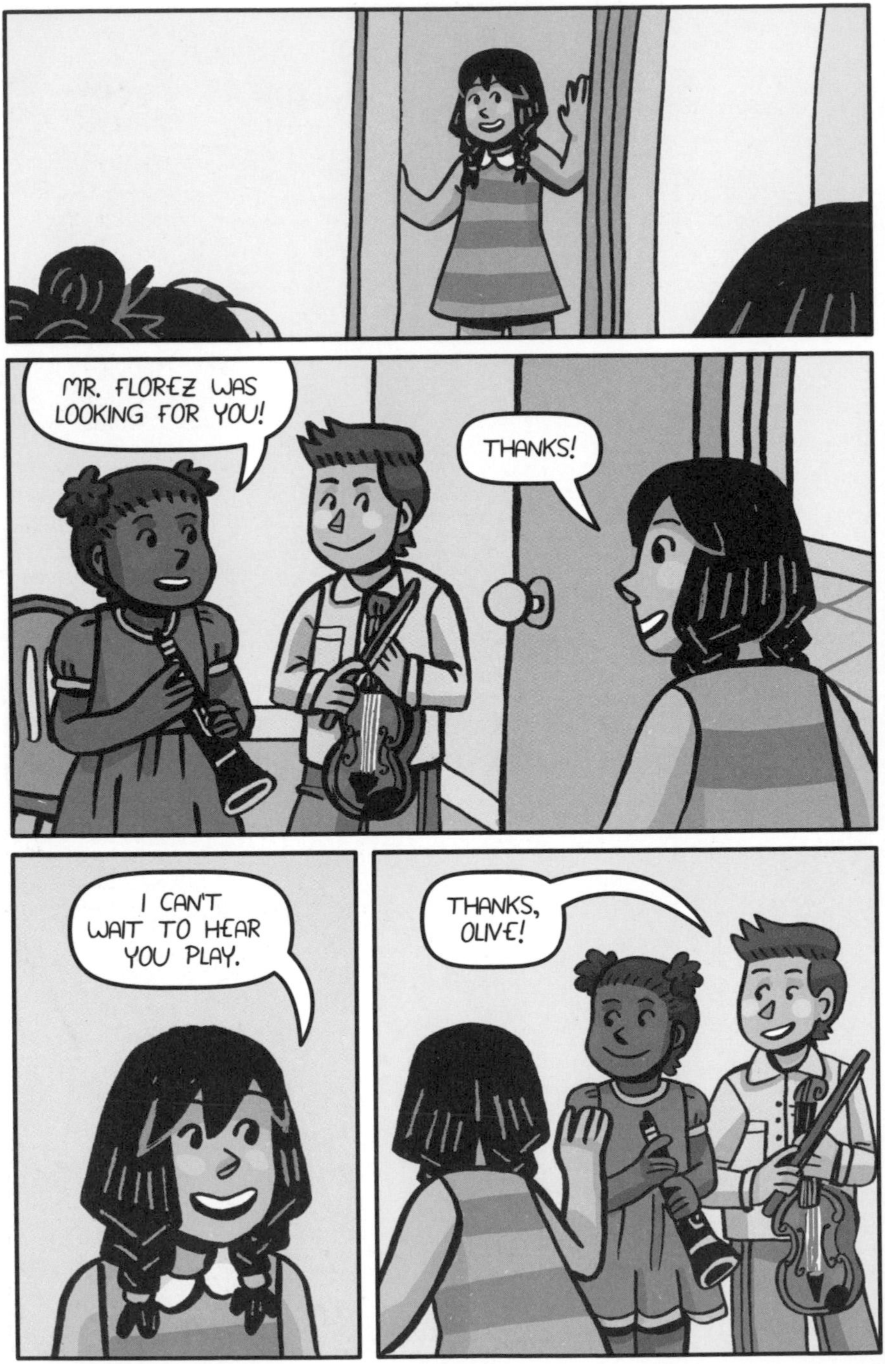
MR. FLOREZ WAS LOOKING FOR YOU!
THANKS!
I CAN'T WAIT TO HEAR YOU PLAY.
THANKS, OLIVE!

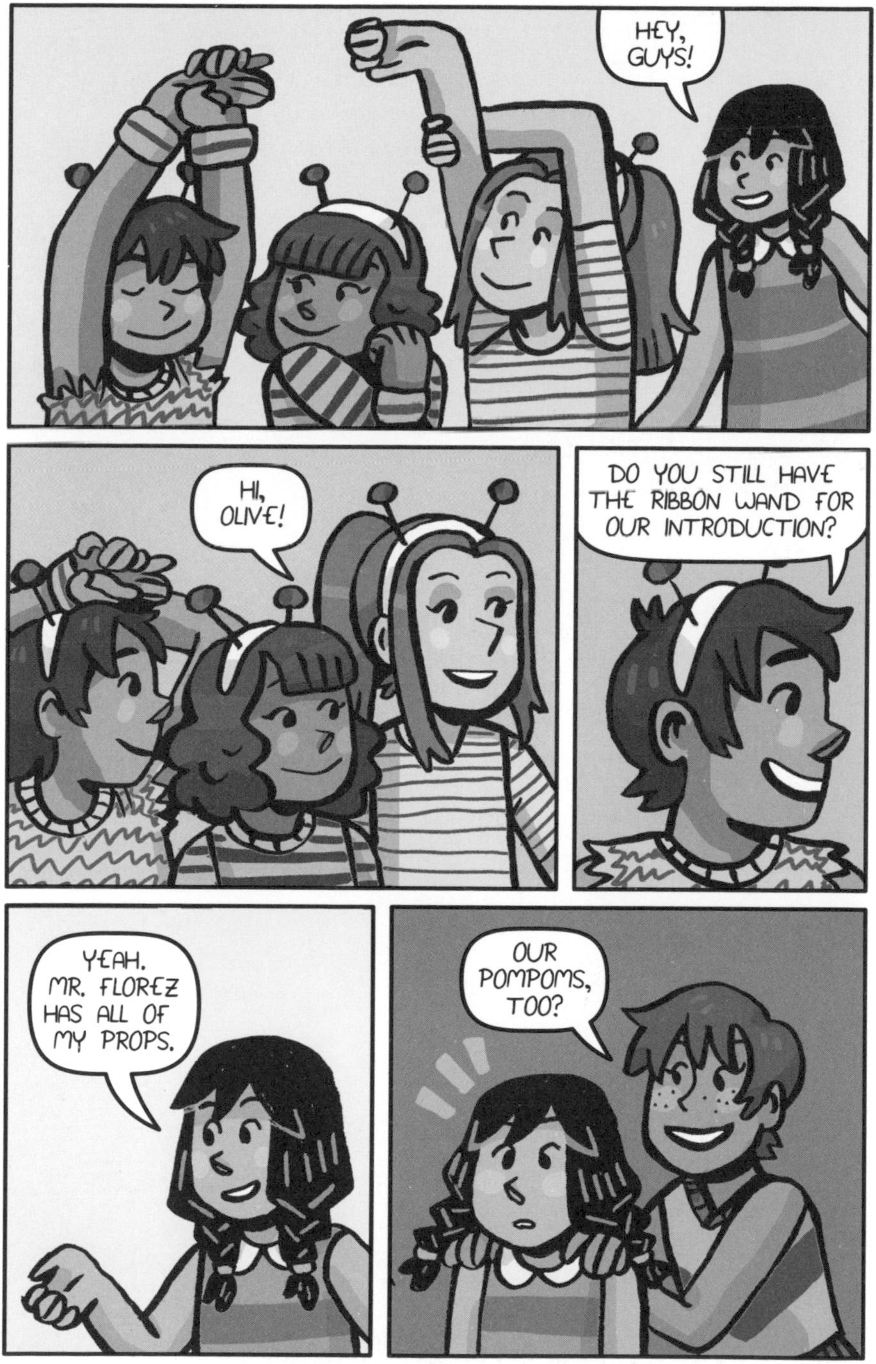
HEY, GUYS!
HI, OLIVE!
DO YOU STILL HAVE THE RIBBON WAND FOR OUR INTRODUCTION?
YEAH. MR. FLOREZ HAS ALL OF MY PROPS.
OUR POMPOMS, TOO?

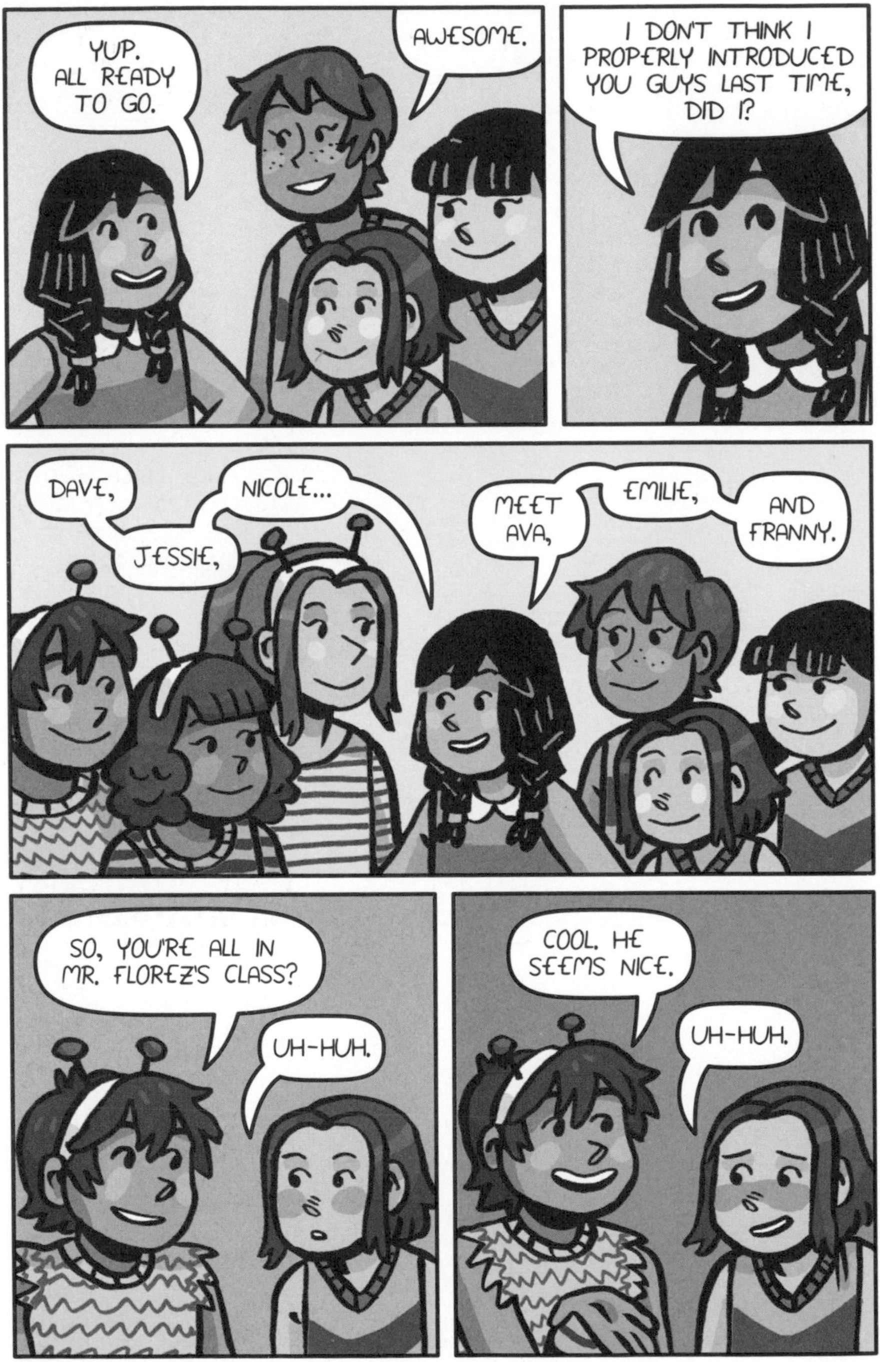
YUP. ALL READY TO GO.
AWESOME.
I DON'T THINK I PROPERLY INTRODUCED YOU GUYS LAST TIME, DID I?
DAVE,
JESSIE,
NICOLE...
MEET AVA,
EMILIE,
AND FRANNY.
SO, YOU'RE ALL IN MR. FLOREZ'S CLASS?
UH-HUH.
COOL. HE SEEMS NICE.
UH-HUH.

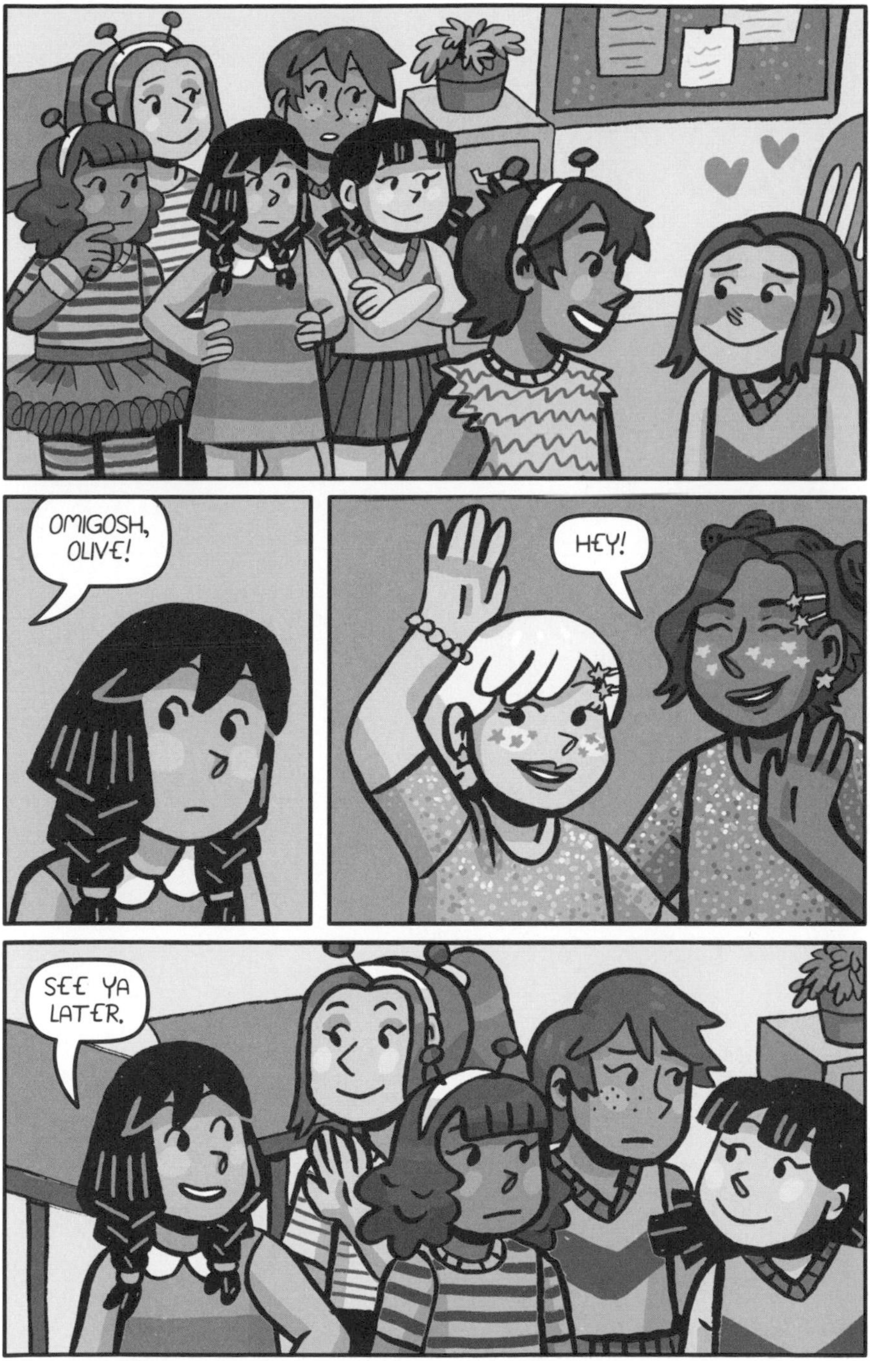

OMIGOSH, OLIVE!
HEY!
SEE YA LATER.

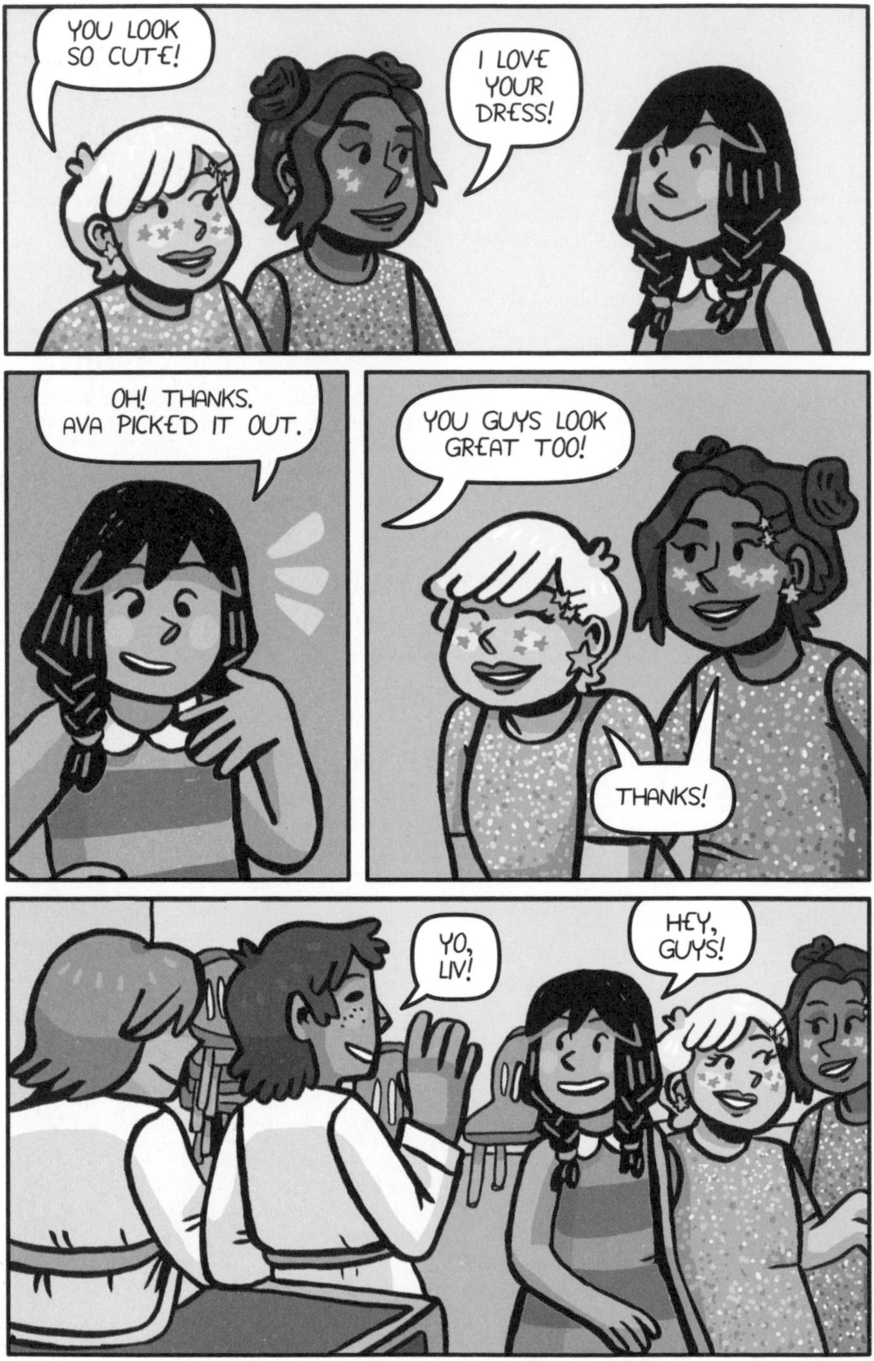
YOU LOOK SO CUTE!
I LOVE YOUR DRESS!
OH! THANKS. AVA PICKED IT OUT.
YOU GUYS LOOK GREAT TOO!
THANKS!
YO, LIV!
HEY, GUYS!

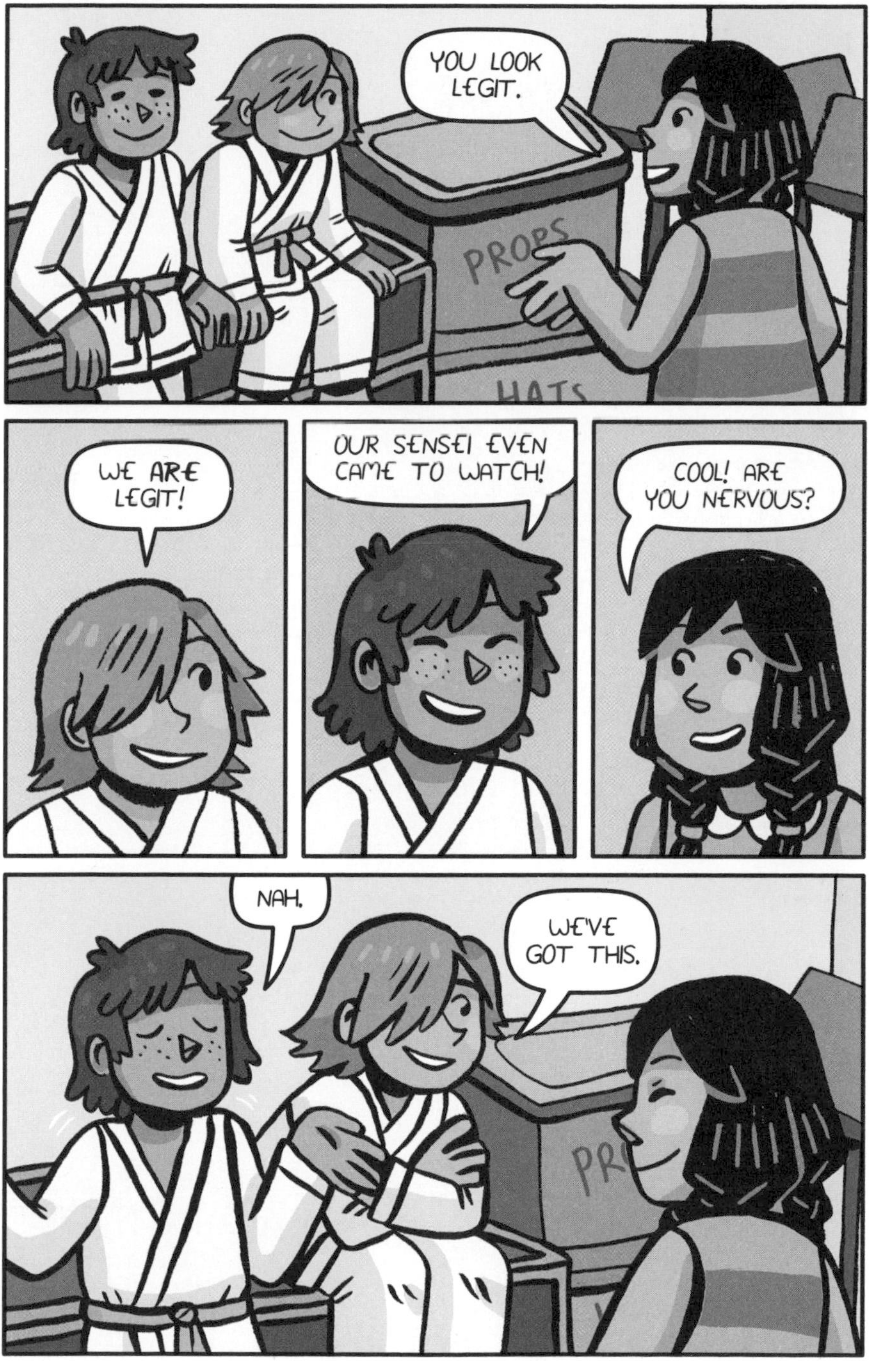
YOU LOOK LEGIT.
PROPS
HATS
WE ARE LEGIT!
OUR SENSEI EVEN CAME TO WATCH!
COOL! ARE YOU NERVOUS?
NAH.
WE'VE GOT THIS.

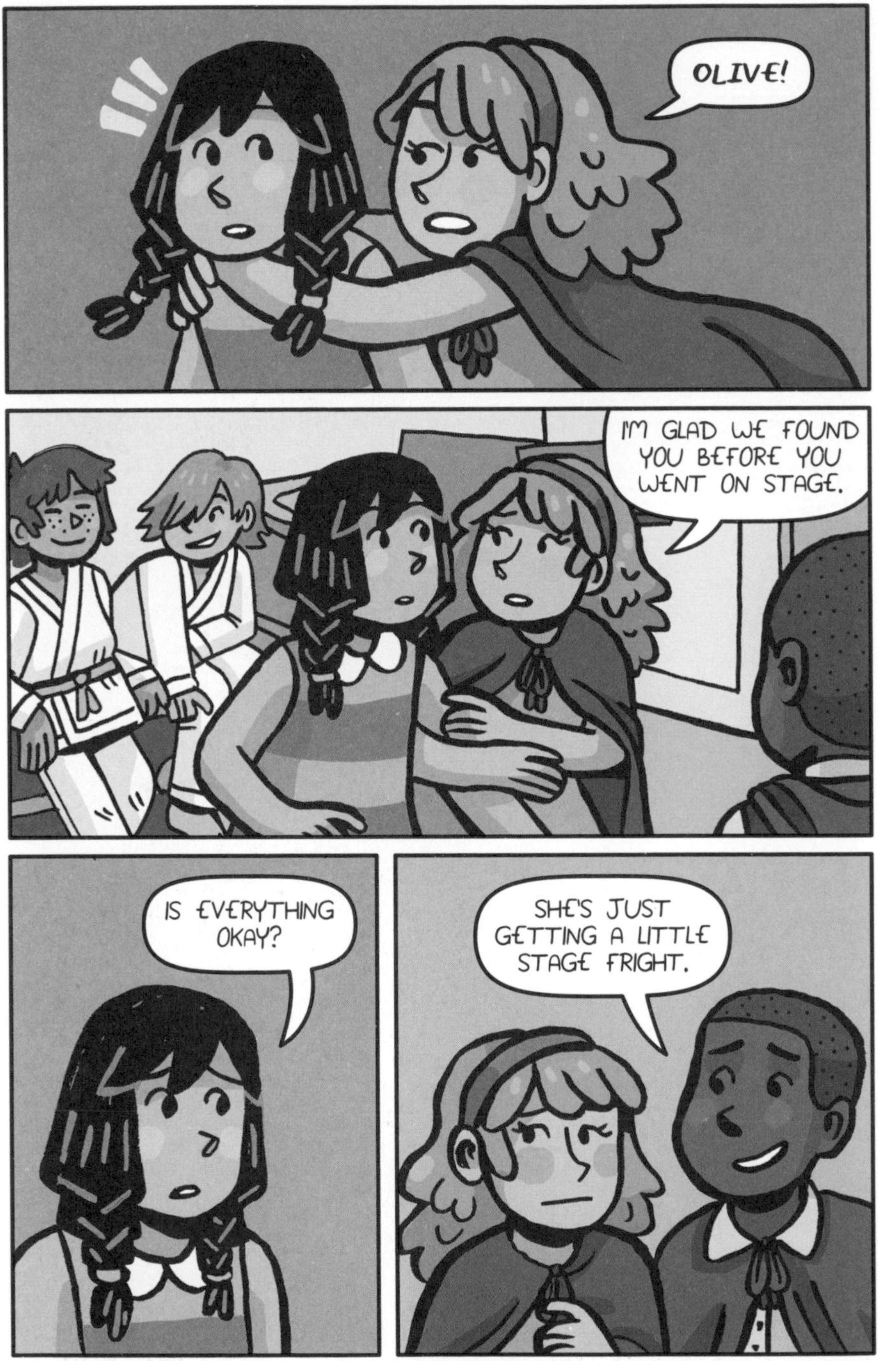
OLIVE!
I'M GLAD WE FOUND YOU BEFORE YOU WENT ON STAGE.
IS EVERYTHING OKAY?
SHE'S JUST GETTING A LITTLE STAGE FRIGHT.

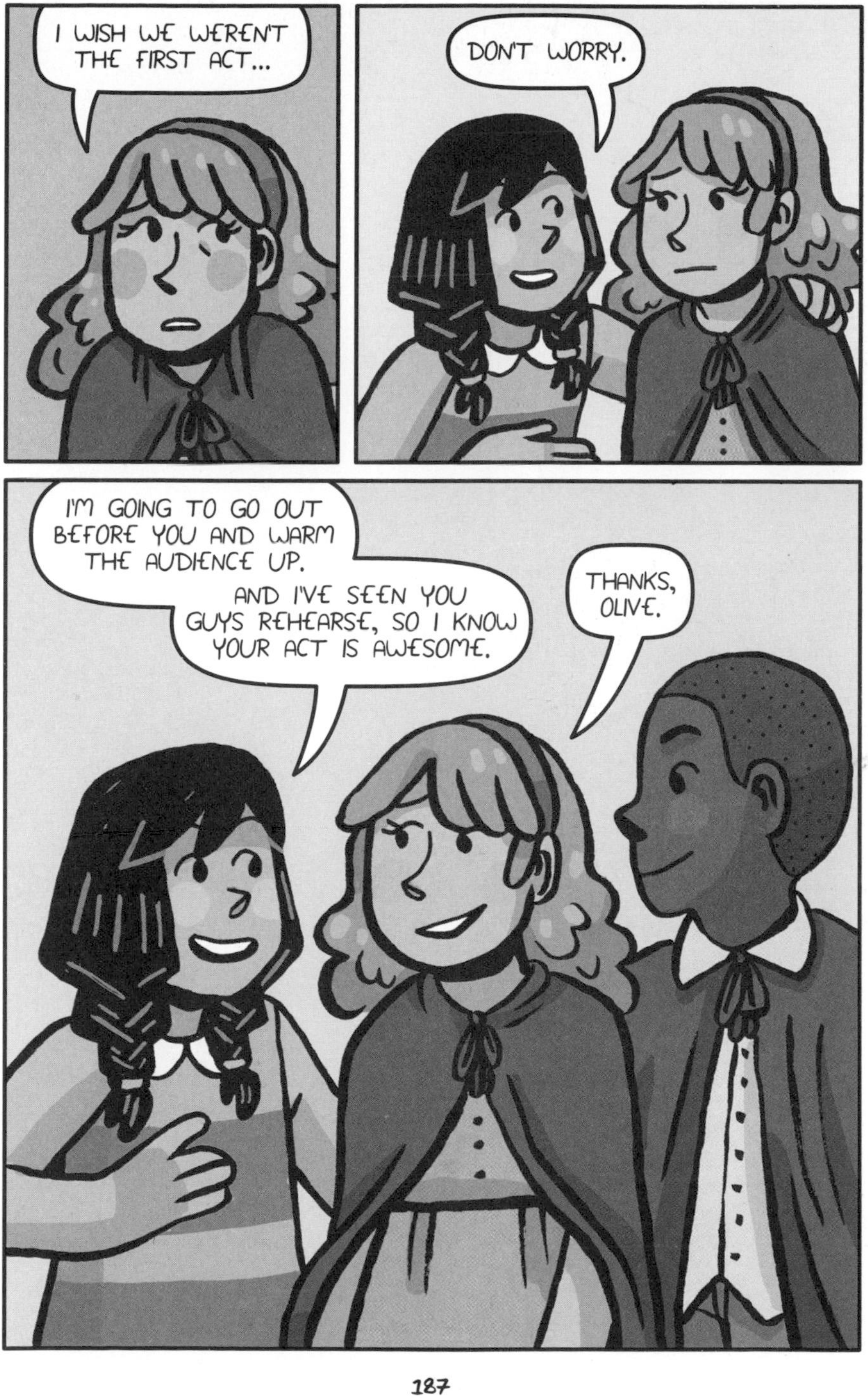
I WISH WE WEREN'T THE FIRST ACT...
DON'T WORRY.
I'M GOING TO GO OUT BEFORE YOU AND WARM THE AUDIENCE UP.
AND I'VE SEEN YOU GUYS REHEARSE, SO I KNOW YOUR ACT IS AWESOME.
THANKS, OLIVE.

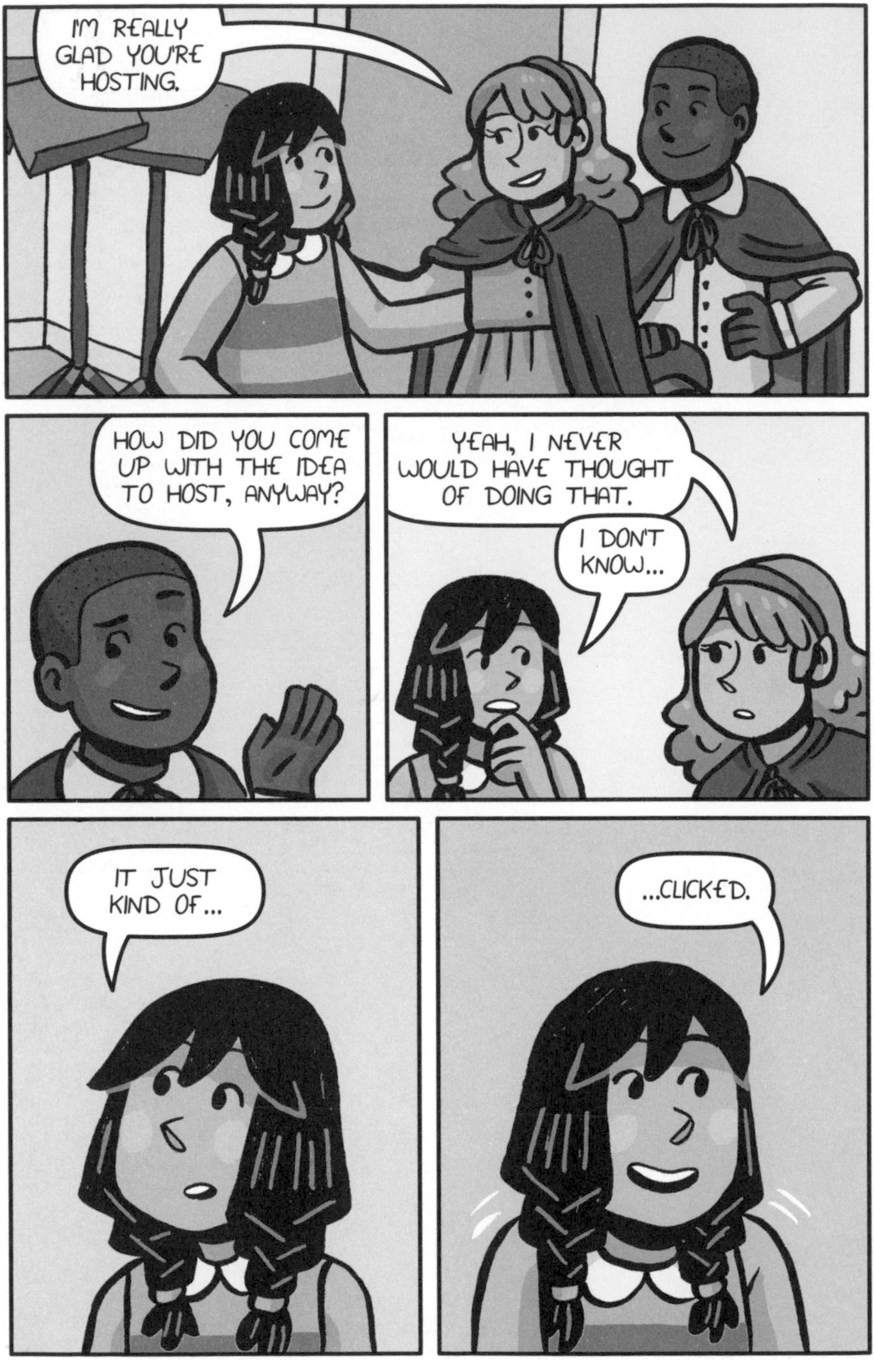
I'M REALLY GLAD YOU'RE HOSTING.
HOW DID YOU COME UP WITH THE IDEA TO HOST, ANYWAY?
YEAH, I NEVER WOULD HAVE THOUGHT OF DOING THAT.
I DON'T KNOW...
IT JUST KIND OF...
...CLICKED.

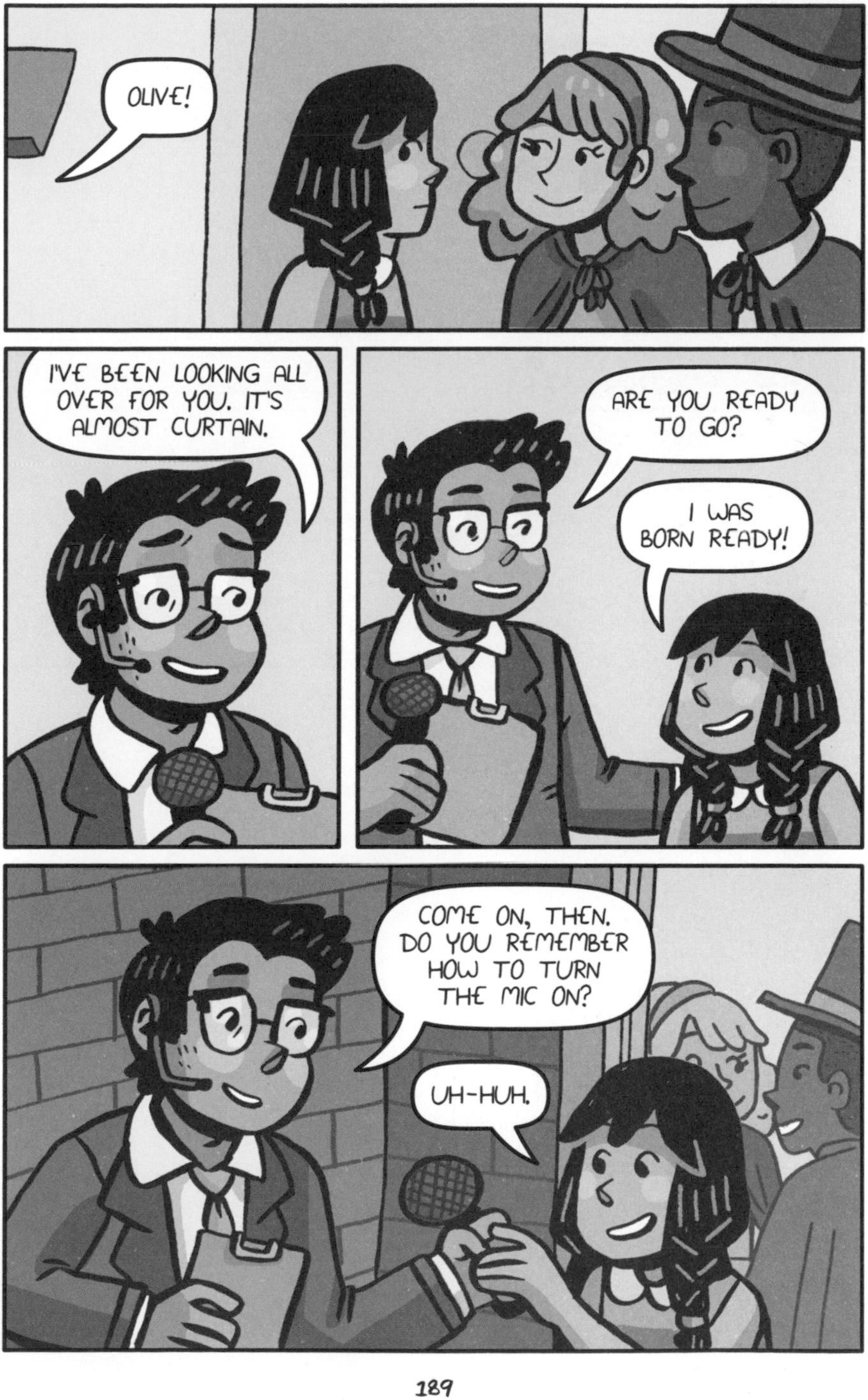
OLIVE!
I'VE BEEN LOOKING ALL OVER FOR YOU. IT'S ALMOST CURTAIN.
ARE YOU READY TO GO?
I WAS BORN READY!
COME ON, THEN. DO YOU REMEMBER HOW TO TURN THE MIC ON?
UH-HUH.

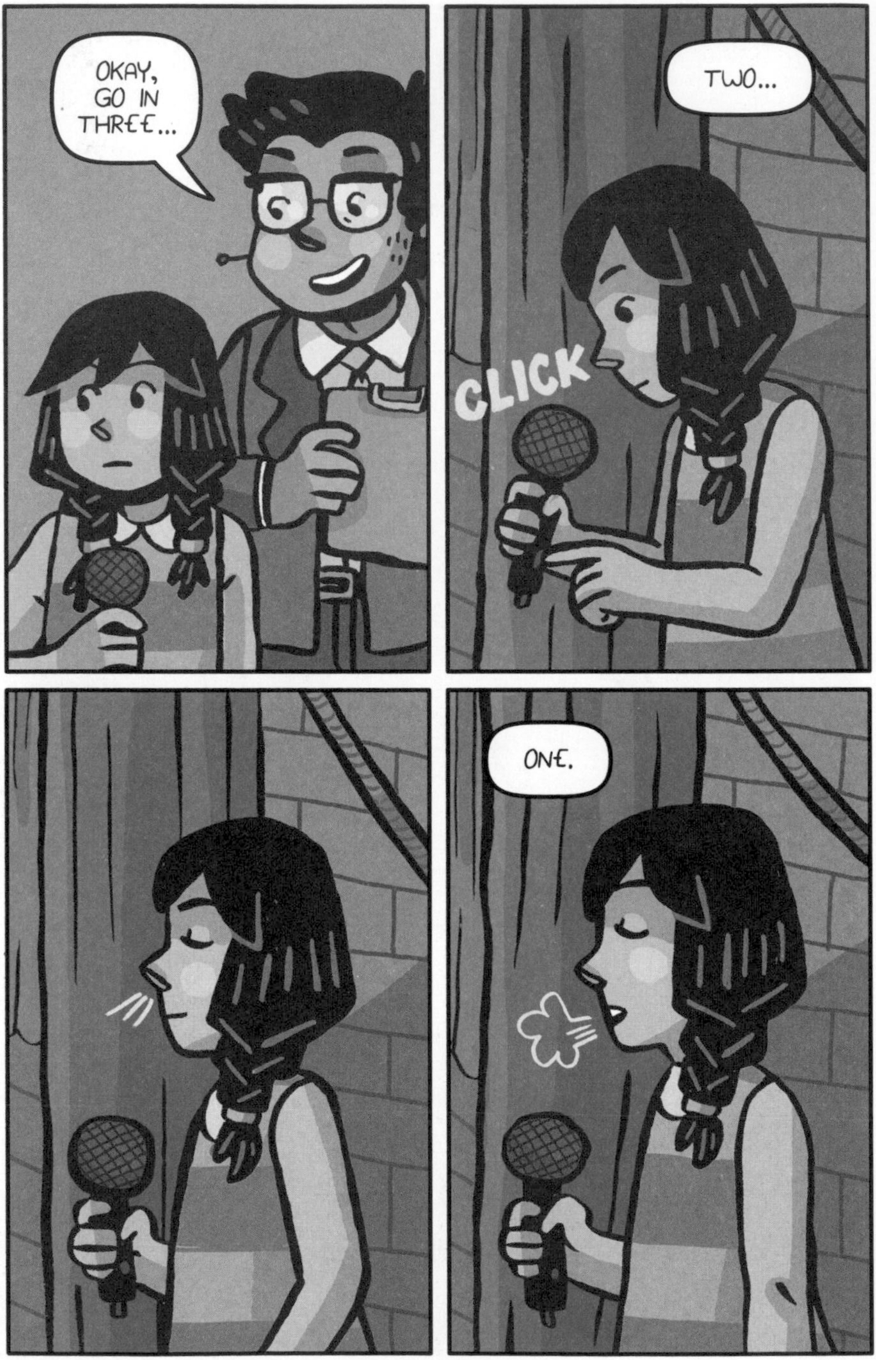
OKAY, GO IN THREE...
TWO...
CLICK
ONE.

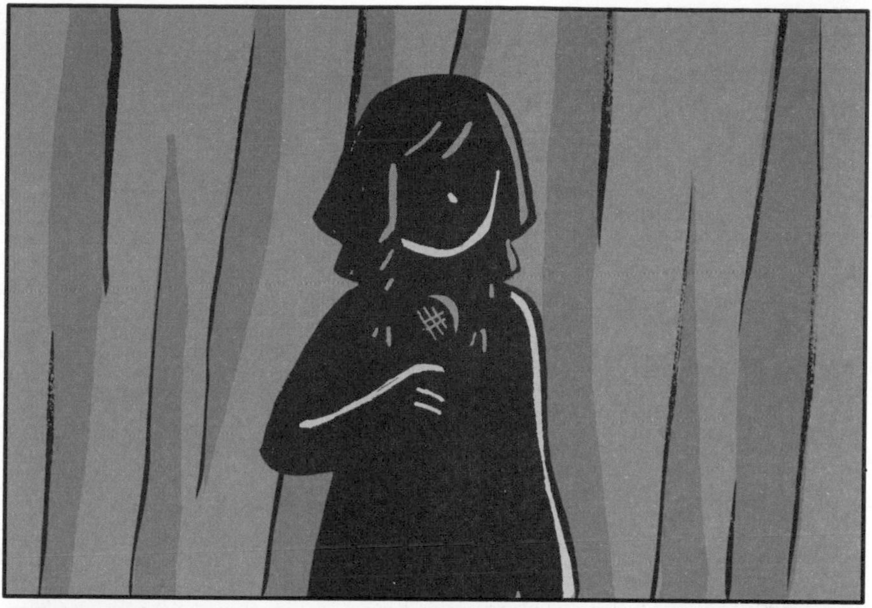

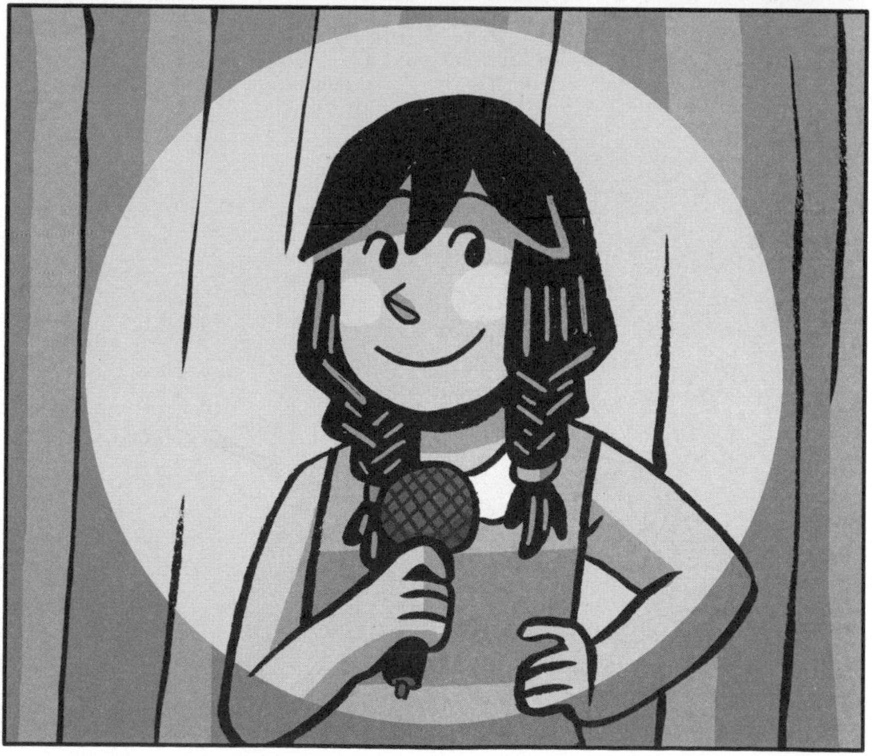

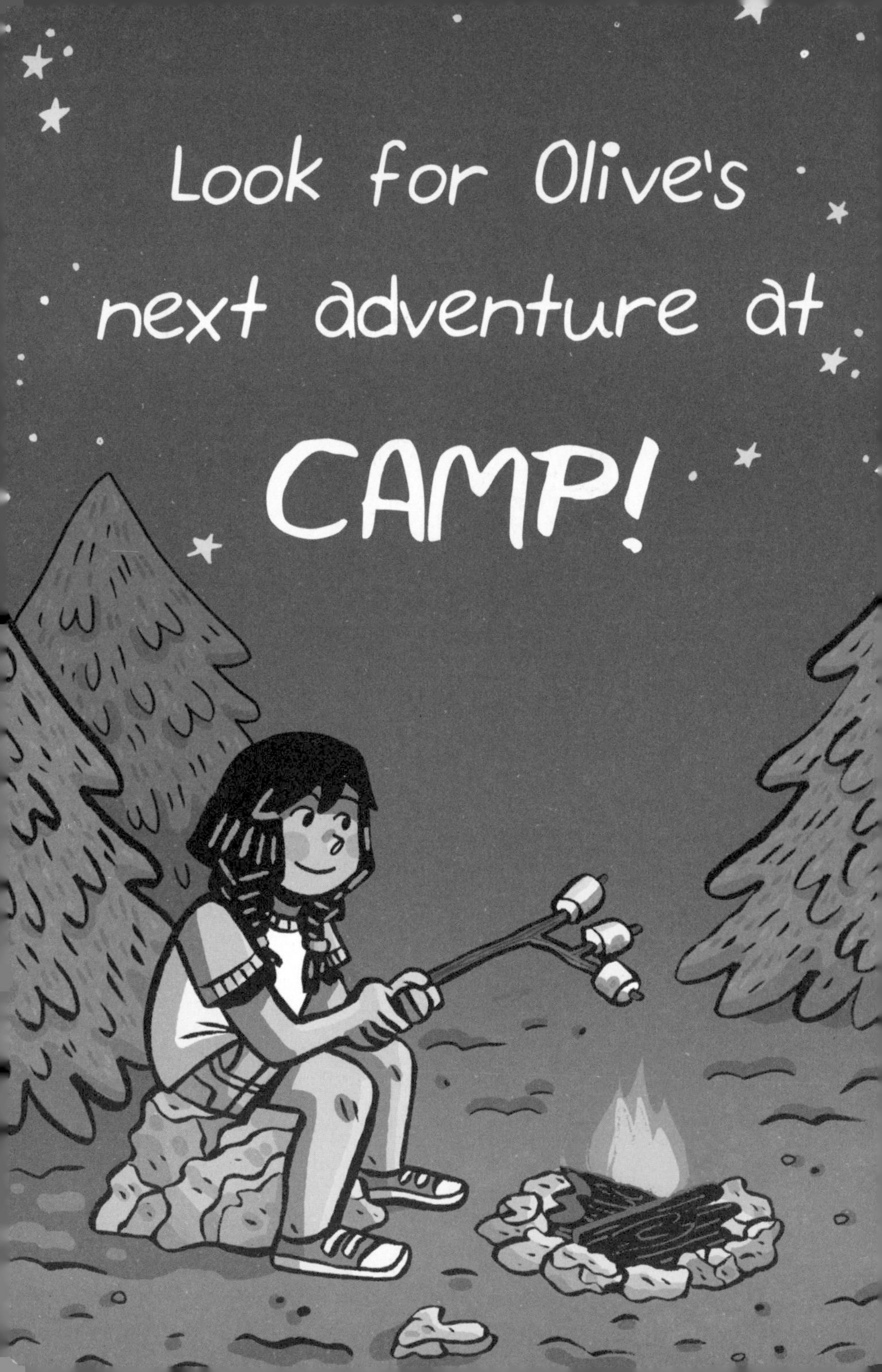
Look for Olive's
next adventure at
CAMP!

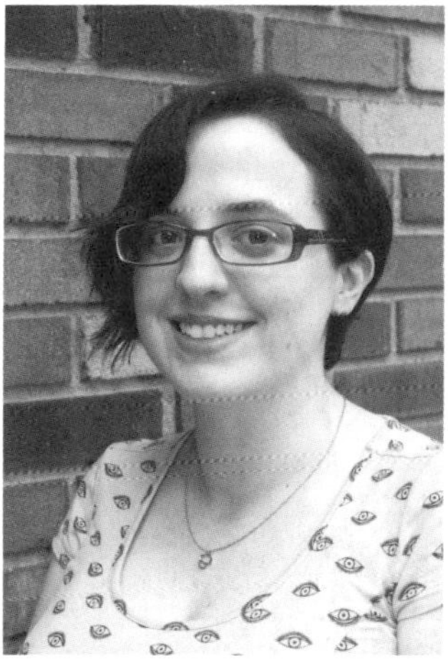

Photo by K Kypers

KAYLA MILLER is an author-illustrator and cartoonist with a BFA from the University of the Arts in Philadelphia. *Click* is her debut graphic novel. She lives and works in New Jersey.

Visit her online at kayla-miller.com.

OLIVE WANTS TO GET IN ON THE ACT . . .
. . . ANY ACT!

Olive "clicks" with everyone in the fifth grade—until one day she doesn't. When a school variety show leaves Olive stranded without an act to join, she begins to panic, wondering why all of her friends have already formed their own groups . . . without her. With the performance drawing closer by the minute, will Olive be able to find her own place in the show before the curtain goes up?

Author-illustrator Kayla Miller has woven together a heartfelt and insightful story about navigating friendships, leaning on family, and learning to take the stage in the most important role of all.

A Junior Library Guild Selection

HOUGHTON MIFFLIN HARCOURT
hmhco.com
Follow us on Twitter: @HMHKids

$12.99/Higher in Canada   1701780
ISBN 978-1-328-91112-4

51299
9 781328 911124